SHADOW BLADE

CHRIS BARILI

WFP
WORDFIRE PRESS

Trade ISBN: 978-1-61475-952-2
eBook ISBN: 978-1-61475-953-9
Hardcover ISBN: 978-1-61475-981-2

Cover design by Janet McDonald
Cover artwork images by Michelle Johnson,
Blue Sky Design
Kevin J. Anderson, Art Director

Published by
WordFire Press, an imprint of WordFire, LLC
PO Box 1840
Monument, CO 80132

Kevin J. Anderson & Rebecca Moesta, Publishers

WordFire Press eBook Edition 2019
WordFire Press Trade Paperback Edition 2019
WordFire Press Hardcover Edition 2019
Printed in the USA

Join our WordFire Press Readers Group for free books,
sneak previews, updates on new projects, and other giveaways.
Sign up at wordfirepress.com

❧ Created with Vellum

DEDICATION

For Mireille. "So as you breathe life into my heart, breathe also wisdom and strength." Je t'aime.

CHAPTER ONE

No one ever noticed Ashai. In his business, being noticed got you killed. So he kept his black hair trimmed just below the ears, flowing free in the style popular with Pushtani men. His nose had been broken once, but its jagged bend was not unusual among these men, who often tussled over matters of honor or family. He wore the long, tan robe of a cloth merchant, nothing more. Though he could afford them, he didn't wear expensive perfumes, nor did he allow himself the luxury of fine jewelry. A simple leather band wrapped around his right wrist—a plain adornment for a plain man. He looked like the average Pushtani, blending in despite having only lived in Dar Tallus two years. No one here knew his true identity. Nor his plan.

They wouldn't until he spilled blood.

The sun hung low in the eastern sky, but already, Central Square baked in its heat. Summers here oppressed a man, body and spirit, the heat baking the trash piles and sewage in the streets until the stench assailed the senses like a foul army. When it rained it merely made the heat muggy, and brought out mosquitoes as big as Ashai's fingers and biting, yellow flies. Yes, with its squat two-story buildings, dark cobblestones, and throngs of people, Central Square acted like a frying pan, grilling up merchants, beggars, and nobles alike.

Ashai slipped through the crowd, angling and sidling at a steady pace, not slowing, despite the packed street. He passed within a finger-length of rich merchants, commoners, and soldiers smelling of sweat inside their bulky armor. The last would have gutted him had they known his true identity. But they marched past, blissfully ignorant.

It helped that he drew lightly on the tiny stream of power his God provided him, taking in its strength and portioning it out to his mind, body, and face. He saw events before the average man, as if time moved slower for Ashai, so he moved through the crowd like it stood still. His features shifted slightly with every step, making it impossible for any two people to describe him exactly the same. Even the deep brown of his eyes —the mark of a Nishi'iti—changed every other step: blue, then green, then gray. Never brown. Not here, where Nishi'itis were beaten on sight. Never brown eyes.

Nishi's power also improved his senses, feeding him bits of conversations, detecting scents only dogs could smell, keeping him alert for any sign of danger.

He stopped outside a spice shop, breathing in the aromas of cinnamon, crushed hot pepper, and Nishi'iti Snow Spice, which made his mouth water. Ashai had grown up on Nishi'iti streets much like these, only without the heat. Or the wealth.

But he lived here now, in the capital city of Pushtan. He no longer slept under bridges or wagons, but in a small flat atop his humble fabric shop. A shop he'd paid for himself, with money he'd earned as a cloth merchant. All part of an elaborate cover story, years in the making. And that cover was so perfect; it was like it had been fated since his birth. Even his Nishi'iti name, "Azha'i," made the transition to the Pushtani version simple.

Nishi always provided.

The crowd milled about like sheep, ringing the fountain in the center of the square. Waiting. For her.

These fools ignored their gods and worshipped a mortal woman. A woman marked to die.

Ashai studied the street entering the square from the north. Princess Makari would come from there for her weekly bout of helping the poor from the safety of her carriage, where the filthy masses couldn't touch her. On occasion, she would step from her coach onto the broiling cobblestones and mingle with her people. Today would be one such day, if her patterns held.

He'd seen her many times, always from afar, and yet her beauty always stunned him. He almost regretted that he would kill her.

Almost.

Out of nowhere, the stench of rotting flesh hit him like a wall of refuse. He glanced to his right, following the odor. There, weaving through the crowd, was a bent, filthy man, with hair like a rag-mop and rags on his back. When his gaze met Ashai's, his eyes flashed silver.

"Nishi strike him." Ashai risked the Nishi'iti curse out loud to protect himself from the foul creature. Shiners were people who fell prey to back alley magic—potions or powders or spells that gave them a contaminated kind of power that mimicked Nishi's gift. But once the corrupted magic sunk its teeth into a victim, it never let go. Most went mad and killed themselves. Survivors were marked with the glow in their eyes for all to see. Abominations.

The first time Ashai had seen a shiner, he'd left the man's corpse on the snow-swept side of a Nishi'iti mountain. He'd never seen one in Dar Tallus. Until now.

The shiner turned and slipped off into the crowd, probably sensing Ashai's true power and fleeing.

Relieved, Ashai stole a furtive glance to his left. A few feet away, a boy of fourteen shifted from one foot to the other, fists clenching and unclenching at his sides. His mud-colored hair stood in all directions, hastily chopped short with a knife, and dirt smeared his face. His green eyes scanned the crowd, meeting briefly with Ashai's before moving away.

Ashai wondered for a moment if he'd chosen the right boy. It had taken just a few copper pieces and a pinch of magic to convince the young thief that the princess's purse made an easy target. Just a gentle nudge, a wordless suggestion, and the young man had smiled at the prospect of stealing from well-guarded royalty. Had Ashai applied a bit more magic, he could have convinced the boy to kill her, or die trying. But Denari Lai did not let children do their killing.

Denari Lai, Shadow Blades, Holy Death—no matter the name, Ashai's order did not just kill. They instilled terror, toppled nations, and destroyed power. Their legend had so grown, that one Denari Lai assassin had forced a foreign king to withdraw troops from Nishi'iti territory just by leaving one of their gleaming midnight daggers on his pillow. The king still died of course—his blood served as the wax that sealed their message.

Denari Lai were hand-chosen by their leader, the Chargh Lai, and fiercely loyal to their God, Nishi. It was his power that gave them the skills to take life in his name. He let them touch him, and in return, they would kill their own children if Nishi condemned them, so long as they spilled no innocent blood.

A commotion near the entrance to the square told Ashai the princess had kept her schedule again.

The boy had noticed, too, as he stood stock still, his emerald eyes staring at the entrance. It would have looked suspicious had every other pair of eyes not been turned that way, as well. Yes, Makari's people loved her. They would mourn her death for weeks. Months, even.

The crowd parted as Royal Guard soldiers in blue armor, helms gleaming in the morning sun, opened a path through the crowd. Trumpets sounded, and a cheer rose from the assembled rabble, rattling Ashai's teeth.

Makari had forgone the usual carriage and royal gown. Instead, she rode into the square atop a white gelding. Leather armor, glistening in black and deep blue, clung to her body, covering every inch of her own pale skin with a hardened carapace. Her midnight-colored hair flowed behind her, and her sky-blue eyes shone as she surveyed the gathered crowd. At her side rode a fortress of a man, dressed in blued chain mail, a long sword swinging at his hip. Captain Marwan Bauti, Commander of the Royal Guard, had accompanied his princess this morning. An unexpected complication.

Behind her walked a dozen servants, all carrying baskets of bread. She'd never done that before.

Things had just become unpredictable. Too many variables. Ashai looked for the boy, hoping to wave him off, but the lad had disappeared into the mass of bodies.

Ashai's gut twisted.

He looked again at the princess, and to his relief, her purse hung at her belt. He hadn't expected it to be there while she wore armor, but she couldn't toss coins to the poor without it.

He caught sight of the boy weaving through the mass of people and followed him. If he couldn't stop the thief, he'd have to improvise.

Makari stopped amidst the throng, her guard fanning out around her, Bauti at her side. She sat tall in the saddle, scanning the sea of people. When her eyes reached Ashai, they locked with his, and his heart stopped. He knew he should look away, but he couldn't. Her gaze held him fast, and for that frozen moment, Makari dominated his mind and his heart, blocking out all else. Then her gaze moved on, and Ashai let out a breath, confused.

He shook himself and moved forward again until he stood just a few paces behind the thief. He felt the tension radiating from the boy as nervousness swept his thin frame. Still, his exterior remained placid, as smooth as the surface of a mountain lake. Perhaps Ashai had chosen the right boy after all.

Makari raised a single, leather-gloved hand and her subjects fell silent. Her voice rang through the crowd.

"Citizens of Dar Tallus, I apologize for my unladylike attire, but I came directly from my sword lessons with Master Bauti, and did not want to keep you waiting while I changed into some stuffy gown designed to impress other nobility. You're working people. Your time is more valuable than royal vanity."

The crowd cheered, and Ashai didn't think any of them—at least not anyone male—objected to the form-fitting leather. While it protected everything vital and left no skin exposed, it clung to her shapely legs and accented her long, elegant neck. He'd never been this close to her before, and had to look away to avoid offending his God.

He took a deep breath. There were new variables—armor, Bauti, and now bread.

He had to focus, but her beauty continued to drag his attention from the details.

"If you will have me," Makari said, "I will walk among you now, and offer help to those in need."

Swinging a leg over the saddle, she dismounted. Bauti joined her, moving to her left shoulder. His hand rested on the pommel of his long sword. Servants carrying baskets of bread stood behind them both.

The boy edged forward and Ashai tensed. He drew a thicker strand of magic, extending his senses further. He could hear the thief breathing now, feel his pulse. He smelled the bread, mingled with Makari's sweet perfume, and the stench from the gutters behind them. He tasted the metal of the coins inside her purse.

The thief worked his way to the head of the line to receive bread, his left hand out, his right hand hanging at his side. Ashai drew within five steps.

Makari turned to receive the first loaf of bread and when she did, the boy's left hand reached for her purse, the right flicking a small blade from his sleeve.

Time seemed to slow as Ashai closed. Three steps. The boy grasped the purse and brought the blade up.

Two steps.

Bauti saw the blade, but reacted too late.

One step.

As the boy sliced the purse strings, Ashai reached him and time returned to normal.

Ashai jumped in front of the knife, knocking the blade upward with his arm, feeling the cold metal bite through his robe and into the flesh of his forearm.

"Knife!" Bauti yelled, shoving Makari behind him.

Ashai allowed his facial features to relax and stop shifting. The thief's green eyes opened wide just as Ashai snatched the knife from his grasp and applied a tiny trickle of magic to his mind, blanking out the boy's memory of him.

Bauti crashed into Ashai, knocking him aside.

"No, don't!" Ashai yelled.

But the captain thrust his sword into the boy's chest. The thief's green eyes opened wide, his mouth forming a circle. Then Bauti jerked his blade free, spraying blood across the cobblestones, spattering Ashai's face. The boy crumpled to the ground, a gurgling sound escaping his lips as his blood pooled between the cobblestones.

Ashai jumped to his feet and rushed Bauti, rage sweeping through him, but the remaining guards drove him to the ground, pinning him down and taking the small knife. Then they twisted his arms behind his back and hoisted him to his feet.

"He was but a boy!" Ashai shouted, straining against the guards.

"And he tried to kill the princess!" Bauti yelled back.

Ashai opened his mouth to reply, but never got the chance.

"Release that man!" Makari stormed toward them, her eyes blazing blue fire. She gripped a curved dagger in one hand. "Release him now!"

The guards released Ashai, but remained close, hands near weapons.

Makari shouldered past Bauti, her eyes falling quickly to the wound on Ashai's forearm. Those eyes, shining with confidence and command, turned his knees to jelly.

"You are injured," she said, reaching for his arm, but stopping short.

"It is nothing, Highness," he said, bowing his head.

"You saved my life, sir, at great risk to your own."

Ashai looked at the body of the boy on the ground. He seemed small now, not threatening. Ashai reached for the boy's body, making the guards tense. He paused, then picked up the purse and extended it to Makari.

"Charity and good will should not be met with thievery, Highness," he said. "He was just a boy and probably meant you no harm. His death is ... regrettable. His family ..."

He let the sentence trail off. Blood ran down his forearm, so he channeled a silent string of magic to the wound to stem the blood.

"I doubt he has any," Makari said. She turned to Bauti. "Captain, summon a healer to see to this man's wound."

Bauti balked. "Highness, we should return to the palace. There may be more—"

Ashai stared at the ground to keep from glaring at the captain. He needed to remember his mission. Emotion had no place here, but the image of the boy's expression as Bauti ran him through had burned itself on Ashai's mind and fueled a fire in his belly.

"Then let them show themselves," Makari snapped, twirling the knife around her fingers and stowing it in a sheath at her belt. "I won't let one boy stop me from helping our citizens."

"I must insist, Highness," the captain said, straightening.

Makari wheeled on him, hands on her hips. She opened her mouth, but Ashai interjected.

"Highness, your captain is right, I fear. Where a boy steals, men may plot worse. I must urge caution, as well. As my mentor always said: 'Small trouble always has a bigger brother.'"

She turned her blue-fire gaze on Ashai, but he lowered his eyes and inclined his head, deflecting her heat.

Makari sighed. "Very well, but I would have the servants distribute the bread and coins on my behalf."

"We have no one to oversee them," Bauti said. "We can try again another time."

Makari looked crestfallen, and Ashai jumped at the opportunity.

"Highness, I am but a humble cloth merchant, but I can oversee your servants here. I promise your money and food will be handed out fairly."

Bauti's eyes narrowed, as if to say, "What are you up to?" Makari, however, smiled.

"That is most noble," she said. "But you need healing."

Ashai tore a shred of cloth off the hem of his shirt and wrapped it around the wound.

"It has stopped bleeding already, Princess. It would be an honor to serve you."

He bowed, his fingertips touching his forehead in the Pushtani way.

"What is your name?" The question came from Bauti, cold and knife-edged.

"Yes, I would have it, too," Makari said. "I want to reward your valor."

"I am Ashai, Princess," he said, holding his bow. He felt the fire of Bauti's glare, but ignored him.

"Ashai? Ashai what? You have a family name, do you not?" Bauti's voice had not softened. If anything, its steel was now forged with anger. Ashai made a mental note to deal with the man later.

But for now, he forced a calmer approach. "No, my lord captain. I was raised in an orphanage in the southern city of Brynn. I was taken in by a kind merchant who raised me well and taught me his business. I have no family name of my own, but should I choose one, it would be his. Larish."

"Well then, Ashai Larish," Makari said, cutting Bauti off, "when you have seen to this task, come to the palace. We will hold a banquet where my father will thank you personally."

Ashai bowed again, keeping a smile from spreading across his face. "As you command, Princess. I would be honored and—"

She had remounted her gelding, turning away, the matter closed. Bauti grinned and leaned close to Ashai's ear. "It will be a very small banquet for a very small occasion. Barely a dinner, really. Do try to dress like something other than a common merchant."

"But my good Captain," Ashai replied, forcing a thin smile, "Dressing above my station would be dishonorable."

Bauti frowned at him and mounted his horse. "You'd do well to remember your station then, Larish. And do not be late. His Majesty has more important things to do than wait on a merchant."

Yes, like planning his own funeral, Ashai thought as they rode away.

The Watcher turned from the bakery's second story window as the Princess and her company galloped away, the towering Captain Bauti watchful at her side. Disappointment simmered in The Watcher's heart at what he'd seen.

Ashai had shown promise, selecting the boy and influencing him with subtle magic. His plan to come under the Princess's good graces was, frankly, brilliant and had worked quite well. He hadn't heard everything that was said, but he read lips well enough to know Ashai would be in the Palace that evening. If he wanted, the King and Makari could be dead by sundown.

His subtle command of Denari Lai magic was masterful, and he moved through the crowd like a shadow. No one in the square would remember seeing him come or go, though everyone would remember him saving the Princess.

But the young assassin had made several mistakes, small things really, but mistakes nonetheless. He'd allowed Makari's beauty to distract him from the all-important mission, to make his heart skip a beat where it needed to be steady. He'd allowed his emotions to get in the way where the boy's death was concerned, and had almost come to blows with the captain.

That would have been an interesting fight, one that probably would have left both of them dead. But a dead assassin couldn't kill a King.

And the boy's death was regrettable, a sin for which Ashai would reckon with God and God alone. Denari Lai were sworn to kill no innocents, and while the assassin did not wield the blade that spilled the boy's blood, he had set the events in motion that left a child dead. A child of the streets, a poor orphan whose only crime was trying to survive in the shadow of a corrupt and opulent empire.

That kind of sloppiness made The Watcher wonder if Ashai would accomplish his mission.

Still, the young assassin found a way inside the palace and would dine that evening with royalty. Barring any further mistakes, his infiltration could well be a success.

The Watcher closed the shutters, moved down the steps with the grace of a cat, and exited the back door of the spice shop, inhaling one last sweet-hot breath of Snow Spice, a reminder of home. He decided further observation would be necessary before reporting Ashai's progress to their superiors. For now, he would continue to observe and stand by as reinforcement. That was what he'd done for all these years. A few more weeks wouldn't make a difference.

CHAPTER TWO

Pachat trudged along the rutted, dusty path, iron manacles slicing into his ankles, the brutal sun smashing down on his shoulders like a giant hammer. Ahead of him, Tryst stumbled, catching himself on the shoulder of the man beside him. He stole a furtive glance at the slave master who marched a few paces ahead, then let out a sigh of relief that the man hadn't seen.

Tryst exchanged a worried glance with Pachat, then resumed the march, their line moving with clinks and clanks, the air occasionally cracked open with the snap of a whip.

It had been a hard day in the mines, but then, they all were. The Pushtani Masters drove them from sunup to sundown, but stopped them early today, making them march back in the brutalizing midday sun.

Pachat almost wished they'd worked them all day. The high desert air cooled quickly after sundown, and walking back was often a treat after a long day sweating underground.

The stark, treeless foothills south of Nishi'iti broke many men, with their lack of water, summer heat, and withering winter cold. But Pachat had survived five long, hard years here, never forgetting the day the Pushtanis had ransacked his village. They had taken him hostage, along with his betrothed, though her fate had turned out better than his.

Kendshi had been taken to Dar Tallus, her Nishi'iti beauty saving her from a miner's life that probably would have killed her. She'd always been a gentle soul, nurturing and kind, and while she had a tough side, this was not her kind of work.

So as much as he missed her, as much as his heart ached, Pachat thanked Nishi for taking his love somewhere gentler. Safer. Here, with the slavers ... he shuddered at the thought.

They rounded the base of a hill and came into sight of the slave camp. It didn't look like much, just a cluster of tents cowering at the base of a crude, wooden fortress. Designed to keep slaves out rather than defend against another military, the walls of the fort were built from logs twelve feet high, sharpened at the top and lashed together by rope and pegs. A few Pushtani soldiers walked the battlements, and a stout keep made of logs peeked over the wall from the center of the fortress.

Nishi'itis did not get to go inside the fort, unless they were being punished. Hangings and beatings took place inside, often for the soldiers' entertainment, but otherwise, slaves lived in tents. So defeated were the slaves that the fort never had to close its gate.

The slaves' canvas shelters formed their own little city around the base of the wooden fortress, nestled like children against their mother's skirts.

They did little to keep out the summer heat, even less to keep out winter's cold. But the slavers knew that frozen slaves did no work, so they provided firewood enough to keep their workers alive.

The slaves marched through the low, outer barriers and into camp just as the sun started its descent in the west, the slave masters stopping them on the main pathway through their tents. They worked their way down the line, unlocking shackles and letting the chains drop to the ground where they stood.

Next morning, the slaves would line up again without being told. Even now, as shackles dropped to the dirt and slaves felt the weight of iron fall from their legs, they stood fast. Their eyes stayed straight ahead. Their hands hung limp at their sides, and their shoulders slumped. These were beaten men, men with broken wills and severed spines.

The slave boss sauntered down the left side of their line, his belly straining the laces of his black leather armor. He patted the whip that rode his thigh, looking each man in the face, daring them to make eye contact.

No one did.

He stopped before he reached Pachat, his pig face twisting into a smile that showed his rotted teeth. He spit a wad of chew leaf into the dirt and held a folded paper above his head.

"I hold in my hand an order from Her Majesty, Princess Makari, heir to the throne of Pushtan," the slave master bellowed, sarcasm dripping from his words like blood from fangs. "Her Majesty instructs me to deliver this letter to a slave, and to do so without delay."

He marched to Pachat's side, and stood with his belly pressing against Pachat's hip. Pachat fought the urge to punch the man in his turned up nose, to make blood gush from the man's face. To knock out one or two of his rotten teeth, and blacken his beady little rat-eyes. The beating he would take would almost be worth it to see Slave Master Cargil crying like a little girl.

But then Pachat wouldn't get his letter.

"Form a circle!" Cargil barked.

Having been through this drill before, the slaves formed a ring without hesitation. Three rings, actually, of forty men each. Perhaps ten guards, armed with clubs and cudgels and whips, mixed into the circles and for a moment Pachat thought how easy it would be to overwhelm the men and take control.

But no. There were real soldiers nearby, with swords and axes. His friends would die.

Cargil shoved the paper under Pachat's nose.

"It's story time, slave," he announced. "It's bad for slave morale if one slave receives something the others do not, so everyone will hear your lover's letter. I'm sure most of them will imagine fucking her tonight, or maybe even as you read to them."

Pachat forced down bile and rage and took the letter in his hands. Kendshi's smooth, flowing handwriting danced across the page, clean and pure. She'd been forced to write in Pushtani, but had mastered it well.

"Come on, slave!" Spit flew with Cargil's words. "We all know your daddy was a Pushtani soldier who lowered himself to fuck your mother. So you can read the language."

Fuming, Pachat cleared his throat and read.

Dearest Pachat,

I hope this finds you well, and that life in the mines has not harmed you. It seems forever since I saw you, since you held my hand and led me from the village the day we were attacked.

Cargil snickered. "I'd make her hold something other than my hand."

The slavers all laughed, but Pachat ignored them. This was Cargil's way of being the big wolf, the dominant male. Responding would only play into his bite.

He read on, instead.

Life here is safe, if not predictable. The Princess is a fair and compassionate mistress, who treats me well. Probably better than I deserve. Overall, I'm happy here, though I miss many things about home. I miss snow in the winter, and the spice we make every fall. I miss shepherd's lamb, cooked over an open fire, and our winter celebration most of all.

Pachat's grip tightened on the paper. They did not celebrate winter—it was a killer far worse than Pushtanis. But during the season, they held a three-day celebration of Nishi's providence, three holy days of prayer and feasting. Three holy days Kendshi was not allowed to celebrate or even mention for fear of punishment.

"Keep reading, slave," Cargil said. "Some of your comrades are just starting to touch themselves."

The princess has agreed to request your relocation to Dar Tallus, though she does not think her father will agree. King Abadas does not like Nishi'itis, especially Nishi'iti men, and every day he's more and more careful about who he allows inside. Still, Princess Makari promises to try. She has a good heart, and I believe she will do as she says.

"Don't get your hopes up, slave. You won't be crawling into your lover's bed anytime soon. That's for King Abadas, should he want to dirty himself with Nishi'iti filth."

Pachat allowed himself a brief glance at the slave master, hoping to lock eyes with him, but the man's back was turned.

This is all I have time for, my love, but know that I think of you daily. Remember that the same sun warms both our shoulders, so we're never really that far apart.

Love always,

Kendshi.

Cargil snatched the letter from his hands, balled it up as tight as possible, and tossed it in a nearby campfire.

"All the princess ordered me to do was to deliver it," he smirked. "She didn't say to let you keep it. And we all know what her father, the king, likes to do to Nishi'iti slop like you."

He ran his finger along the whip at his belt.

This time Pachat did lock eyes with the slave master, his fists bunched at his sides. He took a step forward, toward the black-armored man, and for an instant Cargil looked like he might step back. Then Pachat realized his mistake.

A whip cracked, and fire shot up his ankle. He spun, but too late—the slave driver jerked the whip and pulled his feet out from under him. Pachat hit the hard ground, his breath exploding from his lungs and his head bouncing off the hard dirt.

He started to get up, but Cargil put a booted foot in the middle of his chest and pushed down, keeping his lungs from filling with air. Pachat's arms and legs flailed as he fought for breath, and his vision started going dark. Grinning, Cargil lifted his foot.

"You think to challenge me, you worthless piece of shit?" Breath finally rushed back into Pachat's lungs as Cargil kicked him in the side of the head and went on. "You know the punishment for challenging your masters."

An instant later, they were dragging him toward the whipping pole. Pachat didn't resist.

CHAPTER THREE

The main audience Hall of the Pushtani Palace was modestly grand. At least, that's how her father had described it. The ceiling was tall, but not tall enough to seem ostentatious or intimidate visiting dignitaries. The décor was ornate, but not extreme. The floors were marble, but the walls simple granite. Gilding was kept to a minimum, and light came from oil lamps instead of chandeliers. Here they hosted lesser houses, those who didn't, in her father's mind, deserve the throne room itself.

Her father sat on a wooden throne, on a slight dais, looking out upon the man and woman who had approached. Makari sat to his left, with Kendshi and Captain Bauti like statues behind them. The dark-haired Nishi'iti girl with her tilted eyes was quite the contrast to the white-topped mountain beside her.

Lord Brendar wore the most ridiculous costume Makari had ever seen. He tried to mix-and-match a blue doublet with black vest to represent her family's colors, with purple hose and a flowing yellow cape to represent his own house. It was a shame Brendar's wife had died, or he might have been better dressed. As it was, his sister stood with him, face pale and features pinched, her own dress a muted combination of purple and yellow with a simple blue and black necklace to represent the Royal family.

Not that Makari liked her own dress any better. Her father had insisted she wear the yellow dress—which had been her late mother's—

with purple highlights to honor their guest. The yellow washed out her skin, making her look like she'd been dead for three days, and the purple made every vein stand out under her skin.

She tried to pay attention, acted like she was listening as the old Lord droned on about her beauty, her intellect, and how he would love and cherish her. But the fact remained, Lord Brendar had sons her age. He could no more love her then she could him, so all his words were just wind in the leaves. She found herself staring not at the man, but at the stack of boxes and chests he'd left as gifts. Offerings.

Payment.

"If Her Highness recalls," Brendar said, shifting from one foot to the other, "my estate lies in the north, in the northeast foothills to be exact. On the border with Nishi'iti. I control nearly twenty-five percent of the kingdom's gold mines, thirty percent of their silver mines, and a good portion of precious stones as well. Such wealth will go a long way toward paying down the debt the crown has accrued."

For the first time in an hour, he had Makari's attention.

"Is one of your mines near Trellwin?" she asked.

Her attention seemed to catch him off guard, and he stammered for a moment. Seeing his discomfort, his sister answered for him.

"No, Princess. As my brother said, our holdings are in the northeast, directly adjacent to the Great Chasm. Thus, the crown would have direct control over crucial defensive position, which—"

"Never mind then," Makari snapped. She'd hoped to demand Pachat's release, but Brendar had nothing to do with those mines. "Tell me, Lord Brendar, if I were robbed in the city square by an orphan boy, how would you respond?"

This didn't seem to fluster the Lord as much as her first question.

"I'd have his head. No one assaults royalty and lives."

Her father put his head in his hands, while Makari stifled a grin and let her mind wander back to that day in the square, when she first met Ashai. She remembered the shock on his rugged face when Captain Bauti drove his sword through the boy's chest, how he turned deathly white. That boy's death had touched the cloth merchant, meaning he had something Lord Brendar did not: a heart.

And having a heart made him more of a man than almost anyone in the hall.

"Then I would find the orphanage he came from and burn it to the ground. That should be lesson enough for the thieves to never bother you again."

"You would kill innocent children because someone they knew stole coins from me?"

Brendar's face turned bright red. His lower lip quivered, and his sister again answered in his place.

"What my brother meant to say—"

"Let your brother explain this," Makari snapped. "If I'm to marry someone old enough to be my father, whose only interest in me is power, who will bed me nightly until his heart gives out, I would hear from his own lips why the lives of dozens of innocent children are a just price for the actions of one."

"Princess Makari," Brendar said, drawing himself up and puffing his chest out, "being a woman, you may not know the importance of a strong response to aggression against the throne. One cannot allow commoners to lay even a finger on someone of your stature."

Makari drew her dagger so fast Lord Brendar actually jumped, while his sister squeaked, looking like she might turn tail and run. Makari raised the knife over her head and drove it point first into the soft wood of the table. Her father looked up, winced, and put his head back in his hands. Behind her, Captain Bauti chuckled.

"Makari," her father muttered, "the table was a gift from the king of Slevonia on the anniversary of my tenth year with your mother, the late Queen. Try not to scar it." Eyes smoldering, Makari pulled the knife from the wood and returned it to the scabbard at her belt.

"Never presume that what's between my legs has any bearing on what's between my ears, Lord Brendar. I guarantee I know as much about forceful responses as you, or did you forget who my father is?"

Brendar bowed his head, a look of defeat flickering on his face. He had to have known his chances were small. He was just so … old.

"Those dozens of children you would've killed are citizens of this realm," she continued. "Such violence might work in your duchy, but when you're ruling a nation, you must think of your people's support. And killing children never wins anyone's heart."

Lord Brendar departed with little ceremony, his sister shuffling along behind him. As soon as they were gone, her father slapped both hands on the table, shoved his chair back, and vaulted to his feet.

"Makari, stop this childish behavior! We must find you a suitor, and

Lord Brendar would have been perfect. He's a strong leader, and he controls much of our kingdom's wealth. You could at least have been respectful!"

Makari pushed her chair back, stood, and walked to her father. She took his face in her hands and watched his expression return to normal. The tension in his shoulders relaxed, and he took a deep breath.

Smiling, Makari folded him in a hug and kissed him on the cheek.

"Father, please trust me. I'm not going to marry someone as old as you. I am not going to marry anyone who doesn't make me happy."

Her father put his hands on her shoulders and stared deep into her eyes.

"But you must marry someone," he said. "And you can't keep angering everyone who comes to try or suitors will stop coming."

Makari had half a mind to be even crueler in hopes that suitors would stop coming to the palace. She was tired of being paraded like a prize horse, a fine dress, or prime cow in front of the men her father considered worthy.

Thinking of it fanned her anger, and she lost control. "If you're going to force me to marry someone, Father, you may as well make Ashai a Lord and force me into his bed!"

The entire room gaped at her, even Bauti's jaw hanging down. Heat crawled up her neck and into her cheeks. What in the world had made her say that?

Her father turned away, planting his hands on his hips and pacing toward the far wall. A serving girl dodged him, then dashed for the service door.

Makari kicked herself for letting her words slip. Certainly Ashai had shown courage and humility. And he was handsome, true. But still, that would be like Kendshi marrying Lord Brendar.

The thought made her snicker, and her father wheeled on her, face purple.

"This is not funny!" His voice came out taut as he fought for control. "Marrying an up-jumped lord would weaken our position. Everyone would know his nobility was a gift, a reward for saving your life, and whatever duchy or territory we gave him would be small and insignificant. It would leave you vulnerable to the stronger houses.

"You must understand, Makari. You're a Princess. Your duty is to this kingdom, not to yourself."

Makari opened her mouth to confess her fib, but her father silenced her with a wave.

"We will speak no more of this. Where's the Nishi'iti wench of yours?"

Kendshi appeared, seemingly out of nowhere.

"Yes, Majesty?"

"Take the princess to her chambers and remind her why we have classes in our society."

The King spun on his heel, and marched from the Audience Hall.

Moments later, as they shuffled down the corridor toward Makari's chambers, Kendshi patted Makari's shoulder.

"That was quite cruel of you, princess," she giggled. "One might think you were trying to frustrate your father."

Makari snickered, her hand flying to cover her mouth. Sometimes the half-Nishi'iti woman seemed to read her mind, even peering into its darkest, most hidden corners.

"Did my father actually think I'd agree to marry Brendar? I understand my responsibilities, but I'm a Princess, not a corpse."

"A corpse would be more appropriate for—"

Shouting erupted behind them, followed by the clatter of armored men at a run. Makari and Kendshi exchanged a glance, then ran back toward the hall.

A squad of Royal Guard members, their armor gleaming blue, ran past them, toward the hall.

Bauti's voice thundered over the rest. "Defensive perimeter! No one enters this room! And bring me Lord Brendar and his sister. Now!"

Makari and Kendshi skidded to a stop in front of the guards. Their leader, a grizzled sergeant with a scar on one cheek, raised an eyebrow, and shouted back over his shoulder.

"Captain, does that order include her highness, the Princess?"

Someone mumbled inside the hall, then Bauti appeared behind his men. He pointed at Kendshi.

"The Nishi'iti stays outside, but allow the princess to enter."

Makari narrowed her eyes. Bauti had never singled out Kendshi before. Why now?

She nodded to Kendshi and went inside. Her father sat on the steps leading up to his throne, head in his hands, staring at a box on the marble floor between his feet. When he saw Makari, he scrambled to close the wooden lid and put his foot on the box.

"Father, I already saw the box. Now what's in it?"

"Makari, some matters are best handled by—"

She stomped and used her eyes like daggers to his throat. "If you say 'men,' I swear I'll scream."

"... your father. I was going to say your father. Me. Children shouldn't see some things."

She moved to his side and put a hand on his shoulder, the midnight blue velvet of his doublet smooth and warm.

"I'm hardly a child any longer, father. Aren't you trying to marry me off to men with a foot in the tomb?"

That brought a chuckle, albeit a weak one. With a deep sigh, her father, King Abadas I, reached down and opened the plain, wooden box.

She gasped, and her heart stopped for a beat.

Inside the box, on a blood-red cushion, sat a curved dagger, its blade impossibly black and etched with strange markings, with the darkest granite she'd ever seen as a handle. It was a simple weapon, plain but effective. Efficient, even, as the pommel formed a second, smaller blade. She recognized it immediately: the Denari Lai had left their warning.

Her father would die.

CHAPTER FOUR

M akari apologized to Ashai for the blandness of the palace's smaller dining hall, but inside he cringed at its opulence. Plush rugs warmed the gleaming marble floor, and the high, vaulted ceiling bounced voices in near-endless echoes. Crystal chandeliers lit the room, their light reflecting off gold, silver, and brass. Even the small, cherry wood table, with its ornate carvings and high-backed chairs, sang of royal riches.

Wealth offended God, and this room reeked of it.

Ashai admired the knife he'd just used to slice off a bit of lamb. The edge shone keen and razor sharp. He could do it now, kill both his targets before the guards could react. Child's play.

The fools. It was just two hours from the dagger's delivery—no doubt the work of a second Denari Lai—and Bauti had so tightened security that it was squeezing life from palace residents. To enter this meeting, Ashai felt like he'd been violated rather than searched.

And yet they left all he needed to kill his targets sitting in front of him.

He sighed. Fools.

To his right sat King Abadas Damar, pouring wine into a silver goblet, his snowy beard splayed across the vast expanse of his belly. His red velvet jacket looked ready to burst at the buttons. The king's expression reminded Ashai of curdled milk, as if he'd been left too long in the sun.

To the left, Makari regarded her father with summer-sky eyes shrouded in worry. She wore a ludicrous teal dress with a collar of yellow lace and ruffled sleeves that made her shoulders look twice as wide as Ashai's. But the hideous dress couldn't hide her beauty any more than the night could hide the beauty of the stars.

Ashai set the knife on the table. He'd only been among them an hour, and these people remained guarded. He would wait until they trusted him with all their hearts, then he would cut those hearts from their chests and raise them high to strike fear in every Pushtani.

"Your Majesty," he said. "The lamb is magnificent, but you must have more pressing matters than dining with a simple merchant."

"Simple merchant," the king repeated. His gaze seemed distant, as if he were really quite far away. "Captain Bauti, is this man a simple merchant?"

Bauti lurked near the back of the room, his gaze never leaving Ashai. Ashai avoided eye contact with him, but rage still burned in his heart. Captain Bauti, killer of children, would burn for eternity before Ashai was done in Dar Tallus.

"Indeed not, Majesty. He displayed incredible heroism … for one of baseborn roots."

Sarcasm dripped from his lips like wine from the king's. Makari shot him an icy glare.

"Father, we should raise Ashai to lord," she said, smiling for the first time in an hour. "Grant him lands and a title. Then an orphan from Brynn can spread word of your good grace and smash our enemies' lies about you."

Abadas considered that, dipping a hand-sized piece of bread in his wine, and mashing it into his mouth. Crumbs clung to his beard and tumbled to his belly.

"Hmmm, well, we do have Laramor," he said. "Lord Penter—half-breed upstart—defaulted on his taxes, so I relieved him of his lands and titles. And his head." He burst into laughter, sending bread and wine everywhere.

"Your Grace," Bauti said, "Laramor is on the Nishi'iti border. That lord would face constant attacks by Nishi'iti savages, and even now the slaves are restless. He would need a strong military background and unquestionable loyalty to handle Laramor."

"Never should have trusted that half-Nishi'iti dog." Abadas studied Ashai's face. "You *do* look like there's some Nishi'iti in you."

Ashai shifted in his chair, his hand inching closer to the knife.

Abadas stared at him a moment longer, then shook his head.

"You looked like you might wet yourself," he grumbled. "Makari, I think your dear hero may need to use the privy."

"Father, you're awful!" Makari said, eyes wide. "Master Ashai is a guest. You shouldn't scare him."

Bauti grinned, smug against the wall, his arms crossed over his chest.

"I wasn't frightened," Ashai said in his softest voice.

All laughter stopped.

"You looked afraid," Bauti said. "You smelled afraid."

"Lord Captain, even on Tailor's Row we know of His Majesty's great love of jest and even greater hospitality. He would never harm a guest in his palace. I think perhaps you smelled your own tunic. I don't think it's been cleaned in some time."

Bauti's face turned purple and he puffed his chest out, taking a step toward the table. Abadas's chuckle stopped him short.

"Ah, Bauti, you should stick to crossing blades, not tongues or wits."

Bauti bowed. "Gladly, Sire." The embers in his eyes told Ashai they might very well cross blades someday. Unfortunate for the captain.

"That still leaves the issue of your reward, Master Ashai," Abadas said. "I won't have it said that Abadas Damar doesn't reward his friends or crush his enemies. But how?"

His gaze went distant again.

"Perhaps we should sleep on it, father," Makari suggested. "We may come upon suitable rewards in our dreams."

"Yes," the king said. "Yes, good idea. I shall answer in the morning, merchant."

Ashai inclined his head. "Truly, Majesty, your gratitude is all the reward I need."

"I will escort him back to town," Bauti said, stepping a bit too close for Ashai's comfort. Despite his graying hair, the captain made an imposing figure, just as a mountain imposed, despite the snow on its peak.

"No one leaves the palace tonight," Makari said standing and putting her hand on Ashai's shoulder. Her touch caused a tingle that made him squirm. "Father's orders. We should put Ashai in the guest chambers tonight."

"Done," the king said.

"But highness," Bauti interjected. "What of the threat?"

Abadas considered only a moment. "Put two guards outside his door. If he even peeks out, kill him. Merchant, do not test my gratefulness!"

"Of course not, Majesty."

"I will show him to the chambers," Makari said, offering her arm. "Captain Bauti, you may accompany us if it will make you stop scowling at me."

Bauti's face had just regained its normal color, but now it flushed plum again.

Ashai linked arms with Makari and let her lead him from the dining room, grinning at Bauti as he passed.

Marwan Bauti stalked the corridor like a thundercloud stalking a valley, glowering at everyone who passed, making servants, soldiers, and even some minor lords duck out of his way. He could feel his neck muscles bunching, even as his fists clenched. How dare that common merchant treat him with such arrogance? And Makari was smitten with him! A man she barely knew, an arrogant commoner with no noble blood.

How could the Princess not listen to her trusted, longtime protector? Yes, Ashai was handsome, that much was certain. But something was off about him, and left a gaping pit in the bottom of Bauti's stomach.

He had been by Makari's side since the day she was born. How could she choose a merchant over him?

Still steaming, Bauti turned the corner into an empty hallway and paused. He glanced around, furtive, and made sure he was alone. Then he twisted a sconce a few degrees to the right until a portion of the wall slid backward. A great sucking sound drew air from the corridor, as if life were rushing into a crypt, and Bauti pressed on the slab of marble until it was open enough for him to step inside. Then he slid the panel back into place before anyone could see.

Few people knew about the passages, but Bauti had been in the palace for decades and knew many things most people did not. They'd been built to allow the original Pushtani royal families to come and go without being seen, to add security to their then-tenuous hold on power. They'd seen assassins everywhere then, behind curtains and in shadows and lurking corners, and the passages allowed kings and princes to move without exposing themselves to danger.

Now, though, even the King and Makari did not know of the passages. Only Bauti and one other man.

The man he was going to see.

He had to feel his way along the cool, granite walls, for the torches on the walls were cold. But he knew the way, and a few minutes later, he stood in front of a wooden panel, raising his fist to knock.

To his surprise, the door slid open and there, holding a lit oil lamp, stood Samaran Tan. Pushtan's chief spy didn't look at all like a spy. He was a thick man, with a belly like an ale keg, and shoulders that slouched as if the weight of the world rested there. His blue eyes stared out from under a cliff of a forehead, and his mouth was touched with femininity, a flower bud or a bow in the middle of his face.

"So good to see you Captain," he said, pulling the door closed behind him. "I would invite you in, but I'm currently entertaining company and would not want our meeting to be overheard."

Tan had eyes and ears—noses, fingers, and tongues even—in every crack and corner of the place. If it happened in the Palace, Samaran Tan would know.

"Thank you for seeing me, Lord Tan." Bauti masked the distaste in his voice. He had little like for spies, with their sneaking and lying, but he recognized their usefulness. "Have you discovered the identity of our Denari Lai?"

Tan ran his meaty fingers through his thinning, mud-colored hair. "Good Captain, you know I would come to you right away if I had such information. What is it you really want to see me about?"

Bauti hated feeling like a man saw inside his head, read him like a scroll or a book, but that was how Tan operated. Knowing people was his business.

"I'm sure you've heard we have a new hero in the palace?"

Tan giggled, a child's laugh coming from a near-giant.

"Master Ashai, yes? Quite the brave man, I understand. But since you're here, you must believe him a threat to your dear Makari."

Bauti looked at the floor and shifted his stance.

"My instincts are screaming at me. I don't trust him. I could use any information your people can find. Strictly to ensure the royal family is safe, of course."

Samaran Tan raised his eyebrows. "Of course, for their safety. But I'm afraid my assets are quite busy. Trying to find a Denari Lai is difficult enough without getting involved in this ... affair. You have your own sources, do you not?"

Bauti fought the instinct to strangle the man.

"I will utilize my sources, too, but the safety of the King requires both of our efforts."

"As I said, Captain, my assets are too busy to be involved in—"

Bauti drew his sword so fast Tan jumped back, bumping his head on the wooden door. His hands came up in front of his chest, sausage-like fingers spread wide.

"This is a matter of Royal security!" Bauti growled. "I'd hate to think you don't care about the King's safety. Don't you find the timing of this man's arrival somewhat suspect?"

Tan's lips pursed and he made a clucking sound, like a mother scolding a child, while his wide forehead scrunched down.

"So you suspect Master Ashai could be our assassin?"

Bauti shrugged, sheathing his sword. "He moved very quickly to stop that boy in the square. Too quickly."

Tan considered a moment, then nodded.

"I see your point. I will have my sources look into it and let you know what they find."

"That's all I ask, Lord Tan. That the spymaster does his job."

Bauti turned on his heel and started to march back the way he'd come, but Tan cleared his throat.

"You know, Captain, information is my sword. The next time you draw your blade against me, I won't hesitate to wield mine. And it is just as deadly as steel."

Bauti's throat clenched. He looked back over his shoulder.

"Understood, Lord Tan. Next time I draw steel on you, I'll be sure to use it."

Tan giggled again, the sound turning Bauti's stomach.

"Now, Captain, I need you to leave these passages through a different door. Follow the tunnel to the first intersection, then turn right and follow it to the end. No one will see you. It would be most unfortunate if master Ashai knew we're conspiring against him. Even worse if the Princess found out."

Bauti nodded, turned around, and followed the tunnels. When he reached the door a few minutes later, he stood open and stepped outside to be assailed by the worst reek he'd ever smelled. Sliding the door closed behind him, he stepped cautiously around the middens heap and started up the hill towards the palace gate.

"So you think this is funny, Lord Tan?" His boots squished through the slop under foot. "Remember this when I shove my blade through your heart."

CHAPTER FIVE

Ashai crouched behind a column of rock, staring into the fire-lit cavern beyond. Sweat rolled down his face, soaking his collar and trickling down his back. He fought the urge to shiver as it tingled along his spine.

From somewhere deep within the cave came a loud crack, followed by a wail of pure agony. Next came the clash of hammer on anvil, followed by the smell of smoke, and the sharp tang of iron on his tongue. The sounds of an army being built.

He ducked as a column of soldiers passed by, dark men dressed in dark leather, with studs and spikes and steel rings glittering in every joint. Armed with wickedly curved swords, three-tipped spears, eight-pointed morning stars, and double-edged battle-axes, and weapons he'd never seen, the men marched past his position, grim and foreboding.

Their faces came from a nightmare, dark skin swirled with tattoos and punctured with the same rings and studs and spikes that adorned their uniforms. It was almost as if their armor was merely a second skin, a thick black shell permanently attached, designed to frighten as much as protect. Cold, cruel eyes dark as midnight scanned the cave as the soldiers marched past, column after column, a never-ending line marching up from below.

Some soldiers—maybe one in twenty or thirty—stood head and shoulders above the rest, rippling in muscle and sinew, carved from the mountain itself. Black as night, with eyes the color of fire and fangs that dripped blood, these ones drove the others, barking commands and cracking whips, when needed.

And to make matters worse, they wielded power. Not pure, enriching power, like his, but a corrupt, twisted kind of sorcery that filled his nostrils with the stench of decay, and chilled his skin like the air from a long-sealed tomb.

Ashai had to know where they were going. Something inside him drove him, implored him to find their destination.

He looked down and found himself dressed in the same studded armor, a notched and serrated sword on his hip, a small iron shield in his hand. Without a thought, he ran from behind the pillar and fell into formation, marching in step with the soldiers.

If they found him out of place, no one said a word. They kept marching, onward and upward, driving toward the surface. They didn't seem to tire. Even when Ashai's legs were throbbing, his feet screaming in pain, his back clenching, the soldiers marched on without even a whisper of dissent.

After what seemed an eternity, they rounded a corner and a light appeared ahead. Upon seeing it, the soldiers began to chant, banging sword or axe on shield or rock in a rhythm that grew in speed and frenzy.

They jogged, then cantered. And as the first of their column reached the opening, they broke into a run, releasing a war cry so bloodcurdling, so terrorizing, that Ashai, for all his training and all his conditioning, wanted to hide.

He burst into the sunlight, and dodged to the side, out of line. He crouched again behind a boulder this time and watched as the flood of dark soldiers poured from the mouth of the cave. They became a raging torrent, a never-ending deluge of violence and death, and wherever they went the green of the earth turned brown or black, sunlight turned to shadow, and death settled on land like a shroud.

From Pushtan in the South to Lyres in the north, everything and everyone died.

Ashai sat bolt upright in bed, his sheets drenched in sweat, his breath coming in ragged gasps. The tatters of the dream slipped away into the night, but the image of the soldiers and their masters lingered, along with the shadow of death fallen across the world.

The dream was a sign, but of what? He tried puzzling through, but could not.

He reached for a cup of water he left on the nightstand, his hand shaking so much that he spilled the water on himself.

Makari was clouding his mind. He needed to pray, but he could not do so, at least not aloud, for the guard Bauti left outside the door would hear. He'd been in the palace five days now, and prayed only once. His power was fading, and his body was paying the price.

He gave fleeting thought to sneaking out and paying Bauti's throat a visit with his dagger, but he couldn't afford the indulgence. The captain's death would arouse suspicion and endanger his plans. After God had made them go so perfectly, Ashai dared not ruin them. He would kill Bauti for his sin against the boy, but not before the captain watched his king and princess die.

He rose while the sun still slumbered, and he longed to say his morning prayers in the tradition of his faith: prone, facing the rising sun. But even if the guard would not hear, the one called Tan had spies roaming secret corridors, listening to guests and inhabitants through walls and paintings and wardrobes. It would not do for one to see him praising the One True God instead of worshipping the five false ones that ruled here in Pushtan.

Not that these people were devout worshippers. Their relations with their gods were distant. Aloof. They spent more time worshipping commerce than any of the Five Gods.

So instead, trembling with longing, he went through the physical motions of praying to The Five while repeating Nishi'iti prayers in his mind. As he prayed, he felt his hold on the thread of magic strengthen, the power coursing through him like fire. It felt not like something foreign entering him, but some part of him awakening, filling a void in his soul.

The Power of Nishi cured all.

He reached into the sleeve of the modest purple robe he planned to wear that day. Two thirds of the way down, where he could reach it only with the garment off, he found a small pocket. Inside that pocket, he found a tiny, velvet purse. He withdrew the purse and walked to a small table in the corner of the chambers.

Taking a deep breath, he looked around. There was some danger doing this here, knowing the palace had ears and eyes. But he had to be sure.

Untying the drawstring, he turned the purse upside down and three cut diamonds spilled out onto the polished wooden tabletop. The size of the tip of his pinky finger, each gem was a different shape. A round one represented Abadas, an oval Makari. And a square represented Ashai himself. All three had been meticulously carved so facets twinkled and reflected light in almost perfect proportions. All three glowed the color of the summer sky.

One by one, Ashai brushed the stones with the tip of his forefinger. He held his breath and counted to ten, but nothing happened.

Letting out a deep sigh, he returned the stones to their pouch and stuffed it in the hidden pocket. Had any one of them turned red, the person it represented would have died that day, no questions asked. Ashai found himself relieved they had remained blue, for he had not yet gained his targets' trust. His kill would be less effective.

As the sun came up, he looked around the room, ticking off in his mind a list of sins it held. Opulence. Vanity. Waste. Arrogance. Idolatry. All resided in the high-ceilinged room, starting with its gigantic, ornate bed, carved from fine, dark wood. Silk sheets and a thick comforter had kept him warm, but a simple wool blanket would have done as well and at no offense to Nishi. The gilding on the walls, and the fancy, woven rugs looked expensive enough to feed the city's poor, and the white marble walls gleamed with the dull ambivalence of wealth.

God abhorred wealth.

Ashai sighed and put on the soft, cotton robe they'd given him, frowning at the fancy embroidery and fur-lined collar. So much excess surrounded him. He wondered if it tainted his soul to be around it.

Still, he did God's bidding here. Nishi'itis had suffered too long at the hands of Pushtanis, both in the northlands and here, where they worked as slaves or prostitutes. The deaths of Abadas and Makari would bring Pushtan to its knees, forcing the army to pull out of the northern foothills, leaving fertile land to Nishi'itis. Land his nation needed to survive.

His mission came from God and the Chargh Lai. They would forgive his sins in accomplishing it.

He had just tied his brown silk sash around his waist when a timid knock came at the door. He opened it to find Makari there, dressed in a gown the color of eggplant. Sadly, it was shaped like one too. Pink lace adorned the bodice and puffy sleeves tumbled like waterfalls down her arms, leaving her shoulders bare.

"Highness," he said, bowing. "Your dress is quite …"

Her eyes flashed. "It was my mother's!"

"… lovely. It is no match for your own beauty, of course."

She frowned. "My father makes me wear her things. It's … frustrating."

Ashai inclined his head. "It may help him remember her, Highness. He may see her in you when you wear these."

She gave him a smile then, an expression that made him feel like she'd shared it with him alone, and that no one else would ever see it. For a moment, he felt light-headed.

He cleared his throat and snatched his thoughts back. How did she always distract him so?

"I thought we might break fast together," she suggested. "Without Captain Bauti."

"I would be most honored, Your Highness," he said, following her into the corridor. "I suspect the captain doesn't like me much."

She shrugged, and he glanced at her bare shoulders. Guilt gnawed at him. "Bauti trusts no one, where my father and I are concerned."

"Especially you."

She blushed, and looked out an arched window as she passed.

"It will be hot today," she said.

"Not as hot as Brynn, Highness," he said. "There it gets so hot your feet blister just walking in sandals."

"Surely not!" She laughed, her eyes sparkling. She surprised him by taking his arm again. "I have heard Brynn is cooled by winds off the sea, and never gets hot."

"Her Highness is misinformed." He knew. He'd lived there for years, perfecting his disguise. "When the winds are off the water, the climate is moderate. But in late summer, the wind is often from the east, hot and dry and carrying the yellow sand of the wastelands. Some days, your lungs fill with the dust, and you eat it in your food.

"They say that on those days, you can cook a pig by leaving it outside for an hour."

Makari's heels clicked on the marble floor as they rounded a corner and came to a simple, wooden double door. She opened it and led Ashai into a low-ceilinged dining room, lit by oil lamps and braziers. Plush rugs covered the floor, and a small, sturdy table sat in the middle, three chairs on each side.

Makari closed the door and motioned for Ashai to sit.

"This is the servants' dining room," she explained. "It's bland, I don't think Captain Bauti will look for me here."

She sat across from him, and as if on cue, servants entered from a small door at the back of the room.

She and Ashai dined on fresh melons and grapes, with bread and cheese and nuts she said grew in the palace arbor. They drank a sweet, pink wine, followed by a strong, black tea from Thahr.

Makari peppered him with questions about his childhood, life in Brynn, and his business. And she asked him how he'd worked his way into the trust of the merchant Larish.

"Ah, that was quite the accident," he told her. "I was an orphan. Living on the streets. And I ... well, I stole a bolt of silk from his shop, but tripped on the way out, ruining the cloth. Old Larish made me work a half-year to pay off the debt and avoid the constable. I watched and realized business was poor, so I proposed a solution."

"How did an orphaned boy solve a business problem?"

"I knew the orphanage in Brynn needed cloth to make clothes for their children, so I had him donate the cloth to the orphanage. When the orphanage had the clothes made, the only payment he asked was that they sew his name on the inside of each garment. Nice clothes got more children adopted, and every adopting family saw Larish's name. Since only people with money adopt, business improved. And since that same orphanage had taught me to read and do numbers, I kept Larish's books for him, so he had more time to handle patrons. Before long, business was on the mend and he kept me as his helper. When a robber killed him and his wife, I inherited their business, which I sold to move here."

He winced at the memory of finding Larish dead. He'd been a good man, as non-believers went. Honest and hard-working. He'd deserved a long life, but he liked to think the death, while sad, had helped him reach this point. In his own way, Larish had served Nishi.

Makari studied him a moment, her lips pursed, her index finger tapping on her cheek.

"I think I know your reward!" She slapped the table and bounced up. "Let's go see my father."

And she left in a swish of purple as Ashai struggled to keep up.

Makari marched through the palace corridors, dragging Ashai along by his wrist, the merchant panting and huffing as she jerked him around corner after corner. Finally, she stopped in front of a set of oak wood doors, ornately carved with her family's coat of arms. Two Royal guard members snapped to attention and started to lower their halberds to block the door before recognizing her. The senior man, a grizzled sergeant with a scar under his right eye, cleared his throat.

"I'm sorry, Your Highness, you may enter but your guest may not."

Makari planted her fists on her hips and locked her eyes on the guard's. He actually pressed his back against the wall.

"Do you deem to tell me who I can and cannot take into my father's study, Sergeant?"

"I'm sorry, Princess, but Captain Bauti said—"

Still holding Ashai by the wrist, Makari pushed past the guards and seized the handle on the right door.

"Captain Bauti answers to me! Now stand aside."

She tore the door open while the Sergeant stammered, then she burst into the room, hauling a confused Ashai behind her.

Her father's study had always been one of her favorite rooms in the palace. Large enough to accommodate ten or twelve people, but small enough to remain intimate, the study had been built mostly from dark, warm wood. A mahogany desk, oak tables and chairs. Books lined up on shelves of maple, with posts and rafters of knotty pine. If it weren't for the walls of books, the room would've been more of a hunting lodge than a study. It even had a gaping stone fireplace with a stag's head hung above it.

"Makari, what is the meaning of this!"

Her father jumped to his feet, spilling red wine on his pearl-colored robes. A servant moved quickly to dab the stain. Seated in a circle around her father were his chief advisers. The commanding general of Pushtan's armies, the broad shouldered General Celani. The stoic Minister of Trade, Lord Talbot. The Foreign Minister, the Interior Minister, Samaran Tan, and several others she did not recognize. Even Captain Bauti stood behind her father, his sword uncharacteristically leaned against the wall, chain mail discarded for a blue and black doublet.

"Preposterous!" The blustery Foreign Minister said, slapping a mug of ale on a side table. "Women are not allowed in Royal Council unless they sit the throne. And commoners not at all!"

Ashai bowed and tried to back out of the room, but Makari held his wrist tight.

"Minister Renard, I would suggest you remember I am more than just a woman. I'm also your Princess and the heir to the Pushtani throne. Someday your future on this council—and perhaps in this city—may depend on our conversation today."

Renard paled and inclined his head, picking his mug back up and taking a long pull. She didn't miss his slight glare, or the grin that crept onto Captain Bauti's face.

"Makari," her father said, "I have not yet invited you to this council for my own reasons. What is it you need of me?"

Makari looked around the room, finding every pair of eyes focused on her. She took a deep breath.

"Father, I nominate Ashai Larish for the position of Minister of Finance."

The council erupted in chaos.

"She's not a member! She cannot nominate!" blurted Lord Talbot.

"He's a common merchant!" Wheezed the aging Interior Minister, Lord Neffin. "There is no precedent."

Her father dropped into his padded chair, the leather squeaking through the room. Behind him, Bauti crossed his arms over his chest and gave her a disappointed glare.

"I've interviewed him extensively," she shouted over the din. She'd spoken publicly enough that her tone silenced the arguments for a moment. "He's an experienced businessman who is good with numbers. He turned around his mentor's business. He managed the crown's charitable affairs the day he saved me. And the throne owes him a reward for saving my life. I propose their reward be a Lordship and appointment to this council."

This time, silence wrapped the room like a burial cloak. The Council members looked at the floor, their hands, their wine or ale. Anything but Makari. Finally, Lord Neffin rose and shuffled his way to her side. He placed a gnarled hand on her shoulder, and leaned in so close she could count the gray hairs sticking out of his nose.

"My dear Princess, your intentions are noble, but these are troubled times. An assassin is in the palace. We must only appoint those we know to be loyal to this council."

Makari had always liked Neffin. The old man had been on the Council longer than she'd been alive. He always had a kind word, and rarely partook in the court's mean-spirited gossip.

Letting go of Ashai, she patted Neffin's hand and led him back to his chair.

"My Lord Neffin, Master Ashai placed his life in harm's way to save me. What greater loyalty is there than that? Besides, if he were Denari Lai, my father and I would be dead."

As if to contradict her, Ashai spoke.

"My Lords of the Council are all correct, of course." Makari's head whipped around and she fired icicle darts at him. "I am but a common merchant, not experienced in courtly matters, and a stranger to the palace. Captain Bauti is right to not trust me, and while I am deeply grateful for Her Highness's belief in me, I must thankfully and respectfully decline her nomination for this position."

He sketched a deep bow, then turned and strode from the study. Makari could only stand, steam coming out her ears, and watch him go.

Seeing her distress, her father came to her side and took her by the hand. He led her to the chair beside his own and helped her sit.

"Stay and listen, Makari. Perhaps it's time you saw how the Council does business." He turned to the other council members. "Since the subject has already been broached, let us discuss replacement for the late Lord Merwin, Minister of Finance. I will accept your nominations, hear cases, and make my decision by the end of this council."

What followed for the next hour made Makari want to drive needles into her ears. Every Council member had their own nominee, each one woefully unqualified but well-suited to serve the purposes of the nominating council member. For instance, Minister Renard nominated a weasel-faced man with no financial experience, knowing he would send inordinate amounts of money to the Foreign Ministry. General Celani nominated another general who would no doubt send money to the Army. And so it went for each minister, ending with an all-out shouting match over whose nominee was most corrupt.

Makari glanced at her father to find him with his head in his hands, massaging his temples. Finally, he slapped both hands on the table, rattling glasses and sloshing wine everywhere.

"Enough selfishness! Not one of you nominated someone who will serve the Pushtani kingdom. In fact, the only person who did is not even a member of this council. Therefore, I select Ashai Larish as the Minister of Finance. If my daughter trusts him, so do I. Makari, inform him this hour. This council is adjourned."

Chaos exploded through the room again, but her father ignored it, shoving back from the table, and striding from the room. Makari, still in shock, rose and followed him out, Captain Bauti close on her heels like her own personal thundercloud.

The Watcher moved like a shadow down the hidden passageway behind the walls of the royal palace, careful to make no more noise than a mouse or a cockroach, his presence a mere zephyr in a drafty stone building. Although walls of wood and granite separated him from the denizens of the palace, one misstep would echo down the corridors and be heard where no one knew about the passageways. It would render the passages useless to him if they were discovered.

So he planted his feet with the utmost care, soft slippers barely more than a whisper on the stone floor as he followed the Princess on the other side of the wall. He didn't really need to follow her, for he knew where she was going. Her father had charged her with telling Ashai of his new position. Minister of Finance was a true achievement for the Denari Lai, perhaps a record for working his way into an inner circle in just under a week.

The Watcher grinned as he glided around a corner. Ashai had proven most adept at manipulating the Pushtanis, especially using Princess Makari to control her father. And turning down the ministerial position had been a stroke of genius, making him look reluctant, and lifting suspicion from him.

Perhaps there was hope for Ashai after all.

Makari climbed a set of marble stairs, heels clacking with every step, and The Watcher paralleled her behind the wall, his slippery feet kissing the steps in silence. At the top, she turned to the first door on the right and knocked. The Watcher worked his way to the back of the room, where a pinhole in the wall allowed him to peer inside. Ashai lounged on his overstuffed bed, eyes closed, probably in silent prayer.

A good sign.

At Makari's knock, the assassin rose and walked to the door. He turned and hesitated, a deliberate step designed to make him appear surprised, unprepared. But The Watcher could tell from the smug smile on Ashai's face that he'd known all along this would happen.

Then he pulled the door open, and the Princess stepped inside. Ashai bowed, a deep flowing gesture he reserved only for Makari, and ushered her inside. He left the door open, a sign of respect and courtesy for her virtue. It would not be necessary in Nishi'iti culture, but here in Pushtan, men did not always act with honor. The erosion of faith always resulted in the growth of poor behavior.

Makari spoke first.

"My father has appointed you Minister of Finance," she said. Her face beamed, her eyes glittering with pride. She had no idea she'd been manipulated into this.

Ashai made a grandiose gesture of throwing his hands up, then running his fingers through his dark hair. He turned his back and stalked to the bed, showing some disrespect by not facing his Princess. Again a calculated move, this time designed to show distress had robbed him of his faculties.

Brilliant.

"Your Highness, while I appreciate your faith in me," Ashai said, adding a slight edge to his voice that The Watcher thought somewhat dangerous, "I truly do not desire a position in court. I'm quite happy running a business. A courtly life is not for me."

Makari planted her hands on her hips and fixed Ashai with her iciest glare.

"Are you angry at me? I just got you appointed to a powerful position. You'll have lands, servants, and gold."

Ashai wheeled on her. "Princess, I never asked for those things."

"And you'll be able to see me every day."

Tears glistened in the corners of her eyes. The Watcher sucked in a breath, amazed at the emotional impact Ashai had on her. But it seemed he had miscalculated this time, gone too far.

Then something in Ashai changed, something subtle and almost unnoticeable. In fact, if The Watcher had not been as well-trained as he was, he might've missed it. Ashai's features didn't move, but they softened ever so slightly. It wasn't physical, but emotional or spiritual.

As if the fire in his eyes had gone from a raging flame to a comforting blaze.

Ashai took a step toward the Princess, his hand stopping just short of her forearm.

"I-I'm sorry, Princess. You're right, of course. I'm being small-minded, rude, and ungrateful. I owe you my thanks for your faith in me and for the opportunity to be more than I was before."

He took her hand, swept into an elaborate bow, and kissed her ring.

"I hope that you'll forgive me, for I'm still but a simple merchant. Perhaps, with your help, I can learn to be a proper lord."

No, Ashai had not gone too far. His emotional manipulation of the Princess had simply reached a new level of perfection. She was clay in his hands now, ready to stand and trust him as he carried out God's will. The question remained, was Ashai the person to carry it out? The softening of his heart had been real, a response to Makari's tears that could mean only one thing.

Feelings. A Denari Lai's worst enemy.

The Watcher had seen enough. He stepped away from the hole, and pattered away down the corridor toward his chambers. He had a message to send.

CHAPTER SIX

Pachat swung his hammer, knocking away a chunk of the tunnel wall. Sparks flew. Sweat dripped from his brow and ran down his shirtless back in cold rivulets. That was the problem working underground. He worked hard, but the air stayed cool, so he ended up sweating and shivering at the same time.

Around him, the other miners chipped away with hammers, picks, and chisels, the flickering light of their torches the only source of illumination. Their light threw grotesque shadows that danced like ghosts around the chamber, no two alike.

They'd moved deep into an abandoned shaft earlier that morning, the slavers pushing them to find veins of silver or gold in already explored tunnels. This mine had been stripped bare, but the Pushtani Masters were not ready to give up. Not until they found another vein.

So desperate were they to find more silver, to milk more of the soft metal from the teats of the foothills, that they sent a slender Nishi'iti boy named Vishi into an unexplored tunnel barely wide enough for his eight-year-old frame to squeeze through. The Pushtanis were adamant that more silver existed in this mine, and that it was down the narrow tunnel.

So Vishi had wriggled his way into the shaft fifteen minutes before and hadn't been heard from since. The only way they knew he was alive was that the rope tied around his waist kept moving.

"You, Pachat!" One of the slave masters cracked their whip at him. "Back to work, dog, before I strip the skin from your back!"

Pachat swung the hammer again, smashing the wall with all his might, sending sparks and chunks of stone into the air around him.

Then, as if Pachat's blow had been that of Nishi himself, the ground shuddered under their feet. Debris fell, and a dust cloud rose, making miners and slavers alike mask their faces with shirts or scarves. The tunnel shook for several seconds, then stopped as suddenly as it had started, the roar replaced by the slow hiss of settling sand and men breathing.

Slavers and miners gaped at one another for a long moment, before breathing sighs of relief that they still lived.

Then Pachat remembered Vishi.

He rushed to the hole, grabbed the rope, and gave it three sharp tugs. Nothing happened, no response. The other miners gathered in a semi-circle around him, again holding their breath, everyone no doubt praying in silence for the boy's safety.

Pachat gave the rope three more tugs and waited again. After a pause, Vishi tugged back.

"Vishi, are you all right?" Pachat called down.

"I'm fine." The boy's voice was muffled, as if he spoke into a pillow. "The tunnel didn't collapse, but my torch went out."

"Lie flat and we'll pull you back," Pachat yelled.

Someone cuffed him on the back of the head and he spun to find Slave Master Cargil, a broad shouldered man with an even broader belly, standing behind him. Cargil ran a filthy hand under his flat nose, wiping away a trail of snot.

"The boy can press on. Tunnel's still open."

Pachat stooped his shoulders and avoided eye contact. Angering Cargil wouldn't help Vishi.

"Due respect, Master, but if he can't see, he won't get very far. And the earthquake probably weakened the shaft. It could collapse."

The slaver laughed, spitting in Pachat's face when he did.

"So we lose a slave urchin. We have plenty to replace him with. Get back to work."

Pachat nodded, fighting the urge to punch the man in his broad, stupid nose. Years of work in the mines had made Pachat chiseled and lean, stronger than he'd ever been. He could've killed the man with one swing of his hammer, driven it clean into his temple, and dropped him on the spot. But he knew the result of that, had seen it when others resisted before. The slavers would punish them all for the actions of one.

He turned back to the tunnel and yelled to Vishi.

"Be careful, but try to find the end of the tunnel with your hands."

As they went back to work, dragging their hammers and picks and shovels behind them, the rope moved slowly again into the shaft.

Pachat lifted his hammer to swing when the ground shuddered again, a great sideways lurch that threw men to the ground and made even the slave master brace himself on the wall.

Vishi's rope shot into the tiny shaft, and Pachat dove to catch it. It slipped for several inches through his hands, tearing off skin and making him wince until two other miners grabbed it as well. Then a great rumble sounded, and a cloud of dust exploded from the tiny hole.

The rope went slack, but Pachat kept pulling. A moment later, the frayed end fell from the tunnel.

Pachat raced to the opening. "Vishi! Can you hear me?"

Only the deafening silence of sifting sand came from below.

He called again and again got no answer.

For an instant, silence enveloped the cavern.

Then the slave master laughed, shattering the silence into a thousand pieces. The sound was so offensive, so inhuman and insensitive, that Pachat at first could not believe it.

Then rage swept through him, coursing through his body like boiling water, creating steam pressure that threatened to blow him apart.

He vaulted to his feet, snatched up his hammer off the floor, and charged the slaver. The fat man never saw him coming, never had a chance to ready himself. Pachat's hammer slammed its heavy head into the man's bulbous gut, doubling him over with a whoosh as the air rushed from his lungs. Then Pachat's shoulder took him in the ribs and drove him back against the tunnel wall. Something cracked and the slave master cried out.

But Pachat did not stop. He swung the hammer again, this time at the slave master's head. The man moved just in time, and the hammer crashed into the tunnel wall sending sparks flying. The slaver's fist swept up and caught Pachat under his chin. His head rocked back, his teeth smashing together as he dropped his hammer.

Pachat returned the blow, delivering a sweeping right fist to the slave master's already broken ribs. A weak, wheezing cry left the slave master's lungs, and Pachat pulled back his fist to strike again, but the other slavers fell on him.

They grabbed his arms and dragged him onto the ground, where one man held him so the others could kick him in the ribs and head. He tried to curl himself in a ball, but the slave drivers held on, keeping his body exposed and his head accessible.

Blow after blow cracked his ribs, broke his nose, and made lights dance before his eyes. Then, the men stopped as quickly as they started. They held his ankles and wrists, stretching him out on the ground.

Pachat opened his eyes just as the slave master's black leather boot smashed down on his face and darkness claimed him.

CHAPTER SEVEN

Captain Bauti's chair groaned as he leaned back and put his feet on the desk. Unlike other officials in the palace, Bauti preferred a wooden desk. No granite, no marble, no wrought iron, or steel. Just a simple, functional desk big enough to spread out the papers he needed, but not big enough to appear ostentatious.

He was Captain of the Royal Guard, not prince.

Before him, Samaran Tan shifted impatiently from one foot to the other, making a steeple of his fingers under his chin. Bauti tried not to smile. He'd summoned the spymaster using a common servant. Tan didn't like being summoned at all, much less by a servant. It was not becoming of his position. But Bauti was tired of Tan's games, and thought he needed to be taken down a notch.

He'd been wrong.

"My spies have no idea who the assassins are," the spymaster said, looking down his turned-up nose at Bauti. "But we know they'll be close to the Royal family."

"They?"

Tan nodded his massive head. "Denari Lai always send two. They're cautious people. In fact, I would not be beyond suspecting members of your own Royal Guard, Captain."

He smirked as he said that last part, and Bauti resisted the urge to drive his dagger into the man's forehead. It would look so good sticking out from between his eyes like a horn on some mythical fat beast.

"The Royal Guard is beyond suspicion, Minister. I hand-select all of them."

Tan squeezed himself into an armchair on the wall opposite Bauti's desk. It was a calculated move, taking him just outside Bauti's peripheral vision, a place the spymaster knew would make the seasoned soldier uncomfortable. Bauti had to commend him for the tactic, but refused to shift and give the man any satisfaction.

Emboldened, Tan went on. "Nonetheless, Captain, even you yourself must be suspect until we know for sure. But our chances are negligible. Only one Denari Lai has ever been outed."

"Smart bastards. And cold."

For a moment, Samaran Tan seemed almost insulted, as if he idolized the Denari Lai, or respected them. Then he shook himself, and nodded.

"Brutal killers usually are."

"We should question anyone arriving in the palace in the last six months," Bauti offered. "Perhaps even the last year. Give the dungeon master three days and he'll break even the strongest Denari Lai."

Tan trilled a laugh, a sound that, coming from the mountainous man, it sent a shiver down Bauti's spine.

"While Master Jarne is quite capable, I doubt he could break a Denari Lai. Remember, these are zealots, completely dedicated to Nishi and his will for them. They would rather die in silence and go to heaven than live a bit longer and suffer eternity on fire.

"Besides, we don't want to show our hand too soon. At this point we should observe quietly."

Bauti thought about that. As much as he hated to admit it, the whale of a man had a point.

"What do you think of the Kendshi girl?" he asked.

"She is half Nishi'iti." He tapped his chin with a chubby forefinger. "She's close to the Princess, who adores her, and we really don't know much about her. But I don't know that she's smart enough to be an assassin."

Bauti took his feet off the desk and turned to face Samaran Tan.

"Her stupidity could be an act. But would the Denari Lai use a half-breed?"

"There is a historical precedent," Tan answered. "A half-breed Denari Lai killed a Slevonian general many years ago. He worked his way up from the ranks of the common foot soldier, becoming the general's most trusted officer before slitting his throat.

"Remember, the Denari Lai keep their assassins loyal by feeding them magic. They become addicted to that power, and if they start to stray in their loyalty, the Nishi'iti simply cut them off until they're back in line. Or dead."

Bauti sighed. The system was cruel but efficient, a layered method of creating insanely dedicated soldiers. If religious zeal was not enough, dependence on power was.

"What of the Nishi'iti military?" Bauti asked. "Has their status changed?"

Tan heaved himself up from the chair, his breath whooshing like a bellows. He paced toward the door to Bauti's chambers.

"There appears to be a slight military buildup in the Nishi'iti southern foothills. Our spies report small numbers of soldiers moving south from the capital city, but this could simply be reinforcements due to recent clashes."

"Or," Bauti said, staring at the fat man, "they could be preparations to retaliate for our crackdown on the slave rebellions."

Tan nodded and reached for the doorknob. He paused, tilting his head as if thinking, then raised a finger and looked at Bauti.

"There is one Council member I think we can eliminate from suspicion."

"And who would that be?" As for as Bauti was concerned, anyone Tan brought up was automatically more suspicious.

"Minister Ashai."

Bauti's grip on the arms of his chair tightened and his jaw clenched. He still couldn't believe the arrogant merchant was Lord of Coin. Penny counter. Minister of Finance.

"As far as I'm concerned, Minister Ashai is a top suspect. I already have my men investigating him."

Tan twisted the doorknob and clucked at Bauti like a mother hen.

"I'm disappointed in you, Captain. I expected more efficiency from someone of your background. Ashai entered the palace thirteen days ago, after the threat was sent. The assassin was in place before he came to us, meaning he cannot be the killer. And if he was Denari Lai, our king would be dead."

Bauti fought the urge to rip the arms from his chair and beat

Samaran Tan with them. Infuriatingly, the man was right. His logic sound. Bauti almost wanted Ashai to be the assassin, longed to let Jarne put him on the rack. He just couldn't think of a way around Tan's reasoning.

"I'm sure you can let yourself out," he told the spymaster. "Do try to find out who's going to kill our King before they actually do it."

Tan pulled the door open and fixed Bauti with his watery glare.

"As long as you promise to keep him alive long enough for me to do so. You'll have to take your eyes off the Princess long enough to protect the King."

He slammed the door on the way out.

Bauti lurched from his chair, sending it crashing into the wall. He paced the confines of his chambers, scratching his chin.

As he thought, he calmed. He would keep a guard on Ashai. The new Minister of Finance required protection. There was an assassin in the palace, after all. No one was safe. That guard could keep an eye on their newest Council member.

In the meantime, Bauti would contact an old friend in Brynn. He would see what information his friend could dig up on a cloth merchant named Ashai.

CHAPTER EIGHT

The normal meeting chambers of His Majesty's Royal Council sat three doors down from the throne room along the Palace's main corridor. Closed off by an inconspicuous wooden door, the chamber itself had been kept minimalist. Plain wooden walls with simple, patterned tapestries, a single window at the far end, and sconces holding torches for light. The simple, wooden trestle table itself seated ten people, twelve uncomfortably, and made the room seem to burst at its seams.

Ashai sat on the left side of the table, his head in his hands as he rubbed his temples. It was bad enough that the king insisted he wear black hose and a deep blue doublet, but Ashai's connection to Nishi's gift was fading, and his body showed it. When he looked up, his left hand trembled. He put it in his lap to keep anyone from seeing. He'd missed his morning prayers—the schedule of Minister of Finance began quite early—and now was running low on Nishi's power. The muscles in his neck and shoulders had started to bunch, a slow-moving tension that crawled from the small of his back up his spine to the base of his skull. He clenched his jaw, grinding his teeth.

He needed to pray. Soon.

But the way these doddering old fools bickered and debated over every minor point, this meeting was likely to last to the wee hours of the morning. He looked past King Abadas at the end of the table to see the evening sun setting outside the west-facing window. How long had they been here now? Three hours? Four?

And yet they were no closer to an agreement than they had been when they started.

The entire council had been arrayed around the table. Of course, King Abadas sat at the far end, with Makari to his right in a foppish looking lime dress, the imposing Bauti standing behind them. The rest of the council ringed the table like jackals around a corpse.

"Your Majesty," General Celani said, leaning back in his chair and staring at the smoke-stained ceiling, "the Army is already operating on the thinnest budget we can manage. We have four battalions deployed to the foothills to manage the recent slave uprisings and cross-border raids. That costs money. They've already depleted the local fields and livestock, meaning we have to send them food. And if we don't send them food, they can't fight. And if they can't fight, they do us no good."

Ashai's ears perked up at the report of that many men on the border with Nishi'iti. It seemed excessive to handle simple slave uprisings and cross-border incursions, which most often came from the Pushtani side anyway. He wondered what Abadas was really up to. Or maybe it was Celani. Someone was building up military forces along the border.

"I'm familiar with the cost of soldiering, General," the king said. His voice took on the same sharp edge it always did when he didn't like the tone of the person speaking to him. Celani shrank down a little bit in his chair. "But it's only part of what this government must deal with. Believe it or not, we actually have internal matters to deal with too."

Celani said nothing, at least not out loud. His lips moved as if he were saying a silent prayer. Or a silent curse.

As Abadas droned on, Ashai let his mind wander off. Beside the King, Princess Makari listened with intensity, her blue eyes focused on her father as if reading his lips. Ashai had no doubt she was running numbers through her mind, trying to find a way to pay back their creditors and still meet their financial obligations at home and abroad. She had an extremely sharp mind for numbers. And everything else.

They'd dined together several times since that first night. Each time, Makari found a new secret place where Captain Bauti and the Royal Guard could not follow. Ashai suspected they knew where she went, at least some of the guards, but chose to look the other way. Some understood the Princess needed her time and space, while others were simply afraid to anger her.

Ashai couldn't blame them.

He found himself thinking of her often. Thoughts of her interrupted his daily prayers, which contributed to his weakened magical state. Every time he didn't complete a prayer, or every time one was interrupted, it slowed the flow of Nishi's power and left him weak.

He needed to focus. The girl was beautiful, true. Smart, funny. And independent. Oh, so independent. Sometimes he almost felt sorry for her father.

Almost. The man was still a butcher. And still his target.

"Minister Ashai, perhaps you'd like to join us at this meeting," the King jibed from the end of the table. Ashai snapped out of his trance and found himself staring at Makari while the whole table stared at him. Makari included. "After all, you are our Minister of Finance."

Laughter rippled around the table, with Bauti's irritating snicker rubbing Ashai raw. Someday he would kill that man.

Focus.

"My apologies, Majesty, my mind wandered."

Abadas sat forward and slapped a meaty hand on the hard wooden table. Wine glasses sloshed.

"And based on how you were staring at my daughter, I'll bet we know where it wandered to!"

Even Makari laughed this time, though Bauti remained in any eerie, stone-faced silence.

Ashai allowed himself an appropriate blush, and looked at his hands. "I apologize, your Majesty, as lovely as your daughter is that's not what distracted me. I think we may be able to solve the problem of Pushtani debt to Thahr without taking money from General Celani."

"Is that so?" The general leaned forward on his elbows. "We're all ears, Minister Ashai."

Ashai eased his chair back from the table and stood, clasping his hands in front of his chest and pacing behind the seated men. He stopped in front of Bauti, intentionally blocking the man's view of the King. As he suspected, Bauti shifted slightly to one side.

"The solution may lie in a barter system," Ashai said. "Thahr depends on trade with Slevonia, Neskania, and us. For all of that, they must use the highways that pass through Pushtan and when they do, we tax them heavily. In fact, by my calculations the taxation on their merchants' use of our highways in the last three years was more than we owe them right now.

"I propose we lift the highway tax on Thahr merchants and allow them to use our highway system free of charge for three years. In return, at the end of three years they forgive our debt to them and our two nations are even."

Ashai could have cut the silence in the room with his dagger. Celani sat with his lips pursed in his finger tapping his chin. Foreign Minister Renard looked like he wanted to blow up but couldn't think of something to blow up about. Trade Minister Talbot stared at Ashai, his mouth open, while interior Minister Neffin grinned a fool's grin.

Even King Abadas nodded slowly, a smile spreading like melted butter across his face. In fact, there might actually have been some melted butter in his beard.

"See, my Lords, Minister Ashai has already solved one dilemma for us. Does anyone still doubt the wisdom of his selection?"

Ashai glanced at Bauti in time to see him erase a glower from his face. All that remained of the expression was a turned down corner of his mouth. And a finger that lingered a half-inch too close to the pommel of his sword.

"That's a very innovative solution," said the Trade Minister, his expressionless face not even changing for this. He should've been grinning, since Ashai just made his job that much easier. "But how do we know Thahr will accept this proposal?"

Ashai shrugged. "We don't. But put yourself in their position. They can keep taking promises from us that come with empty bags of silver and gold, or they can take something for free that saves them actual money. And Thahrs are notoriously stingy. I guarantee they know exactly how much money this will save them, and know they'll profit from the deal.

"I think you'll find them more than willing to accept this proposal."

Talbot looked like he might argue more, but Abadas raised a hand and silenced him.

"Lord Talbot, you will press forward with this suggestion. Approach the ambassador from Thahr this afternoon and make this proposal. I want to know by sundown today what their answer is."

"And if they must consult with their own leader?" Talbot spread his hands on the table before him, his face still slack.

"Put some pressure on the ambassador and tell him the offer comes with a time limit of two weeks. That's enough time to send a pigeon and get a response, but little more."

Talbot nodded, and Ashai had to admit the King's finishing touch was clever. It forced the king of Thahr to make a quick decision rather than think it through and possibly have second thoughts.

As if to congratulate himself, the King took a long pull from a wine flagon, wiped his mouth on a napkin, and looked at his daughter.

"Makari, if you would excuse us we have other, more sensitive matters to discuss now."

If the Princess had been a cloud front, in that instant she would've flashed lightning and sprouted tornadoes.

"Father, you told me I could attend Council now to start learning the art of governance. What good will it do me to leave during sensitive matters?"

Abadas shifted in his chair, and looked like he wanted to take another gulp of wine.

"These are matters best attended to by men," he said. Ashai noted he did not look his daughter in the eye when he made that statement, and somehow he thought that was wise. Makari could kill with a glare, mortally wound with her eyes. "These are not matters for the tender heart of a woman."

For a moment, Makari looked like she might explode, her fists bunching on the table. Cords stood out on the side of her neck.

Ashai cleared his throat loud enough for her to hear. She turned her lightning bolt gaze on him, and he gave her a comforting nod. It was a subtle gesture, one designed for her and only her to see. One that said, "Don't worry, I'll fill you in later."

Some of the violence leached from her storm cloud expression, and the lightning bolts faded. She breathed in a deep, cleansing breath, then pushed herself back from the table, deliberate and slow, her dignity on display for all the men to see.

"Come, Kendshi," she said, offering her hand slave the slightest smile. "Let us go discuss more tender things, better suited for our mild hearts. Perhaps sewing, or dancing, or flowers would be better suited for the future ruler of Pushtan than whatever it is my father's going to talk about."

Abadas actually winced, as if his daughter had slapped him on the cheek. But Makari didn't offer him even the slightest look. She simply spun on her heel, put her nose in the air, and marched from the room with Kendshi in tow.

The sound of the slamming door echoed through the small chamber for a full ten seconds after she left, as if every minister there was afraid to speak. Finally, Abadas took a deep breath, sat up straight, and addressed his council.

"As you know, gentlemen, our slave masters in the north report increasing frequency of insubordination, violence, and even organized resistance by Nishi'iti slaves who were led by the tale of this Pachat thug. This cannot be allowed to continue if our mines are to be productive and profitable.

"More disturbing news, however, comes from Minister Tan. I will allow him to explain."

Tan inclined his head, and rose from his chair with great effort. His belly almost hit Lord Renard in the back of the head when he turned, and he struggled to pace behind the ministers as he presented his information.

"My sources in the foothills south of Nishi'iti report numerous instances of Nishi'iti Army units positioning themselves further south than normal. Regiment size units are reported in three separate locations, each one marking a major potential invasion corridor south into our territory. Perhaps just as disturbing is that there is been a marked decrease in cross-border incursions by Nishi'iti raiding parties in the last three weeks.

"This combines with two other factors to look quite nefarious. First, Nishi'iti demands immediate repayment for the gold we've mined from their territory, and by using their people. They made vague threats if we didn't pay in gold. Secondly, as you know, there have been increasing instances of Nishi'iti slave violence in the foothills. Some might call them uprisings, inspired by this Pachat character. Just three days ago a slave attacked his slave master deep in the tunnels and nearly killed him. My sources believe Nishi'iti elite soldiers—the Wanao Lai—may have infiltrated the slave camps to stir up trouble and give their Army reason to move south."

"And what would their goal be?" Celani asked. "Their Army is mostly defensive. We would slaughter them in open combat."

Tan raised a finger in front of his face. "They would not seek to hold land, like most armies, but to recapture their people, steal gold, and retreat deep into the mountains where we could not track them down."

Abadas leaned back in his chair and nodded. "That makes sense. It gets them their gold back, gets their people back, and leaves us no one to work in the mines. That hurts us three times. It would take years of raids into Nishi'iti to come up with enough slaves to work the mines again."

"And yet," Renard complained, "if we move to protect our own people, we are labeled aggressors! Preposterous!"

"Do we care what the Nishi'itis call us?" The King's question silenced everyone in the room. "I don't even want them to think we care. They are bugs to us."

Ashai decided to use the silence to his advantage. He raised his hand, timid as a schoolgirl.

"Your Majesty, I may have a solution that would avoid conflict and protect our image. Your image."

Chuckles around the room told him his idea had been received as poorly as he'd expected, and Abadas's thunderous laughter shook the rafters enough to make him wince. Doubt crept into Ashai's mind like clouds across a midnight sky.

"Master Ashai, you are quite droll!" Abadas roared. Celani and the others looked like they pitied Ashai, except for the smirking Bauti. "I do not, in fact, care even a little what some Nishi'iti slaves think of me or my policies."

Ashai waited for the laughter to die down, then spoke.

"Of course not, Majesty, but what of your own citizens?"

The room fell into a tense silence. Ashai knew he stood on dangerous ground, with Bauti behind him wound tight as any bear trap. So he spoke with the deliberate softness of a priest.

"And your fellow monarchs? Should they not respect you, what then?"

"Merchant, you overstep," growled Bauti. "You're speaking to your king, not some wayward cloth apprentice."

Ashai ignored how his hand dropped to his sword pommel and went on, trying to appear contrite.

"Forgive me, My Liege," he said, addressing the king and intentionally ignoring the captain's posturing, "I mean no offense, but as someone who's been on the streets with your people, and who's traveled far and wide doing business, I know something of how your own people and the people of the world see you. They believe you a capable leader, but somewhat … how should I say it … one-dimensional. They feel you resort too quickly to violence and strong-arm tactics instead of reasoning your way through more diplomatic solutions."

Abadas's face looked like a volcano ready to erupt, red and hot and bulging.

"I have Minister Renard to handle things diplomatically," he said, droplets of spit spraying as he talked. "By the time things reach me, action is required!"

Nods around the table told Ashai he still had an uphill battle, but that didn't matter. He'd never expected the council to adopt this idea—he'd wanted to see how Abadas handled the suggestion. So he made it.

"Your Majesty, this solution solves not only your slave uprising problem and image problem, but allows you to pay back Nishi'iti for the gold Pushtan … procured, and to do so at a substantially reduced rate."

This time, the room's silence was less tense, but just as palpable. He knew he held everyone's attention, so he went on.

"I propose giving small, token amounts of money to select, trustworthy Nishi'iti slaves, telling them they can save it toward eventually buying their own freedom and a trip to the Nishi'iti border. You simply tell the Nishi'iti government you're giving its gold directly to their people. These slaves are the poor, uneducated of Nishi'iti, so there will be no one to track how much money you give them."

Around him, jaws hung open, and faces had gone pale. He fought back a grin.

"This plan does several important things. First, it allows the slaves to feel like they have a path to freedom, reducing their reason for rebellion. It satisfies the Nishi'iti government by simply not giving them an accurate count of how much gold you gave to slaves. Since Nishi'iti has no one here to count it, it's your word against theirs. Everyone else gets to see you handle something with deft diplomatic skill, making your citizens admire you and world leaders respect you. More than they already do, of course."

Now the room's silence fell into such completeness that Ashai could have heard a spider weaving its web in the upper-most corner of the ceiling. After a moment of crackling tension, Abadas leaned forward in his chair, drummed his rings on the wooden tabletop, and gave Ashai a condescending look of understanding.

"Minister Ashai," he said in a low, hoarse voice, "this is why you count coins and I rule the kingdom. I don't need people's respect or admiration—only their fear and obedience."

He turned to Celani and sat up straight.

"General, send another company north to reinforce the slaver companies. Put down any and all rebellions with brutal force. I want heads on spikes, bodies hung from towers, public floggings, whatever your men need to do. Make it clear that any slave—especially any Nishi'iti slave—daring to oppose his master will die a slow, painful death."

Celani nodded his salt-and-pepper head. The King had one more thing.

"Oh, and General?" Celani raised an eyebrow to his king. "Kill Pachat, and use his entrails to strangle anyone else who starts trouble."

"Inform the Nishi'itis that until their assassins turn themselves in and are executed, Nishi'iti gold remains here and Nishi'iti slaves will suffer.

"And as always, My Lords of the council, do not let word of these things reach my daughter. She's still too young for this. Now be gone, all of you. You're giving me indigestion."

Ashai rose, moved to the door, and as he filed out behind Minister Neffin, saw Bauti waiting outside with an additional blue-armored guardsman. The captain caught Ashai by the elbow, none too gently, and nodded at the soldier.

"Due to the threat of assassins in the palace," he said, "I am assigning each minister a personal guard. You're first. Congratulations."

Ashai studied the guardsman, knowing there was no way out of this without looking suspicious, so he gave Bauti the slightest of bows.

"You are too kind to think of my safety so highly, Captain," he said. "I'm sure this man will be more than a match for any Denari Lai."

Bauti's grip on his elbow tightened. "He's not here to protect you. He's here to protect the King and Princess. Should you act against either of them, his instructions are to lop your head off."

The guard's cold, blue gaze told Ashai he'd at least try. He patted Bauti's hand where it kept grip on his elbow.

"You do think of everything, good Captain. Now if you don't mind, I'll move along."

Bauti held on just a moment longer, then turned, and strode away, leaving Ashai to stew in his own juices.

CHAPTER NINE

Makari rummaged through the wardrobe at the foot of her large, four-poster bed, tossing aside gown after gown. The pink saffron? Gone. Lavender silk? Out. Lime satin with lemon trim? She hurled it over her head, knowing Kendshi would catch it, the hand slave scurrying about as her mistress threw her best gowns away.

"Oh, Majesty! Not the gold wool!"

But that one went, too, hitting the marble floor in a pile.

It wasn't that Makari hated the gowns—they'd all been her mother's, and each had been the height of fashion when it hit her mother's wardrobe. A decade or more earlier.

Makari had never really cared much for fashion. In fact, her lack of modern fashion had served her well lately, helping chase off pandering lord-lings.

Until now.

She grabbed a sky-blue dress with a scooping neckline—one her mother had called scandalous at the time, but that now looked conservative—and started to toss it at her servant. She stopped.

Light blue. A subtle but important variation of her family's primary color. The neckline, cuffs, and hem had all been decorated with a silvery, almost gray lace, making the dress more appropriate for winter than early fall, but trim could change.

She dashed to her mirror as Kendshi joined her. The slave held the dress up in front of Makari's figure. The effect stunned the princess. Her eyes popped, suddenly bright and riveting, and her skin went from washed out to shimmering. Instead of flat and dirty, her hair now looked like silken strands of midnight.

"He'll be hungry for you," Kendshi whispered in her ear.

Makari gasped and covered her mouth.

"I don't know who you're talking about! The only man I expect to see tonight is that insufferably boring guard assigned to protect me. And perhaps Captain Bauti, should he check on me."

Kendshi wrinkled her nose, her gold-flecked eyes narrowed. "The captain will hunger, too."

Makari sighed. "He's a good man, Kendshi. He ..."

"He loves you. And not in the way a soldier should love his future queen."

The girl's Nishi'iti accent always made Makari smile. It sounded pure. Innocent. Though she knew first-hand the girl could be quite naughty, where thoughts of men were concerned.

"I don't know what you mean," Makari lied.

Kendshi removed the dress and hung it on the mirror, moving to help her mistress out of the tangerine one she wore underneath.

"Sometimes, when he thinks no one is watching—I am always watching, but he does not know—he looks at you for too long. His eyes look deep into you, past your dress and your skin and into your heart. He looks to see if you love him too. I have seen this look before."

She lowered her gaze, and her lip trembled. The girl fit so well in the palace that Makari often forgot she'd had a different life once, and her own betrothed.

She squeezed the maid's shoulder.

"I'm sure Captain Bauti is just daydreaming," she said, pulling her arms from the old dress and stepping out. The cold of the marble floor soaked up into her ankles. "He's getting no younger, and older people tend to daydream a lot. He might even be napping."

Kendshi giggled at that, a wicked, sly little laugh. "I know what he's dreaming about when he naps, then!"

Makari pinched her on the arm and the maid danced away, snatching the blue dress up again and helping Makari into it before cleaning up. The slave had just re-hung the last of the dresses back in the wardrobe when a commotion sounded outside the chamber door.

Makari wasn't expecting a visitor, so when Kendshi looked at her, she shrugged. Nodding, Kendshi moved to the door, opening it just a wedge. She muttered something, then looked back over her shoulder at Makari, grinning.

"Princess," she said, straightening, but holding the door closed with her hip, "Lord Ashai Larish, Minister of Finance, requests an audience. Should Captain Bauti's guard send him away 'bloodied and broken,' as the captain instructed?"

Makari's love for the girl grew every day. She held wisdom far beyond her seventeen years.

The princess straightened her dress, smoothed her hair—both of which made Kendshi giggle—and leveled her coolest stare at the door.

"Show him in."

When Ashai first stepped into her room, Makari nearly gasped. His eyes held a flinty edge as he glared at the guards—his own guard stood outside next to hers—with contempt. As soon as he saw her, though, his expression softened and a grin broke out across his face. He stood a moment too long, as if drinking in the sight of her in the blue dress, and only when Kendshi cleared her throat did the merchant-turned-minister perform a sweeping bow.

"Your Highness, you look magnificent. That dress is just—"

"This dress belonged to my mother, Minister Ashai," she said. "It is at least five years out of date and will be updated shortly. As a former cloth merchant, you must know this."

Ashai looked the dress over, then let his gaze wander to the open door of her wardrobe, where his eye crawled over the few hemlines sticking out through the opening. He made a pained expression, as if seeing her mother's old clothing drove a needle into his heart.

"I'm only a cloth merchant, Highness, not a tailor. My knowledge of fashion is limited to what materials are popular—"

"Nonsense!" she snapped. "Cloth merchants are always present with tailors when I order dresses, and they're often more informed than the tailors. So spare me the nonsense and explain why you're here."

Caught off guard, Ashai stammered an instant before flashing a disarming smile.

"Perhaps we should discuss things in private?" He nodded toward Kendshi, who made no move to depart.

Makari crossed her arms over her chest and shook her head.

"Kendshi is trustworthy. You can talk in front of her." The slave made a show of pouring goblets of wine for them, but did not hide the smile on her lips. "Someone must preserve my reputation, since my father insists on parading me before a long line of potential suitors. It would not do for us to be alone together. Unless you've come to court me, Master Ashai?"

Ashai's face turned the deep maroon of their wine, and he choked a bit on his first swallow. Makari grinned. So, he was interested.

"Very well, Your Highness," he said, recovering in a hurry. "The meeting did not produce any significant movement on the matter of the slave rebellions in the north foothills. The Pushtani policy will remain the same, and your father did not accept suggestion of a more peaceful method to deal with the insurgency. He will continue to allow the Army to deal with the situation."

Kendshi knocked over an empty goblet, the pewter cup clanging on the floor as the slave-girl gasped. She stared openly at Ashai for a moment before picking up the cup and pretending to focus on her work again.

Of course—her betrothed. What was his name?

"Surely there was more than that," Makari said, giving Ashai an arch of her eyebrow. "You were there for quite some time."

He moved close to her then, not quite touching her, but close enough to whisper.

"The walls have ears." Then he backed up a half step and raised his voice. "No, Princess, the discussions were quite brief. It simply took me some time to get away from the other council members. They all seem to want private audiences with the Finance Minister for some reason."

Makari looked up into Ashai's warm, blue eyes and saw something new, then. Something she hadn't noticed before. Behind the blue hid something dark and mysterious, as if the simple cloth merchant hid some deep secret he sought to share only with her.

The thought overwhelmed her with emotion, making her feel closer to Ashai than she ever had to a man. She admired the strong line of his jaw as he spoke, the jagged line of his nose, and the softer curve of his lips. His was a face she could wake up to every day.

On impulse, she stood on her toes and kissed him on the lips. For an instant—for a single fleeting heartbeat—he kissed her back and Kendshi emitted a low purr behind them. Then Ashai shuddered, eased Makari back, and bowed his head.

"I apologize for my forwardness, Majesty," he said. Her attraction for him waned. He was apologizing for her kissing him! "I will show myself out."

He sketched a bow and left the room in a rush, his personal guard struggling to keep up.

Makari's heart felt like it might rip in two.

"Looks like I scared another one," she said, downing the rest of her wine in one gulp.

Kendshi shrugged. "But you didn't try to stab him. So this one will come back."

CHAPTER TEN

Ashai rose from his knees, the power of Nishi rushing through every vein. From his toes to the top of his head, and from his heart to his soul, God's gift flowed in him, making him tingle with power. He flexed his arms, reveling in the pure strength bulging there, waiting to come out. He stepped to the large trunk sitting at the foot of the bed.

Wrapped in iron bands, the heavy wooden vessel had taken four well-muscled slaves to carry up the palace stairs and into his chambers. He'd made a show of opening the box, showing off the contents of brass and gold, gifts from other merchants he'd told them. Things long ago given to the original Larish, things that lent credibility to Ashai's cover story.

It was hard to believe that had been a month ago. A month and still no kill order. Ashai didn't doubt his God, but he wondered if the order would come before his hair turned white.

A month of seeing Makari. A month getting to know her. Sympathizing with her. Admiring her, even. Since the day she'd kissed him, Ashai didn't know what to think of the princess. She was spontaneous and smart, kind and strong. And of course, devastatingly beautiful.

He'd tried avoiding her by getting caught up in work, and having duties in Trinward, but she went out of her way to corner him, dine with him, or take walks in the gardens.

And Ashai found that he didn't mind. Not even a bit.

He didn't want to kill her. It felt ... wrong.

He squatted by the trunk, took one handle in his right fist, and stood, lifting the end of the trunk almost without effort. Lifting heavy things was nothing to this kind of power. Only being out of touch with Nishi would diminish it quickly. He couldn't let that happen.

He eased the trunk back down, careful not to jar the contents of the concealed compartment in the bottom. Without those, his mission would become very difficult.

His senses heightened, too, just like his strength, so he heard the men outside his door before they knocked. He donned a simple pair of blue cotton breeches and a black tunic, then jerked the door open. Bauti stood there, fist ready to knock again, face a thundercloud. Behind him stood King Abadas, wrapped in a simple gray robe, his family crest embroidered on the breast. He'd lost weight, his belly shrinking, and his eyes looked as if they were sinking slowly into his face. The crown sat sideways on his head, his white hair sticking out from under it in all directions, as if he'd been rushed out of his chambers.

Living in constant danger aged a man a decade for every year.

Next to the king, Interior Minister Neffin wavered, dressed in the white cape announcing his position. He grinned his doddering grin, his milky eyes seeing little.

Ashai sketched a hasty bow. "Your Majesty, Minister Neffin, I was not expecting you or I would've dressed better."

He motioned to the simple, blue pants and black tunic he wore.

"Nonsense!" Abadas bellowed. He shouldered his way past Bauti into the room, Neffin close on his heels. The captain remained in the door, glowering. "We're in our bedclothes! Seems appropriate for this news."

"Yes, yes!" Neffin drooled a little. "Such wonderful news!"

Ashai's stomach did a twist. Unexpected news usually worked contrary to his plans. He liked surprises even less than he liked Captain Bauti.

"It seems the captain does not share your zeal about this announcement," Ashai said.

Abadas shot Bauti a withering glare. "He's just sore because we didn't listen to him. Pay him no mind."

"Minister Ashai Larish, by the power vested in me by the Five Gods and as ruling king of Pushtan, I hereby decree that you shall be granted Lordship over the Duchy of Trinward, a small territory in the east, and granted the lands and titles associated with it."

Ashai opened his mouth to thank the King, but Abadas held up a pudgy hand and stopped him.

"Furthermore, I also decree that as a Lord worthy of such arrangement, you will be wed to my daughter, Princess Makari, forthright."

Ashai's heart stopped and for several seconds he forgot to breathe. Wed? To Makari? That was closer to the King and the Princess than he'd ever hoped to get, deeper in their circle of trust that he could've wished for.

And yet, he didn't think that was why the announcement made him almost deliriously happy.

He'd been spending too much time with the girl since the day they kissed. She was relentless in her pursuit, he gave her that. He admired her tenacity, her refusal to take no for an answer. He tried to avoid her, but when the princess summoned, he had no choice. And in truth, he enjoyed spending time with her.

She was bright, funny, and kind. She had her father's strong will, but lacked his cruelty. She possessed spontaneity without his unpredictability. She'd inherited his leadership skills without his desire for power.

Their meetings had been less than romantic, Makari cautious to keep things appropriate. The handmaid Kendshi always hovered nearby, and their Royal Guard protectors were never more than a few feet away. But Ashai had come to look forward to dining, walking, or just sitting and talking with the princess, and finally he stopped avoiding her.

"Minister Larish?" the king asked. "Don't you have anything to say?"

Ashai shook himself, and snapped his jaw closed, suddenly aware it gaped.

"My apologies, Majesty, I'm quite shocked."

"Do you not find my daughter appealing?" The King's voice took on a hard edge.

"Of course, she's the loveliest woman in the kingdom."

"Is that all you see in her? Beauty?" This time, his voice had sharpened like a razor. But Ashai knew the words were not his own. The king mimicked his daughter.

"As your Majesty knows, Makari and I have spent many hours together in the last few weeks. I've come to know her as an intelligent, kind, and intriguing person. I cannot think of anyone I would rather marry."

"Understand this, Minister Larish, this betrothal was my daughter's idea, but Minister Neffin also thought it wise. My daughter has chased away every other suitor, and I need a strong king to hold the throne when this Denari Lai slits my throat. Makari will rule, not you, and if I hear of you treating my daughter with anything less than kindness while I still live ..."

Ashai inclined his head. "I will cherish Princess Makari and treat her as the queen she will someday be."

"You'd better. The wedding will be in one month. I suggest you be ready."

He spun on his heel and marched from the room, Neffin following him out like a puppy. Bauti lingered a moment, his eyes smoldering embers, his grip on the edge of the door turning his knuckles white. Ashai thought he might break a piece of the thick oak off and chew on it.

"I was against this," he growled. "I still am. I don't trust you, merchant. Don't trust you, don't like you, don't believe you. If you so much as lay a hand on the Princess, I'll have your head."

With that, he slammed the door.

Ashai stood, staring at dark wood for a span of several deep, cleansing breaths. He fought the instinct to pursue Bauti in the hallway and cut his throat. It would be easy to kill the man, he'd never see it coming. But Ashai wouldn't complete the rest of his mission if he did.

When he was sure no one remained outside, he moved to his bed, pulled the small pouch containing the three gems from the trunk's hidden compartment, and dumped them on the soft linen. They glittered and winked at him, blue as Makari's eyes.

Thinking of his soon-to-be wife caused a tickle in his stomach. He tried to chase away the feeling, physically shaking himself, but it would not go away. Just like the image of her bright, blue eyes peering deep into his soul.

What was wrong with him? He was a trained Denari Lai, not some schoolboy, falling in love with every skirt that passed.

He reached out his right index finger, hesitating over the diamond-shaped stone that represented himself. Could the Chargh Lai sense his weak emotions? Could a holy man thousands of leagues away know that Ashai's heart had strayed from the path of righteousness?

He let his skin brush feather light on the surface of the stone, jerking it back as if it might bite him.

Nothing happened. The gem remained brilliant blue.

He held his breath and reached out his first two fingers, touching the gems that represented Makari and her father the King. This time, as soon as he made contact, he felt a tingle, as if the gems themselves had nibbled his fingertips. Both gems turned blood red, pulsing crimson.

Ashai swallowed hard and pulled back his hand. Both Abadas and Makari had to die. That day.

Gathering his magic, Ashai touched the stone representing Makari and sent a thought into the heart of the jewel itself.

We are betrothed. Wedding in one month. Message stronger then. Recommend delay.

Denari Lai rarely questioned their orders, but it was not unheard of. They had operated for centuries, and recognized the need for some decisions to happen on the tactical level. Ashai hoped this would be one of those times.

Withdrawing his finger, he watched and waited as the stones continued to blink their bloody tint. After a moment, both stones turned blue again. Ashai reached out his finger and touched Makari's jewel. A single phrase entered his mind, unbidden.

Well done.

Ashai grinned, happy to have pleased his mentor and his God. His smile lived only briefly on his lips, however. He realized in that instant that he did not want to kill Makari, did not think she should die. Abadas, yes. The man was responsible for countless Nishi'iti deaths, and was as brutal as he was opulent. He stood for everything Nishi wanted struck down in the world.

But Makari, so far at least, had proven the opposite of her father. And as far as Ashai could tell, she knew nothing of her father's cruelty, was ignorant of the brutality inflicted on Ashai's people.

So now, he realized, he had two missions. Kill King Abadas, and convince the Chargh Lai to let Makari take over and rule the kingdom of Pushtan.

Deep in his heart, Ashai's faith fluttered. The Chargh Lai channeled only messages from God, yet Ashai knew Makari did not deserve to die. That meant either God was wrong, or the Chargh Lai was lying.

Both were impossible.

He scooped up the gems and dropped them back in the purse just as a knock sounded on his door. Stashing the purse up his sleeve, Ashai opened the door to find his Royal Guard standing there.

The man nodded his head. "It is time for your lesson, my lord."

"My lesson?"

One corner of the man's thin lips turned upward. "Your sword fighting lesson, my lord. Princess Makari ordered them every morning at this time. She thinks it only fitting that her husband knows how to handle a blade."

Ashai raised an eyebrow. "And who is teaching these lessons?"

This time, the guard's smile dripped with eagerness.

"Captain Bauti."

Ashai looked ridiculous, and Bauti loved it. He'd arranged the lesson at Makari's direction, but her guidance had been minimal. She'd only said she wanted Ashai trained—she didn't say it had to be pleasant. And she didn't rule out humiliation as a training technique.

So they stood in a courtyard behind the palace, the midday sun beating down on the dozen or so men gathered there. Most wore simple cotton pants and tunics, clothing normally worn for training. It was designed to be light and comfortable.

Not Ashai, however. Under the guise of not wanting to hurt the Minister of Finance, Bauti had arranged to have him dressed in an over-padded protective suit. Covering his hips to his shoulders, and running the length of his arms, the suit was thick, heavy, and stiff. The merchant couldn't bend his arms, so they stuck out to the sides like some life-size doll. Rivers of sweat ran down his face as the autumn sun broiled him.

A Royal guard member placed a steel helmet on his head, strapping it into place. It really amounted to little more than a bucket with a slot for his eyes, but it made it virtually impossible to turn his head.

The chuckles that rippled around the other soldiers sounded like music to Bauti. Ashai Larish had caused him no end of humiliation, and he was happy to return the favor.

Bauti hefted the weighted wooden practice sword in his right hand, spinning it with practiced ease so it whistled through the air.

Ashai's helper stepped into Ashai's field of vision.

"The captain will start with the basics. Blocking is essential. His first strike will be a downward blow and you block it like this."

He demonstrated, raising his arms over his head as if he held his own sword. Ashai watched his guard, and Bauti noted his eyes taking in every angle of the man's moves, studying stance, arm position, even the angle of his wrists.

When the soldier stopped, Ashai mimicked the move with near perfection, despite the rigid suit.

"Like this?"

"Why, yes my lord, just like that."

Ashai took the other practice sword, and as soon as his guard was out of the way, Bauti charged, swinging his sword with all his might.

Ashai moved slowly, but his sword came up just in time, wood clacking on wood as he deflected the blow. It bounced off the padding of his left arm.

Bauti grumbled. The merchant had gotten lucky. Had he not raised the block, the blow would have shattered his collarbone.

"I just shaved a pound of muscle off your arm," he growled at the smaller man. "There's not that much there to take, so move faster or you'll be dead."

He swung again, this time coming from the other side. Ashai's block came up slowly and his feet tangled, tripping him. He fell forward and Bauti's blade whooshed over the top of his helmet, missing by a finger's with. The momentum carried Bauti in a half circle so he stopped with his back to Ashai.

He fought to contain his rage. The merchant's clumsiness had caused him to leave his exposed back to an opponent. Bauti prided himself on technical perfection and tactics, on not making such amateur mistakes. To make one in this situation made him angrier.

Ashai flailed on his back in the dirt, grunting as he tried to get up. The guard took him by the armpits and hoisted him back to his feet, handing back his sword.

"You'll have to stay upright to stay alive."

"Thank you for the statement of the obvious," Ashai quipped. "We're not all made to be warriors, you know?"

"No," Bauti said. "Only men are."

He would've missed it had he blinked or look the other way for a second, but the look Ashai gave him just then chilled him to the bone. It was as if the merchant's eyes had frosted over, firing daggers of ice at Bauti's heart.

Then it passed and Ashai smiled a weak, passive smile.

"Some of us were made to count coin, others to kill. Some to marry princesses, others to be alone."

This time, the chuckles of the soldiers were like spikes driven into Bauti's flesh. He charged Ashai again, swinging his sword from right to left at the merchant's ribs.

Again Ashai reacted a split-second slower than Bauti would have, his sword coming up and smacking against the captain's, knocking it away, but throwing the minister off balance. Bauti delivered a boot to his back and knocked him on his face.

The guard helped Ashai to his feet again, and this time the merchant dropped his sword at Bauti's feet.

"Let's be honest, Captain. A Denari Lai assassin is not going to come at me with a broadsword. And the Minister of Finance will never be wearing armor. Perhaps it would be more practical for you to train me in defense against a dagger or a short sword while dressed ... normally."

Bauti straightened, and leaned on his wooden sword, stabbing the point into the dirt and wishing it was Ashai's chest.

"The instructions from the Princess were clear. You were to be trained in the use of a sword. She said nothing about defending against assassins. Perhaps she means to have her new husband fight in a tournament."

The soldiers' laughs echoed off the palace walls this time, lifting his spirit. This was more like he had planned.

Ashai motioned to the guard member to take his helmet off, and then shook out his hair like a woman.

"The padding too," he said. "If Captain Bauti hits me, so be it. He can explain to my betrothed why my arm is broken for our wedding."

It took three men to get the padding off Ashai, but once it was gone the Minister of Finance stood in a plain cotton shirt, just like the ones the other soldiers wore. Sweat matted to his body, and Bauti realized while the man was not muscular, he was lithe and lean, catlike in his build. There was nothing soft about him, and nothing loose. He was a tightly wound spring.

Not at all like a merchant.

He picked up the wooden practice sword and did a poor imitation of Bauti's whistling arc.

"Perhaps now I will move fast enough to not eat sand."

"Or perhaps I'll shatter your collarbone," Bauti answered.

Ashai shrugged. "Maybe, but again you'll have to explain that to the

Princess. She won't like you breaking her new husband before he's even her husband."

"I'm willing to take that chance."

"Then you're a fool."

Rage swept through Bauti like wildfire. He charged again, blade streaking through the air so fast it would cleave through Ashai's practice sword like a hot knife through lard.

But Ashai didn't move. He stood transfixed, sword held before him, point down. His eyes locked with Bauti's.

Suddenly, Bauti realized if he didn't stop, he would kill the Minister of Finance. He had leveled his blow at the man's foolish head, expecting him to try to block the strike or dodge it. No matter his feelings about the man, Bauti remained the captain of the Royal Guard. He could not draw blood on a member of the King's council.

And Ashai knew it.

Bauti twisted his body, tensing his arm muscles to freeze the sword before he could strike Ashai's temple. He lurched to his right, throwing himself off the collision path and pulling his sword back.

His actions put him off balance, perched precariously on his right foot with his left in the air.

Ashai simply stuck out his left foot and tripped him.

Bauti sprawled on the dirt, hitting face-down and feeling the wind explode from his lungs. The pommel of his sword dug into his gut, making him grunt in pain. He rolled quickly to his back, fighting to suck in a breath, but it was as if his entire body had been locked in a dragon's grip. His muscles would not move, his breath would not come.

Ashai stood over him, straddling his body, and reached down, placing a hand under each side of his lower back. He lifted him just enough to stretch the muscles of his abdomen.

Air rushed into Bauti's lungs, as he breathed in great gulps. Ashai nodded to him, removed his hands, and stepped aside.

Bauti lay on his back a few seconds longer, then vaulted to his feet and snatched up his sword.

"Underhanded tricks won't save you in a real fight. Had I not avoided hurting you, I would've taken your head off."

"You're welcome, Captain." Ashai hefted the practice sword in his right hand, then switched it to his left as if both were equally good. He grinned. "I apologize for embarrassing you. But I knew you would not actually hurt me, so I used knowledge of your weakness to my advantage. Is that not part of every battle?"

The soldiers around them chuckled again, this time at Bauti's expense. The captain stepped forward and raised his sword.

"Let's see how you fare this time," he growled.

He stalked closer, dropping to a near crouch. He kept the practice sword in his rear hand, his left in front as if he held a short sword or a dagger. His arms were longer than the minister's, and he could use that.

The two circled one another, Ashai appearing awkward and off-balance, his steps too close together to maintain a solid foundation. And yet, his movements flowed, like a silk flag blowing in the breeze, effortless and smooth. Bauti had the impression the man could drop to a balanced stance in a heartbeat.

Bauti tested Ashai's defenses, thrusting and sweeping. Each time, Ashai danced back or threw up a hasty parry, barely knocking the sword away and losing his balance in the process. He fell twice, springing back to his feet right away.

Tired of playing cat and mouse, Bauti came at him full-on. He didn't charge this time, he simply pressed a steady attack. He began by switching stances, moving his right hand forward. Then he leveled a combination of strikes at the merchant. Thrust, slice right, down sweep, thrust, backhand. The stances came naturally, flowing with decades of practice. His muscles remembered what to do, even if his mind had slowed in sending the commands.

Ashai countered everything with clumsy, awkward, or just plain lucky blocks and parries, and this time did not fall.

Bauti pretended to back off, then launched an overhead strike. This time, Ashai threw a near-perfect overhead block, deflecting the blow and throwing Bauti off-balance. The minister's wooden sword swept around and spanked the captain on his buttocks.

That drew a roar of laughter from the gathered soldiers, many of whom had stopped just to watch. Bauti felt heat rush to his cheeks.

But he also smiled, for he'd discovered something about his adversary. Minister Ashai already knew how to handle a sword. He'd covered it up so far, but slipped in the heat of the moment and shown his hand.

"Well struck, Minister," he said. He would show the grace and honor of the Royal Guardsman, despite his embarrassment. "One would think you'd handled a blade before."

Ashai whirled the practice sword, attempting to flourish but dropping the wooden blade in the dirt. More laughter, just as raucous. At least the men were getting a good show.

"Everyone gets lucky every now and then, Captain." Ashai's smirk mocked him. "I surely possess no skill measurable against your own."

Bauti took his blade in both hands, sank into a saddle stance, then launched himself at Ashai. His two-handed overhead swing, had it struck with a steel blade, would've beheaded the man on the spot. But the blade was made of oak, and it never found its mark anyway.

Ashai simply crumpled, as if he melted inside the cotton clothing and formed a puddle in the dirt. The blade whistled harmlessly over him, as he rolled to his feet behind the captain. Bauti whirled, but too late. The blunt tip of Ashai's practice sword poked him in his right buttock.

"Looks like I got lucky again," the minister mocked.

Now Bauti's suspicions screamed at him. Ashai had received combat training somewhere, elite training. He just covered it with feigned clumsiness.

Bauti attacked again, maintaining his two-handed grip on the sword. He sliced right then left, smashed down and swept up. This time Bauti studied the minister's feet. Ashai stayed on the balls of his feet the entire time, his heels just off the dirt, his steps quick and decisive. The rest of his body looked awkward and klutzy, but his feet betrayed him.

Bauti drove him all the way back to the stone wall of the palace's South Wing. Sweat poured down Ashai's face, and his arm trembled as he raised his last block to fend off an overhead strike. He moved slowly this time, and dipped his sword point too low. Bauti's practice sword slid the length of Ashai's blade and clipped him on the shoulder.

The merchant cried out, and dropped his wooden blade, and fell to his knees. He cradled his left arm in his right, rocking back and forth and moaning as if the arm were about to fall off.

"The blow was not that hard, Minister," Bauti said. "I'm sure you'll be fine."

He offered his hand, but Ashai glared up at him and did not move.

"I assure you, Captain, Princess Makari will hear of this ... assault on her betrothed."

Bauti stepped back and planted his hands on his hips. Behind him, he felt the other soldiers of the Royal Guard closing in until they formed a rough semicircle behind him.

"My Lord Larish," Bauti said, forcing himself to incline his head, "I assure you I meant no harm. I would never knowingly assault a member of the King's Council. This was merely a training accident."

Ashai struggled to his feet, still cradling his left arm, wincing with overdramatic pain.

"I'm sure the soldiers here didn't see it that way," Ashai said. "What about it, men? You saw it, didn't you?"

One by one, the soldiers drifted away, most shaking their heads.

"Looks like you have your answer, Minister. Training accidents happen. You have my heartfelt apologies. Shall I call for a healer?"

Ashai shook his head and turned his back on the captain.

"I'll consider this our last lesson, Captain. I'd appreciate someone more … professional training me next time."

He started to walk away.

"Do you even need more training?" Bauti asked. "You looked competent to me."

Ashai paused for an instant, then marched off toward his chambers.

Bauti smiled, satisfied with himself and his day's work. He'd uncovered some very interesting information about the new Minister of Finance. Not that military training was unusual. Many people had been in the Army at some point, and some even retained their skills. But Ashai Larish possessed advanced skills, and the physical traits to use them. And he was hiding them from everyone.

It was a start, but not enough to take to Abadas. Yet.

On the opposite side of the courtyard, Bauti retrieved his chain mail, tunic, and weapons. He was just dropping his sword belt to his hip when an average-looking man slipped from the shadows of a small doorway and sidled toward him. He stopped a few paces away, seeming to stare at a third-floor window while scratching his ass.

"I have information for you." His lips barely moved. "The small stables in an hour. Bring the gold."

The man strode away and Bauti smiled after him.

The Watcher didn't understand. At first, he thought Ashai had lost some of his abilities, or that the ridiculous armor had slowed him. He should have been able to best Bauti, even dagger-on-sword, but he'd lost. And been embarrassed.

What Bauti had said made sense, though. Ashai had probably faked injury, drawing Bauti in so he could beat him.

But he hadn't beaten the grizzled, old captain. Ashai had lost. Had it been a ruse? If so, it was a gamble. If Bauti saw through the ruse and understood Ashai's fighting skills, it could tip him off to Ashai's identity.

So The Watcher had two questions. First, was Ashai injured? And second, if he wasn't injured, why did he fake a lack of skill?

The Watcher knew exactly how to find out.

CHAPTER ELEVEN

The patrons of the Wooden Cup Tavern did not see Ashai. They saw a dirty, unhealthy looking dockworker, dressed in rags with three days of stubble on his chin and a gob of snot on his upper lip. It took only the tiniest trace of magic to maintain the illusion, but he added physical disguise elements too, allowing him to channel less from Nishi.

The inside of the tavern felt claustrophobic, packed with bodies and smelling of sweat and urine, the dirt floor crawling with the rats and dogs fighting over scraps of dropped food. The customers themselves were an unsavory lot, rough and drawn to violence and easy money. Another reason to disguise himself as a poor man—it kept him from being robbed. And having to kill the robbers.

A plump serving wench smacked a wooden mug of ale on to the table in front of him, sloshing a healthy amount of it onto his pants. He didn't care about the pants themselves, he'd throw them away when the night was done. But it made him uncomfortable, running down his leg and into his crotch. Still, he gave her what looked like a toothless smile and handed her two coppers for her effort.

He scanned the tavern. To his right, a bawdy prostitute sat in the lap of a man who looked like he couldn't afford her, while his friends cheered for him to move his hand further up her thigh. To the left, an obese man with more chins than hair sat at a table, staring into a flagon of wine as if he could find the answers to life inside. Against the back wall, a group of thieves gathered around the table, their heads close together as they whispered.

The fat man was looking at him. Ashai tried to avoid eye contact, but the man nodded as his gaze passed over him, and Ashai recognized Minister Tan.

The table behind Tan sat empty, so Ashai picked up his mug and moved there. He sat with his back to Tan's back, unable to see anything but a shadow of the spymaster in disguise.

"You pick a most unsavory meeting place," Ashai said, pretending to take a drink of his ale. He'd been surprised at Tan's summons, but not shocked.

Tan shifted ponderously in his chair, far too massive for even the plump man Ashai had known in the palace. His disguise was genius.

"Most palace dwellers wouldn't be seen dead here," Tan replied. "And those that would, stand out like a rose in a middens heap."

"Point taken. Why are we risking our necks here?"

"You need information. I have it."

"What makes you say that?"

Tan muffled his titter of a laugh. "No reason to be coy. Anyone can see a certain snow-capped mountain obscures your view, keeps you from the one you want. I have information that should bring that mountain down to the size of a small hill. A bump, really."

Ashai kept his voice low. "I could use some mountain-reducing information, come to mention it."

"That leaves only your compensation method. Information is most expensive."

This time, Ashai laughed. "I am Lord of Coin, Penny Counter, the King's Goldmaster. If anyone can afford this information, it is I."

Tan made a sound like a purr, and shifted in his wooden chair again. "And what of loyalty? That mountain serves the same man I do."

Ashai shrugged. "Perhaps I misunderstood your feelings for one another. There must be an unspoken love between you and this mountain. I know he thinks very highly of people in your profession."

He chanced a look over his shoulder only to find Tan swallowing deeply from his flagon. He didn't even use the wooden cup before him, and somehow spoke at the same time he drank.

"My Lord Larish is quite observant. Perhaps you'd be interested in something under your seat."

Ashai reached under the cushion of his chair and was only slightly surprised to find a leather pouch there. He opened it, and pulled out a half-burned piece of paper. He studied it for a moment in the dim light of the tavern, his skin crawling more with every word, then returned it to the pouch, tucking the pouch into his shirt.

"I assume that handwriting is the captain's?" From the corner of his eye, he caught Tan's barely perceptible nod. "How long have you known of this?"

"It's been whispered about in the corridors of the palace for many years. This particular letter came into my possession a few months ago, prior to your arrival."

Ashai took a drink of his ale, this time for real, wincing as its warm bite slid down his throat.

"And the things he mentioned are possible?"

The letter had spoken of secret passages behind private chambers in the palace. If one existed behind Makari's quarters, he had to assume one existed behind his own as well.

Again the subtle nod.

"Then I thank you, and will expedite all transfers to your ... operations."

He started to get up, but the spy cleared his throat and Ashai froze.

"As you know, the Denari Lai have sent an assassin to kill Abadas and Makari, leaving Pushtan without leadership."

Ashai's stomach twisted like a towel trying to wring itself out. He eased himself back down and took another drink.

"Do you believe this to be true?"

At the back of the bar, two dockworkers started to tussle, one cracking the other over the head with a wooden cup. Ashai tensed, ready for trouble, but both men went back to drinking.

"I do. And as I'm sure you know, the Denari Lai have never failed to kill their targets."

"As Makari is about to become my wife, this is of great concern to me."

Tan stared into the depths of his half-empty flagon again. "I know you care deeply for her. A man in your position may notice certain irregularities in the expenditure of funds. You may also see comings and goings or happenings that are not natural. Bring all your suspicions directly to me. Do not go to Captain Bauti, and certainly do not go to the King or your betrothed. If the Denari Lai know we are on to them, they will execute their plans—and the Royal family—immediately."

"Do you have any idea who the assassin might be?"

The spymaster thrummed his fingers on the wooden table in frustration.

"None."

And you won't until it's too late, Ashai thought, hiding a grin. Instead he said, "Perhaps we should watch the princess more closely."

Taking one last sip of the burgundy wine, the whale of a man rose with a groan, the wooden chair seeming to sigh in relief as his weight left it.

"It's already being done," he said without looking at Ashai. The Pushtani spymaster dropped a handful of coins on the table. "And remember, no one in a royal palace is really who they appear to be."

And with that, he waddled from the tavern.

Ashai leaned back in his chair, stretching his legs under the table, and resting the mug of ale on his flat stomach. What was Tan getting at with that last sentence?

The hair on the back of his neck rose. Someone was watching him. He fought the urge to look around, then downed the rest of the ale and made a show of looking for a serving wench, using that time to search the room.

The feeling came from the table of thieves who'd been huddled together earlier. They'd been looking at him until he beckoned for the server, then they all snapped their heads back into a tight circle and resumed their whispering.

The serving wench was busy, and Ashai didn't really want more ale anyway. He felt suddenly as if he needed his wits about him, and his magic too. So he threw down a few coppers, and stalked from the tavern.

As he suspected, he felt the eyes of the three men crawling up his backbone as he did.

The fall night was unusually brisk, sharpened with a chill blade of winter. Mist slipped from alley to alley on silent cat feet, and the silver disc of the moon hid all but a tiny sliver behind scudding clouds.

Ashai moved at a brisk pace down the cobblestones toward the palace. The rocks had become slippery as the fog made them wet, but thanks to Nishi, his footing remained sure. He moved left, hugging a wall of shops, ducking in and out of doorways and alleys.

He checked behind him several times, but no one followed. He breathed a sigh of relief. Perhaps he'd get home this night without killing.

They jumped him from both sides, two men charging from his right while a third came in from the left. Ashai heard them in time to run a few steps and turn around. It wasn't enough to get away, but it got him out from between them, and put his back to the moon, blinding them.

When he turned to face them, he gasped. At first he thought it was the light of the moon reflecting in their eyes, but when one passed under an awning, out of the moonlight, and his eyes still glowed cold silver, Ashai knew they were shiners.

"Be reasonable, now," the big one in the middle said. He carried a cudgel. The short one on his left carried a hatchet, while the one on the right carried a wicked-looking knife. "Give us the purse and we give you your life."

"You don't want to do this," Ashai said. His senses heightened until he could hear each man's heart beating in his chest, could see them clearly in the silver moonlight. Four. He heard four beating hearts, not three. "You don't know who you're dealing with."

The men tried to surround him, but Ashai backed up, shifting from side to side to keep them off balance. He didn't draw his dagger yet—revealing it would identify him as Denari Lai—but he kept his hand on it, ready to draw. As he scanned his enemies, he caught a glimpse of a cloaked figure in the shadows of the alley. Towering and broad-shouldered, the man was somehow almost invisible, as if shadows were his home.

"Don't matter who you are," the leader said, swinging the cudgel low. "There's three of us and one of you. You can give us your purse, or we can take it. And your life. Either way, your gold is leaving with us."

Ashai measured their movements, watching as they slid from step to step. They moved well, the back alley magic increasing their strength and coordination. But they were undisciplined, untrained. The leader held his cudgel too close to the end of the handle. The small one was too weak to swing the axe effectively, and the last man barely knew which end of the knife to use.

Ashai almost felt sorry for them. Almost.

"My purse, my gold, and my life all remain with me. This is your last warning."

"Take him," the leader shouted.

The other two men moved quickly; almost as fast as Ashai, but not quite. Ashai danced to his left, catching the arm in which the man held a hatchet as it swung toward his head. He whipped out his dagger and slashed across the man's forearm, severing tendons and slicing through muscle. The man screamed, dropped the hatchet, and grabbed at his arm, trying to stop the blood that sprayed forth.

Ashai spun to face the second man, parrying a clumsy thrust with the knife. He shattered the weaker blade, then whipped around and plunged his dagger into the man's ribs just under his right arm. The shiner's glowing eyes went wide, blood trickled from his mouth, and he fell.

The leader looked uncertain now, his moon-like eyes darting from his friends to Ashai and back. He held the cudgel out to one side, and looked for a moment like he might attack. Before he could move, the glow in his eyes flickered like a candle and he doubled over, clutching at his abdomen. Ashai could've killed him then, could've plunged his dagger in the back of the man's skull, but he found himself unable to look away as the man's magic left him.

The attacker vomited, black bile spewing from his mouth and hissing as it hit the ground. Smoke rose from where it pooled, and when he was done, the man let out a long groan. Then he took one look at Ashai and sprinted down the alley, his wounded ally close on his heels.

Ashai sheathed his dagger and glanced around the alley. The fourth man slipped away in the shadows to his right, disappearing between two buildings, graceful and almost wraith-like. Ashai's gut told him he'd seen the man before. But where?

Something else moved, to his right. Ashai made out the shape of a little boy with a lopsided run, distancing himself from the fight.

Ashai's instincts told him to chase the boy, to kill him and dispose of one more witness. But the attackers were more important, and he'd let them go. Besides, unlike Bauti, Ashai didn't kill innocent children.

He straightened his clothing, adjusted his magic to give himself a new face, and walked calmly down the alley as if nothing had happened.

CHAPTER TWELVE

Marwan Bauti marched toward the King's private study, heels clacking on the marble floor with military precision. Servants, lords, ministers, and soldiers alike parted before him, seeing his lightning strike expression and steering wide around him.

He finally had the information he needed to tell the King. He'd hoped to bring Minister Tan with him, for the spy could lend credibility to his claims. But Tan had not been in his quarters and no one seemed to know where he was, leaving Bauti no choice but to do this alone.

The Royal Guardsmen on either side of the double wooden doors snapped to attention as he approached, weapons at the ready. They did not attempt to stop their commander, though they looked uneasy as he reached for the door. Bauti paused and looked at the man on his right.

"What's wrong, Sergeant?"

The Sergeant cleared his throat and scratched his grizzled chin underneath his helm.

"The King left orders that he was not to be disturbed, Captain."

"I'm going to disturb him anyway."

He thrust the door open and stopped dead in the entryway. Seated before the fireplace was King Abadas in a long, blue and black robe, trimmed with fur at the edges and tied with gold-laced rope. The five-pointed crown of Pushtan sparkled on his snowy head, and he rested his hands on his rotund belly. Seated across from him was the very man

Bauti had been unable to find. Minister Tan wore his normal gray cloak, his pudgy fingers interlocked across his lap.

"Captain Bauti," the King said, "Come sit down."

Bauti moved to an empty chair between the two men, feeling trapped and alone.

"I'm glad you're here, Minister Tan," he said, looking at the spy. "I think I know who our assassin is."

The King leaned forward in the chair, gripping the arms until his knuckles turned white.

"Yes, so Minister Tan has told me," the king said in a low, warning voice. "He says you suspect my future son-in-law. Those are serious charges to level against a member of the Royal Council. I hope you have proof."

"My King, consider the facts. Ashai came to Dar Tallus under a year ago, according to my sources. He's made it to your inner circle—a key requirement of the Denari Lai—and we don't know his motives for doing so. He handled the boy in the square too well for a mere merchant, so I tested his fighting skills."

The King sat back in his chair and pointed a stubby finger at Captain Bauti.

"I heard about that little game. You could've killed or seriously injured him right before his wedding. What were you thinking?"

"He moves like a veteran warrior," Bauti argued. "He appeared to be off-balance, and he made himself fall several times, but I never laid a hand on him that he didn't want me to. His footwork was perfect, and when he struck back, it was perfect as well."

Minister Tan shifted in his chair and cleared his throat.

"I happened to watch your little training session," he said. His eyes shifted around the room, never meeting Bauti's gaze. "You thoroughly embarrassed him. You knocked him down several times, and could have landed any number of blows had you wanted to. He scored two very lucky hits on you. I attribute both to your advancing age."

Bauti ground his teeth. He wanted nothing more than to jerk the man out of his chair and smash his face into the wall, but this moment required restraint.

"You should stick to spying, Lord Tan. A trained soldier like myself could see what he was doing without any doubt."

Tan steepled his fingers under his nose.

"Your Sergeant at Arms disagrees. I spoke to several of the soldiers who watched that fight, and they all agreed. Ashai got lucky twice, but otherwise you embarrassed him. You should be proud of yourself."

Sarcasm dripped from his last words like blood from fangs.

"Tell him what you told me," the king said to the spymaster. "All of it."

"My sources in Brynn checked on Ashai Larish, just like you asked me to do, Captain. It turns out the merchant is telling the truth. He did live there for several years, and did inherit his shop from a man named Larish. He sold the shop and moved here when his business was at its highest value. My source spoke to the person who bought the shop."

Bauti's throat tightened. How could this be? Things didn't add up.

"It would not be beyond the Denari Lai's reach to have someone deep undercover for many years to establish a solid story," he argued. "Your source doesn't clear Ashai at all. It simply proves he worked hard to establish cover."

Abadas heaved himself out of his chair and paced the small study, stopping with his back to the crackling fire. Despite the blaze, Bauti felt a chill in the room.

"Captain Bauti," the king said, "your personal feelings are getting in the way of your better judgment."

"I don't understand, Majesty."

Abadas gave him an apologetic look, one that warned Bauti something bad was coming.

"Your feelings for my daughter are widely known throughout the palace. I know that you've loved her for many years, and that your love for her is not always fatherly."

The words punched Bauti in the gut, nearly doubling him over.

"A letter has come into my possession recently," the king said, pulling a half-charred parchment from his robe. Bauti's heart sank. "I assume you recognize this?"

Bauti swallowed hard and forced himself to nod. His cheeks burned with humiliation. He wanted to vomit.

"Your feelings are understandable," the king said. "My daughter is lovely, smart, strong, and will someday be queen. I've been shortsighted in having you guard her so closely, considering your infatuation with her.

But your behavior, especially of late, is unbecoming your position and rank.

"You must understand, Captain, you're simply not in a position to marry her. Or any Princess. I could have ten daughters and you wouldn't be in position to marry the oldest of them. You're a soldier, Captain, not nobility and not royalty. I recognize your loyalty and courage, but your duties in personally protecting my daughter are removed."

Bauti opened his mouth to protest, but the king held up a hand and silenced him.

"You will assign your three best men to guard my daughter. From this point forward your duties consist of keeping me alive, and commanding the Royal Guard. Direct provision of security for Makari is no longer your responsibility. Do I make myself understood?"

Bauti fought to keep his breathing regular, and rubbed his temples with his fingertips. His head felt like someone had driven a spike through it.

"Your Majesty, my judgment where Makari's safety is concerned is uncompromised. Ashai—"

The King slapped his hand on a tabletop, rattling an oil lamp and nearly spilling it.

"Lord Ashai to you!" He snapped. "Or Minister. But you will maintain proper courtesies around the man from now on. No matter your thoughts on him, he is nobility and you are not. He is a member of the Royal Council, just like you. Show him respect. This is where your judgment is compromised, Captain. You're jealous."

Bauti bunched his fists at his side and could feel the muscles in his shoulders and neck tightening. Had he not fought for control, he'd have been shaking with rage. He stared at the letter in Abadas's hand, then shifted a fiery glare at the spymaster.

"Save your dirty looks for someone else," Tan said. "The letter was here when I arrived."

Ashai. Grinding his teeth, Bauti nodded at Tan, then bowed to his King.

"If I might be dismissed then, Your Majesty? I should see to security for the wedding."

Abadas stared at him a moment, then nodded.

Bauti stalked from the room, vowing under his breath to make Ashai pay dearly for this humiliation. He'd served the Royal family for thirty years just to have some upstart merchant supplant him in Makari's heart.

Yes, the Minister of Finance would pay. Bauti just had to figure out how to make it happen without hurting Makari, too.

CHAPTER THIRTEEN

Makari had never liked the palace's main banquet and ballroom, with its marble columns, crystal chandeliers, and expensive tapestries. Ashai's Bestowment Ceremony was supposed to take place in the Chapel of the Five Gods, but ongoing renovations made that impossible. So servants had moved the ballroom's long trestle tables out of the way, replacing them with row after row of benches. Row after row of officials, lords and ladies, and members of the King's council lined the rows, dressed not quite in their best clothes, but something a bit lower. More appropriate to Ashai's station.

Makari frowned. Her father had chosen her dress for her this time, selecting one the color of a pear, with hoops at the bottom and wires intended to sculpt her into a curvier woman.

"I want everyone in that room to see Ashai staring at you," He'd said. "Only you. When your mother wore this dress, I couldn't keep my eyes off her. Or my hands!"

Makari had almost thrown up in a potted plant.

Few of these people had ever seen Ashai, much less met him, and today they would watch him be named Lord and granted lands, even though they were small and unimportant. The event was so rare, so practically unheard of, that she had to go back in their historical records nearly three generations to find the last time it happened.

Makari and her father stood on a hastily constructed platform at the head of the room, a stage so rickety she wondered if would hold her father's weight, much less those of her and Ashai and the priest, who was rather portly himself. Feeling the platform wobble made her say a silent prayer to the Goddess of Love that the chapel would be ready in time for her wedding.

The doors at the back of the room opened and the priest stepped in, dressed from head to foot in a white and gold floor-length robe. Atop his head sat a tubular five-sided hat that looked like a giant crystal on his head. At each point of the pentagon, a tiny bell jingled while he walked.

The points, of course, represented the five gods—the Gods of Love, War, Children, Harvest, and Death—and the bells were supposed to summon their attention as the priest walked. In reality, it made the priest look like a jester in a fancy robe.

Behind him came Ashai, dressed splendidly with the help of his friends in the tailors' district. His black hair had been tied back in a tight ponytail, making his strong nose seem to jut further from his face than it normally did. He wore a short, blue jacket, trimmed with gold over a black tunic, open at the neck. His hose were a deep, midnight blue, with black leather boots shining to his knees.

They'd made good choices, putting him in her family's colors. She could see her father's grin stretching from ear to ear.

The priest stopped just short of the platform, and Ashai stopped behind his right shoulder. The priest cleared his throat, and addressed her father the king.

"Your Majesty, King Abadas the First, Ruler of Pushtan, and Liege over these lands, I present to you for coronation to the title of Lord, Master Ashai Larish. May the Five Gods purify this man's intentions, buttress his loyalty, and ensure his worthiness by giving their blessings to these events."

Abadas bowed his head in deference to the Five Gods and replied, "So let it be spoken, so let it be done. Ashai Larish, approach the stage and kneel before us."

As Ashai mounted the rickety stairs to the platform, Makari realized how long it had been since she'd seen him up close. In the week since her father had announced she would marry Ashai, the former merchant's workload had double or tripled. For weeks prior, they'd shared quiet meals, walks in the gardens, and long discussions of parts of the world she'd never seen. Then, as if he'd been a magician's illusion, he simply disappeared from her life.

She understood that the Minister's job was a busy one. Given the crown's poor state of financial affairs, even Ashai found it challenging to make numbers match. He'd told her one day that paying the kingdom's debt was like filling a bathtub with a thimble. He'd had to find creative ways to fund many things, but he'd had to deny many requests for funding too, as he tightened the Pushtani belt.

Still, Makari felt like her betrothed was a ship with anchor pulled, slowly drifting from her harbor, sailing for the horizon.

She shook herself. She was just being silly, a ridiculous girl with ridiculous jealousy. Her betrothed was an important man, and was bound to have periods of never-ending work.

As he kneeled before her and her father, Ashai managed to give her a sly smile. It wasn't much, just a slight uptick of one corner of his mouth and a fleeting brush of his gaze over hers. But it lifted her heart, and sent a rush of warmth from her chest to her fingers, toes, and cheeks.

"Ashai Larish," her father said in his best public speaking voice, "by the power vested in me by the Five Gods, I bestow upon you the title of Lord of Trinward, with all the titles and duties, lands and responsibilities that accompany it.

"As Lord you have several duties to which you must swear. You must protect your citizens, swear fealty to the crown, pay taxes on time, send troops when requested, and answer to the King or Queen when summoned. Do you swear to uphold these duties in the name of the Five Gods: Love, War, Children, Harvest, and Shadow?"

Ashai looked her father in the eye. "I swear in the name of the Five."

The priest joined her father, and the two men placed their hands on Ashai's head. They muttered a prayer, then stepped back.

"Rise then, Lord Ashai Larish, protector of Trinward and loyal member of the Royal Council. Receive your fellow lords and ladies, as a proper noble should."

The next hour droned for Makari. She stood by Ashai's side, greeting a long line of pompous Lords, snooty Ladies, and other puffed up nobility. Next came Ashai's new staff members in Trinward, including the man he would name Chancellor in his absence while he attended his Royal Council duties. She managed a weak smile when Lord Brendar—who for some reason remained in the city—congratulated Ashai for his Lordship and his upcoming wedding. The man seemed almost sincere.

Makari's mind drifted off. Again her thoughts went to Ashai and their upcoming wedding. There was more than just her loneliness, more than missing Ashai. Something inside her felt off, misbalanced or out of alignment. Almost like the wedding itself was a heavy weight on one side of her body, making her list that direction, pulling her away from safety.

She kicked herself. It was normal to feel apprehensive about a wedding. Every bride who'd ever gotten married had wasps in her belly for weeks beforehand. Kendshi had told her as much just an hour earlier.

She straightened her back, stuck her chin out, and resolved not to think of it. She was no silly schoolgirl, no tittering Lord's daughter, desperate for marriage yet frightened to death of it. Marrying Ashai had been her idea, and it was a good idea. Possibly the best she'd ever had.

Nerves or not, hornets in her belly or none, Makari would marry Ashai.

She'd just have to ignore the nagging little voice in the back of her mind.

The ceremony drew to a close, and Makari took a deep breath, letting it out with a sigh. Ashai offered the slightest touch on the sleeve of her dress, sending a message of assurance. Confidence.

"Shall we have dinner together tonight?" She allowed her hand to brush his, and was surprised when he flinched as if she'd shocked him.

"That sounds lovely," he answered, his voice as distant as his eyes. "But I have a council meeting in an hour, then private meetings with at least three Lords asking for money. After that I must meet with the representative of the bank of Thahr, to which we owe quite a bit of money, so I can try to convince him not to wage war on us.

"If you can wait until after dark, possibly midnight, then I will come to you and we can dine together under the stars."

For a moment, for just a lightning-fast instant, he smiled at her and their eyes met and she knew the man she'd fallen for was still inside. He'd been buried under bolts and bolts of thick cloths called responsibility. She chided herself for not being more understanding. He'd gone from merchant to minister in a few weeks, and by all accounts had handled the transition stunningly. Of course there would be a period of adjustment, where he'd have less time for romance.

She saw all this and more in his eyes, saw the Ashai she knew staring back from the bottom of a deep well, where he fought to keep his head above the surface.

Then the moment was gone, and his attention turned to a gangly young lord who approached and offered his hand in congratulations.

"Lord Renick," Ashai said, "I'm happy you attended. Perhaps you brought the taxes your family owes? Judging by the gold inlays on your jacket, you're certainly not hurting for funds."

The young lord's cheeks flushed and he stammered over his words.

Makari didn't wait to hear what he said. She brushed Ashai's forearm with the tips of her fingers, and left the room. She found Kendshi waiting for her in the corridor outside, midnight hair tumbling down past her shoulders, dark eyes searching Makari's.

"Are you still having second thoughts?" she asked.

"No, Kendshi, no longer. Ashai is a good man, and I'm lucky to be wedding him."

But as they turned to walk down the hallway, arm in arm, the little voice continued to nag in the back of her mind. She doubted it would ever shut up.

The Watcher leaned back from the tiny hole in the ballroom wall. His vantage point had been perfect, directly behind the Princess and her father, able to see every expression on Ashai's face during the ceremony.

He'd acted the part well, as if he'd been to the ceremony a dozen times before. He was contrite when needed, gracious, and for all intents and purposes he looked like any other Pushtani lord.

And yet something bothered The Watcher, something suggesting perhaps Ashai had a weakness. Oh, he'd known this already. He'd seen the way he looked at the Princess, taken note of the subtle change in the tone of his voice, the light in his eye whenever he saw her.

It was certainly understandable. Makari was lovely, and smarter than even her father. Yet when she brushed his hand, the assassin had flinched. Ashai's back had been to The Watcher, but he'd have bet that under the cloak of his magic, Ashai had been blushing.

The Watcher had listened to the thrum of Ashai's magic as only another trained in its use could do. Being grounded in a man's faith, magic served as a tuning fork of sorts. With a trained ear, one could detect the slightest perturbation of tone, the smallest shift in the vibration of the line attaching them to God's power.

Eyes closed, The Watcher let the sound of Ashai's magic fill his heart. A strong, steady note emanated from the assassin, pure and holy and powerful. It sang of righteousness, reflecting the strong faith of its user like a music note reflects the tuning of its instrument.

There. The slightest twinge reached The Watcher, a moment of discord in an otherwise perfect tone. It had come as Makari departed, when her fingers brushed Ashai's arm. It was as if someone playing a lute had stretched a string, warping the note sharper than normal. It lasted but a heartbeat, yet it told The Watcher everything he needed to know.

Ashai's faith had wavered. Even worse, it had wavered at Makari's touch, at the presence of the person he was supposed to kill.

The Watcher opened his eyes and tapped his fingers against his chin as he thought.

If Ashai was having second thoughts about Makari, did it mean he was having them about Abadas too? Was he doubting his God, or simply in love with the girl?

This gave The Watcher pause, for he respected Ashai's judgment and intelligence. If Ashai was having second thoughts, did it mean Makari did not deserve to die?

The Watcher shook his head and started down the passageway toward his quarters. Of course not. Nishi never changed his mind, and never erred. He had deemed Makari and her father must die. Obviously, he had seen inside Makari's heart and knew that she had the same potential for evil as her father, no matter her beauty.

She posed a threat to the Nishi'iti people, and the Denari Lai did not let such threats live.

As he turned a corner, brushing a cobweb from his face, he decided Ashai would need to be ready sooner than they thought. What better place to kill the King than at his daughter's wedding?

CHAPTER FOURTEEN

They came for Pachat at sunup, just as golden rays wedged themselves through the bars on the pit, teasing him with promises of warmth.

He'd been here for three days and three nights, sweltering by noon and shivering by midnight. The pit was too narrow for him to spread his arms side to side, and now it was filled with the stench of piss and the stink of shit. He'd only slept the first night, and then only until the temperature dropped so much his teeth chattered him awake. By the second night, he couldn't sleep without lying or sitting in his own waste, so he stood and did exercises to keep warm. The third night found him too weak to exercise or even stand up, so he'd simply collapsed into the pile of his own making and drifted into a tortured unconsciousness.

He looked forward to the sun slicing through the opening, for morning was the only time of day the pit had any comfort. It warmed enough to be livable, but didn't turn into a frying pan until the sun reached its highest point.

He'd expected another two days, so when guards tossed aside the wooden mesh cover, it startled him, and when they dropped a rope ladder, suspicion came with it.

"We can always leave you down there three more days." The guards were little more than silhouettes peering at him, the brilliant blue northern sky blinding behind them. "But most people don't live past day six."

It took every ounce of his strength to climb out, and it lasted what seemed like an eternity. But when he reached the edge, the guards grabbed him under the arms and flung him on the ground. He lay there on his back, eyes closed as the sun thawed his frozen body, and took in great gulps of fresh air. He knew he should be embarrassed about his nakedness, should cover himself immediately. Nishi frowned on public nudity, but Pachat thought his God might understand in this case.

The guards hauled him to his feet and dragged him to the tent where he and his work crew had lived for years. They heaved him through the door and ordered him to get dressed.

As soon as he was ready, they took his entire crew and led them to the mines. Not just any mine, either. They led them to Lazarakh's Maw, a mine that had gone unused for six years, since a series of cave-ins had killed twenty-two slaves. The logs once used to cover the entrance had been tossed aside, and now the opening gaped like a demon's jaws just waiting for Pachat and his men to march themselves inside.

As they stood staring at the tunnel, Cargil marched up behind them and laughed.

"Thanks to your friend Pachat," he told the group, "your squad is reopening this dormant mine. Your task is simple: find gold. You'll have to clear the blockages, which means you have to clear the bodies too. And we can't spare any timbers for you to shore up the tunnel, so there's a good chance all of you will die.

"Since you're all willing to risk your lives to support the Pushtani crown, I will offer some incentive. If you successfully find even a medium-sized vein of gold, you'll all be moved to the galley. Permanently. Except, of course, for everyone's hero. His Majesty has a special reward in store for the trouble-maker."

Joppish, a scrawny man with a hook nose and a split lip, raised his hand.

"No more tunnel work?"

Pachat winced, knowing what was coming next. The boss marched to stand in front of Joppish, his chest touching the miner's. With no warning, his right fist jumped up and clubbed the man on the side of the head. Joppish staggered to his knees, then fought his way back standing.

"Don't ever speak to me unless I speak to you first, slave," the master said. "But yes, if you find gold you'll never work the mines again."

Rage boiled in Pachat's belly. He called this reward? They'd be slaving in the kitchens and being beaten by the Pushtani head cook instead of slaving in the tunnels and being beaten by Cargil. The cook had grown so enraged at a slave once that he'd held the man's face over an open cook flame until the skin melted off.

Freedom. Being released to go home would've been a better reward.

The slave drivers herded them into the tunnel, where the stagnant air had been fouled with the stench of death.

"If any of you consider running," the slave master said, "we'll be waiting right here. We'll send a messenger when your day is done. If no one comes, just keep digging."

Pachat's crew struck torches and marched into the darkness, coming across the first blockage perhaps thirty paces inside the cave. Pachat was able to reach up and place his hands on the cool surface of the ceiling, and the tunnel was wide enough for four men to walk abreast.

Without a word, they began removing the blockage. It took them three twelve-hour days to clear the rubble, and the three decayed bodies inside. Pachat thanked Nishi that the bodies were beyond recognition, just in case anyone knew them. Still, the sight of their shriveled bodies, broken and left alone for so many years, fanned the flames of his rage. He found himself clenching his fists and grinding his teeth, longing to wrap his fingers around the slave master's thick neck.

They found the second blockage the following day, a jumble of head-sized boulders piled to the ceiling, bone-white remnants of arms and legs sticking out in places. One man turned and vomited against the wall, while another broke down in tears. This collapse had taken place before most of them had come to the mining camp, but the sheer horror of the situation was enough to enrage them.

They took their time clearing this, working with delicate care to avoid damaging the bodies. But it was not just respect for the dead that made them move with caution, but the instability of the tunnel itself. They removed rock after rock, one by one, and anytime they came to a weight-bearing one, they'd move back from the tunnel and tug it free with a rope or lever.

The ceiling collapsed once, breaking one man's leg and bloodying another's head, but two days later, they'd cleared a space big enough for two men to walk through side-by-side.

Pachat stood back, arms crossed over his chest, and surveyed their work.

"We should clear the rest," Joppish said, appearing at Pachat's elbow. "There could be more miners buried in either side."

The other men, ten of them all total, gathered around. Pachat shook his head.

"The rest of the collapse may be holding up the ceiling. If the masters aren't going to give us shoring timbers, then we need to be extra cautious."

"We can't just leave the bodies here," said the broad shouldered Traybin. His square face pinched, his brows coming down until they almost touched the top of his nose. "That's no way to treat our brethren."

"We will get them out later, when we can take our time. Right now, they would want us to live, even if it meant staying down here a little longer."

The men nodded, even Traybin, and muttered their agreement. Pachat faced the men and led them in a silent prayer to Nishi, their lips moving without a sound, hoping their God could hear them even this far underground.

They lit fresh torches and filed two by two through the opening, into the pitch black on the other side. Even the light from their torches only cut through the darkness so far, illuminating the walls and the ceiling but showing nothing but more black ahead of them.

The air here had been still for so many years that the slight breeze created by their opening kicked up dust motes that glittered and sparkled in the torchlight. It smelled stale, and tasted of mold and rotten meat. Pachat led the group at a brisk pace.

"We need to find the last collapse quickly," he told them. "The sooner we find gold, the sooner we're out of this tunnel. The old miners were digging here for a reason. They had to have thought there was gold —or something precious—down here."

They came to the next blockage five minutes later, the wall of stone appearing suddenly in their torchlight, as if it had jumped up in front of them. There was something unusual about this collapse, something different from the other two, but Pachat couldn't figure out what. He motioned for the men to hold their torches near and he moved closer to the wall.

That's when it hit him.

"This is no collapse," he said.

The men exchanged nervous glances, but the closer Pachat looked, the more convinced he was. The stones were almost all the same size, the size of a melon or a child's head. Unlike the other walls, the stones here didn't tumble or clatter away when he touched them. They held tight, as if placed in interlocking positions.

He put his hand on the closest one and tried to pry it free. It took all of his strength to break the rock from the wall.

"Someone built this," he said.

Traybin moved to his side and grasped another stone. He broke it free, but not without effort.

"He's right," the big man said. "Look how regular the spacing is, and how none have tumbled to the floor. Someone built this wall. So, was it to keep people out or in?"

Pachat shrugged. "It doesn't matter. We need to know what's on the other side or none of us will live long enough to care."

They moved faster on dismantling this wall, since Pachat suspected it did not support the ceiling. The even spacing and small size of the stones made light work, and a day later they were through.

The wall had been much thinner than he'd expected, and led to a split in the tunnel. To the left, the tunnel was open and descended farther into the belly of the earth. The shaft on the right, however, was blocked by another collapse.

"I thought there were only three collapses," Joppish said.

"There were," Pachat said. "So someone built that wall after the first collapse."

"So what do we do?" Traybin asked. "Which way do we go?"

Pachat considered, studying both tunnels.

"We'll have to split up," he said. "One group clears the right tunnel while the other explores the left. I'll take—"

"There's nothing to see down this tunnel," said a voice from the blackness to their left.

The miners jumped, raising torches or picks like weapons as a lone man stepped from the shadows. He wore the rags of a slave miner, right down to the steel anklets that would connect him to the others. His black hair looked like it'd been home to a wildcat, but his brown eyes skipped from one miner to the next, finally settling on Pachat.

The man stepped into the circle of torchlight, scratching the stubble on his square jaw as he studied Pachat from head to foot. There was something about him, something that made him look different than the average miner. He was Nishi'iti, like them, and possessed a wiry strength typical of men who worked the tunnels. But he carried himself differently, with his back straight and shoulders pulled back. He held his head high, and when he walked, his foot struck heel-first.

"You must be the leader," he said in Pusthani. The other miners moved to stand behind Pachat, tools ready as weapons. The man studied them and smiled. "Yes, you're clearly the leader."

"And you're a soldier." Pachat spat the words at the man's feet. He had no love of soldiers—soldiers had taken his family. "A Nishi'iti soldier, unless I'm wrong."

The other men tightened their pack behind him, a nervous titter running through their group.

The soldier merely inclined his head. "Correct," he said, switching to Nishi'iti. "I am Commando Suzaht of the Wanao Lai. I've come to set you free."

Pachat laughed, and the others laughed with him. Suzaht did not share in their joke.

"You'll need more than just one Wanao Lai," Pachat said. "There is an entire Pushtani company just in our camp, and a platoon stationed in this area. Even a Wanao Lai cannot beat those odds."

The Wanao Lai were Nishi'iti special troops, elite soldiers with unique skills that bordered on unreal. That would explain how he carried himself.

"Fortunately I did not come here to fight," Suzaht said. "At least not right now."

"You think the Pushtanis will just let you walk us out of here?"

"If I wanted to, I could lead you down this tunnel all the way to a camp where ten more Wanao Lai await. From there, we could smuggle you across the border and take you home."

An excited murmur ran through the men, but Pachat was not fooled.

"But you don't want to."

Suzaht shrugged. "I do, but the time is not right. Allow me to show you something."

He turned and marched down the dark tunnel, Pachat and the other miners swarming behind him. A few paces in, they passed through shoring timbers rigged with ropes and pulleys.

"This tunnel is rigged to collapse," Joppish whispered.

Pachat nodded, but said nothing.

A few paces later, they rounded a bend and stopped, jaws falling open.

Suzaht stood back and gestured with his hand as if showing off a prize steer at auction. Arrayed in the corridor around them were all manner of weapons. Swords, daggers, battle-axes, even spears. Boiled leather armor and steel helms stood in boxes against the walls, and stacks of shields lined the floor. A path wide enough for one man to walk passed between all the supplies and disappeared into the darkness.

"All of this is for you," Suzaht said. He picked up his short sword and spun it in his hand, the blade whistling through the air. "We've been stacking this here for months, preparing for your rebellion. All it took was the slightest suggestion to Cargil, and a day later all of you started digging through the tunnel."

"What do you mean our rebellion?" Pachat asked. He had the feeling the Wanao Lai wanted something from them. "We're not rebelling. Rebellion equals death, slow and torturous."

"You're not rebelling yet, but you will be soon." He pointed to Pachat. "And you will be leading the rebellion."

Pachat choked, and took a water skin Joppish offered. When he washed the sand from his throat, he glared at Suzaht.

"I'm no commander," he said. "That's more your business than mine. I'm a miner now and I was a farmer before. I'm no fighter."

The Wanao Lai moved with the smooth grace of a cat and put his hand on Pachat's shoulder. It felt strong, capable.

"My sources tell me you're the only one in the camp who stood up to Cargil. That makes you a leader, and that's all these men need. On your way out tonight you will collapse this tunnel. We cannot risk the Push-tanis finding this cache. When you come back, you'll work at unblocking the other tunnel. When I get word to you in camp, that's when you start digging toward these weapons again. Once you have them, I'll help you start the rebellion."

Pachat's mouth watered at the thought of a hundred and fifty Nishi'iti slaves rising up against their oppressive masters. He longed for the chance to stomp on Cargil's head, or even better to take it off with a sword. But doubt nagged at him.

"I understand your reluctance," Suzaht said. "There are a lot of armed soldiers out there, which is why your rebellion must be timed perfectly. You'll need the element of surprise."

Pachat looked at the men, the other Nishi'itis who'd come to the tunnel with him. They shifted on their feet, open and shut their fists, and glanced at one another. But under the nerves, hidden like a bear trap in the grass, rage lurked. It would take little more than a spark to ignite their fury. The men were eager, too.

"Suppose we do as you say," Pachat said. "How do we know you won't just abandon us? We might beat the slave masters, but when the Pushtanis send a platoon, we'll have no chance. They're all trained soldiers and we're just rabble."

Suzaht put his other hand on Ashai's other shoulder and peered deep into his eyes.

"By the time the platoon gets here, you will be gone down these tunnels, collapsing them behind you. Five days later, you'll be back in Nishi'iti, where you all belong. With your families."

"Our families?" Traybin's lip trembled as he spoke. "I can see my boys again?"

Suzaht nodded and paced around the small cavern, circulating among the miners. "Of course. You can all be home within a few days of fighting back. Unless...."

As soon as he let the sentence trail off, Pachat knew he'd set a trap. He started to call the soldier out, but Joppish cut him off.

"Unless what? Why would we not want to be with our families again?"

Suzaht stared off down the dark tunnel, his back to the men. He took a deep breath, let it out, and turned to face his audience.

"Because Nishi needs men like you."

Pachat fought back a sigh. He'd seen this coming. Suzaht went on.

"Nishi and the Nishi'iti people need brave souls like you to rise up, throw off the chains of Pushtani oppression, and set the wheels in motion for our nation to take back what these animals have stolen. And in doing so, exact holy revenge in the name of our God and in the name of all his people killed over the decades of Pushtani tyranny.

"If you choose to remain here in Pushtan and fight for our people, Nishi will see to it your families are well-cared for, rewarded even, for the sacrifices you choose to make in God's holy name."

"Some of us do have family here, in Pushtan," Joppish said, looking at Pachat. "We want a chance to set Kendshi free."

Pachat's heart leapt. A chance to save his love? To free Kendshi from the clutches of the King?

"Kendshi is beyond our reach," he said, meeting Suzaht's fiery gaze. "No slave uprising will be powerful enough to free her there."

Suzaht lowered his voice to a conspiratorial whisper. "Don't be so sure. Nishi has taken certain measures to weaken the Pushtani regime and put us in a more favorable position to topple them. Without its head, even the most poisonous snake is harmless."

He paused and let that sink in. Pachat looked around at his men, who listened like children at their parents' knees during story time. The soldier had hooked them all, roped them into his fantasy world, and given them hope. Hope of freedom. Hope of justice. Hope of revenge.

False hope.

"Slaves alone cannot do this," he told the Wanao Lai. "Untrained men against the battle-hardened legions of the Pushtani Army? We'd be slaughtered. We're better off going home."

Suzaht gave him a disappointed look, much as his parents had done when he'd failed to say his evening prayers or when he'd been caught in a fib.

"Who said you'd be fighting alone?" the soldier asked. "There are dozens of tunnels like this, many of them just waiting for scores of Wanao Lai to pour through them, into Pushtani territory. We'd be able to take many of their front-line troops from behind, opening the border for our own army to come across unopposed. We could be in Dar Tallus with few casualties."

Pachat squinted at the man. The Nishi'iti Army was a defensive force, well-suited for defending the rough mountain passes in the southern part of their country, but ill-formed for striking deep into enemy territory. Or at least it had been.

"Are you saying Nishi'iti has changed posture and stands ready to invade south?" he asked, raising an eyebrow.

Suzaht raised his hands to his sides and shrugged again.

"I'm saying that with help, tossing this king from power and avenging decades of abuse is not only possible, but likely. But we need the unrest your uprising would bring. If the Pushtanis are focused on internal strife, they'll be easier to surprise."

Pachat put his hands on his hips. "Don't call it *my* rebellion. I'm no fighter, and I'm certainly not some rebel leader."

The Wanao Lai stepped close to him, putting his arm around Pachat's shoulders.

"You are more than you think. And don't tell me you wouldn't like the chance to run a blade through Cargil's flab and watch him die screaming."

Pachat remained silent, refusing to acknowledge how appealing that image was to him.

"As I suspected," Suzaht said. He turned and started back down the tunnel. "One of you come with me now. I'll collapse the tunnel behind you; tell that bastard slave master he died in the collapse. We will dig most of the way through from our side, so when the time comes, you can get to the weapons quickly."

Pachat didn't hesitate. Rebellion or not, he knew one man who needed to go home more than most of them.

"Traybin, go," he said.

The big miner's eyes glistened, but he stood fast.

"You'll need me in this fight."

"Your family needs you more," Pachat argued. "And there may not be a fight. That isn't something I can decide. It'll be up to the men and women held here. So go, while you still have a chance."

Traybin hesitated. Suzaht stood in the shadows on the other side, holding the ropes to collapse the ceiling.

"Go!" Pachat barked.

Traybin jogged to Suzaht's side. Pachat and the remaining miners sprinted back around the corner the way they'd come, and an instant later, a roar shook the tunnel. As they ran up the shaft, a cloud of dust coated them like soot. Pachat stumbled from the opening, hacking and wheezing, to find Cargil there, whip in-hand.

"Collapse," Pachat managed to cough. "Lost Traybin. Not safe anymore."

The slave master responded with a whip slash across his back and a kick to the ribs.

"Fools!" he shouted. "You'll be back in there tomorrow, clearing that rubble if you want to live!"

Pachat's doubts fell away like snow sliding off a roof, and he had an idea.

"Just before it fell," he panted, "we found it."

Joppish, on all fours beside him, snapped his attention to Pachat.

"Found what, maggot?" Cargil asked, kicking Pachat again, though lighter this time.

"Gold," Pachat lied. "We know where it is now. We just need to get to it safely."

Cargil spit on him and laughed. "Safety is not your concern. So we lose a few slaves. We have plenty of you animals. Gold is all that matters."

As he stalked away, Pachat glanced at his men. Every one of them wore a grim, determined grin.

Rebellion was on its way.

CHAPTER FIFTEEN

The interior of the palace chapel still wasn't ready for the wedding with only a week to go. Scaffolding still lined the north wall, and workers still milled around the rows of pews, sanding, fixing, and painting anything that didn't look perfect. Stonemasons repaired chips in the white marble floor, while five sculptors put the finishing touches on new statues of the Five Gods behind the main altar.

Marwan Bauti watched a glass worker fit a large plate of stained glass into a south-facing window, aligning it so its colored figure of Amari, God of War, would glow whenever the sun shone. The wedding would be a late-day affair, making use of the day's sunlight to warm the cavernous chapel and chase off the autumn chill that settled into stone buildings overnight.

Makari's wedding. The end of his foolish, old man's dreams.

A shout snapped his mind back to the present, and he looked up just in time to dodge a falling piece of stone the size of his fist. It shattered on the floor where he'd been standing, dozens of pieces skittering across the floor and peppering his legs.

Above him, a sculptor shouted down an apology, his chisel glinting in the morning sunlight. Bauti shook his head, but couldn't really be angry at the man. The King had been here just an hour earlier and had made known his displeasure at the slow pace of renovations. Now work took place at a near break-neck pace. It was a gift from The Five that no one had been killed yet, though one mason had lost a thumb due to carelessness, and a painter had been knocked unconscious by falling marble.

He sighed and let his eyes wander over the sculptor's work, then walked away to avoid distracting the man. As he turned, he caught sight of the princess standing near the back doors to the chapel, Kendshi at her side and a handful of ladies chattering away at her like a flock of birds.

Makari glanced at him, her icy blue eyes sweeping over him for an instant. He could almost feel a physical brush on his skin, like she'd touched him from across the chapel. And her touch was cold.

She frowned at him, then looked away, turning her attention back to her friends. Even the half-Nishi'iti girl turned a cold shoulder on him. Bauti felt as if the women had thrust spears into his chest, shearing his heart in two. How had it come to this, that the woman he loved, the girl he longed to protect and with whom he'd been so close for so long, come to hate him?

The answer popped into his mind unbidden: Ashai.

The merchant had poisoned her mind, and that of the king, making them believe Bauti was some sort of frightening old man. Like he was a perverted uncle lusting for his niece instead of a lifelong protector with feelings for a princess.

Stinging from the princess's silent rebuke, Bauti went back to his scan of the chamber, looking for anything that might give an assassin some kind of opening.

He found it in the ceiling.

His gaze stopped on a tiny square opening over the third row of pews, a hole just large enough to put his fist through. He waved over a chubby priest with cheeks as red as wine. The man's deep blue-and-black silk robes swished as he approached. Bauti pointed to the hole.

"What is that opening for?"

The priest squinted a moment, then nodded. "That's a compartment we use during special services. We put a choir member in a tiny space up there so they can sing the words of the Gods and have the voice sound like it's coming from above. It's very moving. Quite dramatic, really. I remember during the harvest moon service last fall—"

"Will you need it during the wedding?"

The man fingered his waddle and shook his head. "No, not during a wedding."

"Not even a royal wedding? You're sure?"

"Quite sure, Captain, quite sure. During King Abadas's wedding we did not use it, and during the Duke of Brynn's wedding, we didn't even have a choir. It was quite somber, actually, which suited the situation, since Lady Tiegan didn't really want to marry the duke. That was an awkward—"

"Seal it." Bauti drove his gaze deep into the man's eyes to make sure he understood the command's gravity. "Cover the hole and seal that compartment before the wedding. I don't want it opened again until this assassin is caught and the threat eliminated."

"But we have the harvest moon ceremony again in just a few weeks, and—"

"Seal it, priest, or it'll be your body covering that hole."

The priest swallowed and scurried off, promising to personally oversee the matter. Bauti made a mental note to check the next day.

Satisfied that he'd covered what could be covered for the time being, Bauti took one last longing look at his princess, and strode from the chapel, plotting all the ways he would make Ashai pay for the pain he'd caused.

Makari let her gaze follow Bauti out, shivering as he passed through the chapel doors and into the bright sunlight. The look he'd given her just before leaving spoke of hurt and longing, both soul-deep. All those years she'd looked at him as a father figure and protector while he'd looked at her as … she didn't want to think about it.

Beside her, Kendshi leaned in and whispered in her ear.

"He's gone, you can relax now."

Makari did feel the tension drain from her, her shoulders slumping a bit, her back loosening. Her heartbeat slowed, and a pain that had been mounting the back of her neck faded.

It made her sad to think of Bauti that way, a man who'd taught her so much, but there was little she could do to change her feelings. She'd hardly believed it when her father had told her of the captain's unrequited love for her, but then he'd produced the half-burned letter.

She'd read it right there, in front of her father, her skin crawling. How long had he been looking at her that way? How long had he desired her the way a man desires a woman?

She shuddered back to the moment just in time for the ladies to beg their leave and go. Kendshi patted her forearm with her warm fingertips.

"You should talk to your father about the ceremony," she whispered.

"What about it?"

Kendshi glanced around, making sure no one stood within earshot.

"You will not be able to enjoy your wedding day if Captain Bauti is in the chapel. Imagine, as you're saying your vows, if he were to look at you like that."

The slave girl winced and shook her head.

Makari hadn't thought of that, and was grateful once again for the girl's clear head and common sense. She hugged her, making several onlookers gasp and bringing a crimson flush to the girl's cheeks.

"Your Highness, not in public! I'm still a slave. Think of your reputation."

But Makari noticed the hand slave couldn't keep a grin from growing on her lips.

"Let them gawk," Makari said, flashing one giggling noblewoman a frosty glare. "You've been more faithful to me than anyone in Dar Tallus, even the good captain. Some days I don't know what I'd do without you."

Kendshi's blush brightened, but she kept smiling.

"Still, Princess, talk to the King. Captain Bauti should not be inside this chapel when you marry Minister Ashai."

Makari nodded and vowed to do so. The slave girl might just have saved her wedding.

CHAPTER SIXTEEN

Ashai stood in the arched window of his quarters, watching the sun set behind the forest west of the palace. Its waning orange rays stretched shadows long, lighting the entire world in fiery orange and red and black. With the forest itself already a quilt of those colors, it looked to Ashai like Nishi had dressed the world in fire to bid farewell to life as Ashai knew it. Or to symbolize the fire he would bring to Pushtan.

Stars already twinkled in the deep blue velvet of the sky, like the jewels set in the gown he'd seen Makari preparing for the big day.

Turning from the window, he surveyed his sparse quarters in the slicing evening sunlight. His bed was a simple wooden frame with a modest feather mattress and simple bedding of cotton and wool. He'd ordered the fancier silks and satins removed, along with most of the ostentatious gold and silver that had once decorated the room. Simple, hearty rugs lined the cold stone floors, with inexpensive tapestries on each wall for both noise reduction and to cover spy holes he'd found.

He'd dressed the measures as an example being set by the new Finance Minister to show austerity and help the kingdom's budget woes. It wouldn't do, he'd told the King, for him to demand deep budget cuts of others while living in excess. Abadas had thought it odd, but had approved the changes. So far, only one or two other minor officials had followed the example, but Ashai had managed to do what he'd wanted: please Nishi by reducing his own opulence. And he'd fooled them all into thinking he'd done it for the betterment of Pushtan.

He'd tried to get similar austerity measures implemented for the wedding, but neither the King nor Makari would hear of it, the Princess actually becoming quite irate at the thought of her wedding being anything less than grand.

Abadas had chuckled and explained to Ashai that the citizens of the kingdom, and especially of Dar Tallus, expected a grandiose wedding ceremony, needed to see the royal family celebrating to excess in order to keep faith that the Five Gods still blessed the Damars and still wanted them in power. Anything less would sow seeds of doubt and misery, making some people see the crown as failing.

And with slave unrest in the north and even some dissent among indentured servants in the capitol city, the throne needed to portray itself as strong and prosperous.

Ashai moved to the humble wooden desk he'd had placed in his sitting area, shaking his head. Abadas was a fool, and a cruel one at that. And if the Five Gods needed wealth to make someone a ruler, they were fools, too. Wealth almost always made for poor leaders, corrupting and devouring their morals and their souls until all that remained were self-serving autocrats intent on doing one thing: maintaining their own wealth and power.

He smiled when he thought of Makari taking over for her father someday. She still made her weekly trips into the city to help the poor, understanding that a ruler's strength came not from money or gold or armies, but from their citizens and the faith and trust they placed in those leaders. She'd be a much better ruler than her father, showing all his strength and decisiveness without the brutality or cruelty. Leadership without compassion was a demon, but Makari had both in ample supply.

Ashai sat in the stiff-backed wooden chair and said a silent prayer of thanks to Nishi for sending him here, and for the Chargh Lai's decision to grant him more time. He'd checked the crystals several times since requesting the delay, but no change. Perhaps the Chargh Lai trusted his judgment and would allow things in Pushtan to work toward Makari's natural assumption of leadership. Nishi must have looked deep into her heart and seen the same pure soul with which Ashai had fallen ...

He stopped himself short, the thought striking like lightning, sending a shockwave down his spine. He nearly bolted from the chair.

He loved her. He'd broken one of the core rules of the Denari Lai: he had feelings for a target. He should have realized it sooner, with the way he found himself thinking of her at odd times, the way he couldn't help but grin when he looked at her. Even the thought of marrying her tomorrow brought a smile to his face.

Guilt coursed through him, making him ask Nishi—again in silence —for forgiveness. He didn't even know if he could kill her father now. The man was evil, but Ashai didn't think he could break Makari's heart that way. She loved her father, and was insulated from this cruelty. The king had worked hard to hide the darker side of his soul from her, giving cruel or violent commands outside her presence.

He'd blinded her to the wrongs of his rule, and thus his daughter still loved him as daughters always love their fathers.

If Ashai killed him, Makari would hate him, and Ashai didn't think he could live with that. Losing her love would hurt as much as losing Nishi's.

Again he kicked himself. Blasphemy! Nothing was as valuable as God's love. Nothing.

So why did he feel like she'd supplanted his God, at least partly, in his heart? And why hadn't God punished him for these feelings?

He rose and kneeled by his bed, tugging the chest from underneath. He had to check the crystals one more time before the ceremony, just to make sure. His hand hovered over the wooden lid, fingers just brushing the smooth surface. He shook his head and pulled back his hand.

An idea crossed his mind again, one he'd had several times in the last few days.

Did it matter what his orders were? He could ignore the crystals, just choose not to check again, and if they'd changed, the second assassin would take care of things. That's why the Denari Lai always sent two, because one man could be compromised.

Of course, that meant Ashai would die, too. Either the second killer would kill him, or the Chargh Lai would send someone else, and neither would accept that he simply didn't know his orders had changed. Failure was failure, and the order did not accept it. Ever.

Still, he thought that death might be preferable to losing Makari's love. Of course, she'd be dead, too, but at least he wouldn't have had to face losing her heart. He imagined an eternity of fire and suffering for him would be more bearable knowing Makari had loved him to the end.

He'd tried finding the second assassin, but he'd found nothing, not even a clue. He shouldn't have been surprised, he knew how deep a

Denari Lai could plant himself. Of course, Kendshi was his first option, but his gut told him the girl wasn't the killer. Oh, she was certainly hiding how bright she was, but that was likely just to keep herself from anyone's attention. As slaves went, she had a pretty good life, and she seemed to genuinely love Makari, something which endeared the half-breed girl to Ashai even more.

Hand trembling, he picked up a stack of parchments from his desk, flipping through the sheets he'd compiled on everyone from servants to nobles to Captain Bauti himself.

Bauti, the one man he knew for certain was not an assassin. Not only had the man been loyal to the family since before they'd become the power in Pushtan, but he was also in love with the princess. In love with Ashai's betrothed.

Ashai couldn't blame him, and unlike others in the palace, he didn't find it repulsive. It wasn't uncommon in Nishi'iti for marriages to happen between older men and younger women. If Nishi wanted a couple to wed, who were mortals to interfere? And he knew well enough that love was more powerful than duty. He couldn't fault the man for falling for the woman he was charged to protect.

No, Bauti was not the second assassin.

Ashai stood and paced back to the window, placing his shaking hand on the cool glass, letting it steady him. His power was flagging. He needed to pray and renew his link to Nishi's Gift. Yet he hesitated. He didn't want his God to see him with weakened faith. No doubt Nishi knew, had seen him falling for Makari, had looked into his heart about Makari. But something about strengthening his link frightened him. It took a moment's thought to realize why: he didn't want to change his mind. He knew that renewing his power would also recharge his faith, erasing doubt in God and planting seeds of hate toward their enemies.

He didn't want to hate Makari, but he couldn't hate his God.

He knew what he had to do.

Ashai opened the trunk lid. Placing aside the contents, he opened the secret compartment in the bottom and gazed upon the crystals that glowed a faint blue. This would be his moment of truth, he knew. If his orders changed, he would face an impossible choice: follow his faith or follow his love.

Taking a deep breath, he reached out his index finger toward the diamond gem that stood for himself. He winced as his skin touched the surface, but nothing happened. The gem's cold blue remained.

His God still believed in him, still loved him.

Encouraged, he touched the square rock representing Abadas. At first, nothing happened. But then the stone's glow faded to bloody red. Ashai's gut twisted, and his finger hovered over the oval gem representing the princess. Did he dare hope that the Chargh Lai would let Makari live? And if so, could Ashai go through with the plan, knowing he would lose Makari's love?

He touched her stone and his heart sank. The gem turned the same color as her father's had.

Ashai jerked his hand back, and tossed his belongings in carelessly. Slamming the lid, he threw himself on the bed and stared at the ceiling. His God had spoken to the Chargh Lai, and the Chargh Lai had spoken to Ashai.

Ashai trembled, not just his hand, but his whole body this time. His worst nightmare was coming true: he had to choose between Nishi and the woman he loved. A day that should have been filled with happiness and love would instead be flooded with blood and death.

How could he decide? What mortal man could hope to choose when faced with this situation?

No one. No man could choose the right thing when both seemed wrong. So Ashai would do what he'd always done when he needed help.

He would ask Nishi.

Kneeling, Ashai faced north and looked toward the sky. This time, he didn't bother to disguise his prayer as Pushtani.

The Watcher hurried through the secret corridors, scurrying to make his way to his own quarters in time to notify his superiors in Tabi Ge Nishi that Ashai could not be depended on. That The Watcher would have to take over killing the Damar family.

He shook his head. To his knowledge this had only ever happened one other time, and that had been the Denari Lai's only failure, over 100 years before. One of their first assassins—a young man much like Ashai —had come to sympathize with the man he was supposed to kill, and had warned his target before the hit could take place. He had, of course, been killed, not by the Denari Lai, but by the very man whose life he'd spared. A sound lesson to which Ashai had apparently paid no heed.

The Watcher paused, putting his hands on the cool stone wall and trying to think. The Chargh Lai would want them all dead: king, princess, and assassin. Yet he would not want anyone knowing that the trusted Finance Minister was actually a Denari Lai killer. That would reveal weakness to their enemies.

The Watcher would have to make it look like Ashai was collateral damage, killed incidentally to Makari's death. He'd planned on doing all this after the wedding, when Ashai had become a member of the royal family, but the orders had come sooner than he'd expected. Now he had to improvise, and improvisation was an assassin's worst enemy.

He resumed his march down the passageway, rubbing his temples. He'd always wondered why the Chargh Lai insisted on sending young men to do these jobs. They were most easily tempted, especially where the guile of women was involved. The Watcher would never have fallen for Makari. Women did not tempt him.

Rounding a bend, he thought about what he'd just witnessed. Ashai had stalled in checking the stones, clearly not wanting to know if he'd been ordered to kill his love or not. When he did see the commands, he'd nearly broken down in tears, his resolve buckling and his faith crumbling like a wall made of sand.

Then he'd gotten careless, saying a Nishi'iti prayer in traditional form, not disguising it as Pushtani. He was fortunate only The Watcher had been in the passageway, or he'd have been dead by morning.

Perhaps that, The Watcher thought, had been his plan. Allow the Pushtanis to capture and kill him, removing the burden of choice from his shoulders, and making it someone else's responsibility.

That would have been disastrous for the order, having an assassin captured and killed before completing their mission. Denari Lai operated as much on fear as on actual killing. The psychological effect of knowing the Order never failed wore on potential victims, making them tear one another apart from the inside. The mere possibility that a target could discover and thwart a Denari Lai would weaken the order's influence.

No, that could never be allowed to happen.

The Watcher reached the door leading into his quarters and paused, peering through a tiny hole to make sure the room was empty. Satisfied, he shoved aside the wall panel and stepped inside. He had some planning to do before the big event tomorrow. If Ashai couldn't complete the task, The Watcher would, even though it would mean his death.

Inside, he slid closed the section of bookshelves, lit the oil lamp on his desk, and poured himself a cup of Lyran white.

He drank it down and shrugged. He would die serving his God and his country, and that was fine. He'd lived long enough anyway.

CHAPTER SEVENTEEN

The inside of the slaves' mess tent smelled more like a latrine than a place to eat, but Pachat had learned early in his time in the camp to ignore the smell and down his food, for he would not get a second chance. After a month, his nose had grown blind to the stench anyhow.

Not that the gruel their masters allowed them was far removed from shit, either.

He looked at the pathetic slop in the small tin bowl before him. Brown and thin, the porridge consisted mostly of rice and water, with a few insignificant spices thrown in to give it some sort of flavor. Sometimes the cooks were allowed to toss in whatever meat or fat was left over from the masters' meal, though it was no act of kindness or compassion by the Pushtanis.

Their captors knew that meat built strength, and that stronger miners dug more each day. The move was always selfish.

Pachat dipped his spoon into the bowl and jerked it back as something moved under the surface. As he watched, a cockroach emerged from the soupy contents of his bowl, its long feelers testing the air while it no doubt drank of Pachat's meal. It didn't seem in any hurry to get out of the bowl, so Pachat scooped it up and popped it into his mouth. The bug panicked, legs moving frantically on his tongue as it tried to fight its way out of the cavern, feelers probing his cheeks and lips, looking for an exit.

Pachat crunched the creature between his teeth, feeling its gooey insides slough onto his tongue. He chewed it until it stopped moving, spooned in a gob of gruel, and swallowed.

Another thing he'd learned early in his internment was to eat whatever he could find that wouldn't kill him. With winter approaching, his body would need all the nutrition it could get to avoid freezing.

He washed it all down with a swig of the weakest, most watered-down ale the masters could find, and looked around the tent.

The men of his crew sat around the same table with him, heads bowed low as they slurped their evening meal. It had been a week since the Wanao Lai had come to them, and no one had spoken of it since. They couldn't afford their captors overhearing, and Pachat didn't want to get their hopes up, either. It all seemed too good to be true, the possibility of going home. The thought of killing Cargil.

Still, they'd followed the plan, working the right-hand tunnel as if they had seen veins of gold, digging silently for hours. Cargil never asked about Traybin's body—he didn't care. What was one more miner's corpse in the tunnel?

Yes, the thought of killing the man made blood rush to Pachat's head, turning him giddy until he downed another spoonful of gruel.

Behind him, another crew took their seats, slapping bowls of the same bland mud onto the wooden tabletop. They ate in silence for a moment before one of them started muttering to the others.

"We outnumber them three to one," he said, swishing a mouthful of gruel around between words. "If we rushed them, they'd be dead."

"They're armed, we're not," replied one of his tablemates.

"We'd lose some men, that's true," the first said, keeping his voice low. "But in the end, they'd be sacrificing themselves in Nishi's name. And when the dust settled, we'd be free."

A general murmur of assent passed around the table.

"How would we get back home?" one man asked.

"Why go home?" the first man answered. "If we stir up every slave camp in the foothills, there'd be no way the bastards could stop us. There are too many of us."

Pachat chanced a quick glance over his shoulder at the leader. He sat facing Pachat, his dark eyes moving around the tent, taking in everyone and everything in a single sweep. He made momentary contact with Pachat, offered the slightest of nods, then turned his attention back to his food.

Pachat hadn't seen him before, with his square jaw and strong nose. His hair hung in dark waves to his broad shoulders.

Odd. One of the first things the masters did with new slaves was shave their heads to check for lice. Infestations had swept through the camp twice since Pachat had come here, and the masters had become affected both times. If the man were new, his head would be shaven.

Pachat went back to eating, turning things over in his mind. He knew in his heart what this meant, understood the man was not a slave at all, but a Wanao Lai. His job was to stir up dissent, setting the kindling for a fire they hoped would sweep through the foothills like wildfire, burning down all things Pushtani.

In other words, he was trouble.

The way Pachat saw it, in any kind of rebellion attempt, more Nishi'itis would die than Pushtanis, even if Suzaht was right about the Wanao Lai supporting them. Some slaves might manage to slip away to freedom, but many more would die without ever seeing their homes again. And being alive in captivity was always better than being a corpse in freedom.

And if slaves rose up, that would likely mean his lover would, too. And Kendshi would end up just as dead as any other slave caught opposing their master. Maybe worse, since her master was the princess.

He finished his meal, dropped the bowl and spoon into a cleaning basin, and started out of the tent when the troublemaker stopped him.

"Suzaht sends his greetings," the man muttered in the common tongue of the southern kingdoms. "Stay ready. Nishi will call on us soon."

Pachat pretended to pour sand from his boot, not looking at the Wanao Lai infiltrator. He didn't know why he'd expected the man to use Nishi'iti like Suzaht had when there were so many Pushtanis around. Speaking their native language was forbidden, and punishment would be severe.

"As long as I get Cargil, I don't care what the rest of you do," he lied. "I'm no soldier."

A Pushtani slaver strode past in his black leather, patting a whip against his thigh, his blond hair tied back in a hasty ponytail. He paused a moment, as if considering speaking to them, but one look from the Wanao Lai sent the man on his way.

"Does he know?" Pachat asked, fixing his other boot.

The soldier shook his head. "They don't have to know what I am to realize I'm not to be trifled with."

Pachat had to agree with him. The man had a certain look, a cool aloofness that made him look both relaxed and tightly wound at the same time. He'd seen the look in many a seasoned soldier along the border before he'd been taken. Only this man had ice behind his eyes, as well, as if his whole being were built around a glacier.

"I told Suzaht," Pachat said. "I'm no soldier, no commander, and certainly no rebel. You have the wrong man."

The other man looked off to the north, his gaze becoming distant. He sighed and started to walk away.

"You don't get to choose your role in history," he said. "Only God can choose that, and only a fool rejects it."

He disappeared into a cluster of workers headed for their tents, ready to turn in for the night. Pachat watched after him a moment, then headed for his own bed. He had the feeling sleep was going to be hard to come by very soon.

CHAPTER EIGHTEEN

Ashai hadn't truly been frightened since the day he'd been named a Denari Lai. With his training, skills, and faith, he could handle just about anything.

Until his wedding day.

He stood on the rickety platform, in front of the altar of the Five Gods, dressed in resplendent blue silk with black highlights, a ceremonial sword at his hip, shifting from foot to foot as he waited for his bride to enter the chapel. The King and the five priests stood behind the altar, solemn and silent.

Before them sat or stood what looked to Ashai like most of the city of Dar Tallus. He knew that couldn't be possible, since the chapel only held two thousand or so seated, but to a man used to slinking unseen through the shadows, being on a stage in front of this many people felt like being naked in Baker's Square.

Behind him, on the altar, sat a rectangular box the length of his forearm, tied with brightly colored ribbons, and painted the blue-and-black of her family. Tan had given him the box already sealed, saying it was traditional for the groom to give his bride a gift at their wedding. And since he knew how busy Ashai was, he'd taken the initiative and gotten it for him. A rose made of solid gold, with leaves of jade and a stem of the finest crystal.

Of course, he'd asked for compensation.

Ashai shifted from one foot to the other, his shiny dress boots ridiculously tight on his toes.

Behind him, King Damar whispered to him.

"Don't look so nervous, Minister. It's a wedding, not a funeral. No one's dead."

Ashai gave him a weak smile, resisting the urge to tell him the irony of his statement. He hoped the man would take his nervousness as normal pre-marital jitters, something that seemed common here in Pushtan. Apparently Pushtani resisted marriage as long as possible.

Not so in Nishi'iti, where marriage was seen as a gift from God, Nishi's blessing that you build a family and honor his name through it. Those unable to have children had been known to commit suicide, feeling that their God had abandoned them or condemned them through barrenness.

Still, Ashai had plenty of reason for nerves on this wedding day. After all, he was going to kill the bride and her father.

He glanced around the crowded chapel, hoping to note something out of the ordinary that might tip him off about the second assassin, but he found nothing. Whoever the Chargh Lai had sent as his backup had done an admirable job disguising themselves.

"As slow as my daughter is going today, you'd think she's having second thoughts," the King chuckled. "Is that what's making you shifty?"

"No, Majesty," Ashai responded with another nervous grin. "I know Makari well enough to know she's not inclined to second-guessing herself."

The king chortled again. "You might just survive this marriage then, Ashai."

Ashai didn't find that prospect likely.

Security at the chapel was tighter than anything he'd ever seen. Royal Guard members lined every wall, their eyes watchful, darting everywhere while their hands rested on sword pommels. Each entrance was guarded by a dozen men, and despite the insult, both men and women—even those in nobility—were checked for weapons prior to entering. The balconies—one on either side—had been sealed off, but for a squad of guardsmen on each.

Outside, Bauti commanded a hundred guards, spread evenly around the chapel, heavily armed, and bristling with tension.

Too bad the killer was already inside.

Ashai pretended to scratch the small of his back, instead feeling the gaping absence of his dagger. He missed the cool, smooth surface of its handle, longed for the company of its simple, leather sheath. He'd had to leave it in his chambers, stashed in the trunk's secret compartment. He'd been dressed by a half-dozen attendants, and couldn't have them seeing the blade. Besides, he knew in his heart he could never slice the soft skin of Makari's neck, nor harm her father.

So he'd decided to do nothing. The second assassin would handle the king. And Ashai would protect Makari.

It twisted his gut to think of betraying his God, but it split his heart in two to imagine life without Makari. Nishi would understand, even if the Denari Lai did not, and Ashai knew his salvation, if there could be one, stood in convincing the Chargh Lai that she deserved a chance on the throne.

No sooner had he thought that than the trumpets blared and the doors opened and Ashai's breath caught in his chest.

Makari stood in the chapel doorway, her midnight hair tumbling past her bare shoulders, landing on the light blue silk of her wedding dress so it looked like the night sky had met the day. The dress was low-cut, showing off her perfect, milk-white skin, and clung to her figure until the hips, where it flared into a blaze of summer sky. Pearls and diamonds winked at him from all over the dress, invitations to look at her hip, her thigh, her breast.

Above it all, her eyes shone like beacons, calling to him, the ultimate traps. Once captured by those eyes, he knew he would never be able to look away again. He'd always known his bride was lovely, but dressed in her mother's old fashions, he'd never realized how completely stunning she was until now.

All thought of Nishi and the Denari Lai winked out, and Ashai's full attention, every ounce of his concentration, fell on the princess as she swayed down the aisle with the grace of a swan. He felt the power of his magic waning within him as he lost focus on the task at-hand.

"Close your mouth," the king whispered. "You look like an idiot."

The rebuke snapped Ashai back to reality enough to close his mouth and smile at the vision walking toward him. It was not enough, however, to make him think of killing her again.

As Makari approached, a little boy dressed in a brilliant green shirt dashed out of a pew, and wrapped his arms around the princess' legs while his parents gasped and looked like they might faint. Makari laughed and bent just enough to tousle his hair.

The boy hurried back to his mother, still beaming at the princess.

Ashai stared at Makari and sighed. How could someone so lovely, so innocent and kind, be an enemy to his people?

Makari came to a stop at the base of the platform and kneeled, bowing her head.

"I, Makari Abadas, daughter to the king, and princess of Pushtan, ask the Five Gods to give their blessing to this union, that they smile on my choice of husband, Ashai Larish, and that the king sees fit to formalize this marriage. I come freely to this union, intending it to last forever, even beyond the veil of death, for what The Five have joined no mortal should undo."

Ashai did as they'd rehearsed, stepping off the platform—gingerly, since it wobbled as he did—and offered his hand. Makari rose and stood before him, radiant and beautiful, her smile radiant.

"I too enter this union of my own free will, and will honor it with my soul. I ask the Church to bind us in the name of the Five Gods as holy and pure, giving us love eternal, and blessing us with many children."

He and Makari mounted the platform again and approached the five priests, arm-in-arm. Ashai's vision danced around the chapel, searching for any sign of the second assassin. He again found none.

His stomach knotted and he fought down bile trying to escape his gut. Sensing his distress, Makari squeezed his forearm and smiled up at him.

It only made things worse.

The ceremony dragged for what seemed like an eternity, with each of the priests offering long-winded prayers to their Gods, asking for blessings on the union. Even the priest representing the God of Death prayed, asking his deity to not harm the couple or their children.

Ashai's feet ached and his back spasmed from standing so long and worrying so much.

Once the priests finished, King Abadas moved to stand before them, frowning through his white bear, his gaze locked on Ashai.

He knew something was wrong.

"Ashai Larish, if I am to offer you a place in my family and trust you with my daughter's heart, I would first see what you bring as your gift to her."

Ashai's head swam as he picked up the box and handed it to the king.

"Your Majesty, with this gift I prove my love for Makari is true, and ask for my place in your family forever more."

Smiling, Abadas opened the box.

The king looked confused for a moment, then the color drained from his face. Ashai tensed as the king turned the box to show him its contents.

The rose had been shattered, and sitting amongst the shards was Ashai's dagger, its cold, black steel gleaming in the bright light of the chapel. Ashai's head swam. How?

The King's face turned purple. "What is the meaning—"

Something whizzed past Ashai's ear and embedded itself in Abadas's neck. Ashai recognized the black feathers of a Denari Lai poison dart. He dove for Makari, tackling her to the ground as a second dart whiffed past, embedding itself in the fifth priest's knee. The king fell to his knees, someone screamed, and all chaos erupted in the chapel.

Guards surrounded the king, lifting his significant mass and forcing their way through the panicked, screaming spectators. Ashai tried to gain his feet, but the rush of people forced him to cover Makari so she wouldn't be trampled.

Then Kendshi was there, pulling fiercely on Ashai's coat, trying to haul both of them to their feet.

"Princess!" she shouted "Makari, hurry. We need to run!"

The slave girl made just enough space in the crowd for Ashai to get up, pulling the princess up with him. Bodies crushed in around them, moving like a mudslide toward the side doors. Ashai and Kendshi tried to let the flow move them out, Ashai holding his coat above the princess to shield her from other darts. But Makari had her own idea of where to go.

"We have to follow the king!" she shouted, lunging toward the king. "Father!"

"No, princess," Ashai yelled. "The king is in good hands, but we need to get you away from here. The assassin remains a threat."

"I don't care, I—"

"You rule Pushtan right now!" Kendshi shouted. "You must get to safety."

Makari froze, her icy eyes meeting Ashai's.

"She's right, love," Ashai said, snatching up the Denari Lai dagger, and showing it to her. "You know what this dagger means. The gift was for you, so the dagger is too. They won't stop until you're dead."

Behind them, the stricken priest howled in agony on the platform. Ashai knew his eyes would start bleeding soon, and his lungs would fill with his own blood. The poison came from a snake found only in the Nishi'iti mountains, and killed within minutes. Abadas was likely dead already.

The crowd stalled a few paces from the door, leaving them exposed and vulnerable. He forced Makari to stoop, hiding her behind her citizens. Two Royal Guardsmen found them a moment later, one of them shoving Kendshi in the chest and knocking her into the mob.

"Get back, slave!" He pointed the tip of his sword at her.

Ashai put his hand on the soldier's chest, but too slow. Kendshi's eyes spit fire as she rushed forward again.

"I serve Her Highness!" she shouted. "I belong by her side!"

Makari tried to intervene, but Ashai pushed her head down, keeping her shielded. He shot the soldier a smoldering glare.

"That slave helped save Makari's life!"

The guard shoved Kendshi again and started tugging Makari away from Ashai toward the door.

Kendshi recovered and rushed the guard, snarling and hammering his breastplate with her fists. Before Ashai could react, the man ran her through.

Everyone froze, staring in horror as Kendshi fell to her knees, blood spreading on the pure white of her dress.

"No!" Makari screamed, knocking the guard aside and easing Kendshi to the floor. She sat on the marble, cradling the half-Nishi'iti girl's head in her lap.

"Captain Bauti's orders," the soldier told Ashai, still holding the bloody sword. "He said—"

Ashai didn't hesitate. He snatched the man's sword from his hand, swung it in a mighty arc, and clove halfway through his neck. The soldier collapsed, and his partner drew his blade, standing over Makari and facing Ashai. The crowd had thinned now, leaving the princess open and vulnerable.

"We need to get her out of here," Ashai told the man. "Now."

The guard hesitated, and that ended up killing him. A dart hissed past Ashai's ear, digging deep in the guard's neck. His eyes popped open and he clawed at the fletching, trying to pull the tip from this throat. But the darts were barbed, and Ashai knew it would do as much damage coming out as it did going in.

Ashai glanced in the direction the dart had come, and he saw its origin immediately. A fist-sized hole in the ceiling stood open, a blowgun protruding through it.

Ashai said a quick prayer to Nishi, felt his magic flare, and moved like lightning. He had Makari on her feet in an instant, even though she fought to remain with her hand slave. His strength far outmatched hers, and he scooped her up in his arms, dashing for the door.

Outside, he found a dark gray cloak on the street, discarded by someone fleeing the chaos. He wrapped it around Makari, the princess no longer fighting him. Her body shook with violent shivers and she sobbed in heaves. Her body went limp, and Ashai had to wrap her arm around his neck to usher her away from the chapel.

He knew he stood out, still dressed in his wedding clothes, so he did something he didn't want to do: channeled more magic. He wrapped himself in a disguise, much the way he had the day he'd met Makari, covering the princess, too. It took more power than he was used to using, but it must have worked, for no one stopped them as he half-carried, half-dragged the sobbing princess through the courtyard.

He had to get her out of the palace. It was the only way to keep her safe, at least for the short term, until he could figure out what to do. The Royal Guard would lock the gates soon in hopes of capturing the assassin, so he headed for the north wall, just a few paces away and packed with a mob of people trying to run to safety.

He fought and shouldered his way through the crowd, finally reaching the gate. Behind him, he heard someone yelling to close the gate, and he looked over his shoulder to see Bauti mauling his way through the crowd, sword drawn, face purple with rage.

He gave brief thought to enlisting the man's help. Bauti knew the city well, and his loyalty to Makari was undoubtable. But the look on the captain's face told him the only thing on Bauti's mind was killing him. Bauti was just a few paces away now, so with one last great surge, Ashai dashed through the gate, tugging the princess into the city beyond. Behind them, the gates slammed closed with a clang.

And over it all, Bauti's voice thundered. "Makari!"

CHAPTER NINETEEN

Bauti had heard the scream from clear across the south courtyard, where he'd been surveilling the chapel roof to ensure no one entered from above. He froze at the sound, as did most of the twenty-five Royal Guard soldiers patrolling the south side of the chapel grounds. The south side held the chapel gardens, a space for reflection and homage to The Five, but the woman's scream sliced through the tranquil air, chilling him to the bone.

He stared a moment at the nearest window, then sprinted for the south door.

"Get in there now!" he shouted to his men. "Secure the royal family and get them to my quarters immediately!"

Yet as the first of his men reached the door, it burst open and a flood of people spilled out, blocking the way. Bauti reached the door right behind his men, shouldering his way through the crowd, sword drawn, until he thrust himself into the chaos inside.

He caught sight of Abadas's body being carted off through the west doors, the ones leading directly into the palace.

"Follow them!" he told his men, pointing. "Protect the king at all costs!"

His men nodded and started fighting their way through the sea of bodies to follow their king.

Bauti searched the room, but caught no sight of Makari. He grabbed an escaping priest by the elbow and spun him around to face him.

"What happened?"

The man's face had turned a ghostly white, and his eyes were wide as platters.

"S-someone killed the k-king," he stammered, drool running from the corner of his mouth. "Poison dart, I think. Priest Polini, too."

He tried to pull away, but Bauti held him fast. The panicked holy man glanced around, searching for threats.

"Where's the princess?"

The priest recovered enough to snatch his arm away.

"Let me go or I'll be next!" He dashed away out the south door, into the sunlight.

Bauti saw the slave girl's body on the platform to his right. One of his guardsmen lay dead beside her, blood streaming from his eyes.

He cursed again. Poison from the ice viper. Denari Lai specialty, though not often used. They preferred killing with a blade. He looked closer and saw the box Abadas had given Ashai to present as a gift to his bride. Shards of the rose's delicate shape littered the floor around the bodies. Tan had shown him the flower, bragging about his taste. How had this happened?

He glanced at the nearby door just in time to see a flash of dark blue silk, with a gray cloak held over the wearer. An instant later, he caught sight of Ashai's black hair.

Bauti reached the north exit in a few bounds, leaping over the fallen and knocking survivors aside as he forced the door open. Most of the audience had escaped this way, apparently, turning the open expanse of the north courtyard into a cattle pen of people.

He caught sight of the gray cloak again, then Ashai's hair as the merchant maneuvered someone under the cloak toward the north gate. Rage exploded in his heart, and his vision went red. His suspicions were right—the minister was kidnapping Makari!

Bounding down the steps from the chapel door, Bauti shouted to his men from across the courtyard. "Stop them! Seal the gates now!"

The Royal Guard reacted as quickly as they could, but the number of people trying to escape made it impossible to close the gate with any speed. Every time they tried, another knot of people would force the gate open again. Yet Bauti was closing. If the crowd just kept pushing forward, kept blocking its own progress, he could catch the merchant and save the princess.

Then Ashai looked back and saw him, his eyes locking on Bauti's. He hesitated, and for an instant, Bauti thought he had him. Then the man ushered the cloaked princess through the gate as it slammed behind him, leaving Bauti with one vision in his mind: brown eyes. Ashai was Nishi'iti.

Bauti cried his princess' name at the top of his lungs as he threw himself at the closed gate.

CHAPTER TWENTY

The sky clouded over and the wind whistled through the streets, buffeting Makari and seeming to work against her at every turn. No matter which way Ashai pulled her, the wind seemed to be in their face, like The Five wanted to slow them down.

Ashai rounded another corner, and she found herself staring into the setting sun, blind to anything ahead of her. But Ashai kept pulling her forward, even picking up his pace.

Frustrated, she stopped and jerked her wrist out of his grasp.

"Where are we going?"

He grabbed her wrist again and tried yanking her forward. She stood fast and put her free hand on her hip. Something about all this didn't seem right.

"Shouldn't we be going to the palace?" she asked.

He shook his head and herded her into the shadows. "The palace is the last place you should be. That assassin will be looking for you to hide somewhere in the palace, and will search every room, every corridor, and every corner to kill you. Out here at least we can keep you on the move, keep him guessing about your location."

She studied Ashai's face, searching for truth in the deep, brown pools. She found only questions.

"How do you know he hasn't given up already?"

He let out an exasperated sigh. "Did you see that dagger, Makari? It was a Denari Lai blade, a warning sent from the deadliest assassin's guild in the world. Sent to you. Denari Lai never fail because they never stop until their target is dead. Right now, your best bet is to keep him off-guard until Bauti and the Royal Guard can figure out who it is and kill them."

Something scurried away under a trash heap to her right, and she took a step into the dim light of the setting sun. Ashai pulled her back into the darkness of the shadows.

"My place is in the palace, by my father's side," she argued, brushing away his hands. "My people will need me if … if my father … until he recovers."

She felt her voice shaking and chose to say no more for fear of breaking into tears again. Ashai stared at her, his mouth down-turned, eyes crinkled with worry. She wiped her nose on the cloak, sniffed, and looked away.

After a moment, he took her hands in his and squeezed them, as if trying to push some of his strength into her through their touch.

"You'll be no good to your father or your people dead," he said, voice softer. "And that's what you'll be back in the palace. Dead."

She sniffed again, finally able to breathe through her nose, as her crying became a distant memory. She regretted it immediately, as the stinks of feces, urine, and rotting meat assailed her senses.

She pinched her nose closed and looked down the alley, into the orange disk of the sun.

"So where are we going?"

"My place," he told her. "My old loft. I keep some things there that will help us, and we can take an hour or two there to rest."

Suspicion crawled like an insect into her heart. Why did he still have a residence in the city when they'd given him quarters in the palace? Then he smiled at her, and she pushed the thought aside. An hour ago she'd been ready to wed him. Why should that change now?

Giving his hands a return squeeze, she nodded and followed him down the alley.

"Then what?" she asked. "After we rest, what will we do then?"

To her surprise, Ashai shrugged. "I haven't figured that part out yet."

A few twists and turns later, Ashai stopped, eyes closed as he listened in silence.

"They're coming," he whispered, opening his eyes. "We need to hide."

He ducked into an even smaller alley running behind a row of shops, went to a back door, and pushed it open, urging her inside ahead of him. He eased the door closed just as the sound of boots clattered outside, steel clinking. He slid a bolt closed and pushed Makari down so they huddled together under the door. The footsteps got louder as a squad of armed men clinked and clanked past, disappearing down the alley. As soon as they were gone, Makari let out the breath she hadn't known she was holding.

She looked around the dim room and saw stacks of cloth against the walls, and spools of thread lining shelves. The muffled sound of snoring tumbled down a set of steps to her right, pointing to the slumbering owner of this shop.

"We need to change clothes," Ashai whispered. "I'd hoped to do it at my loft, but we need to change sooner than that."

He moved deeper into the room, stepping around a pile of cloth on the dark floor. He ran his fingers over a bolt of cloth, letting them linger a moment, as if he missed the feeling. Makari watched him ease forward, realizing he moved with a grace she hadn't seen before, an almost cat-like litheness she'd seen in other men, all of them seasoned soldiers.

"Who are you?" she whispered.

He didn't hesitate, didn't flinch as he stepped through a curtain-covered door into the next room. She followed him, finding herself in a tailor shop, with unfinished items hanging everywhere, and a storefront open to a large street, display windows shuttered for the night.

"I am the man you are going to marry. Ashai Larish, Minister of Finance, and former cloth merchant until you saved me from my boring existence."

He shot her a grin through the darkened room, and for a moment, she saw again the man she'd fallen in love with, the one she wanted to marry. Then he turned his attention back to the task at hand and the moment was gone.

"I know the man who owns this shop," he whispered, tapping his lips. He turned to a wardrobe against the side wall. "Ah, here we go."

He opened the doors and produced a simple cotton dress, dyed forest green with simple silver trim and a high neckline.

"That looks about your size," he said. He motioned to a neck-high privacy screen behind her. "Put it on. We'll have to worry about shoes later."

Makari looked down at the black slippers she'd worn to her wedding and nearly teared up again. She fought it, though, stuck her chin out, and went behind the screen.

Meanwhile, Ashai tossed his jacket into the wardrobe and stripped out of the black silk shirt he wore underneath before turning his back to her. She watched as the shirt came off, admiring the ripples of his back as he shrugged into a plain brown tunic. How had a merchant become that fit? Developed such muscle?

As soon as he unlaced his hose, though, Makari felt heat rise to her cheeks, and she turned away.

When they both had changed, he handed her a hooded wool cloak, again dyed green like her dress. He'd donned tan cotton breeches and a rough-hewn brown cloak, drawing the hood up to hid his face.

"Good thing Master Frollo had customers close to our size," he whispered.

"You will steal from a friend?"

"Oh, believe me, Frollo owes me at least this much. He's notorious for under-paying for materials."

Makari pulled a purse from her old dress and stared counting silver coins into her hand. "We can at least pay him for his trouble," she muttered.

"You carried a purse on our wedding day?" He looked at her with arched eyebrows.

She handed him three silvers, but he held out his hand until she gave him one more.

"Part of the ceremony was supposed to be you and me handing out coins to the poor, just like the day we met."

He looked her in the eye then, and smiled a melancholy smile. He brushed her cheek with his fingertips.

"I'm sorry about all this. What should have been a joyous day has turned into a …"

He paused, listening again, eyes closed. A moment later, he opened them and hurried her behind the changing screen just as the sound of marching men echoed through the street in front of the shop. Holding his finger to his lips, Ashai crouched with her behind the screen.

The footsteps grew louder, mixed again with the chinks and clangs or armor and steel. Peeking through a hole in the screen, Makari saw the shadows shifting in the street outside as the soldiers passed, even caught the faint glint of moonlight on steel.

"Who are you?" The man's voice came from behind them, and she spun to see a wizened old man with a bald head behind them, a cudgel in his hand. "Get out of my shop!"

Ashai moved to show himself to Frollo, but too late. The squad halted right outside the shop. A moment later, someone pounded on the door.

Frollo's eyes seemed to adjust and he recognized Ashai, nodding. He motioned for them to stay put and walked to the front door just as the soldier pounded again.

"Open up in there or we'll kick the door in!"

"I'm coming!" Frollo answered. "Bad enough you wake an old man from his sleep, but then you expect him to move like you young folks."

He jerked open the door, and through the hole, Makari saw a Royal Guardsman she recognized from the palace. He kept his hand on his short sword, and made an imposing silhouette in the flickering light of the torches his men held. Frollo faced him in the doorway, hands on hips.

"We're looking for the man who kidnapped Princess Makari," the Sergeant said, his voice strung with urgency. "Former Minister of Finance Ashai Larish. He's a dark-haired—"

"I know what he looks like," Frollo interrupted. "He used to over-charge me for silk, the crook. And everyone knows what the lovely Makari looks like."

He inched closer to the door, as if trying to force the soldiers to stay outside by blocking their entrance.

"We heard you tell someone to get out," said the soldier. "Who?"

"Oh, that?" Frollo shrugged and motioned to the shop behind him. "That was just … them!"

He bolted out the door as Ashai said something under his breath that Makari couldn't understand. The soldiers stood in shock a moment, then the sergeant bulled his way inside, drawing his sword.

Ashai moved like lightning, bounding from behind the screen, drawing a wicked-looking blade from the small of his back.

"Run!" he shouted.

Makari froze, knowing she should move, but unable to do so. She stood, staring, as Ashai attacked the men coming through the door. He

moved like quicksilver, flowing from one place to another with such efficiency that she wondered for a moment if he was human. The sergeant
died first, his throat sliced from ear to ear, blood splashing the walls and
ceiling. Ashai shoved him back, forcing his dying body into the
other men.

His blade flashed again, cleaving through a second man's knee. The
soldier screamed and fell, making a third man trip. Ashai's eyes flicked to
her before he spun and kicked another soldier in the chest.

"I said run!" he shouted.

The distraction almost killed him, as the man whose knee he'd
slashed managed to thrust at him with a short sword. The blade glanced
off Ashai's shoulder, making him wince, but he skipped away and drove
his dagger into the man's eye.

Makari finally came alive, jumping to her feet and heading for the
back door. She'd almost gained the back room when Frollo jumped in
front of her.

Makari's rage leapt up, a fire in her chest.

Her foot jumped out, almost of its own accord, and caught the tailor
in the groin. Frollo fell to his knees and Makari jumped over him. An
instant later, Ashai was there, shoving her forward while behind them,
the soldiers gave chase.

She burst through the back door into the alley, surprised no soldiers
waited there. Ashai slipped out right behind her, turned right, and
grabbed her wrist. Before he could move down the alley, a figure
appeared ahead of them. Broad shouldered and tall, the man wore a
flowing gray robe, face wrapped in dark material. In his hand was a
dagger much like the one she'd seen in the gift box. The one Ashai now
carried. A Denari Lai blade.

Ashai pushed her behind him and went into a crouch, the dagger
he'd taken from the chapel in his hand. Makari's stomach knotted as she
watched him roll the knife around in a circle, like it was a part of his
hand.

Before she could think about it, the cloaked figure's arm leapt out
and something flashed silver in the air, streaking toward her. Ashai
moved lightning quick, knocking the item out of the air, deflecting it
with his dagger. The object clattered to the ground, skidding to a stop at
her feet. It was a gleaming disc with sharpened, serrated edges. She
winced at the thought of it hitting her.

Ashai backed into her, shielding her with his body as the cloaked figure stalked them. In the shop to their right, the soldiers had recovered and were smashing their way through the back room. Ashai backed her past the door just as a hulking soldier broke through, torch in hand. Makari's heart soared, for standing in the doorway, silver hair shining in the torchlight, was Captain Bauti.

Bauti's gaze skipped from her to Ashai to the cloaked figure, stopping on her as two more men poured from the doorway around him.

"Protect the Princess!" he shouted to his men.

He placed himself between Ashai and the man in the cloak, facing the stranger as his men fanned out around him. Ashai moved to Makari's side, the dagger disappearing under his shirt, and took her hand.

Bauti had four men now forming a semicircle in front of them, blades drawn. The captain himself stood directly in front of her, feet shoulder-width, broadsword ready before him.

The assassin struck like a whirlwind, spinning into the Royal Guardsmen, blade slashing and slicing in a deadly arc. Blood flew from one man's throat, then from the ribs of a second. A third soldier swung at the figure with his sword, only to have the killer melt away and reappear behind him.

The assassin moved unlike anything she'd ever seen, smooth and fluid, disappearing and reappearing as if by magic. Two men were down, and the other two wounded within seconds. A third died with a disc in his throat, leaving just one man standing in front of their Captain.

Bauti moved forward, sword sweeping low as his remaining soldier faced off with the assassin.

Bauti looked over his shoulder at Ashai, his voice a growl. "Get her out of here. She must live."

Ashai tugged her toward the end of the alley. She snatched her arm away and glared at him.

"I won't leave him," she said, picking up a fallen short sword.

"Then he will die," Ashai whispered to her. "If we run, the killer will follow us, even if it means leaving Bauti. We need to draw him away to save your captain or none of us leaves here alive."

She considered as the killer circled the remaining soldier. The dagger flashed so quick she almost missed it, but the soldier let out a gurgling sound and fell to his knees, grasping at his throat.

"Go now!" Bauti yelled, moving to engage the assassin. "You rule Pushtan now, my queen. Run!"

Her heart stopped. She ruled Pushtan. That meant her father ...

The thought spun away from her as she watched Bauti move to obstruct the assassin. Without thought he'd placed himself between her and the killer, forsaking his own safety for her own. How had she ever thought this man's intentions impure? How she must have hurt him with her rejection. If he'd been in the chapel, her father might have lived.

This time, Ashai grabbed her too tightly for her to resist and pulled her toward the end of the alley. Tears running down her cheeks, she followed him.

Looking back over her shoulder, Makari saw the captain feign a strike at the killer, dancing back as the dagger lashed out at him.

"Kill him, Marwan!" she yelled. "Be my hero!"

And then they were out of the alley, sprinting down a street.

CHAPTER TWENTY-ONE

The Watcher slipped into the palace through a drainage grate, one that he'd opened many years earlier for just such an occasion as this—needing to sneak back inside. He pulled the grate closed a bit harder and louder than intended, his irritation getting the better of him. He paused in the ankle-deep water, grimacing at the foul stench of raw sewage. His ribs ached from a blow he'd taken from Bauti's sword, his leather armor preventing a flesh wound, but allowing what felt like a broken rib. He cursed under his breath, then kicked himself for it.

He needed to get control of his emotions. Ashai had disrupted his plan, that much was true, but he hadn't ruined it. The first poisoned dart had found the king, just as planned, and while the ones intended for his daughter had all gone astray, the girl was still missing and would likely remain so for a long time. Ashai knew that as soon as he brought her back to the palace, or went public anywhere, The Watcher would kill her.

In the meantime, a missing princess was almost as good as a dead one. Better in some ways, by allowing him to manipulate certain people. Most people loved Makari and would do anything to get her back. That gave him control over some very important people.

Wrapping the assassin's cloak tighter to ward off the damp chill of the sewer, The Watcher started north, sloshing through the disgusting water while his mind worked through the problems at hand.

He would still have to kill Makari, and of course Ashai, but for the time being, they were out of his way. He would put his most trusted sources to the task of finding them, and he had little doubt that within a few days, both would suffer a fate similar to the king.

Abadas had proven to be his own sort of special problem, one that needed solving too. The viper's poison should have killed him in minutes, but when The Watcher had left the palace to pursue Ashai, the old man had still been screaming in agony in his bedchambers, frightening servants and soldiers alike. He'd always been a stubborn old man, so it shouldn't have surprised The Watcher that he refused to die when he was supposed to. If he still lived, The Watcher would have to slip a little something extra into the poultices and potions the palace healers were no doubt forcing down his gullet. He'd finish the job himself if needed.

He turned a corner, picking up his pace, feeling his way through the dark with a hand on the slimy wall. A message would come for him soon from the Chargh Lai, asking for explanations. It would do no good to miss the chance to explain how he would fix the mess Ashai had created, so he needed to get to his chambers and get out the crystals.

Crystals. He would also need to see to it that all traces of Ashai's affiliation with the Denari Lai were removed from his quarters and destroyed. He couldn't allow news of a Denari Lai defector leaking, couldn't tolerate the image of a failure to mar the order's image.

Or could he?

He paused, tapping his lips with his index finger as he thought through the possibilities. If he allowed Ashai's things to be found, Ashai would be blamed for the King's death, and possibly for Makari's, too. That would remove suspicion from The Watcher, allowing him to follow through with the later phases of God's plan. The order could take its time sending Ashai's replacement, allowing The Watcher to manipulate events in Dar Tallus, like he should have been doing all along.

He moved forward again, smiling in the darkness, quite pleased with the way he was putting things back together here. Nishi and the Chargh Lai would be pleased with him. They might not feel the need to send another Denari Lai this time, if they finally trusted him enough.

His hand brushed cold iron and he moved swiftly up the rungs of a ladder in the stone wall. At the top he paused and listened, pushing up a circular iron cover when he was sure no one was there.

He climbed through the opening and found himself in a narrow space between the back wall of the chapel and the palace proper. Just where he'd planned to pop up. He slid the cover back into place without a sound and shivered in the chill night air. Beside him, an unlit torch hung in a sconce on the palace's granite wall. He twisted it to the right and watched as a section of granite slid back and aside.

It was a tight fit, but turning sideways, The Watcher angled his broad shoulders through and shoved the rock wall back into place.

He set off at once, slipping noiselessly through the hidden passage-ways of the palace, praying to Nishi no one else was using them that night. He wound through the corridors—his rib throbbing now, making it hard to breathe—heading for his chambers. A few minutes later, he slid aside a bookcase and crept into his bedchamber, hand on the dagger tucked under his shirt.

His quarters were, of course, empty. No one, not even the arrogant Captain Bauti, would enter without his permission. Fear wasn't a great motivator, but it made a wonderful deterrent.

He wasted no time changing into his Pushtani robes and stowing the assassin's cloak in a secret compartment behind a second bookcase. He'd built this one himself, needing somewhere to store his Denari Lai things that no one could find. It had taken him a year of chiseling and chipping and building as quietly as he could, but now that small cabinet held his daggers, poisons, clothing, and everything else associated with being Denari Lai.

Even the crystals.

He reached for the velvet purse holding the three stones, but stopped when someone knocked on his outer door. Closing the hidden cabinet with a subtle snick sound, The Watcher straightened his Pushtani attire and moved through the bedroom door into his sitting area. He stood, facing the door, waiting.

When they knocked again, The Watcher moved forward.

"I'm coming," he called. "Be patient."

He pulled the carved wooden door aside to find Neffin, Renard, and Celani outside, all dressed in their wedding attire, wearing shadows on their faces.

Celani stepped forward, trying to peer into The Watcher's chambers. The Watcher let him look—he'd see nothing but a drab sitting area with modest décor, as was fitting The Watcher's station.

"We come bearing dire news," said the general, running a hand over the salt-and-pepper stubble on his head. "His Majesty the King has died."

"And Princess Makari is missing," Renard added.

The Watcher let his hand fly to his mouth in mock surprise, and placed the other hand on the door, as if he might faint.

"May The Five help us," he muttered, motioning for the men to come inside. They stood fast. "What is the matter, my lords?"

The three ministers exchanged worried looks, and Celani held out a scroll with a broken wax seal.

"This is the king's decree, signed by his hand, and affixed with his seal, naming who he wished would assume the role of 'Protector of Push-tan' until Makari assumes her place on the throne."

The Watcher did not move to take the scroll. He'd been there when the king signed it, so he knew exactly what it said.

"If there is anything I can do to assist you in those duties, General, please—"

"It doesn't name me as Protector," Celani said, his words taking on a knife-edged sharpness. "It names you."

The Watcher opened his mouth and let it hang that way, feigning a lack of words. He channeled just the slightest thread of magic and painted his face a paler white than it normally was.

"Me? But, I am no ruler, sirs. I am just a humble servant of the crown. I don't even come from noble blood."

The three men stood, looking at him, waiting for instructions. He looked Celani in the eye and gave him a weak smile.

"Well then. I will need to rely on the exceptional talents of the Royal Council." He managed to sift most of the sarcasm from his voice. "What would you recommend, General?"

A few minutes later, he'd given the orders to lock down the city, clear the palace of all who did not work or live there, and recall Captain Bauti and the Royal Guard to see to palace security. He told the men to convene the council so they could discuss the king's funeral arrange-ments, as well as tend to other crucial business to keep the kingdom alive until Makari was found.

"Thank you, My Lords, for your sound advice and steadfast loyalty to the crown and the nation. Together, we will guide Pushtan through this crisis and see it set on stable ground again. I will see you all in an hour."

They turned to go, but Celani paused and gave him a cautious look.

"Captain Bauti will want to lead the search for Makari himself," the general said. "But his place is here, protecting you."

"I understand completely, General Celani. I will see to it the captain is properly utilized."

Celani studied him a moment, as if trying to decipher some hidden meaning in his words, then sketched a slight bow.

"The king chose well," he said. "In an hour then, Minister."

And Samaran Tan watched him march off down the hall.

CHAPTER TWENTY-TWO

The last rays of sunlight smeared the sky over the western foothills like a bloodstain, red and orange and the black of scab, as if night had slashed the sky with a dagger, leaving its wound to fester.

Pachat followed the line of slaves chained in front of him like a giant snake of flesh and iron. Their breath steamed in front of their faces, and sweat froze into sparkling diamonds on their exposed skin. Behind him, Joppish trudged along, huffing and wheezing as phlegm clogged his chest and nose.

"Back to the tunnels at night?" he whined. "How much work do they think they can get from men who are already exhausted and sick? We spent twelve hours down there already today."

A guard bellowed for them to stop talking, and Pachat shushed the younger man.

"We'll find out when we get there," he whispered. "Anyone who's sick won't have to work. The masters never go down with us anyway. Too dangerous for elite Pushtani soldiers like themselves."

That drew a chuckle from the men around him, and in turn a crack of the whip from the nearest master.

When they reached the opening to the shaft, though, Cargil was waiting, his face only slightly lighter than the bleeding dusk sky behind him. He stood outside the shaft opening, hands on hips, feet wide. He wore a long sword at his belt, which Pachat had only seen one other time, and then for ceremonial reasons.

"Something's wrong," muttered Mishi, a younger man with a hunched back and a limp in his left knee. "Cargil never misses his evening wine and wenches."

A nervous murmur filtered through their group as they drew to a stop in front of the master.

For a long, almost torturous moment, Cargil simply stood, staring at them. Or glaring, more accurately. Joppish started to shiver, his teeth chattering and his knees knocking. Cargil marched up to him and delivered a backhand to Joppish's jaw that sent him reeling.

"Did I give you leave to move, Nishi'iti shit-pile?"

Joppish struggled to his feet, shaking his head. Cargil knocked him down again, this time with a cross to his temple.

"I didn't give you permission to get back up, either!"

Pachat looked from Joppish to the other men, but all stood with eyes downcast. All but one—the Wanao Lai. He'd joined their work crew three days earlier, after an older man had passed away in the abandoned shaft. No one had noticed the old man's death for an hour. The Wanao Lai—Jingsho was his name—had replaced him within the day, dressed in miner's rags.

He hadn't said more than a few words to Pachat since, all benign and work-related, as if their former conversation had never happened. Now he stood straight, staring at Cargil with hate boiling from his eyes. If Cargil noticed, he said nothing.

The slave master walked away from Joppish's crumpled form and paced back and forth in front of their group. He stopped in front of Pachat, standing almost nose to nose with him. Pachat averted his eyes.

"You see, now, this repulsive pig of a slave knows how to show respect to his betters. You could all learn a lesson from this one."

He started away from Pachat, but wheeled without warning and punched him in the gut. Pachat doubled over and fell to his knees, gasping for air. When Cargil stood over him, he stayed down, eyes locked on the dirt before him.

"You want some news of your lover, slave?" Pachat's heart leapt, but he fought down his excitement and kept his eyes on the ground. "Well it seems there's been some trouble in Dar Tallus, trouble stirred up by savage Nishi'itis like your bitch of a woman.

"I suppose I should start by telling you all that a Denari Lai heathen killed our king. Abadas is dead."

Every pair of eyes snapped to Cargil at that moment, and while Pachat expected to see smiles or at least grins of satisfaction, he saw only shock and fear. Fear of the reprisal that would no doubt come their way soon.

"And Princess Makari appears to have been kidnaped by the assassin, who was masquerading as her betrothed. He killed a priest and at least four brave Royal Guardsmen, too.

"What kind of cowardly act was this? Are you Nishi'itis so craven that you need to kill from the shadows?"

Pachat's stomach clenched when Jingsho opened his mouth.

"Says the man whose army steals women and children and makes them into slaves because his own people are too fat—"

A slaver behind him cracked his whip across Jingsho's bare back, making the Wanao Lai cry out, though perhaps more in shock than in pain. He whirled to face the man, but a second master clubbed him in the small of his back. Jingsho fell face-first and lay writhing in the dirt.

Cargil clucked his tongue and kicked the Wanao Lai in the head, then faced the group.

"Since it was your countrymen who killed our ruler and stole his lovely daughter, all of you will pay the price. Tonight, you will work until midnight, when my men will bring you back to observe me punishing every other Nishi'iti dog in the camp. Our whips will sing in Nishi'iti blood tonight, and you'll watch it all. I might even make you do the whipping.

"Then, when that is done, all of you will sleep under the light of the moon, with no blankets, no shirts, and no fires."

"We'll freeze to death," one man said. "Who will work the mines?"

Cargil shrugged. "I'm sure the Pushtani Army will be making a trip or two into your lands to find replacements. Soon. General Celani will replace all of you in a week, and provide my men with women to keep them company."

He turned to go, but stopped and looked back over his shoulder at Pachat.

"Oh, I almost forgot, the precious Kendshi." He grinned from ear to ear, his face twisted and shadowed. "You won't be hearing from her again. The assassin cut her down, too. She got off easily—she deserved a good raping first, the little whore."

Pachat thought he heard his heart shattering. He fell forward on his face, his nose smashing into the cold, solid ground, blood mixing with his tears as the ground swallowed them both. He knew he should be sobbing, crying in great convulsions, but all he could manage were a few tears. His body went numb, as if every emotion drained from him with the tears and blood, hiding in the hard ground where no one could see.

He had no idea how long he lay there before Jingsho kneeled beside him, hand warm on his shoulder. The black leather boots of a slaver appeared before his eyes, and the sound of a whip cracked the frigid air. Pachat had no idea whether or not it struck him, and he didn't care.

"It's time to get up, friend," the Wanao Lai whispered. "There's work to be done. In the tunnel."

Pachat ignored him, willing the slave master to whip him, hoping for physical pain to wash away the ache in his soul.

"Hurry now," Jingsho urged, voice soft but urgent. "We must get to work. In the tunnel. You remember, right? Near the collapse."

The collapse. That spurred memories, something in Pachat's mind, lighting a fire in his heart. The hidden cache. Weapons.

Revenge.

He turned his head enough to watch Cargil's form slip into his tent, where no doubt a whore and a wineskin awaited. Probably a Nishi'iti slave woman, knowing Cargil. She would suffer tonight, as the master took his revenge on her body.

And she would die, just like Kendshi.

Pachat put his hands on the ground and shoved himself up, vaulting to his feet. The remaining slaver eyed him with suspicion, but Pachat ignored him, turning to Jingsho.

"You're right. We have work to do. Let's get to it."

An hour later, all but Jingsho were armed and armored, Pachat donning lightweight boiled leather plates, hefting a curved sword in his hands. Most of the slaves held spears or short swords, and Jingsho went through basic instructions on how to use them. Since all Nishi'iti men served a two-year tour in the Army, though, only the two youngest—Joppish and another boy—had never done so before.

When the training ended, Pachat looked over his crew, now his squad, and shook his head. Even armed, they didn't look like much, and most were sick or injured or weak.

"We need more men," he told Jingsho.

The Wanao Lai nodded and jogged up the tunnel. A few minutes later, he returned with ten more men, most new and thus healthy.

"I told them we'd found a major vein and needed more men to extract the gold." The soldier grinned, teeth white in the flickering torchlight. "I left one man further up the tunnel to watch for slavers."

Pachat nodded and addressed the newcomers.

"Did Cargil tell you the news?"

All ten nodded, eyes wide at seeing slaves with weapons.

"Then you know that tonight, every Nishi'iti slave will be punished for something they did not do. Cargil and his thugs will rape our women, murder our children, and retaliate a hundred-fold for the death of their King.

"But as you see, Nishi did not forsake us. The Wanao Lai brought us weapons and armor enough to stop Cargil's evil, and to strike the chains from our own ankles. No longer will we shiver while they have fire, starve while they glut themselves, or work while they beat us. Once we've broken free, you can return home if you want, back to your families and villages. That's what I mean to do.

"But Jingsho says there is something here for those of you looking for Pushtani blood, or with no one left to go home to. Jingsho is Wanao Lai, and he promises reinforcements if we take this fight to the Pushtani Army."

That brought a buzz of murmurs from the new men, and Pachat's crew joined right in. He felt their excitement flowing like a river through the tunnel. A river that soon would flood.

He quieted them by raising his hands and went on.

"But for right now, let's focus on the task at hand: saving the Nishi'itis here. We may not be elite soldiers, but we are Nishi'iti, and we go with our God. Nishi calls for justice, and we will give it to him!"

A cheer went up from the miners, and Pachat felt a twist in his stomach. He could well be sending every one of these men to their death if the Pushtanis managed to rally.

"There are enough weapons here for every slave to take up arms," Jingsho said, stepping forward. "We will need every slave if we're going to destroy Cargil and the evil that is this camp. We will start as a breeze, but end as a whirlwind, destroying all that stands in our path."

"Do you have a plan, then?" one man asked.

Jingsho grinned. "Of course."

An instant later, a scrawny Nishi'iti boy sprinted down the tunnel, huffing as he slid to a stop in front of Jingsho.

"They're coming," he said. "Four slavers. They heard the cheer and got suspicious."

Everyone, even Jingsho, looked at Pachat, awaiting instructions. Footsteps sounded in the tunnel, growing louder, followed by the clink of metal. Pachat hesitated, seeing the simple, good people before him, all armed but none soldiers.

He knew most of them, and wondered how many would die this night. He wondered if any would actually make it back to Nishi'iti.

"Pachat," Jingsho said, "now is not the time for hesitation."

As the footsteps neared the tunnel's bend, Pachat made up his mind.

"Our salvation starts now."

He charged around the corner, all twenty miners close behind, screaming in their native tongue. In a matter of seconds they over-whelmed the startled slave masters. None even had a chance to cry out before steel found them.

It ended as quickly as it had begun, only Joppish needing to be dragged from the bloody body of a slaver as he hacked and chopped with his short sword at the man's lifeless form.

The new men went back and armed themselves, and when they were ready, they marched to the mouth of the tunnel and stopped.

Pachat turned to the boy who had warned them.

"I want you to remain with the weapons. We will send slaves to you as we find them. It's your job to get them armed and send them back out to fight. If you see any slavers coming, follow that tunnel at a run. It'll take you home. Tell everyone what has happened here tonight. Let our people know it's time to fight."

The boy nodded and ran back down. Jingsho looked at Pachat, an approving smile on his lips.

"See, natural leadership," he said. Behind him, the rest of the men nodded in agreement.

Pachat shook his head, but felt pride swelling in his heart. Not pride in himself, but pride in his people, pride in the Nishi'iti spirit that, despite years of oppression and cruelty, had not broken.

"Where do we start?" Joppish asked.

Pachat took a deep breath and let it out slowly. A third crew stood outside another tunnel a hundred paces away, two slavers whipping one man while the others watched.

"We start right there," he said.

They got within twenty paces before the slavers even knew they were coming, and by then it was too late. The Pushtanis died in heartbeats, and Pachat gathered the slaves.

"One of you take this one through the tunnel to our home," he said, pointing to the whipped man. The skin on the man's back hung in strips while blood oozed from the cuts. "He needs a healer. The rest, go get your armor and weapons."

When they were gone, Pachat turned and looked at the tents fifty or so paces away, listened to the raucous laughter of their captors streaming from the fort, and the tormented cries of the Nishi'itis they punished. He let it all fan the flames in his heart.

"You know what to do from here," he told the slaves. "Stay in groups of at least five and kill all the masters. No one escapes. If they do, they'll bring the Army and we'll be dead."

The men gave grim nods.

"Oh, and one more thing," Pachat said. "Leave Cargil to me."

Cargil's tent sat in the middle of the fort, a large, circular canvas with slivers of light coming from the seams and the space around the flap. An iron stovepipe stuck up from the peak, smoke lifting to the night sky like a flock of birds escaping a predator. Jingsho and three other men followed Pachat as he marched through the tents, their faces as dark as the night and twice as cold.

They encountered only one soldier on their way, since most of the slavers were busy with whores or liquor or both. Even the soldier they ran into had stepped outside his tent to piss, wavering on his feet, and squinting to see the approaching slaves better. His eyes opened wide when he saw them.

"Hey, you—"

Jingsho slashed his throat with a sweep of his curved sword, nearly severing the man's head. The soldier toppled to the ground.

When they came to Cargil's tent, Jingsho stood aside and motioned for Pachat to enter.

"This one is all yours," he whispered. "For Kendshi."

Pachat hesitated, sword in hand. Then cries broke out from the other tents, as his army of slaves attacked their masters. Inside Cargil's tent, a commotion told Pachat the Slave Master had heard the fighting.

"Damn them all!" came Cargil's voice. "What now?"

"Hurry," Jingsho urged. "Before he can arm himself."

Pachat tossed aside the tent flap, shielding his eyes from the light of the interior as he stepped inside. Cargil froze beside a large, crudely built bed, his breeches down around his ankles, his member pitifully small and wrinkled under the hairy bulge of his stomach.

On the bed lay a Nishi'iti girl, no more than fourteen, gagged and naked. Pachat didn't recognize her, but her face was swollen and bleeding, and her ankles and wrists had been lashed to the corners of the bed frame.

Cargil watched as Pachat stalked closer, and he eyed a sword leaning against a nearby chair.

"How did you get a weapon, Nishi'iti pig? I'll have you flogged for this!"

He lunged for the sword, but Pachat was faster, leaping forward and slashing with the short sword. The blade bit into the flesh and bone of Cargil's arm, blood spattering the floor. He jerked back his hand and fell on his backside.

"Guards!" he yelled.

Pachat kicked him in the face, reveling in the sick crunch of bone and cartilage, then pulled back his foot and kicked him in the groin, too. Cargil doubled over, clutching at his man parts. He made a strangled noise in his throat.

Outside, the chaos had risen to a new level, and the sound of fighting barged into the tent. Men screamed in pain. Steel clashed with steel, and Nishi's name rang through the night.

Pachat kicked Cargil's sword across the floor, out of reach, and kneeled on the master's chest. He jammed the tip of his short sword up under Cargil's chin until it drew a tiny droplet of blood.

Cargil whimpered, his eyes wide now, but Pachat held his finger to his lips and cupped an ear with the other hand.

"Hear that?" he growled. "That's the sound of Nishi bringing his justice to your thugs. Listen to them die, Cargil. Listen and know that your fate is the same as theirs."

Cargil swallowed hard. "Please, don't. I can help you. I'll make sure the Army doesn't know what happened here. You and your people can flee home and I'll stall for you. I'll—"

Pachat drove the pommel of his sword into Cargil's jaw, snapping Cargil's head to the side and spraying more blood.

"The only thing you're going to do, you miserable sack of dung, is die."

He raised the short sword over his head with both hands and stared at a spot between Cargil's hair-covered breasts. Before he could bring it down, the girl on the bed mumbled through her gag. Pachat glanced at her and she shook her head, thrashing at the ropes with a fury.

The tent flap opened and Jingsho poked his head inside.

"Hurry, Pachat," he said. "We need you out here."

Pachat nodded and moved to the bed. He pulled a sheet over the girl's nakedness and tugged the gag from her mouth. She looked him in the eye, mouth twisting as she spoke.

"Let me kill him."

"What's your name?"

"I am Fooshi," she answered. "And he has raped me every night for ten days now. I want Nishi's revenge."

Making sure Cargil didn't move, Pachat nodded and sliced through the bonds on her left hand and ankle. In a flash, she had her other bonds undone and sprang from the bed. She dropped a knee onto Cargil's throat. The man tried to roll away, but Pachat pinned his wrist with a foot, and handed the girl a dagger from his belt.

"Be quick," he told her. "Nishi frowns on cruelty."

Her brown eyes sizzled with hatred. "He also frowns on rape."

Sliding down to Cargil's knees, she lowered the blade to his groin. Cargil started to thrash, but Pachat jammed the sword point against his throat and straddled his chest, standing now on both of Cargil's wrists.

Cargil's scream told him Fooshi had started to slice.

CHAPTER TWENTY-THREE

Ashai pulled Makari down to crouch behind a trash heap, wrapping them both in a shroud of magic so they would appear to the passing soldiers as two street people, huddled against the night. He didn't know exactly what they looked like—the magic chose appropriate faces from deep in his memories, and he saw Makari's real face through the spell—but it must have worked, since the two Royal Guardsmen passed them by.

When they disappeared around a corner, Makari pushed Ashai back and stood.

"How did they not recognize us? The big one looked right at me like I wasn't even there!"

Ashai stood and stepped off down the alley, the princess' footsteps falling in behind him.

"That's because they couldn't see you," he told her. "At least not the you they sought."

She caught up to him, eyes smoldering with blue fire, and marched along at his side.

"What's that supposed to mean?"

"Shush now," he said. "I can't disguise your voice like I can your face, and you sound very much like, well, a princess."

"Of course I sound—"

Ashai spun on her, clamping one hand over her mouth and the other behind her head. He put his face close to hers and hissed out his words like a serpent.

"Listen to me, Makari, if you want to live long enough to rule Push-tan. The assassin looking for you is Denari Lai. He uses magic and can see through these thin disguises if he has reason to look close enough. Don't give him that reason. Walk, talk, and act like an old beggar woman or old age is something you'll never see.

"I promise to explain when we get where we're going, but right now my main goal is keeping both of us alive. I cannot do that if Princess Makari Abadas is roaming the streets at my side instead an old hag. Do you understand?"

Her blue eyes lost some of their fire, replaced with fear as she nodded. He removed his hands and led her down the alley.

He twisted and turned them through alleys and streets, making numerous unneeded turns to make sure no one followed. As they went, the buildings became older and squatter, as if time had worn them down. About thirty minutes later, they stood in front of a run-down tavern, blinded by light spilling from doors and windows, deaf from the raucous laughter and music dancing out into the street.

The place's sign dangled by one of its two chains, listing to one side. It bore no words—most of its patrons could not read—only a picture of a duck swimming in a keg of ale.

"The Drunken Duck," Ashai announced. "I keep a room upstairs, hidden from all but the barkeeper. A safe house if you will. No one would think to look here. We'll be safe for a few hours while we rest and change clothes."

"Why would you need a safe house?" Makari asked, narrowing her eyes at him. "You're a merchant and a minister."

Ashai winked at her, hoping to assuage some of the vitriol he knew would come out in the room, when he told her everything.

"Like I said, I'll explain inside. After you."

She rolled her eyes and started for the door. He stopped her with a gentle touch of her elbow.

"Don't forget. You're not a princess here. Just look ... poor."

"I've been a princess all my life. I don't know how to look poor because I've never been poor."

"But you've been among the poor," he reminded her. "Every week for years. Think about the people you helped. Remember how they carried themselves, how they talked, then mimic it until we're safe."

She thought a moment, then nodded. "The boy," she whispered. "The one who robbed me. The one Bauti killed. I remember his eyes. They were ... hopeless. He'd given up. On himself."

Ashai nodded, smiling, as she shifted her stance, slouching and looking at the cobblestones. The changes were subtle, but with his remaining magic, they would be enough.

He led her up the sagging stairs and through the door.

Inside, he took a moment to let his eyes adjust to the brightness and motion, taking in the crowd. More than a few pairs of eyes noticed them as they shuffled across the wood-planked floor, but all looked away, uninterested. Even a young thief—barely more than a boy—in the back corner disregarded them as too poor to make good marks.

The place was larger inside than it looked from the street, with a high ceiling and pillars separating the dozen or so tables. Two serving wenches moved among the unsavory crowd, jumping when pinched or groped, and not always by men. Behind a crudely built bar against the back wall, the bartender watched them come in as he dried a pewter tankard. He was a bear of a man, both broad-shouldered and hairy, but Ashai had known him for years.

He led Makari to the bar and laid down a single copper.

"The hag and I will take your smallest room," he said, giving Daggit the first pass phrase.

"You might not want it," Daggit replied. "Rough crowd tonight. Like to be blood soon."

Ashai tensed. Royal Guard had been here looking for him.

"Is the room warm?"

Daggit shook his ponderous head. "Cold and drafty."

At least they hadn't discovered his hideaway. "Then we'll take our chances."

Daggit nodded and pointed to the stairs to their right.

"You can't miss it," he said. "Plain as a cow in a ballroom."

Ashai wasn't sure what to make of that. It wasn't one of their prearranged signals. But Daggit winked, so he decided to trust him.

He took Makari by the hand and led her up the rickety stairs. They opened into a short hallway, with two doors on the left and only one on the right. Where the second door should have been hung a tapestry with a picture of a cow standing in the middle of a ballroom, shattered glass everywhere, guests distraught.

Ashai chuckled, drew the tapestry aside, and found a door with the word "storage" painted on it. Smiling, he opened the door and found exactly what he'd expected: a storage room. Crates lined the right wall, and shelves the left, bottles and linens and boxes of silverware piled high on all of them. The back wall was lined with pegs, on which hung aprons and smocks and tunics, most in need of repair or cleaning. A single window allowed the light of the moon to enter.

Makari wrinkled her nose, and Ashai grinned again. Jars of pickles filled one shelf, pungent enough to keep even the most inquisitive soldier or constable from exploring too deeply.

Footsteps on the stairs made him usher Makari inside and slide the door closed behind them, letting the tapestry fall back into place. It took a moment for his eyes to adjust to the dim moonlight, but when it did, he moved to the back wall, brushing aside a grease-covered apron. He pulled on the lone empty peg and with an audible click, the wall below the pegs slid inward. Pushing the tiny portal open the rest of the way, he stood aside and motioned for Makari to go through.

"Daggit's made some improvements since I was here last. We should be safe here for a few hours. The assassin will find us, though. It won't take him long to scour the seedier bars in Dar Tallus and find this one."

Makari's expression said she was not convinced, but she stepped through the portal into his room. Ashai followed her, clicking the door closed behind him.

This room had no windows for prying eyes to peek in, so when the door closed, it plunged them into total darkness. He felt around the wall to his right and found an oil lamp on a hook. A minute later, he'd lit the room with dancing golden light. He kept the flame low, to avoid letting light through the door crack, though he had no doubt Daggit had seen to that possibility.

The room was sparse, even by Denari Lai standards. A bedroll spread out on the floor against one wall, a simple pile of thick blankets and scraps of material from his old business, with two pillows. A single chest sat in a corner, and several dark cloaks hung on pegs in the walls. A bench had been built into the closest wall.

He held the lamp up to Makari's face only to find her glaring at him through the darkness.

"Start explaining," she whispered. "Start with why a simple cloth merchant needs a safe house hidden in a storage room, but don't forget to explain how you disguised us. How you learned to fight that way. Oh, and who you really are."

Ashai sighed and motioned for her to sit on the bench.

"I'll stand," she said. "So I can kick you if needed."

He studied her face, knowing she meant every word, and dropped onto the hard seat of the bench. As he set the oil lamp down, his hand trembled and he felt the muscles in his neck starting to bunch. He needed to renew his link to Nishi's power, and soon. He'd seen what happened to men who let their links go cold, and he'd do Makari no good in that condition.

"Perhaps it will help you understand if you see me pray," he told her. "I need to rebuild my strength soon or ... bad things will happen."

Makari opened her mouth to ask a question, but he silenced her with a wave of his hand.

"Just watch, my Princess," he told her. "All will be clear soon."

He stood, letting her sit on the bench, and moved to the center of the floor. He kneeled there, face upturned to the sky, and started to pray to Nishi. He didn't disguise it this time, did not try to make it look like a Pushtani prayer. He used his native tongue, something he hadn't done in months, and yet still felt so natural that it rolled off his tongue like water from a pitcher.

The prayer strengthened his link to his God, and rebuilt the power of his magic inside him. He felt Nishi's hands on his shoulders, felt his God lifting him and renewing his faith. Power coursed through his veins, and a tingling, almost lightning-like feeling, that made him think he could do anything.

His prayer turned to song, chanting the praises of his God, the volume low enough that no one outside the room would hear. He felt the power of his prayer crescendo, his heart beating faster, his senses heightening and peaking.

Then, just before his prayer ended, he felt it. Someone far away was watching him, looking through the power of his link to his magic, and seeing deep into his soul. A dark figure, wrapped in shadow and cloaked in night.

The figure rushed toward him, streaking over mountains and plains, through the trees and fields, only to flash out of existence at the last second. But it had been enough. Ashai recognized who'd been watching him.

He recognized the Chargh Lai. And the Chargh Lai recognized him.

Ashai panicked and broke the link, cutting off his prayer and jumping to his feet. Sweat poured down his forehead and back, and his stomach felt like he'd swallowed a box of needles. Instinctively, he reached for the dagger in the small of his back, but then he saw Makari.

His princess stood before the bench, arms crossed under her breasts, feet apart, tears streaming down her cheeks. Her blue eyes were cold as the winter sky.

Ashai dropped his disguises, letting his features and his eye color return to normal. Brown. Nishi'iti.

"You're one of them." He'd expected her to yell, but the calm, cold tone of her voice chilled him. "You're Nishi'iti. An assassin. That's how you know so much about them, how you hid us. You're one of them."

He dropped back to his knees and buried his face in his hands.

"I am Denari Lai," he cried. "I was sent here to kill you and your father, but I couldn't do the job, so they used another. I was trying to find and stop the other, but I was too late. I managed to save only you.

"So I did the best I could, and got you out of there as soon as … as soon as your father went down."

"You could have warned us," she growled, towering over him. "My father might still be alive if you had. Bauti. My father. Me, Ashai! You could have told me, but you chose to lie instead."

He looked up to see her glaring down at him, fists on hips, face red.

"I couldn't," he told her, unable to meet her gaze. "I knew if I told anyone, you would be taken from me. Our wedding would be called off and I'd lose you, if not my head, too."

"So you chose to let my father die in order to keep this lie of a marriage?"

"It wasn't like that." He rose, going to her and looking her in the eyes. He put his hands on her shoulders and she didn't flinch away. "I thought I could save him, save us all. I thought I could stop the second assassin and keep our marriage. It conflicted with my faith, and was the hardest choice I've ever made, but I chose you, Makari. Us. Over God.

"But know this: I did it because I love you, and because you loved me. All I wanted was to keep that love alive, to live in it forever. I thought if I could stop the second assassin, I could be true to you and explain to Nishi later. He's a wise God, and would have understood, but now I've failed you all."

She stood and stared at him a moment, looking deep into his eyes, considering. Hope flared in his heart. Maybe all was not lost.

Then she punched him in the stomach. The blow came so fast and so unexpectedly that he never had a chance to react. She caught him right under his ribs, knocking the air from his lungs and doubling him over. Then she kneed him in the face, her knee smashing into his left eye, snapping his head back.

Ashai staggered, shocked by the sudden violence, but his reflexes remained heightened from the prayer, and he recovered quickly. Makari came at him with a scream and a volley of punches and kicks and slaps, most of which he managed to fend off. She did strike him once on the mouth, fattening his lip, and one of her kicks connected with his shin in an explosion of pain.

But a few moments later, he'd restrained her, clamping his hand over her mouth again so she couldn't scream.

Eventually she stopped struggling and Ashai whispered in her ear.

"Listen to me, princess. I know you hate me right now, and you're right to feel that way. I've been untrue to everyone important to me, and lied to you all this time. But right now, I am your only hope of survival. The second assassin will not give up until you're dead, and only another Denari Lai can stop him.

"I know what he'll do, and how to counter it. I am the only one who can stand against him in combat, and my only purpose in life is to keep you alive. Bauti can't do that. Tan cannot. Your entire Army can't do what I can. I will kill this second assassin and see you sitting the throne, my love. Even if I don't sit beside you."

She went limp against him, sobs wracking her body, and Ashai resisted the urge to stroke her hair or kiss her. That would only make matters worse.

"After that, do with me what you will," he said. "Torture, beheading, whatever. I've betrayed my love and my God, so once you are safe, nothing remains for me. I'm guilty of my crimes, but saving you is my chance at redemption, if not with Nishi then at least with myself. Please let me help you."

She hesitated, then nodded and he let her go.

This time when she wheeled on him, she jabbed him in the chest with her index finger, but refrained from further violence.

"If my father survives, you will confess all of this to him and he will decide your fate. But our marriage is off. I'd rather marry anyone than you!"

Ashai masked the hurt caused by her words, and looked at the floor.

"I understand," he said. "But your father—"

The sound of the storage room door opening stopped him, making both of them glance at the hidden portal to his room. Barely audible footsteps crept into the storage room beyond, and the door clicked closed just as Ashai doused the oil lamp. He patted Makari's arm, whispering for her to stay quiet, and glided to stand beside the portal, ear to the wall.

Someone shuffled around in the other room, searching for something, first in the shelves, then the crates, and finally along the row of pegs. Ashai slid his dagger from its sheath as someone brushed along the wall, lifting aprons and smocks and letting them fall with soft swishing sounds against the wood. Ashai tensed as the sounds moved closer and closer to the panel, then stopped.

Someone snickered, and the portal hissed open. For a moment, no one moved. Ashai didn't think the other person could see into the dark, and as his own eyes adjusted, he made out a thin silhouette peering into the hole. Ashai recognized the profile of the thief from downstairs and started to creep forward. The boy lunged, tossing an apron that tangled itself on Ashai's blade. Then the thief bolted for the window, crashing through the glass with a shout.

"Close the door behind me!" Ashai told Makari.

Then he was through the door and out the window, giving chase.

CHAPTER TWENTY-FOUR

Makari wasn't about to hide in a safe house while Ashai ran off, so she wrapped herself in one of his cloaks and plunged out the window behind him. She found herself on a narrow roof, and had to jump onto a reeking pile of trash to reach the street safely.

At first she didn't know which way to go, but then she saw Ashai flash around a corner to her right. She ran as fast as her slippers would allow, reaching the corner just in time to see Ashai duck into an alley. A moment later, someone grunted.

Sprinting to the alley, Makari found Ashai on top of a boy no more than twelve, his dagger poised just a hair from the lad's throat. The boy's dirty face scrunched as he anticipated steel biting into his flesh. He looked to Makari for help.

"Don't kill him," she whispered, putting a hand on Ashai's shoulder.

"He saw us," he argued. "We can't risk it."

"I didn't see anything," the boy stammered. "And I wouldn't say anything even if I had."

Ashai pressed the flat of the blade against his throat. "Don't lie to me! You'd have sold that information to the Royal Guard in a heartbeat for a copper."

The thief considered this a moment, then shook his head. "At least a silver bit. Gold, if you're who I think you are."

Makari smiled. The boy had spunk. She pulled on Ashai's shoulder until he lifted the blade.

"There is a better way to gain his silence," she said. She pulled a small purse from her bodice and produced two gold coins, flipping them one at a time to the boy.

He snatched them out of the air, despite Ashai sitting on his chest.

"You have my word," he said, "no one hears nothing from me about you, Your Highness."

Makari held her finger to her lips. "Don't use our names or titles. You never know who might be listening."

"Around these parts, only the Sixth Guild has eyes and ears. Even Minister Tan's people are afraid to spy in this neighborhood."

She nodded to Ashai. "Let him up."

Ashai gave her a dubious look. She couldn't blame him for not trusting the boy. The Sixth Guild was not really one of Pushtan's five trade guilds, but an alliance of criminal elements united against her father's rule. Still, the boy seemed harmless.

Ashai stepped off and let the lad up.

"Doesn't the Sixth Guild want her dead, too?" he asked.

"Only her father," the boy answered, shaking his head. "The king has shown great cruelty in dealing with our people, but his daughter … she shows us kindness and restraint."

"My father dealt fairly with criminals," she argued, tearing up. "You should be thankful he is an even-handed ruler."

"He sends kill squads after us." The boy straightened, as if offended. "He had a thief's hands smashed with hammers, and ordered one family killed for the crimes of their father."

The lies ignited her temper. She looked to Ashai. "I changed my mind. Cut his throat before he spews any more filth about my late father."

Ashai shrugged and stepped forward. The boy paled.

"Sorry, your … miss! I never met your late father, but listened to people jabber about him. They say he used slaves to run the mines in the north, worked them to death, and came looking for more. They say—"

"They say a lot of things that aren't true," Makari shot back. "My father was a good man."

"As you say, Miss," the boy said, inclining his head slightly.

"What's your name?" Makari demanded.

Brushing himself off, the boy faced Makari and smiled. His limbs were tight and sinewy, while his cheekbones stretched the skin on his face tight. When he smiled at her, she saw gaps in his teeth.

"Don't really have one," he replied. "Sixth Guild took me in when my parents died. I was two, and they didn't know my name. Just found me wandering the streets, or so they tell it. Anyway, they came to call me Tisk, because of the sound most people made when they saw me."

His hands fidgeted at his sides, twitching either with nervousness or fear, but his eyes showed neither in the soft silver glow of the moon.

"Well, Tisk, we thank you for your silence," she told him. "And I'm sorry you were misinformed about my father."

She was about to dismiss him when a commotion started back the way they'd come. She looked at Ashai.

"I don't suppose you'll stay here, will you?" he asked. She fixed him with her most forged stare. "Didn't think so. Just keep quiet and out of sight."

The three of them crept to the corner and peered around, back toward Ashai's safe house. Two members of the Capitol Watch—the constabulary of Dar Tallus—stood in the street outside the broken window through which they'd fled, while a Royal Guard member stuck his grizzled head out the window.

Makari recognized him just as Ashai pulled her back around the corner, out of sight.

"We cannot let Bauti see us," he whispered.

"They found your safe house!" Her heart climbed into her throat.

Tisk looked confused. "I thought the Captain of your Royal Guard could be trusted. Everyone knows of his love for you."

Makari felt heat rush to her cheeks and turned away. Had everyone in the city known?

"We don't know who to trust in the palace," Ashai said. "That's where Bauti will want to take her. She'd be in danger there, even more than out here. I need to get her out of the city."

Makari opened her mouth to object—her place was here with her people, the citizens of Pushtan—but held her tongue. Ashai was right. She would be safer out of Dar Tallus for the time being. She couldn't serve her citizens by getting killed.

The boy looked from Ashai to Makari, then motioned for them to follow him. He snuck back to the alley and all three of them ducked behind a stack of crates.

"The city is locked down," he said. "All roads leading out are guarded now, either by Capitol Watch or Royal Guard. They're not letting anyone leave, at least not without a thorough search."

Makari looked at Ashai. "Can your tricks get us through that?"

He shook his head. "Not reliably. My 'tricks' focus on brief glances, keeping people from looking closely enough to see through the magic. And besides, I'm not sure I should use magic right now."

"Why not?"

"No wonder I didn't recognize you in the Drunken Duck," Tisk interrupted. "You used magic to disguise yourself. Are you a sorcerer?"

"He's Denari Lai," Makari answered before Ashai could slip a lie from his lips. Tisk started to back away. "He has kept me alive this far, Tisk. And if he wanted you dead, you'd already be cold. Now Ashai, why can't you use magic?"

Her once-betrothed looked distant a moment, like his mind had traveled far away.

"I think when I prayed, someone saw me. Someone looking for us."

"And now they're searching your secret room?" Tisk said. "Never believe in coincidences."

Ashai looked at Tisk. "We need to get out of Dar Tallus. Soon."

Tisk scratched his chin. "I may be able to help with that. Rather, the Sixth Guild may be able to help. I'll need to talk to some people. Do you know where the Feather Pillow Inn is?"

Ashai nodded. "I've seen it. North of Baker's Square. Three story building."

"That's it," Tisk said with a nod. "Meet me there at dawn, if you can stay alive that long. If I can help you, I will."

And with that he loped off down the alley.

"How do you know we can trust him?" Ashai asked.

Makari shrugged. "I know my citizens."

He studied her a moment, then nodded. "Then let's start moving north. We need to survive the night."

CHAPTER TWENTY-FIVE

Marwan Bauti strode down the dim corridor to Minister Tan's door, where two of his own Royal Guard members stood watch. The men eyed him, but stood aside and opened the door.

The inside of Tan's chambers was brighter than Bauti had ever seen. The man had lit at least a dozen oil lamps around the room, as well as two torches on the wall and a number of candles. It was as if the minister suddenly feared the dark, not that Bauti could blame him. Assassins slithered somewhere in the palace, and neither Tan nor he had a single lead on who it was. So those who remained in the palace —and many had left—looked over their shoulders and into darkened corners as if the shadows themselves were going to leap out and kill them.

Bauti's fists opened and closed, and his jaw clenched. He didn't need to be here. His place was in the streets, searching for Makari, leading his men to rescue her. As long as he was here, at the beck and call of Pushtan's temporary ruler, the princess remained in danger.

He knew what Minister Tan wanted. The rumors had rippled through the ranks of the Royal Guard, reaching him like a wave in a pond reaches the shore. Minister Tan did not feel safe with simple Royal Guard members protecting him. He wanted Bauti at his side day and night.

Bauti wasn't even sure how the man had come to power. The king had never mentioned particular trust in the spy, never even hinted he'd given him such responsibility. Quite the opposite—Abadas had mentioned several times how little a spy could be trusted.

Yet somehow, the man had gotten the king's mark and seal on the writ proclaiming him Protector of Pushtan. It made the hairs on Bauti's neck stand at attention.

The Protector of Pushtan stepped from his bedchambers into the sitting room, his eyes opening wide as if surprised to see the captain. His shoulders seemed more slouched than normal, and his ledge of a forehead seemed to hang lower. Dark circles formed half-moons under his eyes, and he moved as if he were ninety years old, not thirty-two.

"Ah, Captain Bauti, I wasn't expecting you this early. Please, have a seat."

He motioned to a well-padded chair, taking a similar one beside it for himself. Bauti looked at the chair, then patted the broadsword on his hip.

"No disrespect, Minister, but it's hard to sit with a sword on your belt."

"Of course," the minister replied, nodding distantly. "I should've thought of that. Please be comfortable. We have crucial matters to discuss."

"I agree, My Lord," Bauti said. "I have raised your security as much as I dare without taking men from the search for Her Majesty. Surely the men I've assigned, both younger and more capable than myself, can do a suitable job keeping you safe while I look for Makari.

"So far, we've located a safe house they used in the Rat's Den district, and based on what we found there, we believe we were just minutes behind them. If I can keep looking, I'm certain we will have Makari back safe in the palace in a day or two."

Tan looked at Bauti with a strange softness to his dark blue eyes, something akin to pity.

"Take these two, as well," he said after a delay. "Leave my quarters unguarded and find the princess as fast as possible. We need her back in the palace."

Bauti forced his mouth to close so he didn't look as shocked as he felt. He took a deep breath, stalling so he could wrap his mind around the spymaster's request. It didn't make any sense.

"My Lord, I don't see how that's wise. It leaves you completely unguarded, and right now, you rule Pushtan."

Tan flinched, as if Bauti's words had shocked him or slapped him in the face. Like being in charge of an entire nation had never occurred to him before.

"Come now, Captain." He fidgeted in his seat, looking at his hands that sat folded in his lap. "We both know spies make terrible rulers. We're sneaky and untrustworthy, and the citizenry knows this. They'll only give me so much time before demanding Makari take the throne. They love her, and rightly so. Most have never heard of me, which is how I prefer it in this business.

"I think we both know how important the princess is to this nation. If people start to think she's dead, that there's no heir to the Abadas throne, the other noble families will start circling like vultures. It won't be long before some of them move on the carrion.

"We cannot let the throne become carrion, Captain Bauti."

Bauti nodded, his heart soaring at the news. The man showed some brains after all.

"Of course, My Lord."

"You have access to the entire Royal Guard. There is no royalty here for them to guard, so let them go and find it. It won't matter if I and every other person in this palace dies if we lose the princess. Use the Capitol Watch, too. I've informed their commander—Captain Rogroy—that he reports to you until the princess is found. That should give you almost six hundred men, Captain. Two hundred Royal Guard and just under four hundred Capitol Watch constables. Do you need more?"

Bauti couldn't find words, his mind was so jumbled with shock, so he shook his head.

"Excellent, Captain. When you find them, bring me Makari, and bring me Ashai's head. We searched his quarters and found Denari Lai items. He is an assassin, as well. Level the city if you need to, but bring back Makari and kill that upstart merchant."

The announcement didn't surprise Bauti. It made sense.

"My lord, what if Princess Makari forbids me to harm her betrothed?"

She'd done so in the past, after all.

"Do not give her that opportunity."

Bauti sketched a hasty bow and withdrew, closing the chamber doors behind him. He dispatched the two guards to help in the search, then wandered the hallways of the palace, his mind working through all that had just happened.

Something didn't add up about all of this. He hated Ashai—no one would ever doubt that—but if the man was an assassin, why was Makari still alive? The answer was obvious: Ashai loved Makari.

Bauti couldn't fault him on that account, foolish as it was.

And he knew that fact gave him an advantage. A man in love was blind, deaf, and dumb, and would do anything for that love. And that made Ashai the most vulnerable assassin ever. It made him beatable.

And what of Makari? The princess would know by now. She'd seen him fight, had seen the dagger. She would know. She would be hurting.

Bauti longed to comfort her, to tell her it was not her fault. But even if she was back, he could not do so. She hated him, too.

He rounded a corner and found himself inexplicably outside Makari's chambers, the black lacquered doors unguarded and slightly ajar. He thought about going inside, of taking in one deep breath of her, letting her scent linger in his lungs to drive him forward.

But he decided against it. Anyone could be watching, and besides, he had a princess to find. And an assassin to kill.

And as he strode for the nearest city gate, for the first time in days, Bauti smiled.

CHAPTER TWENTY-SIX

Ashai looked out across the dark street at the outside of the Feather Pillow Inn, letting the sounds of bells at the palace chapel wash over him from across the city. He breathed in the aroma of bread baking somewhere below him, as a baker prepared for the crowds that would come in a few hours. He listened to the soft ruffles of laughter coming from the well-lit first floor common room and the soft titter of crickets, carried on the whisper of a breeze.

His fingers traced patterns on the blackened wood of the burned out building in which they'd chosen to spend the night, but his mind was somewhere else, somewhere far away from all of this, where winter would already have thrown a blanket of white over the mountains, bending trees near the ground and wrapping the world in muffled silence.

He wondered if the Chargh Lai knew where he was, if his mentor knew what he had done. But he didn't wonder for long, his mind knowing right away that the man who led the Denari Lai knew of his crimes and had ordered his death. He'd probably known long before the wedding day what Ashai would do, for the Chargh Lai spoke with God, and Nishi knew everything in the hearts of his people. Especially Denari Lai.

Ashai knew now he could never go back, at least not to the order, and probably not to his homeland. His people would never accept him —he was pariah to them now. He still held out hope, though, that he could convince his God that he'd done the right thing, that Makari had a good heart and did not deserve to die. Then maybe he could live out the rest of his short life at peace with Nishi.

Just as painful, he'd lost his place in Makari's life, too. As compassionate as she was, she could never forgive him for this. Would never love him again. And he wasn't sure his God's love mattered one bit without hers.

Makari moved to his side, standing in silence, looking out on the street just as he did. Her presence felt different now, tense and vibrating with hostility. Gone was the feeling of rightness he'd felt with her before, the impression that they were two pieces of the same puzzle, meant to be interlocked forever.

"It will get cold tonight," she whispered. "We need a fire, and the fireplace in this room still stands."

Ashai shook his head. She was right, of course. It would be a cold night. Already their breath fogged in the air before them, and smoke rose from city chimneys.

"We cannot risk someone seeing it. A fire in a building long ago destroyed by fire? Someone would come and look, and they'd probably have swords."

She sighed, irritation dripping from her voice. "Then how do you propose we stay warm?"

He didn't turn to look at her, but he knew the rustling sound behind him meant she'd crossed her arms over her chest or taken on some other confrontational pose.

"I have blankets," he told her. "We will huddle together under them and stay warm."

"I am not getting under a blanket with you! You meant to kill me and my father! You're a Denari—"

He whirled, cutting her off with an angry glare and a quick motion of his finger against his lips. She actually took a step back as if he meant to hit her, and he found the action stabbed him in the heart as painfully as the second assassin's blade would have done.

"I told you already," he hissed. "I tried to protect both of you, but I failed. If I'd wanted you dead, you'd be so right now."

She turned away, her back every bit as cold as the fall air around them. "My father is."

Ashai looked at the floor, kicking at a charred floorboard with the toe of his boot.

"And I'm sorry," he whispered. "But you have to understand why I chose to forsake my vows, to walk away from my country and my order and my God. I did it because I love you, Makari. I turned my back on everything I'd ever known, betrayed a man who'd raised me from a boy, and sinned against the God who'd cared for me my whole life. All because I love you.

"If you believe nothing else I tell you, believe that."

Her shoulders slumped and the rod-straight shape of her back curved ever so slightly. She took in a deep, shuddering breath and sat in a rickety wooden chair by the fireplace, as if it would warm her. A moment later, sobs wracked her slender body. She put her face in her hands and cried muffled cries, her shoulders quaking.

Ashai longed to go to her, to wrap his arms around her and hold her until the tears dried up and the sobs faded. But he knew better. He was the cause of those tears, the reason she shook and cried and suffered. It was his fault.

For a moment he reached out his hand, pausing just short of her shoulder. His fingers shook with a subtle tremor, a quake almost imperceptible when compared to those of the princess. He needed prayer, renewal of his faith and his magic. He'd been cut short last time by the Chargh Lai's appearance, and hadn't fully renewed his link. If he didn't do so soon, he would fall into fever, quickly becoming too ill to protect Makari.

Yet something made him pause, made him wonder if that was the right thing to do. Had he really seen the Chargh Lai before? More importantly, had the Chargh Lai seen him?

It had never happened before, not in all his years of praying and using power had someone else appeared in his vision. If the Chargh Lai was somehow able to see him again, he might alert the second assassin to their location. They could be dead by the time Tisk came for them.

Still, as another round of tremors shook his hand, he made up his mind. The assassin would find them anyway, and Ashai needed full use of his power if he meant to protect Makari.

"Princess, I need to pray and rest," he said, his voice hoarse and barely more than a whisper. "Will you keep watch on the street for a few minutes?"

She moved to the window. "I thought they would find us if you do."

He shrugged. "Without it, I can't fight him."

She nodded and sat so she would be less visible from the street, saying nothing more.

Ashai kneeled by the cold fireplace, turning again his face to the sky, and placed both hands over his heart. He prayed again in Nishi'iti, no longer needing to hide his identity and longing to feel something familiar, something not trying to kill him.

The power of his prayer filled him, the rush of Nishi's power nearly overwhelming him this time. He rocked on his knees, absorbing the shock of the power's impact and maintaining his focus on prayer. He asked Nishi for forgiveness, for God to see the good in Makari's soul, to see her as Ashai saw her and give her a chance.

And he felt his magic renewing, felt the gossamer thread linking him to it building and strengthening as he communed with his God.

Then it happened again. The image of the Chargh Lai appeared in his mind, the mentor and order leader, standing with his back to Ashai at an altar of red and black. Ashai had never seen the room before, and he thought he'd seen everyplace at Tabi Ge Nishi. The Chargh Lai appeared to be praying, too, face upturned and hands on his chest as he chanted and sang. Around him glowed an aura of red and orange and yellow, shimmering like something from a dream, and Ashai knew the man was wrapped in magic, surrounded by God's power.

He felt as if he were violating some sacred moment, intruding on a private moment between the Chargh Lai and Nishi, and he tried to force the images away so he could focus on his own link to God.

But the Chargh Lai spun around, eyes black as the darkest night, lips peeled back to show his teeth, stark white against the red of his lips. His hands left his chest and pointed at Ashai, nails long enough to curl into claws.

Then his mentor laughed, a sound like molten rock gurgling up from the depths, surrounded by the hiss of steam. And for an instant, Ashai knew in his heart the Chargh Lai could see him, too.

Ashai broke the link, toppling backward to the floor, where he lay staring at the stars through a hole in the roof, fighting to regain the breath that had rushed from his lungs.

Makari glanced over her shoulder, then shook her head and muttered something he couldn't understand, something he didn't want to know.

Ashai breathed deep and took inventory of himself. He held his hands out before him, tremor-free, and sighed in relief. His prayer had been incomplete, but it had restored enough of his magic to steady his body, so maybe he could protect Makari long enough to get out of the city. Outside the walls they would be able to generate some distance between themselves and the second assassin, giving Ashai time to figure out a plan.

Inside Dar Tallus, they'd spend so much time looking over their shoulders they'd never find a way out.

Of course, if the Chargh Lai had really seen him just then, it would not be long before the assassin caught up to them.

No one had ever told him magic could be used that way, to monitor a Denari Lai across long distances. He'd always been told it was a private connection between servant and God, something no one else could invade. But he'd clearly seen the Chargh Lai, and he felt in his heart the other man had seen him.

He sat up, shaking his head and running his fingers through his hair. He was being paranoid. It was just a vision, just a waking dream. The Chargh Lai had been an image drawn by his exhausted mind. It meant nothing.

Ashai yawned, and the room spun a bit when he did. He'd been unable to sleep the day before his wedding, and now he'd been up almost this entire night. Sleep was in order.

"Do you need rest?" he asked Makari.

The princess kept her gaze locked on the street below.

"How could I sleep? My father is dead. An assassin is trying to kill me, while another tries to stop him. The man I was to wed is a killer. I won't sleep this night, if ever again."

"Then I must." He lay down and wrapped himself in a blanket, using another for a pillow. He tossed a third to Makari. "Wake me if something happens."

He dropped into sleep like falling off a cliff, plunging deep into the world of dreams, where visions of dark armies of demons and monsters marched from the earth's heart to spread blackness and death.

And as before, he knew even in sleep that the dream was more than a dream. It was the future.

Tan was deep in sleep when the Chargh Lai spoke to him, the leader of his order appearing like a specter, ethereal and floating in the air before him. He did not speak, but reached out his hand for Tan to take.

Tan did not hesitate, grasping his mentor's misty hand, feeling cold slither over his skin like fog over a grave marker. The feeling only lasted a moment, though, and then warmth spread up his arm, to the elbow like he'd immersed his arm in a bath.

The next instant, Tan was swept away from his chambers, leaving behind his incense and warm rugs, finding himself soaring high above the streets of Dar Tallus. Cold autumn air rushed through him, and he knew he was no more solid than the Chargh Lai himself, both men's spirits gone from their bodies so the mentor could show Tan what he needed to see.

They streaked over the homes and businesses huddled against the outer wall of the palace, swept low over the tailors' district, Anvil Corner, and Barley Row, the scent of hops tickling his senses. They passed over temples and brothels alike, the Chargh Lai paying no mind to either, until Tan found himself looking down at the well-kept streets of Baker's Square, where tendrils of smoke wound up from every building, lifting the aromas of baking bread, honey, and cinnamon like prayers to the Five Gods from their poor, misled people.

The Chargh Lai led him down to the street, alighting in front of a three-story inn, its windows dark and quiet, even those on the first floor, where the tavern no doubt sat. A sign hung out front reading, "The Feather Pillow."

The Chargh Lai turned around, leading Tan to do the same, and pointed across the street.

The blackened skeleton of a building loomed, a corpse of what had once been a second inn, before fire had stripped it of its flesh and left its bones to keep watch on the street, cold and dead. Tan's gaze wandered up the charred walls to the second floor, where blackened timbers stood, jagged tips stabbing at the night sky, and only the lower half of the walls remained.

Something moved. He almost missed it, but he looked closer and saw it again. Something gleamed in the moonlight, reflecting some of the silvery light that the ash-covered building absorbed and smothered.

The Chargh Lai tugged him closer, until they stood in the middle of the cobblestone street, staring up at the building. This time, when the shadows shifted, Tan saw her face. Makari. The princess peeked over the remnants of an old window, her eyes like little silver moons against the black of her surroundings. She watched the street, making Tan try to slink toward cover, but the Chargh Lai held tight, and stood fast in the street.

Makari's gaze swept over them once, then again going the other direction, but she showed no sign of seeing them.

The clatter of iron-shod hoofs arose around a corner and the princess disappeared from sight just as a wagon rattled out of a side street, its horses at a canter. It bore down on Tan and the Chargh Lai, barreling toward them at unusual speed for this time of night. Again Tan tried to move, but again his mentor stood fast, pointing at the spot where Makari had been just a minute earlier.

Tan winced and closed his eyes as the wagon ran them down, shuddering as it passed through them like they were nothing more than evening fog. As it thundered out of sight, Makari appeared again, eyes searching, hunkered down more this time to be less visible.

Then a man appeared behind her and Tan knew he had them both. Ashai's eyes looked sunken, and his normally immaculate hair was tangled and wild. He frowned as he looked down at the princess, and Tan could almost feel the sadness in his heart.

A brief moment of sympathy fluttered in Tan's heart. The man had lost everything—his marriage, his home, his order, and his faith. Perhaps most crushing, though, he'd lost Makari's love, the thing that had caused him to betray everything else in his life.

Ashai was a ship lost at sea, floating with the current, but with no rudder or sails. It was only a matter of time before he was crushed against the rocks and sunk forever.

The Chargh Lai lifted one arm to point at the two people, turning his head and looking Tan in the eye. The spymaster jumped back, startled by the marbled black of his mentor's eyes, frightened momentarily by the man who had taught him everything he knew. The man who'd saved him from his former hellish life of brutality and indecent acts and turned him onto the path of Nishi's will.

In that instant, for a frozen moment in time, the Chargh Lai looked different. Darker somehow, as if a shadow floated around him like a dark cloak. Then it passed and the eyes turned brown again and the vision disappeared.

Tan sat bolt upright in his bed, drenched in sweat and shivering, despite the hot coals still glowing in his fireplace. In his mind he held firm the image of the inn's sign: The Feather Pillow.

He knew where to find the princess.

He rose, shrugged his robe over his shoulders, and threw another log on the fire, lighting a candle from the hearth. He slipped out of his bedchamber and into the sitting room, where he lit an oil lamp and clicked open the door.

A lone servant was passing his door, an old man carrying a basket of linens.

"Fetch Captain Bauti at once," Tan told the servant. "Tell him I need him immediately. Tell him I know where to look."

The servant looked confused for a moment, then jogged away. Tan closed the door and grinned as he strode to his desk, admiring his own cleverness.

In all likelihood, Ashai would kill Bauti and Makari, ridding Tan of both problems. If Bauti was lucky, he might kill the assassin and bring the princess back to the palace, where Tan would kill her himself. Either way, Nishi's will was done and the Pushtani Empire would crumble like dry bread, and the rise of Nishi'iti could begin.

The rise of a new Nishi'iti.

CHAPTER TWENTY-SEVEN

The sun had just started clawing its way over the eastern horizon, leaving bloody gashes of red against the purple-and-gray skin of the sky when Bauti and his men stormed the abandoned building. They'd been watching the blackened husk of an inn for two hours with no sign of Makari or Ashai, despite Tan's assurances they were inside.

Bauti had left nothing to chance, putting archers on surrounding rooftops and sealing off every street and alley leading out of the area. Peeking around a corner at the building for hours, Bauti had lost his patience the moment sunlight had warmed his shoulders. With a shout, he'd ordered his men into the inn.

Ten of the Royal Guard's finest crashed through the back door while Bauti led ten more in the front, short swords drawn. They'd cleared the first floor in seconds, tromping up the stairs to the second floor and into the room Tan had described.

They found three blankets piled against the cold stone of the fireplace, and some clippings of Makari's black hair, but the room was otherwise empty.

Bauti cursed and leaned over the windowsill, feeling the burned wood sag under his weight. Down below, a hair-lipped Royal Guard sergeant named Bryston—one of Bauti's best leaders—had ringed the building's front with another ten soldiers, and citizens were gathering to watch the excitement.

"How in Death's name did they know we were coming?" Bauti hammered his fist on the wood, making it crumble.

He knew, though, that they didn't necessarily have to know he and his men were coming. Ashai was smart, and had probably guessed that moving before dawn would be their best chance at avoiding capture. He doubted the Denari Lai would stay in one place longer than a few hours.

He was about to turn away when he caught sight of a boy standing in an alley across the street. He was a young lad, maybe eight or nine, dressed in rags and tatters, with dirt on his face and a nose upturned like a teapot spout.

What caught Bauti's attention, though, were his eyes. More specifically, the way he used them, taking in the entirety of the Royal Guard forces, concentrating so hard his forehead wrinkled.

He was counting. Counting soldiers.

The boy's eyes brushed briefly over Bauti, then snapped back and locked eyes with the captain. He held Bauti's gaze, then took off down the alley.

"Get that boy!" Bauti shouted to the sergeant. "Down the alley, there!"

Bryston and three men sprinted off after the child, as Bauti ran from the room, bounded down the stairs, and burst out the open front door.

The sergeant marched from the alley, grinning under his pale eyes, as his men dragged the boy out between them. He had the look of a captured deer, eyes wide and darting about, searching for an escape route. He struggled against his captors, but his skinny arms were no match for the strength of the soldiers.

They dragged him to his feet before Bauti, and the boy looked up into the captain's eyes. His own eyes were a defiant green, as if green flames licked behind them, and for a moment, Bauti thought the boy might spit on him. He seemed to think better of it, though, and simply wrinkled his nose.

"I ain't tellin' you anything," he said, puffing his chest out. "I'd rather die."

Bauti studied him, then shrugged and turned away.

"Kill him and burn the body in the street," he told the guards. "Make this urchin an example for anyone else who thinks to defy us."

Behind him, the boy swallowed audibly.

"You wouldn't kill a child." His voice was peppered with fear now, undermining the affected defiance.

Bauti turned back around and looked down at the boy.

"I killed a child just a few months ago, or did you forget? You know, the fool of a thief who tried to rob my princess?"

This time, the boy paled. He'd obviously seen the incident, and no matter how bad Bauti felt about it now, he'd do it again to protect his princess. Or to find her.

"What's your name, son?" he asked, softening his voice in hopes the sweet cake would look better than the morning star.

"Chaster, my lord." A look of shame crossed the little man's face. He was betraying someone and he knew it.

"Well, Chaster, you know who I am, so you know who I'm looking for, right?"

Chaster nodded.

"Well then, why don't you save both of us some … discomfort and tell me where she is?"

For emphasis, Bauti ran his finger along the edge of his sword, drawing a tiny droplet of blood. Chaster swallowed again, but shook his head.

"They'll kill me," he said.

Bauti leaned down next to the boy's ear and whispered, "So will I."

Without hesitation, Chaster replied, "It'll last longer with them. And hurt more."

Bauti stepped back and thought about this. Someone had taken in Ashai and Makari, someone of whom this street urchin was terrified. And yet someone Chaster knew, and who knew him in return. Someone brutal enough to use a child for spying. Only one group in Dar Tallus fit that description.

"So the princess and her betrothed are in the hands of the Sixth Guild?"

The boy put his hands up in front of him and tried to take a step back. The guards held him tight.

"I never said that," Chaster spurted, confirming Bauti's suspicions. "But I don't think they're betrothed anymore."

Bauti narrowed his eyes. "Why's that?"

Chaster looked around the group, as if expecting help to arrive. None did.

"You'll let me go if I tell you?"

Bauti admired the boy's pluck. "If what you tell me is of value."

Chaster motioned for Bauti to move close, and his eyes took on a conspiratorial look.

"She's mad at him because he's an assassin, too. He's trying to protect her, but she doesn't care."

Bauti's heart jumped into his throat. She didn't love him anymore! He gained composure and focused on the boy.

"You're certain?"

Chaster nodded. "When their help arrived, I was watching. The man with the princess had a fancy dagger. It was black as night, and he almost killed the one who came to help them. I've never seen someone move like that. So fast. But I recognize the knife from the tales about the wedding, where the king was killed."

Bauti's throat tightened. His doubt washed away—Ashai was Denari Lai. If he didn't find her soon, she'd be dead, too.

"Look, Chaster," he said, putting one huge hand on the boy's shoulder, "do you love the princess?"

He nodded enthusiastically. "We all do. She's good to the poor people."

"Then listen well. If we do not find her, Makari will die. That man is responsible for the king's death, and will cut her throat in a heartbeat if he thinks it in his interest."

The boy considered, scratching his chin. "I don't think so. She was mad at him, but I've seen the way he looked at her before from men, and it doesn't mean he's mad. He loves her."

"What does a child know of love, Chaster?"

"More than most soldiers." He winked. "You see a lot of things, living on the street."

Bauti smiled, despite the knot in his gut. "How long ago did you see all this?"

"Not long before you and your men got here. Maybe ten minutes."

"Let him go," Bauti told the guards.

They released Chaster's arms and the boy was gone in a blink, sprinting down the alley behind him.

Bauti turned to the sergeant. "You heard him. It sounds like they couldn't have gotten far without us seeing them. I want every Royal

Guard and Capitol Watch member down here, searching. Cordon off this entire part of the city. No one leaves. Period."

With a nod, Bryston started deploying his men.

They searched until the sun had dipped low over the Slevonian Forest to the west, and the city's citizens turned from the business of light to the follies of darkness.

Bauti leaned against a brick wall, watching Bryston and his men question an old baker woman with deep wrinkles and milky eyes. He couldn't hear what she said, but the way she kept shaking her head told him all he needed to know.

He'd expanded the cordon by a half-mile in all directions, searched every room of every building. They'd questioned hundreds of people, but still they'd found nothing. No sign of the princess or Ashai.

Nor of the Sixth Guild, though that didn't surprise him.

He knew in his heart they'd let Makari slip through their fingers. She'd be dead by sunup.

The thought stabbed at his heart, a piercing pain that nearly brought tears to his eyes. He couldn't lose her. He'd failed her in so many ways already, from failing to see Ashai's true nature to letting his feelings for her blind him. He should have been in the chapel where he could have protected the king and Makari, but his foolish heart had made him write that letter, had affected his judgment and biased him in his duties.

He'd known he was too old and too common for Makari, but he'd allowed his dreams to fester, to spread like an infection through his heart and his soul. He knew he was at the end of his usefulness as a soldier, he supposed, and had been looking for someone to put their faith in him again. Someone to love him as the man he'd once been.

Never mind that he'd guarded Makari as an infant, seen her grow up and blossom into the beautiful young woman she'd become. He'd hoped his loyalty would be enough, that she'd love him as a protector and thus as a man.

He'd been wrong, and it would likely cost her life.

Bryston broke away from the old woman and strode to Bauti, saluting as he approached.

"Report, Sergeant." Bauti didn't really need the report, but the sergeant was a stickler for procedure.

"Sir, I believe the assassin has managed to slip Her Highness out of this sector of Dar Tallus. We should expand the search to the surrounding areas."

"Agreed. Double the cordon and search areas. Search all night. Time is not on our princess's side."

"We will need more men, Captain."

Bauti frowned. "I will request regular army troops from General Celani."

He didn't trust regular foot soldiers. They were too easily bribed. He'd hand-selected every member of the Royal Guard, and he knew Rogroy ran a tight group with the Capitol Watch, but using the regular army for internal situations was unwise. They were trained to take and hold land, destroy things, and kill people, not to exercise caution and protect citizens.

Bryston shared his concerns, judging from the look of doubt that crossed his face, but he nodded nonetheless and marched off to carry out his orders.

Bauti spent a few more minutes seeing to the arrangements, then set off on his own down a narrow side street, walking west into the setting sun. He needed time to clear his mind, to make sure he was focused on the task at hand. Bauti had never been one to dwell on the mistakes of the past, but this failure bothered him more than most. It was selfish, an adherence to his own desires rather than those of the people he served. In thirty years as a soldier, twenty in the Royal Guard, and eight as its commander, he'd never let his own needs rule. Until this incident.

Maybe he was getting too old to command.

He wandered for what seemed like an eternity, dusk's grays and blues and purples fading to the pitch black of night. He passed numerous patrols, all of them offering salutes and salutations, which he acknowledged, but he tried to keep to the darker streets and alleys, not wanting attention, needing his solitude.

It was in one such alley, ripe with the stench of shit and the stink of rotting food that the hairs on the back of his neck stood on end. He'd felt himself being watched many times. It was an instinct borne by most seasoned soldiers, one you didn't survive long without.

He'd learned not to ignore it.

Keeping his pace, Bauti let his eyes wander to the shadows around him, looking for even the slightest motion or glint. Controlling his breathing, he listened for anything out of place in the sounds of the city, tiny noises that might tip him off to someone coming for him.

He sidestepped a trash heap, wove around a stack of crates, and found himself at a dead end, the alley ending at the back of a building, a single wooden door at its base.

He was reaching for the door handle when the cold kiss of steel jabbed at the base of his skull and a hand clamped over his mouth. He froze.

"I can kill you with one thrust." Ashai's voice was hushed, barely more than a whisper. Bauti marveled at how silent the man had been, kicking himself silently for not hearing his approach. "But I don't want to. Do what I say and you'll live to see Makari."

Taking a calming breath, Bauti nodded.

"Keep your hands out in front of you and open that door slowly."

He obeyed, wincing as the door creaked through the alleyway. The interior was even darker than the street, but Ashai pushed him inside, where he removed Bauti's sword belt and dropped it to the floor. Next came the dagger on his right hip, followed by the one he kept in his boot. Unarmed and blind, Bauti felt naked and vulnerable, as helpless as a child.

Ashai shoved him against a rough, cold stone wall, then removed his hand from Bauti's mouth. The knifepoint slid down to rest between two vertebrae in the small of his back.

"One wrong move and you'll never walk again." Ashai's voice crawled hot across Bauti's neck. The tip of the blade pierced skin, drawing a trickle of warm blood to emphasize his point.

"I understand."

"Light it," Ashai said.

Behind them, someone rustled and the sound of flint striking broke the silence. Sparks flew, and then a warm yellow light filled the room. Bauti could see only the speckled gray of the stone wall, but the next voice that spoke made his heart leap.

"Captain, I order you to not harm this man." Makari's commanding voice was unmistakable, even with his back to her. "He has done me no harm. In fact, he likely saved my life more than once. Hear him out."

Trembling with anger at the minister, Bauti could only nod.

"Yes, Your Highness."

"Your word, Captain," Ashai ordered. "I'll have your word before I release you."

Bauti reigned in his anger, took another deep breath, and nodded. "I give you my word that so long as the princess commands it, I shall not harm you."

The blade eased away from his back, and Ashai released him.

"Turn around and see that she is unharmed."

Hands in front of him, Bauti turned.

Makari stood against a stack of beer kegs, wrapped in a plain, gray cloak, her hair chopped short in uneven swipes. Dirt marred her perfect features, but her ice-blue eyes stared out at him, from red-rimmed lids.

He nearly passed out with relief. His princess was unharmed. Instead, he fell to one knee and bowed.

"Highness, how may I make up to you my failure?"

For a long moment, Makari didn't move or speak, and Bauti kept his head down, afraid of what he might see if he should look up. Then she stepped forward, and Bauti felt Ashai stiffen, ready for anything.

But the princess put her hand on Bauti's head, warm and soft, and spoke.

"If loving me is a failure, Captain, then fail all you want. I should have trusted you."

Tears stung his eyes, and Bauti squeezed them shut. He would not let Ashai see him weep, but the burden lifted from his heart was so immense, he barely kept his composure. Makari forgave him. Nothing else mattered.

"Rise now, Captain." She stepped back. "We have much to discuss."

Bauti stood and faced Ashai, hate boiling up in his throat. He eyed his weapons on the floor a few feet away, but the Denari Lai shook his head.

"Not until I know I can trust you."

"I gave my word," Bauti growled back. "Perhaps one of your kind doesn't understand how binding that is."

To Bauti's surprise, Ashai lost his composure for an instant, doubt clouding his eyes. But he recovered in a heartbeat and masked his emotions.

Of course. That *would* hurt him. The man had betrayed an oath to his God, an oath to kill Makari, and instead he protected her. It would be a sensitive subject, and Bauti tucked it away in his mind for use later.

"So you're Denari Lai." He did not phrase it as a question.

"I was. No longer. The Order now seeks my death as well as Makari's."

"So you're really just protecting yourself, not her."

Ashai tensed, and Bauti readied himself for a strike. No doubt the man could kill him before he could even reach his sword, but the attack never came. Ashai took a deep breath, uttered something in Nishi'iti, and shook his head.

"I am protecting someone I believe should live and rule this nation. If you know about Denari Lai, then you know we swear not to harm innocents. I believe, despite what my God has told me, that Makari should live."

"Then why are you dragging her around the streets of the city instead of keeping her safe in the palace?"

He stepped forward, fists bunched. Did Ashai think him a fool?

"Because her father was not safe in the palace, so why would I believe she will be?"

This time, Bauti let emotion flicker on his face, the guilt at having failed Abadas punching through his mask long enough that he knew the assassin had seen. He expected a cruel smirk or at least a sadistic grin, but Ashai did neither. He just stood and stared, face impassive.

"Captain Bauti, the palace is compromised." His voice was softer than Bauti expected, almost comforting, as if Ashai knew the pain he felt. "Even the entire Royal Guard cannot protect her if she goes back there right now. Out here at least she has a fighting chance."

Bauti wanted to argue, to scream that he was wrong, but the princess didn't give him the chance.

"He's right, Marwan." Her use of his first name made his throat tighten. "Right now, the best way for me to stay alive and have some hope at assuming the throne is to stay hidden until you can find and kill the other Denari Lai. If he doesn't know where I am, he cannot kill me."

Bauti fought down all the protests that jumped to his tongue, knowing they were all moot. Makari was right, and he could not let his personal feelings put her in danger. Not again.

Sighing deeply, Bauti inclined his head to his princess. "Of course, Princess. I suppose I should call you Queen now."

Ashai held a finger to his lips. "Let us not dwell on titles for people trying to stay hidden."

Irritated as it made him, Bauti knew the assassin was right again, though he would not let the man know it.

"Who rules in my absence?" Makari asked, ignoring Ashai's warning to be careful. Bauti grinned as the Nishi'iti rolled his eyes.

"Minister Tan rules by royal decree. Your father signed a writ before his death naming Tan Protector until you return."

Ashai raised an eyebrow and the princess narrowed her eyes.

"Something sounds wrong about that," said Ashai.

"I agree." Makari nodded. "My father never trusted the Minister of Spies. He told me so many times. Why would he appoint him Protector instead of someone like Celani or Renard?"

"Never trust a spy," Ashai said.

"Nor an assassin," Bauti added, satisfied to see Ashai flinch. "They're cut from the same bolt of cloth, to use a term you might understand."

"I'm impressed, Captain. You used some big words. Try not to—"

"Enough!" Makari put her fists on her hips and fired bolts of blue lightning from her eyes. "This kind of bickering won't get us anywhere. Let's focus on the immediate priority: getting out of the city."

Ashai held Bauti's gaze just long enough to be clear he wasn't backing down, then looked away.

"You're right. We need to find a way to get to the Sixth Guild."

Bauti almost burst, managing only to keep his voice to a low rumble, like thunder in the distance.

"The Sixth Guild? Have you lost your mind? They'll kill her. They hate the royal family!"

Ashai paced the room, his back to Bauti. The captain thought briefly about going for his weapon, running the man through, and apologizing to Makari later. Her smoldering blue glare deterred him.

"Not true, Captain," Ashai said, turning around to face him. "They only hate Abadas. His cruelty hit them harder than anyone not from my country, but his daughter treated everyone with kindness and compassion. The Guild has already promised to get her out of the city, but we need to find a way to get to them without your soldiers catching us."

"I could order them out of this area," Bauti offered, resigning himself to getting Makari out of Dar Tallus. "Have patrols reduced to old levels."

Ashai shook his head. "They'd suspect something, and it would cue our second Denari Lai. We'll need to get you a disguise and try to sneak out of here to someplace less covered in swords and armor."

"I kind of stand out," Bauti said. "And none of your clothing will fit me."

Ashai looked him over, holding up a thumb as if measuring him for a cut of silk or cotton.

"You are quite large, but not unmanageably so. Stay here and I'll find you something."

He moved for the door, Makari dousing the lamp as he did.

"You mean you'll steal it." Bauti let the disgust he felt drip from his words like sewage.

"I prefer to call it long-term borrowing, Captain. But to ease your troubled conscience, we'll leave something in payment if you like."

And with that, he melted out the door into the night. Makari followed him before Bauti could stop her.

Sighing, the Captain of the Royal Guard crept out into the night.

CHAPTER TWENTY-EIGHT

The night sky over Dar Tallus split open like an overripe fruit and poured rain on the three fugitives just after midnight. The rain started with a deluge, sheets of water blowing sideways in their faces, blinding them to the streets and alleys around them. A few minutes later, it tapered to a soft, steady downpour. It switched back and forth for an hour, Ashai leading them from doorway to doorway, finding as much shelter as possible as they worked their way west.

Makari found herself shivering after the first downpour, soaked to the bone, the chill autumn air penetrating her clothing and her skin. Her clothes clung to her body, making it difficult to move and impossible to do so quietly.

A few minutes after they left hiding, Ashai slipped inside another tailor shop and emerged with a thick, wool cloak large enough to cover Captain Bauti. It didn't disguise the clinking noise of his armor and weapons, but the rain was enough to cover that, and the cloak made him look like a commoner, albeit a very large one. As long as no one got close, the disguise would work.

For her part, Makari spent most of the time keeping her mind off the cold and the rain by trying to sort through her feelings for the men accompanying her.

She wondered if she could really trust either of them. The answer was easy with Ashai. No. He'd lied to her from the beginning. For all she knew he was lying now and planned to kill her at his first opportunity.

She did think he loved her, in a strange, twisted way. He'd forsaken his God for her, to hear him tell it. But could she believe it? She decided she could not.

Bauti was a bit harder puzzle to solve. She didn't doubt his love for her, nor his loyalty. He'd proven time and time again that he would give his life for her if needed, and he'd shown his love in more ways than one.

But that love was the wrong kind, a selfish love that put into doubt her ability to trust his judgment. Would he obey her when she most needed him, or would he place his own needs before her, placing her and the kingdom in danger? His poor judgment had already cost her father's life.

She wiped at a mix of rain and tears on her cheek. Her father was gone to the Five Gods, stolen from her before his time. He hadn't been perfect, she knew. He'd sought to hide his cruelty and other faults from her, but Makari saw some. Her sources throughout the government told her things Abadas had sought to deny her, and she knew he'd been a brutal leader at times. Perhaps more than she'd realized. And perhaps crueler than she could imagine.

Yet despite all that, she also knew he, more than anyone else, loved her. A father's love for his daughter was more brilliant than the finest jewel, more valuable than all the gold in the foothills, and more powerful than the power of the Denari Lai.

True, her father had some blemishes, but she'd valued him for no other reason than the love he felt for her. Unselfish, simple, strong.

Now, with him gone, she felt alone and small, dwarfed by the world and surrounded by men whose feelings for her were far more complicated and harder to trust.

It was enough to make her want to hide. But princesses didn't hide, not when their people needed them.

Finally, as they neared the outer perimeter of the cordon, the rain pulled back to a misty drizzle, allowing them a moment's respite. Ashai pulled them into a darkened alley.

"We have to be careful now. The power of Nishi can disguise us to a certain degree, but anyone who looks too close or too long will see through it. Draw as little attention to yourselves as possible. The first checkpoint should be about a minute down that street. Stay close to me, no more than arm's length. With any luck, we will be through the checkpoint quickly."

He led them back out into the street just as a squad of Royal Guard stepped out of another alley. Everyone froze, shocked to find the other party in the streets. Makari's heart thundered in her chest, and the tension crackled like a lightning.

The patrol moved first, fanning out and forming a semicircle to block their route down the street. At first she thought Ashai would reach for his dagger, or that the soldiers would charge them. Either would have ended in disaster. As good as Ashai and Bauti were, the odds were ten against three. Her party would not fare well.

A slender officer she'd never seen before took a step toward them, his hand on the pommel of his short sword. Ashai's fingers brushed over the handle of his dagger where it hid under his cloak. Closing her eyes, Makari said a silent prayer to the Five Gods to prevent violence and protect both men.

To her surprise, Bauti stepped forward and drew back the hood that hid his face. He let the front of his cloak fall open, revealing his chain mail and sword underneath.

The Royal Guard soldier stopped in his tracks, his eyes opening wide. He snapped a salute to his chest, then stiffened as his eyes found Makari and Ashai.

Bauti wasted no time turning on them. "Lieutenant Gartka, I'm glad you found us. We're trying to stay alive long enough to get back to the palace. I found the Princess and the Finance Minister. Has the assassin been captured yet?"

In response, the soldiers drew their weapons, the Lieutenant stepping between Bauti and Ashai, sword leveled at Ashai's chest.

"The assassin is right here, Captain. Lord Tan declared Minister Ashai to be an assassin, and says he's responsible for the king's death."

Bauti whirled, drawing his own sword and pointing it at Ashai, putting himself between the assassin and Makari.

"I should have known. Seize him!"

The soldiers ringed Ashai, and to Makari's surprise, her former betrothed simply shot Bauti a fiery glare and raised his hands. For some reason she'd expected him to fight, to kill at least a few of the Royal Guardsmen.

Gartka eased behind Ashai, slipping the Denari Lai dagger from his waistband.

"Just where Lord Tan told us we'd find it, Nishi'iti bastard!"

He punched Ashai in the small of the back, dropping him to his knees. He pulled back his sword hand to run Ashai through, but Bauti stopped him with a hand on his elbow.

"He is more useful to us alive."

Gartka looked confused. "But Lord Tan told us to kill him as soon as we find him. He's too dangerous to lock up."

"To whom do you answer, Lieutenant, the spymaster or your commander?"

Gartka straightened and sheathed his sword. His men did not let their readiness flag, though, eyeing Ashai like a cornered snake.

"Lord Tan rules Pushtan right now, Captain. I—"

"Tan only rules until Princess Makari returns. Who do you suppose that is?"

He pointed at Makari. She stood taller and cleared her throat, fixing Gartka with her most powerful stare.

"Lord Tan no longer sits the throne." It felt good to say it, like pure power pumping through her body. Like she was taking her natural place in the order of things. "In fact, he and I will be having an in-depth discussion of how that writ came into existence, since my father did not trust our Master of Spies enough to inform me of this promotion.

"Captain Bauti is right. We will need this killer alive, because there is a second assassin. We must find him, and Ashai is our only hope of doing so before he kills again. Do I make myself clear?"

Gartka swallowed hard and nodded. Makari fought back a grin. She'd been out of control long enough. It was time to take command. Still, she gave Bauti an icy look and waved him to her side as his soldiers bound Ashai's hands behind him.

"We will discuss this decision back in the palace," she whispered. "Assuming I live long enough. Your orders were to help get me out of the city, not place me back in the assassin's sights."

Bauti didn't look at her, keeping his eyes on their new prisoner.

"Trust me, Highness. I'm trying to keep you alive."

Ashai didn't struggle, allowing the men to bind him and gag him, showing no emotion at all as they searched the rest of his person for weapons.

"I suppose I don't have much choice, do I?" she muttered to Bauti.

Once Ashai had been bound and gagged, Bauti stood before his men.

"You have before you the only Denari Lai ever captured alive, but one remains loose in the city. We've already survived one attack by this other assassin, and he will no doubt try again to kill Makari. When that time comes, you must kill him first. Or at least give your own life trying. She is our nation's hope now, its right and true ruler. Without Makari, chaos will reign."

He lowered his voice, looking around the street furtively.

"We must get her quietly back to the palace without drawing attention to her or our other prisoner. Princess, raise your hood and stay in the middle of our group. Keep your head down and your voice low. Maybe we can keep you hidden long enough to get back."

He locked eyes with Gartka. "Back alleys and side streets, Lieutenant. And quickly."

Gartka nodded and formed up his men.

As they started out down the street, Makari glanced at Ashai. His expression had changed, going from angry and red to pale and nervous. Perhaps even frightened. He looked at her, but did not make eye contact, as if he didn't see her, his gaze distant.

Behind his back, his hands had started to shake.

Ashai felt the tremors in his hands as they started moving and he hoped for the first time that they'd actually get back to the palace soon. He'd channeled power for hours, disguising them during their move. He'd drained more than expected from his well of power. The longer he went without renewing his magic through prayer, the more helpless he would be when the second assassin showed up to finish his job. And even with Bauti, eleven soldiers would not be enough to stop the killer. They'd probably not even see him before he hit. They'd just see Makari drop dead, a dart in her neck or a dagger in her back.

He'd thought about fighting them, about trying to get him and Makari away and off to safety, but had decided not to risk it. Had he been wounded, his ability to protect Makari would have been reduced, putting her in more danger than she was, and he couldn't allow that. Still, he would deal with the traitorous Bauti as soon as he could. The man had given his word to his princess, and again betrayed her to do what he thought was right.

Sort of like Ashai had betrayed his God, trusting his own judgment over Nishi's.

He had trouble focusing now, his mind wandering to a place of self-loathing and pity. He'd lost so much in just the last few hours. Makari's love for him had disappeared like a candle being blown out, and he had only himself to blame. He'd lied to her, and had a hand in her father's death. Unforgiveable.

The tremor spread for a moment up through his elbow and into his shoulder. He disguised it as a shiver from the cold, not wanting the soldiers to know he weakened, that he was vulnerable.

Even that—his encroaching impotence—was his fault, the result of betraying Nishi and the Chargh Lai, both of whom had saved him from a pointless life of crime and poverty. He'd broken his vow to the order, a group he had considered family. Closer than family, he'd thought—at least the order wouldn't have left him on a street corner in the middle of winter for someone else to find and raise, something his own family had done.

And yet he'd betrayed his Denari Lai family, all for his own selfish reasons.

He could have survived that, though, had it not been for losing his God, as well. Ashai had spent enough of his life in solitude that he could have gone on without his brothers from the order. A Denari Lai assassin was an autonomous unit, trained and sculpted to go his entire life without contact with his fellow Nishi'itis. As long as he could connect with his God's love and power, a life alone in the wilderness would have been happy for him. Nishi made everything acceptable, loving his children and keeping them safe so long as they served him faithfully.

But Ashai hadn't done that. He'd turned his back on the God who had given him life and everything that went with it.

Ashai was the worst kind of betrayer.

He shook himself, driving the thought away. Now was no time for guilt. He still believed, perhaps more than ever, that Makari deserved to live. Killing her would have violated his oath to Nishi to spare the lives of innocents. He merely needed his God to see that, and had to trust that he would.

Ashai had to focus on staying alive long enough for that to matter.

He wiggled his hands in their bindings, using magic to loosen the knot until he knew he could slip out when the time came. It took only a trickle of magic, barely enough to feel, but it used precious power from an already emptying pool.

Still, the rope was loose now. Maybe it was worth it.

Now he needed the right time. He'd kill Bauti first, then Gartka. That would leave the soldiers leaderless and confused. Then he would fight his way out of their midst and if needed, drag Makari to safety. He didn't like the idea of using the Sixth Guild to escape—robbers and cutthroats were less trustworthy than spies—but he knew for sure the palace was not safe. They'd be better off taking their chances with the crooks.

Bauti led them into a narrow, dark alley, reeking of excrement and filled with skittering rats. Ashai readied himself to make his move. The space was too narrow for the Royal Guard to effectively use their swords. They'd be reduced to using daggers and fists, and in that fight, Ashai had a distinct advantage.

They'd gone perhaps ten paces into the alley when Bauti stopped, raising his hand for his men to do the same. Gartka joined his captain immediately.

"Is something wrong?"

Bauti responded with a smashing blow to the lieutenant's jaw, snapping his head back. He followed with a gut punch, doubling Gartka over, then a knee to the face. Gartka hit the cobblestones already out cold.

For a moment, no one moved. Then the men figured things out and went for Bauti.

Ashai moved lightning-quick, slipping his bonds, and grasping his magic. He kicked the nearest man in the back, sending him sprawling. Time seemed to slow down. He saw what each man was going to do before he did it, and responded with cat-like speed and accuracy. With only fists and feet, he felled two soldiers before they even realized he wasn't tied up.

He and Bauti moved like predators in the dark, confined space, easily besting the less capable, now confused soldiers. In a few seconds, only three remained standing, daggers drawn. Bauti faced off against one, while the other two went for Ashai. They never saw the princess coming from their left until she drove the pommel of a dagger into one man's temple. Ashai picked up his dagger and turned to face the other.

The soldier lunged, sweeping his blade at Ashai's mid-section. Ashai knocked it away with his own dagger, then kicked the man in the groin.

When he bent over, Ashai clubbed him on the back of the neck, right below his helmet, with his elbow. The man fell unconscious.

Bauti had finished his man, and the three fugitives took a moment to check themselves over.

"No one hurt?" Bauti asked.

"Only them," Ashai said, pointing to the unconscious soldiers.

"I hope you didn't kill any," Bauti said. "They were only following orders."

Ashai shrugged. "I may have broken one man's neck, but the rest will just wake up with headaches."

"Then we'd better get going," Makari said. "Before they do wake up."

Ashai paused only long enough to slip his dagger into its sheath at the small of his back.

"I thought you'd turned on us, Captain," Makari said. "That I was going to have to discipline you for disobeying. Good thinking."

Bauti looked hurt. "Not all men break their oaths."

Ashai ignored the jibe and concentrated, listening with his magic-enhanced hearing. He held up his hand for silence, and the other two stopped talking. In the distance he heard footsteps. Marching, with mail and weapons clinking and clanging.

"Patrol coming," he said. "About two blocks away."

"How do you ... never mind." Bauti started off down the alley. "I don't want to know."

Ashai was tempted to keep his grip on his magic, knowing it could well warn them about approaching trouble. But he would need the tiny remaining amount more if they had to fight again, especially against the second assassin, so with a sigh, he let go of Nishi's power and jogged after Bauti and the princess, his hands shaking as he ran.

He needed to pray soon, but he remembered what had happened the last time he'd done it, and decided it could wait.

Something occurred to him as he caught up to the other two.

"Who told you where to find my safe house?"

Bauti eyed him sidelong. "Tan. His spies located you and he told me."

Pieces of a gigantic puzzle fell into place in Ashai's mind. The Chargh Lai had seen him during his prayer, and had told the second assassin: Tan. It all fit. Tan had access to almost unlimited information, and could easily have known who Ashai was all along. Tan had missed the wedding, allegedly sick in his chambers, but now he was well enough to run a nation. And Tan had used the Chargh Lai's information to send Bauti and his men after Ashai and Makari.

And the Chargh Lai was tracking him through his power, through his connection to Nishi.

He should have known, should have seen it. He'd let his love for the man ruin his judgment. His loyalty to the man who had saved him had shrouded him in a fog of denial, making it impossible to see even that which had been right in front of his face all along.

"I'm a fool," he muttered.

Bauti nodded. "If you think you can keep her safe better than I can, then a fool you are."

"That's not what I mean. I know who the second assassin is."

Bauti stopped at the near end of the alley, peering out into the street. When he pulled back his head, his brow was wrinkled with concern.

"You think it's Lord Tan?"

"I don't think it," Ashai answered. "I know it. And he's tracking me through my connection to God. We need to get inside. There's something I need to do."

Bauti studied him a moment, then nodded. "Follow me."

Bauti led them down a series of twists and turns, ending in yet another alley. But this one was cleaner, lacking the huge, stinking trash piles Ashai had grown used to, the only obstruction a stack of three crates outside a narrow, wooden door. Light seeped out from around the wood, inviting and warm through the misty rain.

The captain knocked once, and someone scrambled inside. Something crashed, and a man's voice spit out a curse. A moment later, the door opened.

In it stood a stooped, wrinkled old man, with wispy white hair and eyes pale with age. He squinted at the three of them, then took a step back.

"Marwan. It's been a long time. I'd thought you'd never visit again."

"Hessig, I'm sorry for my neglect. But it was ..."

Ashai had never seen Bauti at a loss for words before, and it intrigued him. Who was this old man?

"Too painful, I know," Hessig finished for him. "Well, come in then, before someone sees you."

Hessig's flat was a tiny space, consisting of a small, brightly lit room with a table, two chairs, and a cot covered in ragged blankets and pillows that looked like they'd been used by Hessig's father. It had no windows, no kitchen, and as far as Ashai could tell, no privy. A small pantry took up the right wall, and from it, the old man pulled a flagon of wine and four tin cups, handing one to each. Ashai refused his at first, but the old man insisted.

"I know your God doesn't allow you to drink, but in this case I think you should make an exception."

"How did you know?" Ashai asked.

Bauti chuckled and patted Hessig on the back. "Hessig here was sniffing out Nishi'itis back when I was your age. He found more of your spies than anyone else I know."

"Back when the Master of Spies was focused on the right kinds of threats," the old man added, rolling his eyes.

Ashai took the cup and let Hessig pour. Thankfully, the old man went easy on him, doling out only a small portion. Ashai sighed. He would need something to drink if he was going to do what he'd come here for.

"So you know who Tan really is?" Bauti asked his old friend.

Hessig shook his head. "Never met the man, and you know I need to see him to know. Even then it's not exact. I knew your friend here—who used to be our Finance Minister, unless I'm getting rusty—is Nishi'iti, but I don't know much more. He's a guarded one, keeps his face neutral, so I'd normally guess he's a spy. Given recent events, though, I'd put him in a bit more sinister profession."

"He is what you suspect," Bauti said. "And so is Tan."

Hessig chuckled and handed Bauti a cup, pouring him twice as much as he had Ashai.

"Well now, it seems the rats are kicking the cats out of the palace. Abadas never did have a knack for choosing people around him."

As he handed Makari her cup, he bowed his head and lowered his voice.

"Majesty, excuse me if I miss certain formalities, but I'd hate for someone to overhear a foolish old man mentioning your name or title too loud."

Makari gave him a radiant smile and took the cup, letting him pour for her as much as he wanted.

"Do I know you, Master Hessig? You seem familiar."

"You were just a babe in swaddling when I left your father's service. I'd know you anywhere, but I'm shocked you have any recollection of me. No, on second thought, I should have expected that. You took your mind from your mother, thank The Five."

"Hessig once refused to identify a Nishi'iti in the palace because your father suspected them of stealing from the kitchen. Your father had him beaten and removed from his service to live in squalor here. Hessig had been a land-holding lord, but Abadas stripped him of all lands and titles. He had nowhere to go."

"Eh, I make do here," Hessig said. "Fifteen years and counting now."

Makari touched his hand lightly and the man practically glowed, his eyes brimming.

"Thank you for helping us, Hessig," she said. "I will not forget it."

Hessig inclined his head again, lingering that way this time, as if relishing the moment.

"We should move on quickly," Bauti said. "It's bad enough your father forced Hessig into this life, it would be tragic for him if a patrol found us here."

The old man shrugged. "My life is almost done anyway, Marwan. A few days less won't matter."

"The captain is right," Ashai said. "I need to do one thing, then we can move on."

He removed his boot and twisted the heel off, exposing the hidden wooden vial there. Bauti tensed, but Ashai waved him off and popped the stopper off the vial.

"Don't worry, Captain. This particular potion is for me. It would be quite harmless to Makari."

Taking a breath, he tilted his head back and poured the white powder into his mouth. It sizzled and popped as he took a gulp of the wine to wash it down.

The effect hit immediately, as the link to God's magic severed, cutting him off from Nishi, leaving him with whatever magic still resided in him. He shuddered, feeling even more isolated and alone than before. Prayer would hurt until the drug wore off, making it impossible to even attempt a renewal.

"What did you do?" Concern resonated in Makari's voice, surprising him.

"I suspect our whereabouts are being monitored through my link to our God's magic. That's how Tan knew where to send the captain and his men. This powder cuts me off from that link, making me impossible to track."

"It also makes you vulnerable," Hessig said. "Weakened."

Ashai nodded, impressed by the man's knowledge. "For now. It only lasts a day. After that, I can pray again and renew my strength. Of course, the Denari Lai will know where I am the moment I do."

Makari and Bauti looked at one another.

"Promise me one thing, Captain Bauti," Ashai said.

Bauti studied him with cool, blue eyes. "What?"

"If we don't make it out before this wears off, and I become a danger to her, kill me."

Bauti gave him a long, hard look. "Done."

CHAPTER TWENTY-NINE

Tan sat back in the cushioned chair in front of his fireplace, putting his bare feet up on an ottoman and warming them before the flames. Ache clawed its way up from the arches of his feet, into his ankles and halfway to his knees. His calf muscles knotted, bunching and grunting in pain, as if they had their own voices to lift in protest.

It had been a long time since he'd taken to the streets for any reason, much less in the thin, light slippers of a Denari Lai. Oh, he'd kept himself in shape, certainly, as much as he could without drawing attention to himself. But nothing substituted for actual work in the field, moving along the cobblestones, tiled rooftops, and back alleys of Dar Tallus or any other city.

Still, he'd done better than he might have expected during his foray outside the safety of the palace, moving well through the city and managing to fight decently for one so long out of practice. Not as well as he would have done in his early years, when he'd first come to the city, fresh out of Denari Lai training. But well enough.

And he'd managed to kill Abadas, even if Makari had gotten away. All in all, it might have worked out for the better. With Makari on the run, he had the chance to show the resolve of the Nishi'iti people and the Denari Lai. By waiting and killing Makari later, he would not only show that his order and his nation would not give up, but create two separate traumas for the Pushtani people. First they lost their king, an event known to leave entire nations directionless and weakened.

But Makari's disappearance offered the Pushtani people hope, a candle in the window of the royal palace, left to guide them back together. People would rally around her as soon as she was found, emotions rising like a wave, lifting the citizens up on a kind of euphoria. Then he could kill her, cutting her throat in front of advisors, families, and nobles. Her blood would harden and become the rocks on which the wave of emotion would crash, smashing hope into bits.

Tan grinned and lifted a cup of Slevonian White, letting its bouquet dance upon his nose, preparing to savor the fine fluid's trek across his palate. As the cup touched his lips, someone knocked on the door. He lowered the cup to the table and looked over his shoulder.

"Enter," he called.

A lone Royal Guardsman poked his head inside, looking apologetic.

"My Lord Tan, a messenger. He says he comes from the old city?"

Tan inhaled sharply. That hadn't taken long.

"Send him in."

Tan was expecting one of his spies, so when a lieutenant from the Royal Guard entered, blood running down his temple and his left arm in a sling, Tan rose and hid his surprise.

"Please, lieutenant, take a seat. You look badly injured. What happened?"

"My Lord Tan." He inclined his head, but made no move to sit. "I am Lieutenant Gartka. I bring disturbing news. Captain Bauti has turned."

Tan raised his eyebrows. "What do you mean 'turned,' Lieutenant?"

"My squad was on patrol in the western sector, near the Gate of the Setting Sun when we encountered three people, all cloaked and looking suspicious. One of them was Captain Bauti, who claimed to have captured Minister Ashai and rescued the princess, both of whom were with him.

"But as we tried to get them back to the palace, Bauti and Ashai attacked us and got away, taking Princess Makari with them."

He kneeled and lowered his head.

"I'm sorry, My Lord. We failed."

If there was one thing Tan had learned during his time in Tabi Ge Nishi and his training as a Denari Lai, it was that salvation—real or imagined—created one of the fiercest brands of loyalty he'd seen. So he limped to Gartka, placed his hand on the man's blood-matted brown hair, and smiled.

"You do not fail unless you quit. Now rise and face your new responsibilities, Captain Gartka, Commander of the Royal Guard."

The look on Gartka's face as he stood could have illuminated even the darkest chamber, and Tan knew he'd gambled right. This man was his now.

"My Lord, surely I do not deserve this honor."

"I will determine who deserves what, Captain. And I say a man with the courage to come before me and admit a temporary defeat is worthy of command. That is, assuming your defeat was, in fact, temporary?"

Gartka straightened to attention. "Yes, My Lord!"

"Good, then get out there and lead the Royal Guard until the princess is back in the safety of the palace."

"And the other two, My Lord?"

Tan pretended to think about his answer a moment. "Kill them both."

Gartka saluted and strode from the room, a full inch taller than he'd been when he entered.

Tan returned to his comfortable chair, putting his feet up again and taking a long drink of the bitter, white wine. He'd never thought much of sweeter wines, preferring the harsher, tarter tastes of dry wines. Life wasn't always sweet, and bitter wines seemed truer to the nature of the world, and the nature of his enemies.

He knew the Royal Guard would not find the trio again. With both Ashai and Bauti leading, they would disappear into the fabric of the city, indistinguishable from any other thread woven in. He could not keep the gates sealed forever, for commerce would falter and the people would soon rebel. He needed to remain in control at least until Makari was dead. Then it would not matter who ruled Pushtan—the empire would topple.

So it would be up to him to find the three fugitives, either through his spies or through his … other methods. Since his spies had been silent so far, he knew what he had to do.

He set the cup back on the table and moved into his bedchamber, closing and latching the door behind him. He'd gone to great lengths to be sure this room was secure, with no way for anyone to spy on what he did here. Holes had been sealed, walls covertly thickened and the craftsmen discreetly disposed of. He'd even placed subtle magical wards around the room to alert him should anyone try to eavesdrop.

No one ever had, but he could never be too careful.

He retrieved the three jewels from a secret compartment in his wardrobe, kneeled, and placed them in a row on the floor before him. Both the diamond representing Ashai and the oval representing Makari still glowed bloody red, marking those who still needed killed. The round gem representing Abadas, however, had turned black as coal, marking the end of the king's life, and rendering the gemstone no more than a simple, pretty rock. Tan pushed it aside, as it would do him no good now.

Taking Makari's jewel in one hand and Ashai's in the other, Tan marveled at the ambient warmth radiating from them. To anyone but a Denari Lai, they would feel cold and lifeless, but he could feel the lifeblood of Nishi's power pulsing in them, making them feel like embers in his palms.

Hugging the stones to his chest, Tan turned his face up toward heaven and prayed, hoping the Chargh Lai would hear him. He'd never initiated contact this way before. Always in the past, his mentor had contacted him during prayer or once in a dream. This method was theoretical only, and counted on the Chargh Lai to be in prayer at the same time, the connection of the gems boosting Tan's power enough to contact his mentor. Tan possessed neither the strength nor the skill to enter the other man's dreams, so he had to count on this to work.

At first, nothing happened, other than Tan feeling the rejuvenating power of magic pumping through him. The pain in his feet and legs disappeared, replaced by a warm, relaxed sensation, as if he'd just gotten a rubdown.

The link renewal was exhilarating, and he reveled in its cleansing, purging feeling, but he needed more. Without help from the Chargh Lai's ability to track Ashai through their connection, he knew he had little chance of finding the other assassin at all.

He waited, even after he no longer needed more magic, but still nothing happened. He was about to give up when the Chargh Lai appeared in his mind, a larger-than-life version of the man who had trained him all those years before.

The Denari Lai leader looked exactly as he had when he'd trained Tan, though that was likely a trick of Tan's mind, drudging up the newest memory he had of the man. Full, round cheeks and an ample chin belied the cold, deep brown of his eyes, and his broad shoulders seemed fit to carry the weight of the Nishi'iti people, as they so often had.

Words were not possible in this medium, so the Chargh Lai communicated in a series of images. The first showed Ashai and Makari fleeing the safe house where Bauti and his men had failed to capture them. The second showed brief snippets of the fight where Ashai had tapped into Nishi's magic to defeat the Royal Guard patrol.

That was crucial. The more Ashai tapped into the power of Denari Lai magic, the easier he was to track, so the last image punched Tan in the gut. It showed Ashai seated on a bench, an aura of magic around him as the power of Nishi washed through him. Then he ate something, took a drink, and the aura winked out. Then the entire scene went black, and the Chargh Lai faced Tan again.

Tan knew what the scenes had meant. Ashai had temporarily severed the link to his magic, a bold move, but also brash and foolish. It left him weak and vulnerable, unable to fight as more than a mere man. And by the time his link re-established itself, he would be suffering from the symptoms of Yanagat, the illness that overtook ones needing the touch of Nishi's magic to survive. It would not kill him, assuming he allowed the link to re-establish itself, but he would be unable to win against Tan in a battle.

The Chargh Lai looked deep into Tan's soul, his iron gaze sending one very clear, very emphatic message: find him.

Then the Chargh Lai was gone and Tan stopped his prayer.

He rose and put the stones back in their hiding place. He knew what he had to do, as much as he didn't like it. He had to find them himself.

Which meant taking to the streets again.

His feet ached just thinking about it.

CHAPTER THIRTY

The fourth day of the rebellion dawned clear and cold in the foothills, silver sunlight spreading across the land and turning frost into sparkling diamonds, like the mines had spewed forth their own gems without a single slave lifting a pick or hefting a shovel.

Cargil had finally died the night before, his screams tapering first to sobs, then to whimpers, then to silence.

His had been a slow and agonizing death, one that left Pachat feeling sorry for the man in the end, and disgusted at how quickly good men and women turned into unholy monsters when revenge was an open door before them. Almost every miner and slave in the camp, even some who weren't Nishi'iti, had gotten their licks in. The Slave Master died missing fingers, toes, an ear, his tongue, and numerous other body parts, not to mention the ones Fooshi had taken that first night.

No one deserved to die that way, not even someone as horrible and evil as Cargil. It had turned Pachat's stomach, but when he'd tried to stop it, Jingsho had intervened. The slaves needed this, he'd said. They deserved a chance at revenge, and would turn on Pachat if he denied them that much.

Now Pachat wished he'd ignored the Wanao Lai, for by allowing the slaver's gruesome death, he'd taken part in the killing. He went to bed at night wishing he could wash the blood from his hands, blood that he knew would return the next day should the horrors continue.

They gathered now outside the once-abandoned tunnel, huddled together against the morning chill, breath steaming in front of their faces. Nearly 300 strong now, having been joined by slaves from nearby camps, people they'd not even known existed until a Wanao Lai soldier led them in the previous morning. Even using the now empty tents of the Pushtanis, they'd barely had enough shelter for them all, and now they gathered, waiting for word from Pachat, their reluctant leader.

Pachat glanced over his shoulder at the gaping darkness of the tunnel behind him. No one had been allowed inside since the first night of the uprising, Jingsho appointing ten slaves to guard it and keep people out. The weapons were gone, and he said he feared people leaving before the fight was done.

Even Pachat—the supposed leader of this rebellion—had not been allowed inside, though he'd gotten close enough to hear voices filtering out through the twists and turns.

A tense buzz filtered through the gathered throng as his people—his army as Jingsho had called them—anticipated word on going home. They all knew that the tunnel behind Pachat led to Nishi'iti, to freedom and the possibility of seeing their families again. Frankly, he was shocked none had broken for the opening yet, though some eyed it longingly, clearly eager to be gone from the land of their long-suffered hardships.

Jingsho stepped up beside him, his breath warm on Pachat's ear.

"Are you ready?"

Pachat shrugged. "Do I have a choice?"

He knew what the Wanao Lai wanted him to say, what their instructions were from their homeland. Word from their emperor, passed through the Wanao Lai, was simple and yet devastating. It would break their hearts, and cost many their lives.

"Nishi always gives us choices," Jingsho whispered. "It's up to us to make the right ones when the time comes."

Taking a deep breath, Pachat nodded and raised his hands for silence. The other slaves stopped their mumbling and listened.

"My friends! We stand here before God and the world free men and women, cut loose from our bonds, standing astride the chests of our one-time masters, knee-deep in their blood. We are no longer slaves!"

A cheer went up, but Pachat's heart didn't lift like he'd thought it would. Using words provided by the Wanao Lai didn't seem natural to him, like he was a puppet whose mouth was worked by the fingers of yet another master. Still, he went on as he'd been instructed.

"Behind me sits your road home, a chance to return to Nishi'iti and live again as free people of the One True God. Taking that tunnel means never again hearing the sound of a slaver's voice, never feeling the cut of their whip or the thud of their boots on our bodies. That tunnel leads to freedom and safety, but before you take it, I ask you to consider this.

"We already know we were not the only slave camps in these foothills. We found one another with the help of our Wanao Lai brothers, and in doing so, strengthened our numbers and our position. Even now a company of armed Pushtani Army soldiers marches toward us, bent on returning us to a life of slavery. If a company doesn't work, they'll send a platoon, after that a battalion if needed."

Some in the crowd looked at one another now, fear and uncertainty on their faces for the first time since ripping their freedom from the iron grip of their captors.

"So it's understandable that we all want to run through that tunnel and flee back to safety. Nishi sees this in our hearts and understands. He thinks no man or woman a coward for wanting to do so. None.

"It is our actions, not our thoughts, that define us to our God, and now he asks that our actions take a different route, one of his choosing rather than our own."

He paused to gather his thoughts. This would be the tough part. Jingsho put his hand on Pachat's shoulder to steady him, so Pachat gathered his strength and continued.

"Just as our two camps were unaware of one another, so are there other slave camps in these foothills that don't know of us. These are fellow Nishi'itis, held against their will much as we were, forced to labor in dangerous conditions, treated with cruelty and violence, held down, and stepped on by brutal and uncaring captors. There are dozens like Cargil out there, countrymen, all with their boots on the necks of our fellow Nishi'itis.

"Now our God asks us to help him free them. True, we could all flee into that tunnel and save ourselves, but Nishi and our emperor, Rinshai ho Nishi, ask us to delay our return to freedom and comfort. They ask us to march east and south, freeing slaves as we come upon them, sweeping like an ocean tide across Pushtan in a wave of righteous outrage and holy power.

"Our God and our Emperor ask us to take this fight to the Pushtanis until every last Nishi'iti slave is able to run down this tunnel to freedom, or better yet, to walk back across the border without fear of pursuit or harm because our oppressors are too broken to follow. God asks us to free our people, so how can we turn our backs?"

The last part lacked the conviction he'd hoped to infuse into it, and the crowd's reaction was lukewarm at best. A few clapped, one or two cheered, but most looked frightened, ready to flee. These weren't soldiers or Wanao Lai. They were farmers and shop owners, millers and bakers. They were straw soldiers holding weapons, waiting for the enemy's fire arrows to set them ablaze.

"But we're just slaves," said one man from the front row. "How can we stand against trained Pushtani soldiers?"

Jingsho eased Pachat aside before he could answer and spoke to the crowd.

"We have brought help."

Out of the tunnel stepped a handful of men, perhaps a dozen, all dressed in the gray-and-black camouflage uniforms of the Wanao Lai, Suzaht in the lead. Bristling with weapons, they all carried themselves with the same cool confidence as Jingsho and Suzaht, appearing both outwardly calm and wound tight as bear traps at the same time. They fanned out behind their leader, arms crossed over their chests, and surveyed they assembled slaves.

Pachat gave Jingsho an irritated glare. The Wanao Lai had failed to mention this part of his plans, and Pachat didn't like being deceived.

"A dozen soldiers?" shouted one slave from the front row. "Even the mighty Wanao Lai will need more than twelve men to accomplish what you propose. We're talking about an entire Battalion of Pushtanis!"

Suzaht took Jingsho's place and stared out across the assembled slaves and rebels, his eyes shining with pride.

"But we have almost three-hundred men, all of whom will be trained by these dozen elite warriors. Surely what we have, when trained, will be able to face a company of Pushtanis. And our numbers will grow as we move camp to camp, scooping up more courageous men like yourselves, all of whom are being trained by Wanao Lai as we speak."

"Where is the Nishi'iti Army, then?" shouted another man, this time somewhere in the middle. "Why don't they come to our aid?"

Suzaht smiled, an expression that made Pachat want to vomit.

"All in due time, friend! The Army prepares to help us, but as you know, our military is small, and built mostly for defense. They cannot hope to defeat our enemy here without significant help from loyal Nishi'itis already behind enemy lines. Us."

Pachat surveyed the assembled crowd, finding only a few looks of skepticism. These men and women, he realized, had been abused and trampled on for so long now they were willing to listen to anyone who told them what they wanted to hear: that revenge was theirs for the taking.

As Suzaht and Jingsho went on answering questions from the rebels, Pachat felt less and less important, his misgivings about the whole thing making him feel like an outsider to the people he was supposed to lead.

He stepped back behind the Wanao Lai and slowly worked his way around to the back of the throng of slaves. When no one was looking, he slipped away and sulked back to his tent.

He knew what he needed to do. These men would take their justice —or their revenge, since the line between them was razor-thin—here, where their most egregious abuses had been inflicted. Here they would free friends and loved ones, kill the men who'd hurt them, and set fire to a realm that had oppressed them for year after year.

But Pachat had no one here to free, no one at all, and his justice was south, where Kendshi had died. He knew his road led there, and was one he must travel alone.

He pulled a rough wool blanket from his bed, spread it on the floor, and put his clothing in the middle of it. He would need to find food to take along, but the kitchen tent was on the way south out of camp, so he'd stop when he left.

He bundled his things, tied the blanket closed, and hefted it over his shoulder when the tent flap opened and Joppish stepped inside. The rail-thin slave had done well in the fighting, proving capable with a spear, but his split lip had reopened, and he walked with a limp. He paused in the doorway, then stepped inside and let the flap drop.

"What's this?"

"This war is not for me," Pachat told him. "I must find the man who killed Kendshi and spill his blood. Only when he bleeds to death at my feet can I go home."

"I'll go with you then. You can't do this alone, Pachat."

Pachat hugged the wiry man, patting the back of his head as if he were a child.

"I have to. And this is likely a one-way trip, my friend. The chances

I'll live are thin." Joppish pushed back and started to object, but Pachat silenced him. "Your place is here. Your wife is in one of these mines, Joppish. Find her and take her home."

Joppish wiped at his hook-nose and sniffled, turning away. But he nodded.

Pachat stepped past him to the door, then paused. "Don't let them lose sight of home, Joppish. These Wanao Lai have their own reasons, their own agendas in the war they're starting. A nation cannot survive on warriors alone. It will need farmers, smiths, tinkers, tailors, coopers, and more.

"That's who we are. We're not Wanao Lai, and we never will be. That's not Nishi's path for all of us."

And with that, he slipped out the door.

CHAPTER THIRTY-ONE

A shai brushed a cobweb from his face, wiping the sticky lattice on his shirt as he paced the confined space of the wine cellar. His hand shook, the tremor climbing up his arm and into his shoulder and neck. He reached the back wall, shelved and lined with bottles and casks, in four steps, then wheeled about and paced back toward the narrow flight of steps they'd come down an hour earlier.

"You're going to wear a ditch into the floor," Bauti griped. The big captain sat on a keg of ale, looking like he could use a mug of the stuff. "Sit down and wait."

Ashai ignored him. Bauti could never understand what he was going through, how his body and soul ached for the touch of Nishi's gift, a gift he needed. Depended on. Bauti could not feel the tremors and convulsing muscles that came from the gaping, dark chasm that formed the void where God's power once lived.

It was something one who'd never held magic's power then lost it couldn't understand.

So Ashai paced the room again, trying to ignore the growing weakness flooding through him. His mind wandered back several years, to a mountain slope in northern Nishi'iti, overlooking the tumbled ruins of an ancient temple. He remembered a shiner, with his glowing, silver eyes and crazed look, and he shuddered. The one-time Denari Lai had gone astray and been cut off from Nishi's gift, so he'd sought it in back alley magic, and that magic, while temporarily powerful, left an even larger hole in one's soul than Nishi's power, abusing the body and destroying the mind.

He'd killed the shiner, as was his assignment all those years ago. Killed him with pity in his heart. He could not let himself become that man, but if he couldn't renew his power without being discovered, he might not have a choice, at least not an acceptable one. He had to protect Makari, no matter the cost.

"It's been an hour." The princess stood in the shadows at the back corner of the tiny room, wrapped in the same cheap wool robe, her eyes piercing through the dim light, sweeping past Ashai to light upon her captain. Her lifelong guardian. "They should be here."

Bauti smirked. "If they haven't already sold us out to that lecherous Tan. These are criminals, highness. Thieves, cutthroats, purse lifters. Hardly trustworthy people."

"They're all we have right now," Ashai reminded him. Bauti shot him a reproachful glare. "The palace staff is compromised, including your Royal Guard, and anywhere we go, people are looking for us. The Sixth Guild is our only hope of escaping the city alive."

"He knows that." Makari still did not look at Ashai, keeping her eyes on Bauti instead. Her cold aloofness sliced at Ashai's heart, but he knew he deserved it. "The captain's never been known for his patience."

She offered Bauti a smile to prove she meant it in jest. Bauti barely grinned in return.

"It's not patience bothering me now," he grumbled. "It's sneaking around and running away. I should be in the palace, running my sword through Tan's traitorous heart. This dishonorable shadowy stuff is for spies and assassins."

His eyes swept over Ashai, but the assassin refused to let the man see him flinch.

"They'll be here soon," he said, pausing his repeated treks across the dirt floor. "Tisk wasn't lying. And the Sixth Guild has more to gain by helping you than by turning you in. They know they can trust Makari to live up to her word and pay whatever debt she has to them. But Tan would simply lie to their faces and send the Army to kill them."

"Typical assassin." Bauti didn't look at Ashai this time.

Makari shook her head at him, though, a gesture Ashai caught out of the corner of his eye that he wasn't meant to see. It made his heart leap with hope. She was defending him, so maybe he hadn't completely lost her yet.

Tisk had run across them as they snuck through the streets on the west side of the city, telling them word had gotten out about their location and that they needed to move quickly. The boy led them east, into a wealthier part of the city, and stashed them in the cellar before trotting off to bring help.

"I'll be back," he'd told them. "Sit tight. No one will look for you here."

Ashai had to agree—the hiding place was quite clever. So far, they'd stuck to poorer parts of town, where hiding was easy and shadows more common. Moving to a well-lit, less risky part of the city went against their established pattern, and would take time for Tan or the Royal Guard to figure out.

The wine cellar belonged to a wealthy merchant named Ulwood who sold fine spices and flavorings from around the world. He was a stout man, who apparently owed the Sixth Guild a great deal, for he never flinched when Tisk told him to shelter three fugitives and keep them hidden at all costs.

Now that merchant slept in the house above them, his snores occasionally slipping down to the cellar as he kept his equally portly wife awake with his rumblings.

"Are you sure I can't just kill Tan and take her back to the palace?" Bauti asked. Ashai was surprised at the almost friendly tone he took with him.

"You could try, but even I had a hard time fighting him, and I had the same training he did. Besides, even if you killed him, the Denari Lai would just send more and more until the princess was dead. We ... they never give up, and they never fail. It is God's will."

Bauti rose and stretched, a move as much of impatience as discomfort. "So we're supposed to stay on the run for the rest of our lives? Why keep her alive if she can never lead her people?"

Ashai had thought this through hours earlier and knew what he had to do.

"No, I need to reach the Chargh Lai and convince him to let Makari live. If I can show him her heart is pure, there's a chance he'll change his mind."

"I've never known a zealot to be swayed by reasoned argument," Bauti stated. "What if you cannot convince him?"

This was the part Ashai didn't like to think about. It would be his final betrayal, the one that would end with his eternal suffering.

"Then I'll have to kill him."

A heavy silence fell over the room, like a blanket soaked in oil, as all three found themselves lost in their own thoughts. Then footsteps thudded on the upstairs floor and the silence became tense.

Muffled voices came through the floorboards, and a moment later, the door at the top of the stairs opened, flooding the basement with bright light.

Ulwood tromped down the stairs, each one groaning under his weight. Behind him came the lighter, more nimble Tisk, a grin stretching his freckled cheeks as he looked over the group.

The third visitor swept down the stairs with the grace of a dancer, tall leather boots brushing the steps as if stepping on them was only a suggestion. Dressed in black silk, the man stood almost as tall as Bauti, taller counting the wide-brimmed hat complete with crimson plume. He was thin and wiry, without as much as an ounce of fat that Ashai could see. Black leather gloves covered both hands, the pinky finger on the left missing.

He scanned the room with eyes as dark as Ashai's above a nose that would have made a hawk proud. Thin lips curved up into a smile under a long, brown mustache. At his hip he carried a curved sword, silk streamers dangling from the pommel.

He didn't wait for introductions, but strode up to Makari, chest puffed out, smile dazzling white. Bauti stepped between them, hand on his own sword. The newcomer stopped and turned the same charming smile on the captain.

"My apologies, Captain Bauti." His voice sounded as smooth as the silk he wore. "I mean the princess no harm. In fact, I would help her escape this city and live long enough to rule."

Bauti didn't budge. "And you are?"

"Ah, forgive my poor manners." He palmed his forehead as if he'd committed some great sin of etiquette. "I am Tomar, Head of the Sixth Guild."

He bowed, sweeping the ornate hat off his head with a flourish, then stood and planted it back on with a twirl.

Bauti straightened, fixing the man with a glare. "We've been looking for you for—"

"A decade, yes I know. The late King Abadas—my condolences, Princess, though you'll find no tears shed by the Sixth Guild—had been trying to kill me for ten years." He rubbed at the stump where his left pinky should have been. "Obviously he failed, but his chief questioner made sure I'd never forget my brief stay in the king's dungeon.

"We hope to form a more ... cooperative relationship with Her Majesty."

Makari shouldered past her long-time protector and looked up at Tomar, eyes flashing. The thief lord actually stepped back, then dropped to a knee, something that made even Bauti gasp.

"Princess, the Sixth Guild is at your service. We have men ready to smuggle you and Captain Bauti out of the city and get you to a safe location until you can assume the throne."

Makari glanced at Ashai. "And what of him?"

Tomar shook his head. "We cannot take him. He is Denari Lai, and tied magically to his order. He endangers all of us, you most of all. We should ... be rid of him as soon as possible."

Ashai's first instinct was to kill the man on the spot, assuming he was able to do so in his weakened state. And if he did, it would use up the power he'd saved for fighting Tan. Besides, despite the man's preposterous proposal, Ashai found himself liking Tomar, even trusting him. For some reason, he didn't doubt the man's motives toward Makari.

To Ashai's surprise, the princess defended him.

"Ashai has protected me well. Dangerous as he might be, I am alive now because of him. I would not look kindly on any harm coming to him."

The tone of her voice left no room for argument, but apparently Tomar didn't listen well.

"Be that as it may, Highness, I cannot allow him to come with us. Should he use his magic, or even say a prayer, the second assassin will know."

Ashai stiffened. "How do you know that?"

Tomar shrugged and brushed off the question as if it was silly. "You don't live long in my business without superior intelligence. My sources, though, are my business."

He scratched the tuft of brown hair on his chin.

"You're forgetting one thing," Ashai said. "Without me, none of you will have a chance against a trained Denari Lai. I'm the only one who can fight him, and you know it."

Tomar considered a moment, then raised his hands at his sides. "Perhaps, but in order for that to matter, the second assassin would have to find her. Where we're going, he won't."

This time, Bauti stepped in.

"I wouldn't gamble on that. You know who the second assassin is, right?"

Tomar looked at the floor. "No, to this point, my people have not determined that."

"Tan," Bauti spat, like the name tasted bad. "The Lord of Mice and Birds, King Abadas's spymaster. If anyone can find her, it's him."

Tomar's handsome brown hair scrunched downward toward the elegant bridge of his nose.

"Now that is problematic, isn't it? It seems, then, that we are at an impasse. I cannot allow Ashai to endanger my people, and the princess cannot survive without him."

For a moment, the group stood, facing one another in silence. Then Tisk broke the ice.

"Why not knock him out?"

All five adults looked at the boy like he was crazy.

"He'll hardly be any good to us unconscious," Tomar scolded. "Put your head back on, Tisk."

"My head is on perfectly straight," the boy argued. Ashai liked the fire with which he made his point, but didn't relish the thought of being knocked out. "If you use Semuli Root on him, he'll be out cold, sleeping like a grandfather, and unable to use his power, pray, fight, or cause other trouble. When you need him, you use a little Slevonian red pepper and he'll be wide awake in no time."

"What are you talking about?" Bauti asked.

"It's quite ingenious, actually," said the spice merchant. "In large amounts, Semuli Root is a powerful sleep potion, especially when mixed with wine or ale. Our Nishi'iti friend would sleep quite soundly for several hours. Slevonian red pepper, in addition to being delicious on chicken, is strong enough to jar a sleeping bear. One puff in his face and Minister Ashai will be on his feet, ready to fight."

Ashai had to admit, the plan had merit if the merchant was right. Sleeping deeply might even help him handle the lack of magic better.

As one, everyone looked at Makari, and in true form, she didn't flinch.

"Do it. And lock him up when we get there, just to be safe."

"Very well," said Tomar, looking to Ulwood for the spices. "Our next stop will be Sixth Guild's stronghold. Princess, I hope we can count on your discretion about its location?"

For the first time in hours, Makari smiled. "Master Tomar, if you get me safely out of the city, I'm likely to forget a great many things, the location included."

CHAPTER THIRTY-TWO

I t turned out the Sixth Guild had been hiding all those years right under their noses. Or under their feet, more accurately, Makari thought.

The Semuli Root worked just as Tisk had promised, and with Ashai suitably limp and drooling, Bauti and the thief-lord lugged him to the back wall, the one lined with shelf after shelf of fine wines. Ulwood moved three wine bottles in quick succession, causing the shelves to slide a few feet left, revealing a tunnel opening. The rotund merchant ushered his guests inside, bid Tomar farewell, and watched as the shelves slid closed between them.

The short, dark tunnel led the group into the city sewers, a dingy, underground labyrinth of tunnels, most foul-smelling and damp. Fortunately, the guild had built wooden catwalks over the canals, allowing them to keep their feet out of the slop that gurgled and flowed through the tunnel's floor. Tisk led them through with the ease of someone who'd made the trip many times. The stink so permeated everything that Makari had to breathe through her mouth to avoid throwing up.

After a confusing series of twists and turns, they'd come to a brick wall that rose two-thirds of the way to the tunnel's ceiling. The wall looked out of place from the gray stones and rough, rocky ceiling of the tunnels, and had obviously been built many years later.

It took the three men some time to lift Ashai's motionless form over the wall, but once they did, Makari saw how the guild managed to live down here.

On the other side of the wall, sewage no longer flowed, the trench filled in with newer cobblestones, forming a kind of street or walkway. The unmistakable flickering orange of torch light guided them around a bend to find a passage completely lined with sconces, bright and clean.

Tisk then led them through more twists and around more corners until the stench fell behind and Makari could breathe through her nose again. Gradually, as they pressed on through the tunnels, people appeared. At first they were shifty men, tucked back into the shadows, watching them pass with beady eyes. One man dressed in rags actually stepped forward to block their path until he saw Tomar. Then he whistled ahead down the corridor, nodding respectfully to his leader.

Tomar, of course, recruited the man to carry Ashai with Captain Bauti, but he never asked anyone to take the captain's load. It was a subtle shot, but Makari saw it for what it was: a status play. Tomar's way of showing Bauti who was in charge down here. The captain didn't complain, though, lugging Ashai's left side in silence through the echoing passage.

To further secure his dominant position, Tomar walked beside Makari, offering her his elbow in an exaggerated show of courtesy designed to get under Bauti's skin. Makari had seen this kind of primping and preening her whole life, as lord after lord vied for her affection, each one looking to outdo the other.

If Tomar thought she was some silly girl to fall for his charms, well, let him believe it. It would give her an advantage when she needed it.

As they moved, population picked up, and soon she started seeing crude shelters built against the walls, or cave-like dwellings carved into them, blocked off by curtains. Occasionally, a child's dirty face would poke out long enough to survey the group, then duck back inside.

Before long, they found themselves walking down the main street of an underground city, surrounded by thieves, beggars, pickpockets, and con artists. Makari saw a few men she thought might be assassins, though not Denari Lai, and even some prostitutes who winked and flirted with Tomar as he passed.

"At first, just active guild members lived here," the thief-lord explained, speaking only to Makari, as if the two shared some great secret. "For years only the city's criminal element resided in these tunnels, keeping everyone else out through fear and violence.

"Then we realized that chasing away those who needed help only increased the chances someone would run to the Capitol Watch or to Captain Bauti here, and we'd all be dead by sunup. So we started welcoming the city's street dwellers, or some of them at least. Not all found us, and not all who did were welcomed."

He made a slicing motion at his throat.

"But before long, we had quite the city going down here. It's a rather nice arrangement. They get shelter, the guild gets use of their abilities as bakers, tailors, smiths, and so on."

As if to prove his point, they passed a shack built against the wall with the smell of fresh-baked bread pouring out. Makari's mouth watered and her stomach rumbled. She realized it had been a day since she'd eaten.

As if sensing her hunger, Tomar motioned to the baker, who brought them all chunks of a warm, dark bread.

"How do your people not get robbed every night?" Bauti asked. "They live behind cloth doors, surrounded by criminals day and night."

Tomar didn't even look at the captain, as if the question barely deserved an answer.

"Believe it or not, captain, we have our own honor code down here in Sixth City. No stealing from tunnel dwellers. Ever. It's a crime punishable by exile or death."

That silenced her protector, who didn't seem to know what to think about a society of criminals policing themselves.

At one point, Tisk broke off from their group without so much as a word, just disappearing into a crowd as if he'd never been with them at all. Tomar took over leading the group, but only for a few minutes before they came to a tunnel branching off to the right, guarded by two sly-looking men with staffs in their hands and long knives in their belts. Neither even acknowledged Tomar as the tall man strode past them, the rest of the group in tow.

Just inside this branch of the sewers stood a wall with a heavy iron-bound door. This too was guarded by armed men, but these two smiled and nodded as Tomar approached. One even opened the door for him, eyeing Ashai's motionless form suspiciously. He was a small man, wiry and rugged-looking, with hard, gray eyes and a wicked scar across his forehead.

"Ritter, see to it that Captain Bauti is given quarters suitable to one of his stature. Or as close as we can come."

The guard nodded, again locking his gaze on Ashai. "What about that one?"

His voice gurgled as if someone had cut his throat, the sound of blood running.

Tomar gave Ashai a once over, waving his hand dismissively. "Lock him up in our strongest cell."

"What about me?" Makari asked as two more guards showed up, taking Ashai's weight off the other two men.

Tomar made another overdone show of courtesy, bowing to her with a flourish of his feather-topped hat.

"Why you, princess, will be sleeping here, in my chambers."

He opened the door and motioned for her to enter. Light spilled out, and she caught site of dark wood and crimson rugs.

Makari raised an eyebrow, but didn't budge. He seemed to catch himself, straightening and clearing his throat.

"I will be taking up temporary quarters, of course. Something nearby, should you need me for anything. And I will station my own personal guards outside your door, in case any unwanted visitors show up."

Bauti, of course, was the first to protest, stepping forward, chest puffed, chin defiant.

"I should be close to the princess. I am charged with her protection, not your cutthroats and thieves."

Makari winced at the vitriol in his words, but Tomar wheeled and strode up to Bauti, jamming his finger at the man's chest.

"You might get away with demanding things in the palace or even on the streets, Captain, but down here you'd do well to remember who's in charge. And don't forget, you're travelling with the worst cutthroat of all, so take care in tossing out insults to the rest of us."

Bauti's hand fell to his sword hilt and instantly four more of Tomar's men materialized out of the shadows, clubs and long daggers ready. Tomar made no move for his weapon, but Makari had no doubt he could draw it quickly. Perhaps faster than Bauti.

She tried to step between them, but neither man would move. To her surprise, it was Ashai who broke the tension.

"Gentlemen, please, don't kill one another in your attempts to keep the princess alive. Neither of you would serve her well dead or wounded."

The assassin stood, though shakily, on his own, the guard beside him backing away with fear in his eyes. He knew what kind of danger he was dealing with.

All eyes turned on Ashai, several men stepping back cautiously, weapons trained on the new threat.

Makari's heart stopped when she saw her former betrothed, and her hand flew to her mouth.

Ashai had turned pale, his skin white as pearl, eyes sunken. His hands shook so hard it reverberated up his arms and into his shoulders, where she could see the cording of the muscles as he fought for control of his body. When he spoke, a thin stream of spit ran from the corner of his mouth.

"Fear not, friends. I have no magic, and my strength, as you can see, is gone. This is the effect of the drug I took to repress my magic. It will be several more hours before that drug wears off, and even then I am no threat to you. We both seek the same thing—to keep Makari safe so she can rule Pushtan."

As he finished, his strength fled him and he stumbled. Bauti was the first to his side, propping the assassin up under one arm.

"If you have no magic," Tomar asked, "how are you awake? The Semuli root should have kept you unconscious for hours."

"Sometimes things interact poorly," Ashai answered, easing away from Bauti to stand on his own. "In this case, the Semuli root must have interacted with the drug I took and wore off faster. Either way, I give you my word I'll harm no one so long as we're both fighting for Makari's life."

"The word of a Denari Lai means nothing here! As long as you live, you're a threat to all of us!" He motioned to his guards. "Kill him."

"He has fought valiantly to keep me alive," Makari found herself saying, almost against her own will. "And his order swears no harm to innocent life. Please don't harm him, at least. That little I ask."

Tomar paced, turning his back on both men, twirling one end of his moustache between thumb and forefinger. He paused and looked at Makari.

"Because the Sixth Guild, myself included, have profound respect for you, princess, we will let him live. But he will be locked up, and we will restrict access to his magic our own way."

Ashai's eyes narrowed at that comment, but he made no move to protest. Tomar turned to one of the guards.

"Fetch Grekkyl," he ordered. "Have her meet us at the holding cell."

The guard took off at a jog.

Tomar led them all to the outskirts of the underground settlement, past all the dwellings and structures, and into an otherwise empty passage lit only by a single torch. Here the sewer stench permeated, making Makari cover her nose and mouth with a handkerchief, though it didn't help as much as she'd hoped.

The passage ended in a cell, a small cave carved from the rock and closed off with iron bars as thick around as her wrists. Beside it stood a bent, gnarled old woman in rags, her eyes bright blue, hair little more than wispy strands of cloud falling from her head. With one hand, she leaned on a cane that looked as gnarled as she did.

She stepped aside as the guards tossed Ashai inside the cell none-too-nicely and slammed the door. The Denari Lai fell to the dirt floor, unable to stand on his own. He sat up, spitting sand from his mouth, wiping at his face with trembling hands.

"This one is dangerous," the old woman croaked. "You were unwise to bring him here, Tomar. He may be too strong for me."

Tomar stopped, towering over the old woman, but smiling fondly.

"Everyone, meet Grekkyl, resident hag of Sixth City, conjurer of magic, seer of the future, and healer extraordinaire."

"And your grandmother," Grekkyl reminded him. "You always forget that part."

"I don't forget, Grammi," Tomar said, his voice softening and taking on a tone of respect. "I choose not to mention certain things—"

"Oh nonsense, you forgot again. It's okay, we old people are used to being forgotten. Though it hurts for my own blood to call me a hag."

Tomar sighed a little too hard, but still smiled down at her.

"Can you keep him from using his magic?"

Grekkyl studied Ashai for a moment, her eyes gazing into the cell while one hand played with a brittle-looking strand of hair. She nodded.

"For now. He believes the drug he took blocks his magic, so he's keeping himself from using it. He could, though. If he wanted. If he realized its true source. I could slow him down, but I couldn't stop him. My magic is almost gone."

"Old fool," Ashai said from his cage. "Power comes only from Nishi, and Sai powder blocks my link to him."

Grekkyl laughed, a dry barking sound that echoed through the chamber like a raven's caw.

"Tell me, killer. If your God, the one you call all-powerful, gives you that power, how can a simple powder block it?"

Ashai hesitated, then stammered an answer. "As long as this powder is in my system, I cannot link to Nishi."

Grekkyl clucked and sat on the floor in front of the bars.

"Much to learn, much to learn. Stop trying to link to a God. Link to you."

Ashai closed his eyes, and Makari let herself hope for a second that it might work. But as he concentrated, the tremors shaking his body worsened. After just a few seconds, he let out a deep breath and opened his eyes. He wavered on his feet, unsteady and weakened.

"You're wrong. Nothing's there."

"Not wrong, boy. You're not trying hard enough. Your walls are too high, doors too thick. You must be able to see your own magic before you can touch it."

Without warning, Ashai collapsed on the dirt floor, his entire body shaking and twitching. His legs kicked. His arms pumped. His head pounded itself against the floor.

"Help him!" Makari shouted before she could stop herself.

Everyone turned and looked at her, the hag grinning from ear to wrinkled ear. Bauti gave his princess a disappointed look, and Tomar's brow had wrinkled, as if he didn't understand her. Still, none of them moved.

"Please, he's going to die!" Makari pleaded. "Help him!"

It was Grekkyl who finally acted, smacking a guard on the shoulder with her knobby old hand.

"Open door. Now, boy!"

The guard looked to Tomar, who nodded permission, then unlocked the cell door and tossed it aside. Grekkyl stepped inside, kneeled beside the quaking Ashai, and placed her hand on his forehead.

"He needs magic," she said. "His drug isn't wearing off fast enough. Princess is right: he'll die without it. I can help...."

She looked at her grandson, who rubbed his temples with his forefingers, looking at the dirt floor.

"He truly is our best chance to beat Tan," Bauti offered, voice quiet. "And he hasn't harmed Makari yet."

Tomar considered a moment longer before letting out an exasperated breath.

"Give it to him."

Grekkyl reached inside her shirt and produced a pouch, closed by drawstrings.

"Bring water," she ordered.

Tomar responded, scooping a ladle of water from a bucket on the wall. He held it out for his grandmother, who opened the leather pouch and poured a tiny amount of a fine, golden powder in.

Then she took the ladle.

"You must hold him still."

With Bauti holding his legs and Tomar himself holding his head, Grekkyl forced his mouth open and poured the contents of the ladle in. Ashai choked and sputtered, spitting out a good bit of the fluid. But then he swallowed hard and the hag stepped back.

"Let him go now. He'll calm."

The two men released Ashai and stood, both looking down at him. Then all three exited the cell, Tomar closing the door behind them. Ashai's tremors had softened already, his body mostly still but for twitching in his hands and feet.

"What did you give him?" Makari asked.

Grekkyl smiled, a sad expression on her wrinkled face.

"Some call it 'back alley' magic. Gives access to power within him for a few hours, allows him to rest and to fight if needed. If he lives."

"If he lives?" Makari exclaimed. "What does that mean?"

The hag patted her on the shoulder, gnarled hand lighting softly for an instant.

"Powder lets him see magic within him, but wears off quickly. Leaves him wanting more and more. And it consumes a little of him every time."

"And that can kill him?"

Grekkyl nodded. "Kills most. But Ashai is not most. Stronger. Smart. Don't worry about your love, child. He'll hold on."

Makari felt herself blushing and turned away.

"He's hardly my love anymore. He was sent to kill me."

When she turned back around Grekkyl was still staring at her. The hag nodded, then sat herself in front of the cage wall to keep an eye on Ashai.

"All go now. Will do what I can, teach what he will learn. Faith is strong in this one, and faith clouds judgment. But I will try."

"Come, all of you," Tomar said softly. "Eat and rest. Regain your strength and let my grandmother do her work."

He exited, the guards with him, but Makari lingered, staring at Ashai's now motionless form in the cell. She tried to put her finger on her feelings for him, but all she found was a jumble of emotions, tangled as a robin's nest.

A gentle hand on her elbow made her turn to find Bauti's blue eyes studying her, concern on his face.

"She'll take care of him, Highness. Let's go get some food."

With one last, wistful glance at the man who'd been her betrothed, Makari nodded and let Bauti lead her out of the chamber.

CHAPTER THIRTY-THREE

Hours later, Marwan Bauti stood outside the tiny cell, staring over the hag's balding head at Ashai. The assassin lay still, seizures stopped and breathing steady. But something else had changed about the man, and not in a good way. He seemed haunted, as if he were dreaming some great nightmare, but was helpless to thrash or spasm or even wake up.

Then, as if someone had dumped a bucket of cold water on him, Ashai sat bolt upright, arms flailing in front of him. Eyes still closed, he scraped his hands over his body frantically, brushing away imaginary bugs or spiders, then crawled to the back of the cell and sat with his arms curled around his knees and his face turned away.

"It won't be long now." Grekkyl didn't even turn to look at Bauti, keeping her eyes on the man in the cage. "His body and soul want to reject the new magic. He built his life around faith and this magic threatens that."

Bauti said nothing, concentrating on the assassin. He hated Ashai, but he knew they needed him. And they needed him full-strength.

Slowly, as if possessed by something dark and shadowed, Ashai lifted his face and turned his attention on the hag. Bauti gasped. Ashai's brown eyes now shone a brilliant gold, an unnatural kind of glow, alien and frightening.

"That's why they're called shiners." Grekkyl laughed and wiped her nose on her sleeve. "He will live now, and can use magic. But his master cannot track him."

Ashai jumped to his feet and rushed the bars at the front of the cage, grasping the iron in his hands and pressing his face into a gap between two cords of iron.

"What have you done to me? This is evil, a sin! Nishi will never forgive it. You've sentenced me to an eternity of suffering."

Grekkyl studied him for a moment, then shook her head and made a clucking sound. "Eternity was already decided. I saved your life. So you can save hers."

"You gave me Shiner magic! Once you use this, you never go back. It devours your soul."

"I only gave you a small dose." Grekkyl shook her head. "And will not give you another. I will teach you to use magic of your own. It's the only way you will live."

Ashai rattled the bars as if trying to break out, then paced to the back wall of the cell again. He put his forehead against the rock and grabbed his hair with both hands. His wail started low in his throat and rose like a wave, louder and larger until it crashed upon the cavern walls, ceiling, and floor. He screamed for several seconds, until Bauti almost had to cover his ears. Then he stopped and dropped to his knees.

"If you're done now, we should start." Grekkyl still hadn't changed positions, sitting on the dirt floor with her legs crossed, fiddling with a strand of her white hair. "You must learn. Or you must die. And if you die, the Princess dies."

Ashai didn't even look her way, staring at the dirt floor in silence.

"Very dramatic," Grekkyl said over her shoulder to Bauti. "Most just cry or sleep."

"He's had a rough day," Bauti joked, but the hag ignored him.

"What do you want?" she asked Ashai.

His reply rumbled like a far off storm. "Magic."

"What do you need?"

"Magic."

"What do you have?"

Hesitation. The assassin still stared at the floor, but he didn't answer right away. Bauti smiled. Grekkyl was growing on him.

When Ashai finally answered, even his voice shook. "Sin."

"Wrong, wrong, and wrong." The hag's voice bounced along like a child skipping through a meadow, ignoring the radically emotional tone of her student. "You want the girl. You need to see inside yourself. You have magic. No such thing as fake magic. Power is power."

Again a pause, but this time Ashai turned his head and glared at the old woman, golden eyes intense and focused. Bauti knew that if the bars were not there, he would rip Grekkyl in half. If she noticed, she didn't let on.

"You can't get true power from a powder," he said, lips curling in a snarl. "This brings only corruption."

"Where does power come from, then?"

This time his eyes narrowed, as if he felt cornered, like she was backing him into an emotional corner.

"Only from God," he answered.

Grekkyl jumped to her feet, surprisingly nimble for one so old, and clapped her hands over her head.

"Finally! Right answer! Not complete, but more right than wrong. See, I can teach you."

"You taught me nothing. Your questions are ridiculous."

Grekkyl moved to stand just a foot from the bars, hands clasped in front of her, eyes locked on Ashai.

"Then listen. Learn." She tugged at her ear. "I will teach you what you need to save the princess.

"Magic comes only from God, true. Gods. All Gods have power. They give some to people so people can do what Gods want. They try to give it to good people, but sometimes even Gods make mistakes. So some bad people have power."

"Nishi makes no mistakes."

"Nishi told you this?"

Ashai scrunched his brow, then shook his head. "The Chargh Lai."

"The Chargh Lai is wrong."

For an instant, Ashai's eyes flashed brighter and Bauti thought he might reach through the bars and wrap his fingers around the old woman's throat.

Grekkyl did not look afraid, though. Instead she smiled.

"See? You're close. Almost used magic. Your magic, inside you. Your powder blocks it. Your faith blocks it. Mine unlocks it like a key to a treasure chest.

"You know the Chargh Lai teaches you wrong about magic?"

Again Ashai smoldered, ready to melt. The hag went on.

"When you don't pray or use magic, you become sick, right?"

Ashai nodded reluctantly.

"Because I am out of touch with Nishi."

She shook her head, white hair flying. "Because the Chargh Lai made you need magic. Body. Mind. Soul. You need magic, the Chargh Lai gives magic that is already yours. Makes for very loyal subjects."

Ashai jumped up, face turning red, eyes burning like tiny suns.

"You lie! The Chargh Lai saved me. He is my bridge to God, and taught me everything I know."

"He taught you Makari is good?"

Bauti fought back a grin. She'd cornered him.

"No," Ashai said, eyes on the floor.

"But you know she's good?"

He nodded. Bauti crossed his arms over his chest. This was entertaining. Part of him felt sorry for Ashai. The man's whole world had been turned upside down, and Grekkyl was now turning it inside out, too.

Then he remembered why Ashai had come to Dar Tallus in the first place and his hatred for the man returned in a flash.

Grekkyl raised her hand, palm up, in front of her. She closed her eyes, jaw clenching, and focused. A tiny orange flame leapt to life just above her outstretched hand, dancing and wavering, its light lost in that of the larger torches.

Ashai stepped back, gold eyes wide. Grekkyl closed her fist and gave him a sad smile.

"You thought only Denari Lai used magic? Only Nishi'itis? Shiners?"

Ashai remained silent, so the old woman went on.

"My power was great once, but I let it wither. Rot. Like fine wood, it needs tending and care, and I was a young mother of a very … mischievous boy. No time. So I didn't practice and my power shriveled like a grape in the sun. But my body did not. No illness. Why?"

Ashai shrugged and turned away, his face a mix of confusion and hurt.

"Because I control my magic, not someone else. I used whenever I wanted. A lot. So I never needed it. You use power only when your Chargh Lai tells you to, and how he tells you. You believe magic can be taken from you, so you come to crave it.

"I know magic lives in me, just smaller now. I never miss it. Never crave. So I built strong mind to use or not use. And I used all of my power, in all the different ways. The Chargh Lai teaches you only one way to use it—to kill. Another shackle on your mind."

Ashai kicked at the dirt with the toe of his boot. "What does your powder do, then? How does it give magic?"

This time, Grekkyl gave a sly smile. "You felt it, didn't you? Inside you, like the fire at the middle of the world."

Ashai nodded slowly. "How?"

"Powder doesn't give you magic. Powder gives you freedom to use it. Frees your mind, soul, body. But it taints that power, and you come to need it. Without it you get sicker. So you must learn to touch magic without it."

A tear rolled down the assassin's cheek, and Bauti knew he'd come to realize, even if he wouldn't admit it, that most of his life was a lie. Again he felt pity for his enemy.

"Your problem is your faith. It blocks you from your inner power. Soon, it will block what the powder allows, too. Faith in a God opens a window so you can see power, touch it perhaps. Faith in yourself opens a door you can walk through to seize it."

"Will it help me save Makari?"

She nodded.

"Then teach me."

CHAPTER THIRTY-FOUR

Ashai kneeled in the dirt of his cell floor, sweat matting his hair to his head, temples throbbing from the effort of concentrating. He squeezed his eyes shut, driving his consciousness deep inside himself, searching for anything to suggest magic lurked somewhere within. He didn't need a blazing fire, or even a wavering candle. Just a spark would have done, would have kept him going. Sustained him. Given him hope.

He found only darkness and cold. He couldn't even find the contamination of the back alley magic now. And since they were still hiding from the Denari Lai, he'd taken more of the powder that cut his link to Nishi. He was powerless.

"You're trying too hard," Grekkyl snapped. The old woman could use her voice like a riding crop, smacking him on the rump. This time it snapped his concentration like a twig underfoot.

He opened his eyes and let out a breath he didn't know he'd been holding. His body relaxed and he slumped against the damp rock of the cell wall.

"How can I be trying too hard? I'm not finding anything. Either I'm not trying hard enough or there's nothing there."

He'd been at it for hours, but had yet to even see a trace of power in him. He couldn't even find the tainted back alley magic that kept the Yanagat at bay.

She clucked and leaned against the bars of his cell, wrinkling her nose and eyeing his chamber pot dubiously.

He'd been in the cell three days now. Or so she told him. He hadn't seen the sun since coming here, and had lost all sense of time. Of course, her lessons—and his continued failure at them—made even a few minutes seem like an eternity.

It didn't help that he felt more alone than he'd felt since living on the streets, before the Chargh Lai had swept him into the Denari Lai. The hag was his only regular visitor. He spent most of his time alone, even his guards staying out of sight around the corner. When Grekkyl came, it was only to teach him to find his own magic. She'd given him smaller and smaller doses of the back alley powder, and he could feel tremors starting again in his fingers. He was running out of time.

Tomar had come once, and stayed just long enough to sneer at Ashai and tell him stories of how he'd romanced the Princess. Ashai didn't know how much of them to believe, so he ignored them all.

Tisk had visited once, though the boy had only said he was going into the city to get information about patrols and so forth. He hadn't returned, and Ashai was worried about him.

Surprisingly, Bauti had visited three times already. He never stayed long enough for real conversation, but he had brought food once, with a skin of ale and a wedge of hard cheese. Ashai had seen something new in the captain's eyes before, and never would have expected: concern. Pity definitely. Perhaps even compassion. Oh, the hate still lingered behind the slate gray of his eyes, but for once it wasn't Bauti's predominating emotion. Perhaps his heart had thawed a bit.

Unlike Makari's. The princess had yet to visit, though he'd heard her often enough in the corridors outside, flirting with Tomar, giggling at his jokes. It made Ashai want to throw up, but his chamber pot was far too disgusting to put his face anywhere near it.

"What happens when you try to pull a mule where it doesn't want to go?" Grekkyl's voice brought him back to the present.

"It pulls back," Ashai answered. "Refuses to go."

"And if you are gentle? Offer a carrot?"

Ashai didn't answer her. He knew what she was getting at and didn't believe it. There was no magic inside him to coax out, and he couldn't use Nishi's gift. So he had to count on the powder. Makari's only chance.

Grekkyl sighed. "Ignoring it doesn't make it false, assassin."

Ashai's temper was dry tinder, and her sparks threatened to ignite it.

"Insisting doesn't make it true," he argued. She opened her mouth to argue, but Ashai had heard enough. "No! No more of your lies! The only true magic comes from God, not from inside me, inside you, or inside anyone else. We are but vessels for God's will, *the God*, Nishi. The only time those vessels possess magic is when God channels it through us. I've tried it your way over and over again, but it doesn't work. You're wrong."

Grekkyl stepped close to the cage, pressing her raisin-like face to the bars. "Then how do you explain what I have shown you? The fire in my hand, my glamours? How?"

"Parlor tricks," Ashai spouted, turning his back on the old woman. "Cheap illusions performed by hundreds of tricksters and charlatans every day."

"You know that is not true."

"Leave me."

"You know in your heart—"

"Go! Now!"

She sucked in a harsh breath and stepped back from the bars. "You can yell at Captain Bauti next."

As she strolled around the corner and out of the cavern, Bauti's chain mail clinked in. Ashai didn't even have to turn around to know she'd been right. Bauti had a sound and a presence all his own, and it intensified down here in the confined space of the tunnels. He smelled of steel and leather and sweat, and the measured sound of his breathing rarely changed pace.

"What do you want?" Ashai picked at a scab on his forearm.

"I want you to learn how to use magic. Your own. Nishi's. Back alley garbage. Whatever it takes to fight Tan. I want you to prove to me you really are a changed man, and that you have Makari's best interests at heart. I want you to stop pouting like a petulant child and live up to what is needed of you."

Ashai wheeled on him, hoping the gold of his eyes would show his rage at the captain's implication. Ashai had seen the glowing gold of his eyes once, looking in a tin of water where his reflection had stared back at him. It had startled him at first, but he should have expected it. How many shiners with eyes of gold had he killed?

Bauti, however, held his ground, and Ashai sighed.

"I already failed to do what was required of me, Bauti! I failed my order, my leader, and my God. I failed Makari, too. My betrothed. You could even say I failed Abadas. So don't lecture me about how I'm failing now. I no longer care."

Bauti drew a dagger from his belt and picked at the dirt behind his fingernail. "For someone who doesn't care, you sound rather emotional."

Ashai spit at his feet. "Take your condescension and go."

"You know she still cares for you, right?"

Ashai's heart skipped a beat and his throat tightened. He'd never expected to hear such a thing, especially from Bauti.

"She told you this?"

"She didn't need to. I can see it in how she looks at you. How her eyes get distant when she says your name, and how her hands fidget when someone says your name. She's mad at you, might even hate you a bit. But she still loves you."

Ashai beat down the tiny glimmer of hope that tried creeping into his heart, chasing it out like a rat or a cockroach.

"She hasn't looked at me in days, so how would you know? She's spending all her time with Tomar, the charming thief lord. She barely even remembers me."

Bauti shook his head and paced the tiny cave. After a moment, he turned his flinty gaze on Ashai.

"You know I don't think much of you, assassin. I loathe sneaky, back-stabbing killers like you. No honor. But for all the bad things I think you are, I never thought you were a quitter."

Ashai spit at him again, this time with less fervor.

"Easy for you to say. You didn't fail her. You haven't lost everything. You still know what you believe in, what's real and holy and righteous. I have none of that, not even my faith. I have nothing."

"Didn't fail her?" Bauti stopped his pacing and the gray of his eyes turned to ice. "I failed her and her father. I failed them before the wedding started, before the first dart flew or the first blade flashed. I failed her by putting my feelings ahead of her welfare, by letting my foolish old man's emotions cloud my judgment.

"Don't tell me I didn't fail her, assassin. My failure led to her father's death. And now here I am, consorting with thieves and cutthroats, keeping Makari from the throne. I've been declared a traitor by a man I should have known was plotting against the people I was sworn to protect. I have no job, no home, and no lands or titles. Tan stripped them all.

"What I do have is my heart, killer, and that heart tells me my purpose in life right now is keeping the rightful heir to the throne of Pushtan alive long enough to someday lead us all. I thought you'd found the same purpose in your heart. Maybe I was wrong."

He turned and stalked to the entrance to the cavern, then stopped and glanced back at Ashai.

"She needs you. Without you, she'll die. That's when you will have failed her."

As he stomped out, Ashai slid to the floor and cried.

CHAPTER THIRTY-FIVE

S amaran Tan allowed the other ministers to take the seats in his sitting room. Outwardly, it was a show of courtesy and humility, but it also put him in a power position, using his already tall frame to tower over the now-seated lords. Only General Celani seemed to realize what was going on, slipping a warning glance in Tan's direction, but sitting nonetheless.

Neffin looked like he might fall asleep on the general's shoulder as the two took the small sofa, and Trade Minister Talbot grimaced as he sat in a stiff wooden chair.

The last to file into the room was the recently promoted Captain Gartka, leader of the Royal Guard. The man's wounds had been stitched and administered to by the king's own physician. Tan had seen to that. And Gartka now served Tan with a loyalty bordering on fanatical.

Tan paced the room for a moment, selecting his first target, then moved to stand directly behind the upholstered chair holding the well-rounded form of the Foreign Minister. Renard shifted uncomfortably in his seat, trying to keep Tan from standing right behind him, but subtle shifts on the spymaster's part made him give up quickly and sit, pouting.

"My Lords, thank you all for coming on such short notice." Tan coated his voice in as much honey as he could. "I know you're all busy, so I will keep this short. We stand on the edge of a dangerous cliff, as most of you know. The citizens of Dar Tallus are growing restless. We must find Princess Makari. Now. And I need all of your help to bring her back."

Of course, Renard muttered under his breath something Tan could not understand. Samaran let it slide. It wasn't time to humiliate the Foreign Minister. Yet.

"I don't understand how we can possibly help you, Lord Tan." Talbot's expression was as passive as ever. Tan hated not being able to read the man's emotions, but respected his ability to hide them so well. He would have made an exceptional gambler. "You have an entire network of spies throughout Dar Tallus and the world. What more could I give you?"

Tan smiled at the man, the expression a mask for his own irritation at Talbot's shortsightedness.

"A network of traders, merchants, and craftsman in the city and worldwide, of course." He shifted his weight to remind Renard he still stood behind him. "Just as Minister Renard has access to a huge web of diplomats and royalty around the world, and General Celani commands military units throughout the nation.

"Gentlemen, those are thousands upon thousands of eyes, ears, and minds that could and should be looking for her."

"Won't that destroy our story that she's in mourning for her father?" Tan was surprised Neffin had hit on that point. He'd expected someone more acute to do so.

"That cover story is no longer working anyway. The people stopped believing that the instant we sent teams looking for her throughout the city. Word will spread that she's missing and the citizens will start to doubt our ability to keep peace and prosperity for Pushtan."

"Don't you mean *your* ability to do so?" Renard had timed his shot perfectly, waiting for just the right moment to undermine Tan's authority. Fortunately, Tan had prepared for it.

"If they don't trust the man at the top, they won't trust those under him either, Minister. How did you do getting Thahr to accept our proposal on the highway tax, by the way?"

Even from above, he could see Renard's plump face turn the color of a plum.

"I had them convinced until all of this took place."

Tan put his hands on Renard's shoulders, giving them the slightest squeeze, his fingers just brushing Renard's chubby neck. The Foreign Minister swallowed hard and Tan allowed himself a satisfied grin.

"Then I will discount the information my sources sent me about how you hated the king's order so much you ignored it. Obviously, you have only the best interest of our great nation in mind. You never would have lied about it."

A thick, tense silence hung in the room until Neffin cleared his throat.

"So what would you have us do, Lord Tan?"

Tan steepled his fingers under his chin and let his gaze touch on each of the men in turn, showing each what he hoped was a humble-looking smile.

"I would have you help, my lords. Spread word through your own networks that Makari remains in the city, likely in control of the Sixth Guild, and listen to the replies. Ask questions, seek answers, and dig. We must find the princess as soon as possible."

"No one will be willing to cross the Sixth Guild," said Talbot. "At least not in my circles, where businesses depend on not being robbed, burned, vandalized, and so on."

Tan had anticipated this possibility.

"That, my good Lord Talbot, is why I am offering a reward to anyone who brings me information that leads to the rescue of Princess Makari. Not only will we line their pockets with gold, but we will grant lands and titles—those formerly possessed by our Finance Minister—to whichever person's tip leads to the princess."

Silence descended on the room again, but this time without the tension as each man tried to scheme a way he could get those rewards rather than some common merchant or soldier. These were not men known for kindness or philanthropy, but for ambition and power and pride. None were likely to let pass an opportunity to gain more land, more money, or more titles. In fact, he was counting on their greed to drive them.

To his surprise, Renard was the first to rise from this chair, turning so his considerable belly stood between him and Tan.

"We will move on your wishes at once, Lord Tan. Makari must take the throne immediately."

Celani was next, stiff and formal, but not as hostile as he had been at first.

"Agreed. I will have regular army units surround the city's walls in concentric rings. No one will leave without our permission."

Tan inclined his head to both men as the others rose. He bid them farewell, and ushered them from his chambers, satisfied that he'd accomplished his goal. Makari would be back soon, and dead, while Tan had ensured these men would soon be at each other's throats over the reward. He'd divided what remained of his enemies.

He sipped from a cup of fine Neskanian liquor, a powerful clear liquid with more bite than taste, then slid aside the bookcase that hid the passages behind his room. A few minutes later he stepped out of a second hidden door into a dark corridor, lit only by candles mounted on the walls. Ahead of him stood a wide, black door of thick oak planks, banded with iron. He pounded three times on the wood, paused, then knocked once more.

The door whooshed open and the stale air from inside assaulted his senses, cold and damp and filled with the crisp scent of iron and blood. The man who stood aside to admit him was a dark creature, dressed in bloodstained leather from head to toe, an iron mask covering his face like a second skull.

They stood inside a round room with a high, domed ceiling and torches blazing on the walls. Instruments of torture hung on the stones like statues built to honor the dark cruelty of man, tools thought of and used by only the most twisted minds known to man. In the center of the room sat a wooden table, its surface angled up so that Tan could not see who lay on it, though he didn't need to. He'd held him there while the man in the mask had strapped his wrists and ankles to the wood, spread-eagle.

On the floor at its base, a puddle of blood had formed.

"How is our guest, Jarne?"

The torturer shrugged and grunted, the only communication his tongueless mouth could muster. The sound echoed back to them from the long, narrow corridors leading away from the chamber, the halls holding the Shadow Cells, as they were called. The cells into which people went and never returned.

Tan walked calmly to the other side of the table, taking in the young man strapped there, naked and pale against the dark and bloodstained wood. He tried to look at Tan, but both eyes had long-since swollen shut, and he'd do just as well trying to see with the freckles scattered across his nose as he would through his eyes. He opened his mouth to let out a gurgling moan, his broken teeth like stalactites in a cavern.

The rest of his body was covered in tiny cuts, each one administered by either Tan or the torturer, and piercing holes, where red-hot needles had been pushed into his flesh. His left hand hung mangled at the strap.

Tan approached and pushed his finger against a spot where a red welt marked the entry point of a needle. The boy grunted in pain, grimacing until his nose bled. Then Tan stepped back, wiped his fingertip on his robe, and used his silkiest voice.

"Now, you're going to tell me where the Sixth Guild is holding Makari and the others," he said. "Or I'm going to instruct Jarne, here, to turn you into a girl. Slowly."

The torturer stepped up and placed the cold steel of a sharp knife against the boy's testicles. The lad started to sob.

"Now, now, no need for tears," Tan said. "This can all be over with a few short words. Just tell me what I need to know, and I'll end this. Come on, it's time to trust me, don't you think, Tisk?"

CHAPTER THIRTY-SIX

In the end, Makari had refused Tomar's chambers, opting for a simpler, plainer tent in an adjoining cavern, putting her between the thief master and her lifelong protector, Bauti.

Tomar had seemed genuinely offended, but only for a moment, recovering quickly and resuming his playful flirtations while his men put up her tent. Or at least she thought they were playful. Surely the man didn't think there could be romance between a crook and a princess, especially not a princess about to become queen.

So she played along with what she thought was a show put on for his followers, and for the two men who'd accompanied her. Tomar loved irritating Bauti and Ashai.

She kicked at the edge of a fancy rug Tomar had insisted be placed inside her tent, noticing for the first time the scene displayed in the steady yellow light of her oil lamps. It showed a knight, armor stained with blood, prone at the feet of a queen who stood over him wielding a sword as if to chop off his head.

The rest of the tent was plain, just as she'd requested. A plain, narrow cot, though Tomar had slipped in a feather pillow and warm comforters. Wood table and chairs, a flask of wine and a tin cup on the table. And a lacquered night stand holding one of the three lamps that lit her tent.

Her feet ached and she dropped into one of the wooden chairs, resting her elbows on the table and propping her chin in her hands.

What to think of the men who'd brought her here?

Tomar was a scoundrel, no doubt, but she also knew he cared deeply for his people. Everything he did—from locking up Ashai to flirting with her—were meant somehow to help his people, to keep them safe. She respected him for that, even though she knew someday she might have to lock him up.

Then there was her bodyguard, the man with whom she'd trusted her life for all of her seventeen years. Had he proven enough of himself to regain his place as her sole protector, or were his feelings still too strong? Could she trust him to do what was right, instead of what kept him near her?

The worst part, she thought, was that Bauti didn't really love her the way he thought he did. He simply loved that she made him feel young again, that with her he could forget his graying hair, lined face, and slowing reflexes. Love was the perfect disguise for infatuation, and Bauti had worn it proudly.

She sighed and rubbed at her temples, inhaling the sweet smoke of a wood fire somewhere down the tunnels. Voices peeked in through her tent flaps, murmurs from other parts of the Sixth Guild tunnels.

How had she fallen for the assassin? How had she not sensed the danger he posed, not only to her but to her nation, her citizens?

She'd thought long and hard about that since coming to the tunnels three days earlier. That was why she hadn't gone to see him—she needed time and space to clear her mind, to sort through the events that led her here without him being able to smile and divert her thoughts.

Tears filled her eyes as she longed for Kendshi. The slave girl would know what to say. She always did.

At first, Makari felt stupid and immature for falling for Ashai, like some foolish girl just starting her moon blood and not knowing up from down. Surely only a fool would fall for a man sent to kill her.

But she'd reasoned herself through those feelings as soon as she realized he'd actually fallen in love with her. Like Bauti's loyalty, Ashai's love for her was something beyond doubt. He'd forsaken too much for his feelings to be anything less than love, true and strong.

Love was also the perfect disguise for hate, and while it hadn't been intentional, Ashai had donned the mask and hidden his true face from her for months. Of course she'd missed his true intent. There was no seeing around someone being in love with her. It formed a great, wide wall from horizon to horizon, through which she saw nothing but that love.

She rose from the chair again and paced her tent, shivering a bit at the cool, damp air sliding across her skin.

She'd been vulnerable to Ashai's kind of love, too. So many times had she rejected lords who'd courted her, men who'd come bearing gifts of gold and silver, lands and titles, resources and power. But none had borne the gift of love, and Makari had come to believe after years of being paraded before them, that no one would love her for who she was. They could only love the power and prestige that marrying her would bring.

So what Ashai had offered had blinded her to everything else, even making her ignore Bauti's warnings about the man.

Having sorted all that out, Makari was left with one thing to discern: her feelings for Ashai.

That, of course, was a far more difficult puzzle to piece together. Figuring out other people's feelings was easier than looking inside and seeing your own for what they really were.

She picked up the flask and prepared to pour herself a cup of wine. Maybe the spirits would help clear her mind so she could think better.

A commotion rose outside. Men shouted, including Tomar. She was reaching for the tent flap when the thief master barged in. He seemed to realize then that he'd violated her privacy, bowing quickly, without his normal hat-flourish.

"Highness, there's been an incident. Would you accompany me, please?"

Tired of being dragged around by men, Makari planted her fists on her hips.

"Where to, Tomar?"

"To the holding cell. We're going to execute your assassin."

Makari struggled to keep up with Tomar as the tall thief strode through the corridors toward Ashai's cell. She'd come this way many times, just to change her mind at the last minute, unable to look the assassin in the eye.

Now she had no choice.

They rounded the corner into the assassin's cavern at the same time as Bauti, who came from the other direction. His shirt was soaked with sweat, and his sword bobbed at his hip. He'd been training, and someone had thought to get him, too.

In the cavern, they found a ring of a dozen crooks gathered in front of Ashai's cell, most holding clubs or staffs, though one trained a crossbow on her former betrothed. The men shouted obscenities and threats at Ashai, while Grekkyl stood, feet wide and hands in front of her, the only thing between the mob and the now-open door on Ashai's cell.

Bauti shouldered his way through the throng and stood beside the old woman, drawing his sword in a slow, threatening move that made several thieves step back. Tomar tried to stop her, but Makari moved to stand beside her captain, one hand on the dagger at her waist.

"What is the meaning of this?" She left no room in her tone for questioning or doubt.

"He killed one of us!" shouted a stocky man with a cudgel at the front of the group. "We take that seriously down here, and we'll have his head for it!"

Grekkyl flinched, her hands jerking as if she sought to throw a spell at the men. They backed up another step.

Makari turned to Ashai, nearly gasping at the golden glow in his eyes. She fought to maintain her composure. "Well?"

Ashai showed no fear, glaring at the men through the door, almost daring them to attack. Even unarmed, she knew he'd kill at least two or three of them, even without access to power or magic.

"They're talking about the boy in the square," he said. "The day you and I met."

"But—"

Ashai cut her off. "He was trying to kill you," he said. "I'd do it again if I had to."

Beside her, Bauti shifted his stance. Why was Ashai not telling them the truth?

Tomar moved easily through his men and stood before Ashai. Anger radiated from him in waves, rippling the air in the tiny cave.

"I knew you were trouble," he breathed, his voice serpentine. "That boy you killed was a friend, someone I was training. He had no parents, no family, so we became those things for him. We thought he'd gone missing until his body turned up in a drainage ditch.

"We should have killed you the moment you came here. I'll remedy that mistake now."

Makari wheeled on the big thief, fixing him with her most penetrating glare.

"You'll do no such thing! Ashai didn't—"

Ashai interrupted her again, this time giving her a look that pleaded for cooperation. "They're right, princess. I deserve death. Killing that boy violated even my own vows."

An angry murmur washed through the gathered mob, and they inched closer. Makari ran into the cell and put herself in front of Ashai.

"What are you doing?" she whispered.

Ashai tried to move her out of the way, but she stood her ground and brushed his hands from her shoulders. He sighed and whispered for only her to hear.

"Bauti will take care of you. Without my magic, I'm useless to defend you, and with it, Tan will find you. You're safer with the guild and the captain. Let them do what they will to me. It'll end my suffering."

She slapped him. She didn't mean to, but his words enraged her so much that her hand leapt from her side and smacked him across the cheek, snapping his head to the left with a crack so loud it echoed.

Ashai took his time returning his gaze to the gathered men, offering an irritated look at Makari, but she didn't care.

"You're not quitting on me! You quit on your order. You quit on your God. And you quit on yourself, but I will not let you quit on me! You owe me that much, Ashai. For all the harm you've done to me, to my family, you owe me your life. I'll decide when and where you give it!"

He opened his mouth, but Bauti made whatever he was going to say moot.

"I killed that boy, not the assassin. I ordered my men to dispose of the body in a manner fitting a common thief. Blame me."

Every pair of eyes in the room, Makari's included, turned on the captain. The man with the crossbow moved his aim back and forth between Ashai and Bauti, unsure now what to do.

Tomar moved to stand toe-to-toe with Bauti, his nose just an inch from the captain's, his face contorted.

"You'd better be lying, Captain, or you'll be leaving these tunnels in pieces."

Bauti neither flinched nor stepped back. He met Tomar's gaze with steel resolve.

"I killed that boy."

Makari felt tears rushing to her eyes and she moved to Bauti's side.

"I beg for mercy," she pleaded. "The boy approached with a knife. He stole my purse, but Captain Bauti thought he meant to harm me. He only killed him in my defense. If you have any love for me at all, please spare his life."

Tomar let out an exasperated growl and turned away, tugging off his hat and running the fingers of his other hand—the one with the missing digit—through his hair. He paced through the gathered crowd, muttering to himself, then strode back to stare down at her.

"I will spare his life." Makari let out a sigh, but he wasn't done. "But he must leave the tunnel at once and return to the streets. And I will have his word he'll not reveal our location."

"Done," Bauti said before Makari could even nod.

"You're still sentencing him to death," she complained. "Up there, his own men will kill him. Or Tan. He'll be dead within a day."

"Princess, listen to me," Bauti said, grasping her shoulders so tight she couldn't help but look up into his slate-colored eyes. "You need Ashai to keep you alive. He's the only one who can deal with Denari Lai. I'm too old and too slow. I can't disguise us like he can. I can't kill a Denari Lai, and my face is easily recognized. He's your best chance."

Ashai stepped forward, standing beside Makari, his voice low. "Nonsense, you fool. I didn't kill the boy, but without me he never would have tried to rob her. Now I'm only good to Makari if I somehow find a way to use some power other than Nishi's gift. Either a tainted lie of power, or one that doesn't exist."

"Then choose one and use it! Kill Tan the next time you see him. Once he's gone, even if your order tracks your normal power, they won't have anyone to do anything about it. And if Tomar gets you out of the city, you'll have a fighting chance."

Makari wiped at her tears, holding tight to her captain's elbow. She'd been so mad at him, felt so betrayed, that she'd never considered what it would be like to lose him. He'd watched over her since the day she was born, a constant presence, reassuring and solid. Despite all they'd been through in the last weeks, she still couldn't imagine losing him forever.

But he was right. She knew it. Ashai knew it. And it was too late now anyway. Tomar stepped forward and took Bauti's sword from his hand.

"I'll return this to you once we get to the surface. The more of your own men or Capitol Watch scum you kill, the better for all of us down here."

Bauti turned to Ashai and let his flinty gaze bore into the assassin's soul. "Keep her alive, you murderous bastard. I don't care if you have to use your magic, God's magic, back alley magic, or the power of The Shadow itself, keep her alive. Put her back on the throne, or all of this is for nothing."

Tomar handed Bauti off to the mob.

"If he resists on the way out, bring me his head."

But Bauti followed them out like a lamb to slaughter.

Tomar turned his attention on Ashai. "I heard what you said to him. I should kill you, too, but I gave the princess my word. And believe it or not, the word of a thief does mean something."

Ashai nodded at him, and Tomar gave his grandmother a kiss on the head.

"Get him ready," he told her. "We leave at sunset, and he'll need to have some kind of magic if he's going to protect her."

He left without waiting for the hag's reply.

Ashai reached for Makari's shoulder, but stopped short, his hand wavering in midair.

"Makari, I ..."

He didn't finish, and she didn't acknowledge him. Vision still blurry from tears, she stormed from the cavern.

CHAPTER THIRTY-SEVEN

A shai sat in the dirt at the back of his cell, kicking at roaches with the heel of his boot. The mob had dispersed quickly, shutting and locking his cell door as their anger dissipated, even Grekkyl leaving, telling him he'd be free as soon as he used magic to pick the lock on his door.

That had been over an hour ago, by his estimate, and still he sat alone in his cramped, dank cell, his mind wandering into dark caverns and tunnels that left him somber and forlorn. They'd put too much faith in him to protect Makari. Without power or magic, he would be helpless against any Denari Lai. His senses and reflexes would be normal, unable to compete with the magically enhanced body of a Shadow Blade. They'd just as well throw a seamstress at the assassin. She'd have the same chance of success.

And if he didn't grasp some sort of power soon, no matter the type, he'd become worthless, crippled by tremors and Yanagat.

He no longer even cared where the magic came from. He knew he couldn't tap into his old power—the effects of the drug kept that link cut. So he'd have to use the tainted power of the dust the hag had given him, no matter its effect on his soul. Unless she was right about a power inside him.

He closed his eyes and tried again.

He drove his consciousness deep into himself, plunging into the dark of his soul, searching for the thread of power he needed. He pushed through murky shadows inside himself, seeking any light, even the tiniest pinprick against the black night that had engulfed his soul. He didn't care anymore which source he found. Back alley magic would do. He just needed power.

Then he saw something. Out of the corner of his mind's eye, just on the periphery of his awareness, something shone for an instant. He reached for it, driving his awareness toward the point of brightness with all his might.

But as soon as he turned his attention on it, the spot of light blinked out and he was left in the pitch black again.

Frantic, he propelled his mind in all different directions at once. It was there, and he'd been so close! Maybe Grekkyl was right after all. If he could just focus on that point, that beacon of magic and hope, he might be able to grasp it.

A disturbance broke his concentration, shouts echoing through the tunnels outside his cell. He opened his eyes as the cries became more desperate, mingled with shrieks of fear from women and children.

Jumping to his feet, Ashai rushed to the front of his cell, grasping the cold iron bars and staring out into the cavern beyond. The shouts grew louder and more frenzied, and he picked out the distinct noise of people running, fleeing something.

"Hey, what's happening out there?" No one responded.

One of his guards—a weasel-faced man with shifty eyes and thin lips —slipped into the room. He held his long dagger in one hand, a club in the other.

"They've found us! They're here for you three."

"Who? Denari Lai?"

The guard shook his head. "Capitol Watch and Royal Guard. Hundreds of them. They're pushing toward us from both ends of the tunnels. We're trapped in the middle."

Ashai's stomach turned and he looked deep into the man's beady eyes. "Let me out. Please, I can help. I can fight."

The guard considered, looking at the keys hanging on the stone wall a few paces away, then shook his head.

"No one trusts you."

He turned and jogged off, ignoring Ashai's pleas to come back.

Ashai's heart pounded, threatening to burst from his chest. If they found him here, they'd kill him on the spot. Tan would have given orders to kill all three of them, knowing they'd figured out his identity by now. He couldn't risk them exposing him before the princess was dead.

Makari!

He rattled the cell door, trying to rip it from its hinges, but of course they held fast. Iron bested muscle every time.

He paced the dirt floor, panic rising in his throat. He was trapped, helpless not only to save himself, but to save Makari. And with Bauti gone, she had only Tomar to protect her. The thief master stood no chance against Denari Lai.

She was as good as dead. She needed him. Him. Ashai. Only he could help her.

He closed his eyes again, thrusting back his doubts and fears. He dove deep inside himself, fighting through dark and shadows, searching out that tiny dot of magic that had taunted him before. This was his only chance at life, not just for him but for Makari too. Despite all that had happened, he still loved her.

The light appeared out of nowhere, a tiny sun wrapped in inky clouds. His power, tainted by back alley magic. It was all he had, his only shot at power, so he thrust his mind toward it. A wall sprung up in front of his consciousness, a thick sheet of black and swirling gray, blocking the magic from sight.

He recalled Grekkyl's words: *Faith in yourself is like a door.*

That was it, he understood. His faith in Nishi stood between him and the back alley magic, a wall of belief and dreams and ideology meant to keep him bound to Nishi. Bound to the Denari Lai for his soul's salvation.

But Ashai's salvation no longer mattered. Only Makari did. She needed him. She had faith in him, and that gave him faith in himself.

He lanced through the wall, shattering it into a million shards, and the light blazed behind it, pulsing between dark and bright. He reached for the magic, and this time it didn't flinch away.

Heat hit him first, a wave of fire that scorched his soul and burned his mind, making him cry out in pain as it swept through his body, as well. Ice followed, a rush of death's own cold that left him shivering. Sludge coursed through him as the sinfulness of this outside magic contaminated him, but he no longer cared. He held the back alley magic tight to his soul, mind, and body, hugging it to him like a man trying to tame an angry cat.

His senses sharpened, the sounds of the battle crisp and clean on his ear. He smelled the iron tang of spilled blood, tasted the dust of the tunnels. His limbs took on new life, no longer lethargic and heavy, pounding with strength and vigor and pure power. Under it all coursed the spiritual waste from the back alley powder, but there was nothing to do about that now. Makari needed him.

He opened his eyes, looked at the lock, then shook his head.

"No time for old hag's tricks," he said.

Seizing the bars on the cell door, he ripped the door from its hinges and stepped out into the cavern. He seized his dagger from a stand by the wall and held it up to let the torchlight dance along its polished surface, glitter in its jewels.

The guard rushed inside, weapons ready, but stopped with eyes wide when he saw Ashai.

"I told you I can help fight," Ashai said, reveling even in the soiled magic that had given him new life. "I suggest you get out of my way."

Without hesitation, the man stood aside and Ashai sprinted from the cave.

He had no idea where Makari was, so he just ran, trusting his gut to guide him. He burst around a corner into a battle, the tunnel filled with bodies slashing and hacking at one another. Steel rang, men screamed, and the sharp smell of violence filled the air. But nowhere did he see Makari, so he turned and ran the other way.

Out of nowhere a Capitol Watch soldier sprung up in front of him, leather armor gleaming red with blood. Ashai ducked under a swipe of his short sword, driving his dagger up into the man's gut below the navel. He slashed up, snatched the knife back, and ran on as the man's insides spilled onto the cave floor.

As the sounds of battle behind him faded, Ashai ran across Grekkyl. The hag tried to slip into a crowd of people moving slowly away, but Ashai grabbed her by the elbow and spun her around to face him.

"Where is Makari?"

"I don't know, killer. Gone, I think."

"She escaped? Did you see her?"

She shook her head.

"Use your magic," he commanded, squeezing her arm tighter. "Find her using magic."

She snatched her elbow out of his grasp and pushed him back, anger flaring in her eyes.

"Your magic is stronger than mine. You find her. I cannot."

"My magic doesn't work that way, Grekkyl. You know that."

She laughed at him then, a dry, scraping sound like stone on stone.

"All magic works however you command it. You didn't listen to me, Shadow Blade. Magic is you, part of you. Yours to command like an arm or a leg. So command it."

And she was gone, melting into the crowd. Ashai stood, staring after her, wondering how to do what she'd said.

He thought about how he commanded a disguise or how he used his magic to fight, but those things just came. They simply happened, and always had since the Chargh Lai had introduced him to Nishi's power. He didn't work any spells, didn't make any magical motions. They just happened. At first, he thought them and they happened, and in time they'd simply come when he needed them.

Frustrated, his mind wandered to Makari, to her safety. He wondered if Tomar had managed to get her out, or if the thief master had betrayed her. Images of her lying in a pool of blood flashed in his mind, sending a chill down his spine.

Something tugged at his mind, a subtle pull forward, like a child tugging at the sleeve of his consciousness. He thought of Makari again, picturing her face, those stunning blue eyes, and the pull strengthened. Instinctively, he followed it, weaving his way through the knots of thieves and other criminals shuffling ahead as the sound of fighting drew nearer behind them.

The more he walked, the stronger the tug became, and he knew in his mind he was getting closer, so he pressed on. He shoved through a group of ten thieves marching stolidly the other way, weapons drawn, as they moved to the battle. To their deaths, he knew. Still the tug urged him forward.

Suddenly it changed, pulling to the left. He stood in the middle of the tunnel, carts full of wares to either side. On his left, a fruit cart stood beside one selling blankets and rugs, and as Ashai looked at it, the pull got so strong he almost stepped that way against his own will. He stood between the two carts, staring at a tapestry hung on the cavern wall. Following the pull, he swiped aside the tapestry and found a narrow passageway leading into the rock. Glancing behind him, he slipped into the side tunnel and followed it in the dark. A few minutes later, he reached another tapestry. Gently, he eased one edge to the side and peered out into another corridor, empty but for a squad of thieves waiting, weapons drawn.

Taking a deep breath, he stepped out into the tunnel and faced the men.

They jumped a little, weapons coming up, then tensed when they recognized Ashai.

"I need to find the princess," he said, striding toward them, taking a lesson from Makari's book on command. "I assume she went this way?"

They exchanged confused glances, clearly not sure how to handle this. He decided to capitalize on their momentary lapse.

"Speak quickly, men! Tomar sent for me, so unless you want to answer to him, you'd best point me toward Makari. The second assassin is loose in the tunnels, and both of them will die without my help."

One of the men finally took control. "Down this tunnel. They passed perhaps two minutes ago, so you can catch them if you run."

"Good man," Ashai told him. "If anyone wearing armor tries to follow us, your job is to buy us time to get away. Pay with your lives, if needed, but Makari must live long enough to get out of the tunnels."

The leader nodded, and Ashai took off at a jog.

The tunnel wound left, then right, then left again, and the farther he went, the fewer torches lit the way. Eventually, he slowed to a walk, unable to safely keep his pace. Slowing allowed him to hear the voices, muffled and quiet, coming from the tunnel ahead of him. The same direction the pull on his mind demanded he go.

He crept forward, dagger drawn, drawing on the strange and soiled-feeling power to keep himself quiet, and to wrap himself in shadows. The voices grew louder, and before long he came to a bend where he knew they were just ahead.

Doubling his disguise, he peeked around the bend and saw them. Makari stood, arms crossed over her chest, eyes firing blue icicles at the thief master, who glared down at her.

"We will go back for him!" Makari snapped. "I won't leave him to die."

"Going back is dying, princess. You're safer with me than you are with him."

He took a step forward, as if to intimidate her. Ashai grinned. Tomar didn't know her as well as he did.

Makari's eyes frosted over and she jabbed her finger into the thief master's chest.

"I'm beginning to doubt I'm safe with you at all. You're in this to serve yourself, not me."

"Without me, you'd be dead right now!"

Their argument raged, but another sound yanked Ashai's attention away from them and back the way he'd come. The distant ring of steel on steel, and muffled shouts.

Their pursuers had found them.

Ashai dashed around the corner.

"Sorry to interrupt this lover's spat, but we need to go. Now!"

"Ashai!" For an instant, he thought Makari might run to his arms, her face lit up with joy. It lit a fire in his chest, but then it was gone, and the wintery glare returned. "Master Tomar here was just telling me—"

Ashai grabbed her wrist and started pulling her down the tunnel behind him.

"Tell me about it some other time, Princess. Right now, there are some very angry men coming behind us."

Tomar grabbed her other wrist and pulled her back the other way.

"She's going with me!"

Ashai eased up on Makari's arm and held his finger to his lips. The other two fell silent and the sounds of fighting echoes softly off the cavern walls.

Tomar's face reddened. "You led them to us!"

"Don't be a fool," Ashai shot back. "They would have found you eventually, anyway. But the squad you left will only last so long against the numbers hitting them, so we need to go. I assume this tunnel leads out of the city?"

Tomar glanced back over his shoulder, toward the sound of the fighting, his face going from red to pale in seconds.

"My people," he muttered. "What have I done?"

Ashai released Makari's wrist and grabbed Tomar by the front of his tunic.

"Tomar, these soldiers aren't interested in your people. They want Makari and me. If we lead them out of the tunnels, your people will have time to scatter."

Tomar considered a moment, brow furrowed, then nodded. He regained his composure, the self-confident swagger returning.

"Yes, of course. This tunnel leads us outside the north perimeter of the city wall, opening up into an orchard. And there's a section we rigged to collapse behind us. We could cut off pursuit from behind."

The sounds of fighting ceased behind them, replaced by the clank and shout of soldiers running through the tunnel.

"How far?" Ashai asked.

"Perhaps two miles. Hurry."

He led the way, releasing Makari as if her presence no longer mattered to him. Ashai understood, then, read the man like a scroll. Makari had been a way for him to advance the plight of his people, a chance to improve their lives and give them status they didn't have. But with their very lives threatened now, the princess became less of a power play and more like bait to lead the wolves out of the henhouse.

They jogged ahead in silence, only the sound of their breathing breaking the black stillness of the tunnel. There were no more torches now, but Tomar never slowed, keeping his pace for a good five minutes. Then he skidded to a stop, Makari running into him from behind. Only Ashai's magically enhanced vision allowed him to stop before hitting her.

The thief master bowed his head and listened, then shook his head.

"Just my imagination," he said.

But Ashai heard something else and raised his hand for silence.

The sound of their pursuers was faint, still distant, but there was something else, too. The measured, soft sounds of breathing, somewhere ahead of them. He strained further and picked out more than one.

"It's a trap," he whispered. "People are waiting ahead of us."

Tomar looked back, then ahead. "Can you tell how many?"

"At least ten," he answered. "Maybe more. Around the next bend."

Tomar straightened and drew the wicked-looking sword at his belt.

"Then let's spring their little trap and find our way out of here."

Ashai nodded, hefting his dagger. He noted that Makari had drawn her own blade, ready to fight. His instincts told him to hold her back, to keep her from the fight. She was the most important of them all. If she died, all they did was for naught.

He also knew she wouldn't listen to him, so he chose not to waste his breath.

Behind them, the sounds of pursuit grew.

Ashai snuck to the edge of the tunnel's curve, Makari behind him with Tomar trailing. He could hear their heartbeats now, including those of the men lying in wait. He gathered as much of the back alley magic as he could, readied his blade, and swept around the corner, the other two in tow.

They managed to surprise their enemies, a squad of Royal Guardsmen waiting in the dark, blind to everything more than a couple feet from their faces. Before they knew what hit them, Ashai had dropped two, slashing their throats and ripping the short sword from the hand of the second.

Makari and Tomar fought well, considering they were as blind as the soldiers, but it was Ashai who did the most damage. He became a whirl-wind of steel and death, both blades flashing out as he tore through the remaining soldiers. In less than a minute, the entire squad was down, and the three fugitives stood, covered in blood, panting, while voices rose behind them.

"Time to go," Ashai said. Blood ran from a slash on his shoulder, but he used his power to stem the bleeding and blunt the pain.

"Not so fast, I'm afraid." The voice sounded familiar, and a moment later, more men stepped into view from the tunnel ahead. Torches flared as at least twenty Royal Guard blocked their way out of the tunnel. At their head stood Gartka. "I don't suppose Captain Bauti is with you? I wanted to talk to him about our last encounter."

Ashai's heart dropped into his stomach.

"You're trapped now, Nishi'iti." Gartka seemed quite proud of himself. "Surrender the princess to us and we'll show mercy."

"What makes you think I want to be surrendered?" Makari locked eyes with the Royal Guardsman and picked up a long sword from a fallen soldier. Confusion flickered on Gartka's face. "Look, Lieutenant, if I go back to the palace I'll be dead within minutes. The second assassin is there, and we know who it is."

The men running up behind them clamored to a stop, boxing them in. Gartka straightened, as if offended.

"Lord Tan promoted me to captain, since Bauti is a traitor. I suppose you're going to tell me that he's Denari Lai like the Finance Minister here?"

Ashai watched the group behind them inching closer as Makari answered.

"Exactly, Captain. Tan is the second assassin."

Laughter rippled through both groups of men, and Gartka actually lowered his sword an inch.

"You expect me to believe—"

"I don't care what you believe, Captain," Makari barked, making Gartka jump, "but I do expect you to obey so long as I am princess."

"Minister Tan warned me you might be sympathetic to the assassin." Gartka turned to his men. "The princess is under the Denari Lai's power. Look how his eyes glow. He's using magic to control her. Kill him and the thief, so the princess can be free."

Makari rolled her eyes. "Tomar, when I assume the throne, remind me to have the captain here beheaded."

"Gladly, highness."

With a wave of his hand, Gartka ordered his men to attack.

Ashai leapt to meet the onslaught, running his short sword through one man's midsection, then ducking under a second soldier's slashing blow and slicing though the tendons behind his knee. He rose from that and opened a third attacker from groin to navel while hacking off a fourth man's sword hand.

Behind him, he heard Tomar and Makari engaging the second group of soldiers, but he couldn't spare a moment to look, sliding under the legs of another attack, and burying his dagger in the man's spine. The next man slipped past Ashai's defenses and landed a blow with the pommel of his sword to Ashai's shoulder, making him drop the short sword. Ashai slit his throat in short order, but he'd lost the sword and couldn't pick it up.

Still, it was enough to drive Gartka's men back for a moment, and Ashai used the time to pick up a morning star one of the soldiers had dropped.

Sidling back, Ashai repositioned himself between Gartka's group and the princess, who had engaged a man from the second group. Tomar stood beside her, knocking aside blow after blow from three men.

Ashai knew it was hopeless. As the two groups pressed closer together, he and his companions lost ground until they stood, back-to-back-to-back, facing ten times their number.

"It's over." Gartka grinned as he spoke. "Even a Denari Lai can't beat ten-to-one odds. Surrender."

Tomar whispered in Ashai's ear. "The collapsing apparatus is about twenty paces further on. If we can break through their lines ..."

Ashai nodded, but stayed focused on Gartka. "Maybe you girls in the Royal Guard surrender, but a Denari Lai never does."

Gartka's grin widened as he sensed victory at hand. He raised his hand to start the fighting again, but someone interrupted.

"Under my command, they would already have killed you, Ashai. I think the Guard is going soft!"

With a yell, Captain Bauti fell on the second group of soldiers, a handful of thieves at his side. Gartka took one look at Bauti, howled in rage, and rushed to attack his former commander, leaving his men alone.

Ashai and Tomar made good use of the distraction, plunging into the thinner line of men standing between them and freedom. Confused, the Royal Guardsmen parted like water, and in an instant, Ashai pulled Makari through their lines and into the open tunnel behind. The three of them turned to fend off a weak attack by a few guardsmen, but for the most part, the soldiers were wrapped up with Bauti and his men.

Slowly, defending all the way, Ashai led the other two backward, step by step, toward the trap behind them. For a moment, Bauti disappeared from sight under a wall of mail and armor, but then he burst through the rear of their line, bloodied and battered, but standing like a mountain between the soldiers and the fugitives.

"Run!" he shouted over his shoulder. Gartka and two other soldiers hammered blows down on the captain, but he fended them off, holding ground as best he could. "Get her out of here!"

Tomar felled the last of the men pursing them, but Makari stopped in the middle of the tunnel, staring at her captain. Ashai grabbed her arm and tried to pull her along, but she fought back, tears streaming down her cheeks.

"No! We can't leave him!"

Bauti fought valiantly, but Ashai knew it was only a matter of time before he went down and the soldiers broke free.

"We have to go, Makari!" he spun the princess around and looked into her eye. "He is giving his life for you one way or the other. Don't make it be in vain!"

With one last, forlorn look back, she shoved her way past Ashai and ran.

Tomar found the lever for collapsing the tunnel, and all three of them waited there, hoping Bauti could break free.

Ashai called to him. "Run, captain! Now!"

Bauti heard, dropped one soldier, drove Gartka back a step, then turned and ran.

But the old warrior was wounded, and speed had never been his strong suit. He made it halfway to his friends before a guardsman with a crossbow stepped forward and fired. Bauti straightened, then fell to his knees.

A cheer went up from the soldiers as they surged forward, Gartka at their head. Bauti, against all odds, staggered to his feet and ran again, plunging ahead for another ten paces before stopping.

"He's right under the fall point," Tomar said, hand still on the lever. "He'll be buried!"

"Wait for him," Ashai ordered. "Come on, Bauti! Run!"

But Marwan Bauti, Captain-Commander of the Royal Guard of Pushtan, Protector to King Abadas and Princess Makari, stood, faced his enemies with a crossbow bolt between his shoulders, and raised his sword.

"Do it!" he shouted back. "My life for yours, Makari!"

He threw himself against the rushing soldiers, cutting down one, then another, before being swept under a sea of steel and flesh.

Only Gartka didn't join in the destruction of Bauti's body, standing back and glaring at Ashai with hate in his eyes.

"Men!" he shouted. "Capture the princess or die trying!"

Makari moved like lightning, shoving Tomar aside and pulling the lever.

The cavern shook, a series of snapping sounds made the soldiers stop and glance around as pebbles and dust fell from overhead.

It was Gartka who figured it out.

"It's a trap! Retreat!"

But he was too late. In a rush of stones and dirt, the tunnel collapsed right above Marwan Bauti's motionless form.

CHAPTER THIRTY-EIGHT

A shai almost had to carry Makari through the dark tunnels out of the city. The princess shook with sobs, her grief at Bauti's death nearly crippling. Even Ashai felt as if losing the captain placed immense weight on his shoulders, a weight that pushed down on him, bending his back, and slowing his steps. Bearing most of Makari's weight didn't make it any easier.

But Tomar would not stop or even slow, hefting a torch before him and moving quickly through the tunnel. When Makari fell to her knees and sobbed, he took her under one arm with Ashai under the other, and they half-dragged her through the winding passage.

At some point, the tunnel became a sewer again, and the three sloshed through ankle-deep muck that reeked and clung to their clothes, its stench weaving into their hair as if it would become part of them.

They went on that way for what seemed like an hour, but then rounded a bend and faced a stone wall. The slop around their ankles flowed through a knee-high space under the wall, disappearing into darkness.

"We have to go through that?" Ashai asked.

For the first time since the battle had begun, Tomar grinned.

"If we had time, I would let you do that just to see you covered in shit, killer. But time is our enemy right now."

Handing the torch to Ashai, he felt around on the wall, touching individual stones, a look of concentration on his face. Finally, one stone wiggled a bit, and a section of the stone slid back with a *hiss-whoosh* of air.

They stepped through and Tomar closed the hidden door behind them. They stood now at a fork in the tunnel, one route straight ahead, the other branching right.

"You just passed out of the city of Dar Tallus," Tomar said. "Go straight and the tunnel will lead you into a field north of the wall. About a half mile from there is a stand of trees, inside which wait a handful of my men. They will give you horses and supplies."

"What about you?" Suspicion nagged at Ashai's mind.

"I'm going back." He pointed to the tunnel that went right. "I can't abandon my people."

Makari stepped up and planted a kiss on the thief master's cheek, standing on her toes to do it.

"Thank you, Tomar. I promise that when I sit the throne of Pushtan, I will remember your courage and the help you gave us. Family Abadas is in your debt."

Tomar gave one of his signature bows, complete with a flourish of his now-battered hat. Then he turned to Ashai.

"I've done all I can do, Shadow Blade. I still think I should have killed you, but she's your charge now. Don't let her down."

And with that, he took the torch and sprinted down the tunnel, out of sight.

Just as he'd said, the straight tunnel led to an open field, and Ashai paused just inside the mouth of the tunnel—hidden by a cleverly placed boulder—and scanned the darkness around them. The field sloped down, away from the hill on which Dar Tallus sat, with the line of trees at the bottom, a half-mile away. Lone trees dotted the hillside, skeletal in the light of the moon.

The night sky stretched horizon-to-horizon, bejeweled with stars, distant clouds lurking on the horizon, as if afraid to encroach on the moon's territory. Ashai's breath steamed in front of his face, and his cheeks stung a bit with the crisp fall air. But nothing moved in the field ahead, nor in the woods, so he motioned for Makari to be quiet, and stepped from behind the boulder.

The two followed a footpath barely visible through the tall, swaying grass, making as little noise as the breeze slipping through around them. Ashai strained to listen, to use his enhanced senses, to catch a scent or a taste on the air of anyone lying in wait. But his senses seemed dulled, blunted, as if he wore cotton in his ears and up his nose.

He raised his hand to the side and frowned as it tremored in the dark. The back alley powder was wearing off. He felt it in his muscles, too, as his legs felt leaden now, his arms weak and soft.

"Faster," he said. "I'm growing weaker."

"Isn't that a shame." The voice slipped from the darkness like a dagger from a sheath. "I was hoping to face you at your strongest."

A figure rose from the grass in front of them, tall and broad-shouldered, silent as the wind. Wrapped in his Denari Lai robes, Tan made an imposing figure, a towering shadow against the already black background of the night sky. His dagger glinted in the moonlight, gripped in his right hand, ready for use.

Ashai dropped to a crouch, drawing his own blade, though the hand in which he held it shook so much the blade flashed in the silver light. He pushed Makari behind him, whispering to her.

"When the fighting begins, run for those trees. It might be your only chance."

"That will not help you." Confidence oozed from Tan like sweat from pores. He knew he had them in an impossible spot. "It will only slow your death, princess, and anger me. You'd do better to remain here and help this sorry excuse for an assassin. Sorry excuse for a Nishi'iti, as well. Our people do not turn on their God, Ashai. You're one of only a few to make that mistake in as long as I've lived."

"Ignore him," Ashai told Makari, "and do as I say."

"I'd rather stay and fight," she said. "A leader doesn't run from a fight."

"And a corpse cannot be a leader."

To that she had no reply other than to nod her head in silence.

Tan began to circle them, his blade gleaming, dark steel like a blade of night. His movements were strong, cat-like. Smooth as water over rocks, and as sure of himself as Ashai had once been. Tan's eyes never left his enemy, locking on Ashai with the force and intensity of a predator.

"And don't think your little thief friends hiding in those trees will be much help, either." He pointed his dagger at Makari. "I'll shred them and leave them for wolves to dine on."

Even though Ashai was expecting it, Tan's attack still caught him off-guard. The man lunged, his blade flashing out in a wide, quick arc. Ashai managed to dodge it, dancing backward as the steel whistled by in front of his chest. The spymaster drew back, grinning like a cat grins at a mouse.

"Good to see you still have some reflexes left. I was worried this might be too easy. Boring."

"Glad I didn't disappoint you. Could we get on with this or are you going to fight with your tongue like an old woman."

Ashai had chosen his words carefully, selecting a passage from Nishi's word that most devout Nishi'itis would recognize, especially a Denari Lai. A story about a coward who never fought, choosing to talk his way out of fights even when God ordered him to arms.

Tan's grin faded and his face twisted in anger. "You would insult me? One who has forsaken God and his order? You'll die more slowly for that!"

"And still you're talking."

This time, Tan's attack came with a fury born of hatred and rage. He became a whirling blur, arms and legs striking and slashing, slicing and stabbing so fast it was all Ashai could do to stay on his feet and fend them off. In fact, it was more than he could do, as Tan's blade scored hits on his shoulder, forearm, and thigh. Ashai's dagger never bit into anything more solid than the man's robes, his reflexes too slow to be on offense and defense at the same time. Without his magic, he couldn't see the moves coming, but Tan could. It made it impossible for Ashai to hurt him.

Tan drove Ashai back several steps, until Makari had to skip out of the way. Then the bigger man pulled back, as if to admire his handy work.

Ashai panted, his breath coming in gulps, blood running warm down his arm, back, and leg. Bleeding at this rate, there was no way he would maintain enough strength to fight. He channeled a tiny bit of what magic remained in him to slow the bleeding. He couldn't stop it, couldn't heal himself even a little, but it would have to do. He needed everything left in his body, mind, and soul to survive the next onslaught.

Tan struck again, this time moving like lightning with a single thrust toward his right shoulder. When Ashai moved to deflect it, the spymaster reversed his momentum, changed directions, and slashed down at Ashai's left knee. The blade bit deep into the flesh just above Ashai's kneecap, pain flaring and shooting up his leg. Tan drove the blade deeper, the hot steel carving through flesh and bone, stopping behind his kneecap.

But the spy had miscalculated. Ashai twisted sideways in pain, and when Tan tried to yank back the dagger, the bones had locked it in place. The pain was horrific, and Ashai screamed as fire erupted up and down his leg, but the hesitation slowed Tan down enough for Ashai's blade to find an opening in his defenses.

Thrusting the blade up, Ashai drove his dagger into Tan's ribs, just under the arm that held the knife in Ashai's knee. Tan cried out, but finally jerked his blade free and danced away.

"Hope I'm not disappointing you," Ashai taunted, showing off the blood on the steel of his own dagger.

Tan didn't look up, his face tense with concentration. He was healing himself. Ashai had to attack while he had the chance.

He lunged, but his body refused to cooperate. As the last of the back alley magic gave out, every muscle in Ashai's body tensed, making him as rigid as a log. Even his breathing locked up. Unable to put his arms out in front of him, he fell face first to the ground.

Makari reached him first, sliding to a stop on her knees, trying to lift him up. She struggled, but in the end had to settle for rolling him over.

Ashai wished she hadn't done that, as it made the darkness swirl and pitch for him, as if the ground under him was a boat on the ocean. Bile rose in his throat, and he forced it back down by sheer force of will. He tried moving his arms and legs, but nothing responded, or at least not that he could feel. It was as if his limbs were made of stone.

Makari cradled his head in her lap, and a moment later, Tan stood over them both, his dagger dripping with Ashai's blood.

"What a touching moment," the assassin said, his voice mockingly soft. "I could kill you both right here and everyone would think it a murder-suicide by a distraught lover."

Something moved in the shadows behind Tan, but Ashai couldn't see what it was. He could barely focus on the assassin, and felt himself sliding toward unconsciousness.

"Of course, that wouldn't send the message our order wants to send, would it? We're supposed to kill our targets from that inner circle for all the world to see, not fall for them and try to whisk them off to a life on the run."

Again the shadows behind him stirred, and for a moment, Tan

looked over his shoulder as if he sensed something there. Then he shrugged.

"No, I'll need to make this statement a bit more blatant and destroy your body, Ashai. Burn it, I think, so that no one ever knows you died. As far as the nation knows, you'll be back in Nishi'iti, reporting to the Chargh Lai of your success."

A sapling of a woman rose from the grass behind him, little more than a silhouette against the night sky. She raised her hands in front of her and the wind kicked up, tossing white hair around on her head as if it had a life of its own.

Tan sensed her now, and wheeled, but it was too late. Light flashed from her palms, striking him in the chest and launching him through the air. He landed somewhere out of sight, a muffled whump followed by a groan.

Grekkyl kneeled beside Ashai, eyes glowing in the moonlight.

"Oh Grekkyl," he moaned. "What have you done?"

"Find your magic, killer! I can only slow him. Powder won't help me long."

"You're right about that, hag!" Tan rushed the woman, dagger flashing, but Grekkyl moved faster than Ashai would have thought, rolling away in the grass.

Tan overshot and skidded to a halt, searching the grass, using his enhanced senses to look for her. She popped up behind him somehow, palms flashing again. This time, he grunted but held his ground, wheeling on her. He slashed at the old woman, but she countered with more magic, deflecting the blow with another flash of light.

"Hurry!" she yelled.

Makari stared down into Ashai's eyes, her blue gaze diving deep into his soul, pleading.

"Ashai, look for your magic. It's there."

"It isn't."

"We're going to die if you don't at least try. I'm going to die, Ashai. If you have any love for me at all, find your power and use it. Use anything, even Nishi's power. Just save me. I need you, Ashai!"

Her need drove him, lit a fire in his heart.

Closing his eyes, he plunged inward, seeking the familiar power. She was right. Even if he used his old power, the power of Nishi, it didn't matter. Tan had found them already, even without magical guidance.

The time for hiding and sneaking was over. It was time to fight.

Prayer leapt from his lips, loud and strong, no longer afraid of being heard. Free.

He smashed through the last remnants of the powder that kept him from Nishi's magic, shattering the wall like it was simple glass. Behind it pulsed the thread of power he knew so well. In a single move, he grasped the thread and felt pure strength flood him, cleansing his body of weakness and soil. The rigidity in his muscles disappeared, his limbs moving again, flexible and strong. The dizziness retreated, and his senses kicked into a gallop. He smelled his own blood, and that of Tan. He saw Makari as if the moon was the sun, and he felt every blade of grass pressing against his body.

Somewhere behind him came Grekkyl's labored breathing. He could tell from sound alone she was weakening.

He jumped to his feet, pulling Makari up with him.

"Take Grekkyl and run for those trees."

She opened her mouth, but he kissed her on the lips, a long, passionate kiss that threatened to envelop them both. At first she pushed away, but then she kissed him back, her hand finding the back of his neck.

He broke away. "Don't argue. Just this once, do as I say."

She nodded.

Ashai picked up his dagger and turned. Grekkyl lay in a heap on the ground under an oak tree, Tan towering over her, dagger lifted.

"See, woman? You're old and weak. Time to die."

"We don't kill the innocent," Ashai shouted. Tan froze, knife over his head, eyeing Ashai sidelong. "Or are you forsaking our vows, too?"

Tan paused only a heartbeat before launching himself at Ashai.

The fight went differently this time. Ashai moved like he used to, sensed strikes before Tan made them. He countered and parried, slashed and cut, moving like a shadow through the night. Tan, while skilled, was bigger and slower than Ashai, and had spent much longer away from their order, unable to train as they'd been taught. Where the fight had been unfairly in his favor last time, now the odds fell to the younger, faster assassin.

By the time they separated, both panting and out of breath, Tan bled from a half-dozen cuts, including one over his eye that let blood flow into his vision.

"You know the Chargh Lai can find you now," Tan growled. "He will send more and more Denari Lai to kill both of you. You won't have a chance."

He tossed his dagger back and forth between his hands, but the movement was slow, and he nearly dropped it more than once.

"Let them come," Ashai said. "I'll kill them, too."

"Not, you won't. They'll cut you off from Nishi. Forever. They're probably doing so now."

Makari had hefted Grekkyl to her feet, and the two of them shuffled off toward the trees, the princess slowed by the older woman's weight.

"She'll never love you again," Tan went on, circling Ashai. A slight limp plagued his left leg. "She cannot love what you are. She hates you for what you've done."

The words hit Ashai like fists, slashed at his soul as sharp as any knife, sending pain through his chest.

Tan stalked closer.

"Think of it, Ashai. You've lost everything. Your home. Your order. Your God. And now your love. You're doomed to spend the rest of eternity alone and burning."

Ashai's hold on his magic slipped as his faith faltered. His knees shook and he nearly fell.

Meanwhile, Tan moved still closer.

Then Makari yelled for him. "Ashai, hurry! Soldiers!"

At first he didn't understand, but then he heard the battle cries. Tan looked first, and Ashai's gaze followed. Behind them came an entire company of soldiers, torches held high, swords drawn as they charged forth from the tunnels. At their fore ran Bryston.

Tan attacked while Ashai was focused on the soldiers, but Ashai's improved senses allowed him to somersault over the sweeping dagger and roll to his feet behind Tan. Tan wheeled, blocking down with his blade just as Ashai thrust it toward his lower spine.

With his free hand, Tan grabbed Ashai's wrist, hurling the smaller man through the air. Ashai struck a tree, which drove the wind from his lungs, making him drop his dagger. As he slouched, gasping for air, Tan charged him, blade raised. Ashai rolled to his left, but couldn't move fast enough, and Tan straddled his chest. The ebony tip of his dagger glistened with Ashai's blood. Ashai felt his power flicker, felt Nishi's gift fading from his body. Panic seized his heart, and he froze.

"Time to end this, traitor."

He stiffened, then, face contorting in pain, back arched. His empty hand scrabbled at his back, and when he half-turned, Makari's dagger was there, buried in his shoulder to the hilt.

Ashai seized the opportunity, arching his own back and thrusting up with his hips. He managed to lever Tan upward just enough that he rolled free. A glance told him the soldiers were mere paces away.

Ignoring the dagger in his back, Tan rose, clearly in pain, and glared at Makari, who stood nearby, hands on hips.

"That's for my father, you son of a whore!"

Tan started for her, but Ashai was ready. Snatching up his dagger, he launched himself at the backs of Tan's legs, driving his shoulder in while wrapping his arms around the big man's shins. Helpless, Tan crashed to the ground face-first.

Ashai felt exhaustion rushing in as the Chargh Lai severed his link to God. His mentor's laugh echoed through his mind. Power gone, Ashai had only one chance left to save Makari.

He rose to his knees, held his dagger over his head, and plunged it into Tan's lower back, severing his spine before jerking the blade out. The spymaster shuddered, managed to roll over, and lifted his bulk up on his elbows. As he studied his useless legs, his bladder let loose.

"I'll find you, Ashai. And will send a hundred Denari Lai after—"

Ashai swept his dagger across the man's throat, blood spraying in the night. As the Spymaster of Dar Tallus fell dead, Ashai said a silent prayer, then ran for the woods.

He ran as fast as he could, but still the soldiers gained on him, closing the distance until Ashai knew he couldn't reach the trees in time. As the void of Nishi's power swept through his body, Ashai slowed. What was the point in running? Tan was right. He'd lost everything.

He dropped from a jog to a walk. He didn't deserve to live.

Then Makari stepped from the woods, a handful of thieves behind her.

"I still need you! Run!"

Ashai's heart leapt, and suddenly his legs worked again. He found himself sprinting for the trees.

Each thief raised a bow and fired. Over and over again they shot, arrows arcing over his head. Behind him, yells turned to cries of pain, and after the third volley, Ashai reached the trees and looked behind him. The soldiers were running the opposite way.

When he raised his arm, his hand shook. Grekkyl appeared, offering a vial full of pink powder and a flask of wine.

"The powder will still your shaking for a while. The wine will … make you feel better."

He did as he was told.

It was gone. The thread that connected him to Nishi's power was not just out of reach. It did not exist. It was gone. Forever.

Doubling over, Ashai fell to his knees, his vision blurring, and his head throbbing as if about to implode. Darkness closed in from all around him, an empty cavern as cold and dead as a grave. As he pitched forward, though, right before he hit the ground, he felt something else inside him. Something bright and hot, burning deep within him, hidden behind wall after wall, stashed away behind shadow upon shadow of his own sin. He reached for it, finding hope and possibility there, but it was too late.

Darkness claimed him.

CHAPTER THIRTY-NINE

They kneeled along the edge of the woods, the evening sun raking low from behind them, turning the shadows of the trees into black giants, stretched across the plains before them. Makari inhaled, savoring the scent of the woods, of pine and loam and leaves rotting underfoot. Her breath crystallized before her face, and even through the thick gloves she wore, her fingers tingled with the encroaching cold.

Beside her, Ashai's expression was grim, as dark as the growing dusk around them. Except for his eyes, of course, which glowed gold.

She followed his gaze across the open plain north of Dar Tallus, taking in the sheer enormity of the Pushtani Army as it marched north, steel glinting in the waning light. Banners whipped in the cold, autumn wind, a wind that stayed out of the woods, preferring the easier traveling of the grassland beyond. The army wound north along the King's Highway, a shining, silver snake longer than anything she'd ever seen, stretching as far south as she could see.

"I wonder if this is what they wanted," Ashai said, his voice low and dangerous. "If the Chargh Lai and the others wanted war."

Even in the woods for three days, they'd heard the rumors of war, the thieves bringing them information on a frequent basis. Celani had convinced the royal council that the assassination and the uprisings were preludes to a Nishi'iti invasion, and with their pride already prickling, they'd been eager to send in the army to settle the score.

"Is there any way we can stop them?" She asked.

Ashai said nothing, but the look on his face said there was not.

"A war will make it hard to cross into Nishi'iti." Grekkyl had come to stand behind them, her tiny frame more bent than normal. Her battle with Tan had drained her, but she stayed with them to help Ashai learn to use his power.

Ashai nodded. "I'll have to go through Neskania and cross the western border. That should throw off the Chargh Lai's searching, too."

"At least they can't track your old power." Makari almost regretted bringing it up.

"It was never really mine. I was merely allowed to borrow it, and the terms of that agreement are no longer acceptable ... or available to me. Now I either learn to use what's truly mine, or we're all dead."

She couldn't argue that, so she let the matter drop. Rising, he drew them both back into the trees where their squad of thieves waited. Ashai walked up to the leader, a stocky man with a low forehead and hands like hams at the ends of his arms.

"Any word of Tomar's fate?"

The other shook his head. "None. The Sixth Guild has not been in touch with us yet, so we must assume General Celani and the Capitol Watch are cracking down. But there are no rumors of his capture, either."

"Encouraging," Makari told him. "I hope he was able to help his people."

A smile split the man's square face.

"Your supplies and horses await further back in the trees," he told them. "Enough food to last you at least a couple of weeks on the road. We must leave you now and return to the city to find Tomar and rebuild."

Makari nodded. "Tell him we owe him a great debt, and I *will* repay it someday."

As one, the thieves bowed, then slipped off into the woods, disappearing as if they were part of the trees themselves.

"What now?" Grekkyl stood, hands on hips, as if she expected a full detailing of their plans.

"Now we head west," Ashai told her. "We aren't safe anywhere in Pushtan, so we'll follow the woods all the way to the swamps of Lyres. Crossing them will be difficult, but I know a man who can help."

"And once we're free of the bogs?" Makari asked.

"Then I will stash you away at a safe location in Lyres. I know many people there. I'll make my way into Nishi'iti and try to get to the Chargh Lai without being killed. He'll listen to me. I'll convince him to lift the order to kill you and give you a chance to do better than your father did in treating our people."

"You think I'm just going to stay somewhere while you go off and try to save my life? You obviously didn't get to know me very well."

Ashai started to argue, but Grekkyl stepped in. "The best way for this Chargh Lai to know Makari is to meet her, face-to-face. He will not take the word of a shiner. No insult intended."

Ashai winced at the term. "None taken. The word is accurate. I am a shiner, for now. By the time I get to Tabi Ge Nishi, though, I hope to not need the dust anymore, so my eyes should be normal. And I should have power the Chargh Lai does not control.

"But with you two along, there is no way I'd even make it into the city. We'd all be killed long before reaching the Chargh Lai."

"Then you'll have to learn to use your own magic and disguise us well," Makari told him. "I'm not spending weeks or months locked up like a deer in a clearing, sitting still for the Army or whoever to kill me."

"And you need me to teach you," Grekkyl added. "You cannot learn in time on your own."

"I really don't think—"

Makari raised her hand and silenced him.

"I am not offering you a choice, Ashai. You betrayed me once. I'm not sure I trust you again, so until I do, you're staying in arm's reach. Period."

Ashai sighed deeply, then raised his hands helplessly at his sides.

"Then we go together." She thought he might have smiled a bit at saying that, and it made her glad as he went on. "But you must do as I tell you, princess. You're not the expert at covert affairs. I am."

"Within reason, I will."

He shook his head, but she'd left him no choice and she knew it. Together, they started off to find their horses.

EPILOGUE

He staggered along the narrow, muddy path, rain soaking his clothing and further clouding his already blurry vision. He no longer knew where he was, had lost track days ago. Or was it weeks? He no longer knew that, either.

In fact, most of what he knew, most of what he could remember, he repeated over and over again under his breath, a litany of repeated words forming a lifeline to his past.

"Dar Tallus. Kendshi."

There was another word, but he couldn't remember.

Kendshi. He knew her, a face floating in the eye of his mind. Beautiful eyes, dark and deep like pools. Long, midnight hair. Blood. Blood everywhere, smearing her face and staining her blue, silk robe.

She was dead, murdered. He remembered now. He had to find the killer. Kill them.

But he didn't know who they were.

Ahead of him loomed a forest, a dark line gashing against the slate gray horizon. Maybe the trees would keep the rain off, so he wandered in that direction, plodding along, focused on putting one foot in front of the other.

He'd started to shiver earlier in the day, as the cold rain pounded him and his feet turned numb, his boots soaked beyond the point of drying during his brief nightly stops. He knew what the shivering meant, at least in the back of his mind he knew, somewhere distant and protected, but equally out of reach. He'd taken a fever, which made sense in that dark corner of his mind. The nights were cold now, the rain turning to snow or ice, pelting his skin, and making him seek shelter in whatever way he could.

His options were limited, though. He wasn't sure why, but he knew he couldn't let anyone see him, couldn't ask for shelter. He knew people were a danger to him, would send him back where he'd come from. Back to the place he'd fled. The place of death.

So he had to stay hidden, out of sight, and often that meant he defined shelter as a stand of trees or an outcropping of rocks. The foothills had plenty of both, but neither really did much to keep the rain off, and without a fire, he'd never been able to get truly warm or dry.

Thus, with the sun just touching the western horizon, he shuddered and quaked, and struggled to recall his own name.

Just outside the woods, he slipped and went down, body cracking through a thin layer of ice and plunging him into deep, cold mud. His already drenched clothing became heavier, weighted down with the gray-ish-brown slop, and he had to fight just to climb back to his knees.

As if to mock him, the rain stiffened, pouring down harder than ever, nearly driving him back down on his face. But the trees were close now, close enough he could make out each one rather than just a mass of brown and green, and their promise of shelter gave him the strength to stand and start moving forward again.

The wind howled and shifted, blowing in his face, trying to keep him from reaching the woods, but he leaned into it and forged ahead.

"Dar Tallus. Kendshi."

One foot ahead of the other, slowly, like a turtle making for a rock, Pachat finally reached the edge of the trees. He stopped, peering into their shadows, straining to listen for any sign of movement. For a moment, almost like he was dreaming, he thought he heard voices muttering deep inside the woods. He craned his neck forward, putting his head near the closest tree.

The sound went away and he shook his head. The fever was playing tricks on his mind.

Almost as soon as he entered the shelter of the trees, his body warmed. The canopy overhead filtered the rain and seemed to warm it, too. He took a deep breath and shuddered as he let it out.

He walked a few paces deeper into the woods, looking for a spot he could build a shelter and a fire. He saw a copse inside a circle of rocks ahead of him, and started for them. Something moved to his left, little more than a flicker of light. He looked, but saw nothing.

He needed that fire. Needed to rest.

He managed to trudge to the rocks, stepping inside the circle and dropping to his knees. Before him, a circle of smaller rocks ringed a pile of wet ash, and someone had woven pine boughs from several nearby trees together to form a crude roof that kept all but a fine mist from soaking the little circle.

Beside the fire pit sat a stack of dry firewood and kindling.

Someone had been here. Recently.

Movement made him jump back to his feet, spinning around to the right. His head swam, and he almost fell again. Somehow he managed to remain upright, and when the world stopped spinning, he found himself facing an old woman.

She stood outside the circle of boulders, drops of rain dripping on her from the trees above, her white hair matted and dingy. She stared at him with eyes of brilliant blue, her face a prune with a nose. Her hands hung limp at her side. She said nothing, simply staring at him with those snowy eyes.

"Dar Tallus. Kendshi." It was all he knew.

She seemed to consider that a moment, then turned her head and called back over her shoulder.

"He's not armed. Better come here."

Two more people melted from the trees, one man and one woman. His heart thundered in his chest and he fought he urge to flee. He needed help, even if it meant capture.

People who could hurt him. Could take him back to darkness and death.

His hand strayed toward his belt. There had been a weapon there once, long ago. Where had it gone? Distant memories flashed. Men, many of them. They'd surprised him. Taken everything. Weapons. Food.

Left him hurt and wandering.

He touched his fingers to his temple and found a large scab, and pain.

"Who is he?"

The man spoke. Gray robes, dark eyes. Black hair matted to his head.

A curved dagger in one hand, sword in the other. Something seemed familiar about him.

He stepped forward, moving like a stalking cat, smooth and fluid. Dangerous. Pachat stepped back, hands coming up.

"Don't know," said the old woman. "Looks like he's one of you, though."

That confused him. How could he be one of whoever the dangerous man was?

He swayed on his feet, nearly falling again, steadying himself by sheer force of will.

The man squinted at him and nodded. "Escaped slave. From the uprising."

Beside him, a younger woman stood, cowl of her forest green cloak up around her head, hiding her face, but the curve of her hip through her leather pants gave her away as a woman. A longsword rode at her hip, a dagger in her belt, too.

"Kill him." Her voice was cool, commanding, and yet somehow, her voice calmed him. Soothed him. "We cannot risk being identified."

"Dar Tallus. Kendshi."

The young woman stiffened, her head snapping up inside the hood.

"What did you say?"

"Dar Tallus. Kendshi." His teeth chattered this time, though he didn't know if it was from fever, cold, or fear. And what was that third word?

"Kendshi? What do you know of Kendshi?"

The man put his hand on her forearm and held her from stepping closer.

"It is a common name for us. It doesn't mean anything."

The woman shook off his hand and stepped closer anyway. The man's eyes started to glow, a frightening gold light appearing as if they were tiny suns.

Then he remembered, the third word crawling from his tired lips. His name, lost for days, returned to him.

"Kendshi. Dar Tallus. Pachat."

He felt her gaze lock onto him, knew she was searching him for answers.

"Pachat. Is that your name? Pachat?"

His mind swam, and fear flared brighter in his heart. She knew him.

She would take him back. He inched backward, waiting for a chance to flee without being killed. Or taken back.

But the woman in the cloak did not come closer. Slowly, she lifted her hands to the edge of her hood.

"I knew someone named Kendshi." This time her voice softened. "And she had a lover. A betrothed named Pachat."

"Nishi save us," muttered the dangerous man, eyes flashing in the dim forest light. "It's him. Of all the people to run across in the forest of eastern Thahr, we find the one man wanted as much as we are. The slave who started the uprising."

The woman stepped slowly forward, and as Pachat's stomach tensed, she drew back her hood. Eyes as blue as the winter sky stared at him from a face so pale and perfect he thought there could be no such beauty anywhere else in the world. A face familiar to him, one he thought he knew. Trusted.

"Do not fear," she said. "I knew your Kendshi."

She moved forward and took his hands in hers.

"Kendshi?" he croaked.

She was his betrothed. Now he remembered. She'd been taken, too. And killed. How had she died? His memories faded.

"Yes, your love. She was my dearest friend in all the world. She served me well and faithfully, and I will do anything in my power to help her love."

"Served? Help?" Pachat did not understand.

She smiled again, and all his worries washed away.

"It is good to meet you, Pachat." She stared into his eyes and her mere attention seemed to warm him. "My name is Makari."

ACKNOWLEDGMENTS

I wrote this book as a "back up thesis" for my MFA degree, a feat I never would have considered possible without the mentoring and encouragement of the faculty of Western State University. Specifically Russell Davis, Michaela Roessner, J.S. Mayank, Stacia Deutsch, Candace Nadon, and Mark Todd. You showed me what I was capable of, and made me reach that potential.

And once written, it might never have seen the light of day without the support and enthusiasm of Kevin J. Anderson and the folks at Word-Fire Press. They believed in Shadow Blade from the moment I submitted it, and have worked furiously to make it an amazing book. Thank you.

ABOUT THE AUTHOR

Chris started writing stories in his early teens, and he hand-wrote (yes, with a pen and lined notebook paper) his first novel in 1982. He transcribed it using an IBM Selectric II typewriter the next year, then hid it in a box in his attic, where no one would ever find it. He worked as Co-Editor of *The Tempest*, the first-ever literary magazine of Lake George Central High School in upstate  New York, and won Literary Student of the Year for his graduating class in 1984.

When not oppressed by his day job, Chris writes all kinds of stories, and has published fantasy, science fiction, horror, western, and paranormal romance, with his first crime story coming out in this year's inaugural print edition of *Toe Six Magazine*. He is author of the self-published, weird western *Hell's Butcher* series, with Book One (*Hell's Marshal*) twice ranking in the top five of western horror on Amazon.

Chris believes that while storytelling is a talent, the tools and craft of writing well can be taught, making education crucial. Thus, Chris holds a BGS in English from University of Nebraska at Omaha, and an MFA in Creative Writing, Popular Genre Fiction, from Western State Colorado University. Chris is lucky enough to live in the gorgeous state of Colorado, so he gets plenty of inspiration from the Rocky Mountains. That setting lends itself to staying active, and Chris is both an avid mountain biker, and a second degree black belt in karate.

IF YOU LIKED ...

IF YOU LIKED SHADOW BLADE, YOU MIGHT ALSO ENJOY:

Shadow Warriors
by Nathan Dodge

Blood of Akhilles
by R.M. Meluch

Awakening
by Raymond Bolton

OTHER WORDFIRE PRESS TITLES

Our list of other WordFire Press authors and titles is always growing. To find out more and to see our selection of titles, visit us at:
wordfirepress.com

CPSIA information can be obtained
at www.ICGtesting.com
Printed in the USA
LVHW092129110619
620926LV00004B/43/P